Sign up for our newsletter to hear
about new and upcoming releases.

www.ylva-publishing.com

Other books by Andrea Bramhall

Standalone:

Rock and a Hard Place

Just My Luck

Norfolk Coast Investigation Story

Collide-O-Scope

Under Parr

The Last First Time

The Last First Time

Andrea Bramhall

Dedication

To the victims of the 2017 terror attacks in Great Britain.

22 March – Westminster. Six dead, forty-nine injured.
22 May – Manchester Arena. Twenty-two dead, 250 injured.
3 June – London Bridge and Borough Market. Eight dead, forty-eight injured.
19 June – Finsbury Park Mosque. One dead, ten injured.

Your loss is felt by an entire nation.

To the emergency services and police involved in each attack—we thank you for all you do. Including all the times you keep us safe and we don't even know it.

Acknowledgements

Astrid, Daniela, Michelle, and all the rest of the fabulous team at Ylva, thank you for trusting in me and this series. I know you found this one to be especially difficult. I hope you think it was worth it.

Glendon, I truly love this cover. Thank you for making my vague idea a reality.

Louise, for believing in me and almost convincing me this was worth writing when I was convinced it was a steaming pile of horse shit, thank you. I know I'm a pain in the arse when I'm writing...well, most of the time to be fair...but I couldn't do it without you.

To our friends who worked at the Manchester Arena in the aftermath of such horror, there are no words that can ease the pain of what you saw, what you dealt with, and what you worked through for the sake of others. You are my heroes.

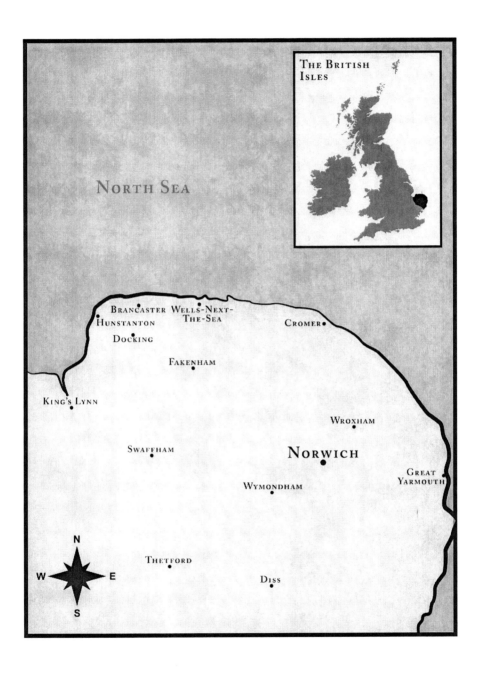

THE BRITISH
ISLES

NORTH SEA

BRANCASTER WELLS-NEXT-
THE-SEA
HUNSTANTON
CROMER
DOCKING

FAKENHAM

KING'S LYNN

WROXHAM

SWAFFHAM
NORWICH

WYMONDHAM
GREAT
YARMOUTH

N
W E
S

THETFORD

DISS

Prologue

The sun reflected off the windows, obscuring the view of the shop inside. Still, Nadia was hyperaware of the products on display. She shuffled her feet and coughed but didn't move towards the door. In the window, she caught the reflection of Saba's easy smile, as if she frequented sex toy stores all the time.

"Have you been here before?" she asked quietly, her breath coming in white clouds in the cold air. Snow lay in icy, dirty clumps at the edges of the pavement, melting in the gutters to murky puddles.

"Yes. I've been watching it, studying it. For our mission." Saba didn't even seem phased—by anything. It was as though she had surrendered to the will of God already, as though he moved her, directed her, and she was but his instrument. She was calmness itself, at peace with where she was, with what they were doing. It seemed almost as though the ultimate consequences of their actions were not to be their last. As though Saba had all the time in the world, and these weren't her last few moments in it.

Nadia couldn't help but admire her and wished she could be as composed or as resolute. They wanted the mission to be a success; they'd planned for it, prayed for it, and, it seemed, watched for it too. She still wasn't sure she'd have been able to step foot inside this cesspit of human perversion to properly prepare, the way Saba had. But it was Allah's will that they strike. And Allah's will would be done.

Christmas carols blared annoyingly over loudspeakers, pouring out of every shop on the High Street. But this was the shop they had picked—the one that they had to destroy. The one that had destroyed so many hopes and dreams, so many lives. The very symbol of all that was wrong and festering in the society of infidels and kaffirs, with its mockery of wholesomeness displayed in the window for all to see. Children walked by and stared at the skimpy outfits. Red, barely-there-lace, green ribbon, and black fishnet stockings covered a mannequin in a lewd representation of a sexy Mother Christmas. This was the right thing to do. This was the only thing they could do. The weak and morally corrupt had taken the sweet and innocent symbols of their own defective religion and fouled it beyond redemption.

But perhaps it would be enough for her redemption. To atone for her own weakness. To want, to desire, another woman's husband was a sin, one Nadia had fallen foul of. With all her heart, she wanted him for her own. But he was not free to be hers. And for her crime, her life was forfeit. At least in her martyrdom he might remember her name, if she could face her judgment with courage in her heart and purity colouring her soul.

"Are you ready?" Saba asked.

Nadia rubbed her hand across the protruding mound beneath her burqua. It had been cannily crafted to look like a developing pregnancy. Not an experience that would be in her future. Hers—theirs—was a higher calling, a calling unto God to mete out his wrath and bring justice in his name. This was her judgment day, and her entrance to heaven was ordained. No matter what other sins she had committed, she was a soldier. A warrior earning her place on the battlefield of icons and the rank stench of commercialism.

She glanced through the window again at the dozens of women touching scraps of cloth, giggling at squirming silicon objects, and grinning lecherously at goods piled high on shelves.

"Are you ready?" Saba asked again.

Nadia nodded. "Allah's will be done."

"Insha'allah." Saba mirrored her gesture with her own "bump" and slipped her hand into her pocket. She pulled out a small switch and waited while Nadia did the same. She touched the two black boxes together—as the kaffirs did with glasses of alcohol when toasting good fortune—then turned towards the door. "Insha'allah," she said again as the automatic doors slid open and they stepped foot inside the devil's den.

CHAPTER 1

Gina glanced into the shop window at the Ann Summers High Street store and cringed. Stella seemed to have no such qualms. She looked a little excited, no, giddy at the prospect of walking into the adult shop.

"Have you been in here before, Stella?"

"Gina, I've been married and divorced three times." She turned to look at her. "Of course I have." She led Gina past a couple of pregnant Asian girls staring at the window display and through the automatic doors. "I wouldn't have survived without a good vibrator."

Gina shook her head, trying to dislodge the image Stella had firmly placed there. It wasn't working. "Thanks. Thanks a lot."

Stella shrugged unrepentantly. "You invited me on this little shopping expedition."

"Yes, for your advice. Not insights into your sex life."

Stella lifted one blonde eyebrow and picked a skimpy gold bikini from one of the racks. "I think turnabout's only fair play." She checked the sizing label and dropped it back on the display rack with a sigh.

Gina frowned. "What are you talking about?"

Stella twirled her hand around. "You've asked me to come and help you pick out a Christmas gift for your girlfriend, Kate, my work colleague—the one I take the piss out of all the time and the one who returns the favour whenever she can. You don't think you've put the odd image or two into my head?"

Gina swallowed. She hadn't thought about it like that. "I'm sorry. Maybe this was a bad idea."

Stella laughed. "It so was, and in January, Kate is never going to live this little expedition down. But in the meantime, I can keep a secret, and you said you needed some help."

"Yes."

"So what do you need help with?"

"Well, I haven't exactly bought a gift for a girlfriend before."

Stella nodded. "No, me either."

Gina frowned. "I thought you were straight."

"I am. Hence why I've never bought a gift for a girlfriend before." She rolled her eyes at Gina.

Gina chuckled, partly at Stella, but mostly at her own nervousness. "Right. Yeah. Sorry."

Stella shrugged. "So why did you invite me here?"

"Well, you're her friend. I thought you might have a little insight."

"Into her taste in sex toys?" Stella's voice rose an octave. "Why the hell—"

"No. Lingerie." Gina pointed towards the racks of silk negligees and short robes.

"Oh." Stella's eyebrows dropped from her hairline, and she blew out a heavy breath. "Well, that's better, I suppose, but I still don't know how much help I'll be in this department. I mean, yes, we're friends, but we're work colleagues first. We talk about police stuff and take the piss out of each other." She shrugged. "I don't know what her tastes in this stuff are. Surely you're better placed to know about that. You're her lover, after all."

Gina's cheeks burned, and suddenly the carpet beneath her feet was incredibly interesting.

"Oh. Wow." Stella wrapped her hand about Gina's arm and tugged her close. She whispered in her ear, "You haven't slept with her?"

Gina knew that even her ears would be red by now. She shook her head.

"But she *is* your girlfriend, right?"

Gina nodded.

"And we're here." Stella twirled her finger again to encompass the whole shop. "So is Kate the one stopping you two from doing the deed? Do you want to use this gift to entice her into your bed—"

"No! She's been amazing about it all."

Stella said nothing, but the question was clearly written on her face. She might as well have said the words. *Why the hell not, then?*

"It's me."

Stella smiled gently. "Well, if it wasn't Kate, then I figured it had to be. I am a detective, you know."

"I know." Gina snorted a soft laugh, desperate to hide her embarrassment, and shook her head. She had no need to be embarrassed about her issue. It was something she was dealing with, something she'd made huge amounts of progress with in a really short time. With the help of her counsellor, Jodi, and Kate's patience and understanding, of course.

"Want to talk about it?"

Gina did, but she didn't at the same time. Her counselling sessions with Jodi about the attack Ally Robbins had carried out on her had been going really well. She was coming to terms with the scars that she carried as a result of Ally's knife skills, and every day, she felt a little more like her old self. More like a woman who could be desirable. Less like the patchwork monster of Frankenstein fame. She'd made huge steps forward and knew she was ready to show Kate how she really felt about her. To share herself with her. But they'd waited so long now that she wanted—needed—it to be special.

Kate had told her about how she'd wanted to savour their first kiss before it had happened. To build up the anticipation and make it last, because they would only ever have one first kiss. And she fully intended that first kiss to be the last first kiss she ever had. Gina thought the idea was so very beautiful that she wished she'd had the forethought to savour it the same way. It was something she'd never even considered before. In the past, she hadn't sought a relationship. She'd never expected anyone to stick around, anyway. Not with a precocious nine-year-old like Sammy as part of the package. Instead she'd sought out the occasional fling, and speed rather than memorability had been the order of the day.

Not anymore. She wanted this time, her and Kate's first time together, to be perfect. The last first time. This—Kate, their new relationship, their future—all meant so much to her.

She knew how she felt about Kate—knew she loved her already—and this would be the first time she'd make love to a person she was truly in love with. This was the first time it really mattered. Her string of one-night stands and weekend flings may have satisfied her physically—sort of—but not one of her previous lovers had touched her heart. Touched her emotionally.

As far as she was concerned, Kate had already claimed her in every way that truly counted. Sex alone didn't equate to the feeling of intimacy she got when she was alone with Kate. It was something she'd never experienced before. Something that wasn't about the way someone touched or kissed. It came more from the sentiment behind it. She felt more—everything—when Kate simply held her in her arms than she had when other lovers had brought her to orgasm.

And Gina knew that part of the reason for that was the way Kate had refused to even contemplate the kind of connection Gina had become used to. *More than a weekend*, she'd said. *I want more than just a weekend.* No one had ever asked for that before. They'd simply taken what she offered and then gone away. Just like she'd wanted. Just like she'd expected. Once in a while, there had been someone with whom she'd hoped for more, had asked for more. *Sure, babe*, they'd said, then never called. So Gina had never asked anyone again.

But Kate had refused to even contemplate a relationship like that with her. *More than a weekend*, she'd said. And that had only been the start. Not only did Kate want more than a weekend, she wanted forever, and she was prepared to wait until Gina was ready to give her that. No rushing, no pushing, no pressure.

Well, Gina was ready now. No matter what demons she had to battle to prove it. "It was just everything that happened with Ally," she told Stella. "I needed some time."

Stella nodded and gave her the time and space to say more if she wanted to.

"To adjust." She shrugged. "You know how it is."

"I get it." Stella pulled down on the collar of her shirt to show the edge of a puckered pink scar. "I got caught by a glass breaking up a fight when I was still in uniform. This was before we all wore stab vests all the time. Tells you how old I am." She chuckled. "Anyway, after it healed, I was very self-conscious about it. Didn't help that my husband at the time was a prick who couldn't look at it and keep it up. Said the scar made me look manly." She let go of the fabric. "Reason enough for divorce number one, isn't it?"

Gina nodded but didn't say anything. Stella looked anything but manly. Heading north of forty, she was an attractive woman: blond hair that hung just below her ears in a short bob and was still blond, blue eyes that sparkled with intelligence and mischief, high cheekbones, a strong jaw, and a slightly large nose. Her large bust and hips pointed to a few extra pounds, carried in all the right places, and her ex had to have been an idiot.

"Took me a while after that to trust a guy enough to let him see me without my clothes on. So, yeah, I get it. But the scar Carl inflicted—"

"Carl?"

"Ex-husband. Anyway, the scar he inflicted, reacting that way, was much worse than the one I still carry on my chest."

"Exactly."

"But Kate's being supportive?"

Gina smiled and nodded. "She really has been. She couldn't have been any better."

"Good. Cos I happen to know she's got a decent collection of brand marks of her own."

"I know. She showed me most of her scars, trying to show me that they didn't matter to her at all."

"Did she show you the one shaped like a fish?"

"On her hip?"

"Hip? Is that what we call that part of the body now?" Stella asked with a laugh.

"She said it was on her hip, sort of. I haven't seen it. She said she was saving it. You've seen it?"

Stella wiggled her eyebrows and grinned. "It's a beauty."

"Where is it?"

Stella shook her head. "Nope. I'm not going to spoil her surprise for you."

Gina stared at her. "Tell me."

"Nope."

"Please."

"Uh-uh."

"You have to."

"Why?"

"Because she's my girlfriend."

"Then get her to show you."

"But why have you seen it and I haven't?"

"Well, Gina," Stella said and leaned forward to whisper in her ear. "I've seen the lovely Kate in all her glory."

Gina's eyes glazed over as she imagined the picture of Kate in all her glory. Green eyes shining, red hair glistening in the gentle light as one item of clothing after another disappeared from her body until nothing remained. She could imagine the tiny freckles that would cover her shoulders. Could imagine kissing them all and hearing Kate's breath hitch in her chest. She could imagine tracing her fingers over each rib as she explored Kate's body and made it her own.

"Wake up!" Stella snapped her fingers in front of Gina's face. "Trust me, whatever you were imagining just then, and I do believe it was the lovely Kate in all her glory, the real thing is so much better." Stella smiled. "She's a gorgeous hunk of woman. If I were into girls, I'd have been in there like a shot."

Gina licked her lips. "Bitch."

Stella laughed. "I live to serve."

"How have you seen her naked?"

"Changing room at work. She has a tendency to get herself into all sorts of messes. Haven't you noticed that?"

Gina nodded, still trying to get her brain to function properly again. "Yes."

"Well, since I've seen the goods, perhaps I am better equipped for this shopping expedition than I thought."

Gina closed her eyes, sighed, and chuckled. "Fine. Let's get started." She cast her gaze over the rack of red lace negligees and immediately dismissed them even as Stella picked one up and held it against her clothes.

"This is nice."

"If you're a working girl."

"I am a working girl, Gina," Stella said with an evil grin.

"Not that kind of work." She plucked the hanger from Stella's fingers and put it back on the rail. "If you're looking for yourself while we're here, I'd say look for something with a bit more, I don't know, class, maybe."

"Meow." Stella pretended to paw the air with her fake claws.

Gina tossed her hair over her shoulder, kept her head pointed slightly towards the ceiling, and moved on to the next rail. A deep-forest-green satin baby doll negligee seemed to call to her. It was simple in its design: soft lines, solid colour, wide shoulder straps. It wasn't until she held it up that she noticed how short it was. On Kate's curvy body, this would barely cover the, erm...important...parts. Her mouth watered.

"Oooo." Stella's chin rested on her shoulder. "Is that what you mean by classy?" She rubbed a handkerchief across Gina's chin. "Drooling, babes."

Gina laughed out loud and slapped her hands away. "Is that what you two do all day when you're supposed to be catching criminals?"

Stella frowned as if deep in thought, then nodded solemnly. "Yes. But I swear we make the boys do some work while we take the piss."

"Uh-huh. Do I look like I was born yesterday?"

Stella opened her mouth and Gina slapped her hand over it.

"Don't answer that."

Stella's eyes twinkled, but she nodded.

"Anyway, I happen to think this would be perfect for Kate."

"Yup." Stella nodded. "For both seconds you'll let her wear it."

"Oh, I don't know. I might let her keep it on a bit longer than that." She turned the hanger in her hand. "I can reach everything I need without—"

Stella put her fingers in her ears and rocked her body forwards and backwards. "Too much information, Gina. I've still got to work with her. You know, catching criminals?"

"You said you left that to the boys."

"Pft. Please. Without me and Kate, they couldn't find their way to the coffee shop, never mind find a criminal." She wandered away a little and rifled through another rack of lace scraps and satin straps. "Oo. Here, what about this?"

Stella lifted up a black, midthigh-length, modestly cut robe. But the fabric was so sheer that Gina could see Stella's hand through it as she lifted it towards the light.

"No, I prefer this one for Kate." She flicked the green dress towards Stella.

"I meant for you." She held it against Gina's torso. "If you're still a bit nervous."

Gina understood what she meant and was grateful for the thought, but the more she considered it, the more she realised that it was essential that she was able to face Kate without hiding behind something...even if that wasn't very much.

She needed to know she could show every aspect of herself to Kate. Emotionally and physically. Letting Kate see that last barrier between them fall, allowing herself to be that vulnerable, was important to her, and it was important to Kate too. She needed to know that Gina was truly able to move past it all and fully embrace their relationship.

But Gina had to admit the idea of being shrouded by the voluminous sheer fabric as she kissed Kate and ran her fingers up Kate's arm made her tingle with delicious delight. Well, if Kate was going to be wearing the green satin number, why shouldn't Gina start out wearing the black one? As long as it came off easily enough. She glanced at the wide sash belt and smiled. No problem.

"Thanks." She lifted the second garment from Stella's hands and folded it over her arm. "Seen anything you fancy?"

Stella laughed. "I've got plenty of batteries at home, thanks."

Gina snorted a laugh and shook her head as she walked to the counter and got in the queue. "You're incorrigible."

"I do my best."

"So does that mean you're single at the moment?"

Stella eyed her suspiciously. "Possibly. Why?"

"Well..." Gina drew it out.

Stella shook her head. "I don't do blind dates, other coppers, or girls. I decided a long time ago that I need to be the only drama queen in my relationship, so don't try setting me up."

"I was going to ask if you'd babysit Sammy for me one night so I could seduce my girlfriend."

"Oh."

The look on Stella's face was the perfect mixture of delight and disappointment. Gina wasn't entirely sure how she could have managed that.

"Of course."

There was only one staff member on the checkout, and the queue seemed to be at a standstill.

"When did you have in mind?"

"Hmm." Gina pulled her wallet out of her handbag and slipped out her card. "Well, do you have any plans this weekend?"

"Nope."

"How does tomorrow night work for you?"

"Sounds good. If you want, Sammy can stay at mine. We'll have a girly night in."

"Do not let her watch *Nightmare on Elm Street* again."

"It's a classic."

"She's still having nightmares, Stella."

"She said she loves scary movies."

"She's nine!"

"So Chucky's out?"

"I swear you only do this to wind me up."

"Maybe."

"If it's not a PG, she can't watch it."

"What about a U?"

Gina laughed. "Then she wouldn't want to watch it."

Stella cocked her head to the side. "Fair point. Jesus, what's taking so long?" She stood on her tiptoes and craned her neck to see over the people in front of her. "Fuck."

CHAPTER 2

Stella pulled Gina close and whispered in her ear. "Head for the door, and put the hangers on a rail as you go. Don't look back. Just walk slowly and get out."

"What's going on?" Gina spun and her eyes fell on two women draped in black cloth.

Each had an arm raised in the air, a small black box grasped in their hands. Thumbs poised over a switch. They looked to each other and then grasped the cloth and uncovered their pregnant bellies.

Except they weren't pregnant bellies.

Small blocks of silver tape were strapped to a vest that hung low over their abdomens. Wires protruded from them and slinked up their shoulders, out of sight.

"Is that...?"

"A suicide vest?" Stella whispered hoarsely.

Gina nodded, unable to tear her gaze away.

"Yes," Stella confirmed and shook Gina until she was looking at her again as she dragged her closer to the door. "Now do what I said. Get out of here. When you get outside, call Kate—"

"Why? What are you going to do?"

"We don't have time for this. Just do it. Call Kate and tell her to get—"

"For Allah!" A woman's voice rang out above everything else in the shop, then a loud bang cut off the words.

Gina was forced to the ground.

Stella's body was heavy on top of her, her hands thrown over her head.

Glass shattered, fragmented, splintered apart, and disappeared. She could hear people screaming through the ringing in her ears. Vaguely. Sort of.

Cloth and metal fell on them from what seemed like every direction.

She closed her eyes, only to realise they were already closed and she was merely scrunching them tighter. She didn't want to see anything around her. Hearing it—or rather not hearing it—was terrifying enough.

Then everything was silent.

Except it wasn't. She could hear everything—the cries of terror, the moans of pain, and the concussive roar of air being forced too quickly into spaces too small for it to fit made her ears throb. But everything she heard seemed far too far away for it to be real. It was like she was listening to a muted TV that was making the sounds in her head rather than her actually hearing them.

Stella's lips were moving, but Gina couldn't make out what she was saying. It was just movement she couldn't make sense of.

Just like the smell that invaded her nostrils.

There was the metallic scent of iron pervading the air, almost strong enough to hide the other scents that Gina didn't want to think about, yet couldn't ignore. There was a rotten-egg aroma of something sulphurous that she could guess at, but she desperately wanted that guess to be wrong. The scent of explosives, residue, whatever the fuck it was that experts called it—she didn't know and she didn't care—filled her nose and hung heavy in the air. It had to be that. Nothing else made sense.

But above it all was an acrid, burning odour that clung to every molecule she sucked into her lungs and stuck to her tongue. She could taste it. It smelled like meat burnt on a BBQ. And the horror of that began to sink in. There was no BBQ. There was no meat. There was nothing cooking but human flesh. And Gina fought the urge to vomit, the vile burning of stomach acid inside her far more preferable to her palate than the tang of anything else around her.

For a moment—one blessed moment—everything around her went black and cold and silent. So silent that Gina wondered if she'd gone deaf. Every noise seemed to stop. All she could hear was her own heartbeat and her own laboured breath, and all she could taste was the fear and blood on her tongue. The thoughts in her head seemed so overly loud, as though she were screaming them rather than thinking. *I'm so sorry, Kate.*

She held her breath. *I wish—*

"Stay down," Stella whispered into Gina's ear, and the world rushed back in a cacophony of raucous screams, wails, and cracking glass. The resounding boom of falling bricks and debris seemed to echo for a split second and then disappear. It was the terrifying howl that brought Gina fully back to the present. The holler of a woman screaming, "My legs! Where are my legs? Oh my God. Oh my God! My legs!"

Gina tried to control her breathing, her voice, and her rising panic. Now was not a good time to have another panic attack. Now was not a good time to freeze. If she could hear Stella, she was still alive, and they would be fine. They had to be. "Stay down?" she whispered, and she could hear the confusion in her own voice.

"Yes."

"Why?"

"Because I don't know if that explosion was both of them or just one. If it wasn't, and they think we're all dead, then they might not detonate the second bomb."

"Oh God."

"Listen, we need to call for help, and we need information."

"You don't think someone will have already called the police?"

"I am the police, Gina. The more information I can get to the relevant people as fast as possible, the better it's going to be for everyone." Her words were slurred, and her hands were clumsy as they slowly moved across Gina's body.

"Need your...phone. Mine's in my bag, and I'm...not sure where... dropped it somewhere."

"Back pocket of my jeans."

"Right." Stella moved her hands across her hip.

She shifted slowly to give Stella enough space to slip her hand behind her back and pull the phone from her pocket. Her abdominal muscles complained at trying to hold her weight up off the ground... and Stella's. "Who are you going to call? Kate?"

"No. Detective Inspector Timmons."

"Your boss?"

Stella nodded, and her eyelids fluttered.

Gina bit her lip. Something was wrong with Stella. Something was very wrong. "But I don't have his number," she whispered, hoping the words would somehow help Stella focus.

"S'okay...know it." Stella placed the handset on Gina's chest before freezing again. "Passcode?"

"2601." Gina could hear the tiny chirp as Stella pressed the numbers and unlocked her phone.

Gina's hearing was starting to return to something approaching normal. Or maybe she was just getting used to the incessant ringing and everything sounding like she was listening to it through water.

"DI Timmons, it's Goodwin...Major incident...sir, Ann Summers, Ki-King's Lynn. H-high Street...bomb. Multiple...multip casualties..."

Gina lifted her head and looked at something other than Stella for the first time. She wished she hadn't.

Both of the women were gone.

As was everything she remembered of the shop.

Racks and rails of clothes were shredded. A glass display shelf beside the counter had shattered, and hundreds of chocolate penises littered the floor. Red ribbons tied the squeaky cellophane closed. Shards of plastic and twisted hunks of metal created a gory avant-garde sculpture park the likes of which would haunt her dreams for the rest of her life.

Screams drowned out whatever Stella was saying into the handset on her chest, and Gina tried not to think about the scene around her. Gina wanted to be at home. No, she wanted to be at Kate's. She wanted to be with Kate. And Sammy and Merlin, Kate's adopted border collie. Oh God, Sammy! What else was she going to put the child through? Gina wanted to be wrapping presents and hiding them before she got home from school. Even wading through the mountain of paperwork on her desk would be nice. She wanted to be anywhere but here, lying on the floor at Ann Summers, wishing she'd bought Kate's gift online.

"Yes, sir…still in the shop. Haven't heard anything more to suggest the other bomber is still—"

"She's gone too," Gina said quietly.

Stella looked at her, clearly trying to focus on Gina's face. One pupil was blown. Gina didn't know how Stella was still conscious. "You sure?" Her words were even more slurred.

Gina nodded, and Stella shifted off Gina's body and flopped onto her back. The movement was clearly the last straw for Stella. Her eyes rolled back in her head as she dropped Gina's phone.

Gina turned onto her side, and quickly grabbed the phone as she placed two fingers against Stella's neck. Her pulse was strong and steady; at least that was a good sign.

"Hello? Goodwin? What the fuck's going on?"

"Mr Timmons, this is Gina. Stella's injured. She's passed out. We need…" Gina looked around as she ran her spare hand over the back of Stella's head.

Everywhere she looked there was carnage, destruction like she had never imagined before. The screams of the women had faded into the background, and Gina could no longer tell where one stopped for breath and another began, as they blended together in a macabre choir of agonised screeches. And Gina waited, expecting the panic to take over, expecting her body and mind to shut down. But it didn't. The images—every vile, horror-inducing image—registered instead. Every fragment of it branded itself into her brain.

There was a woman slumped against a wall, perhaps fifteen feet away, trying to sit up. She lifted her legs to leverage their weight against that of her body, but the attempt failed. So she tried again. And failed. Again. Each failure caused her to slump further to the ground. But she continued to try.

Gina knew she'd fail. She was always going to fail because there simply wasn't enough weight in her legs to leverage her body anymore. Instead of knees and calves, and feet, there were ragged wounds of muscle, sinew, and bone pumping blood into a pool around her. Each time she raised the stumps they squirted a river of red across broken glass and twisted hunks of metal. But with each attempt, the distance of the spray lessened significantly. Logic and far too many movies and TV shows told Gina that meant the poor woman was bleeding to death, and there was nothing she could do to help her. Nothing. But Gina's mind simply couldn't comprehend it. She couldn't accept that something like this could happen in real life. It just...couldn't.

Her hands shook, and she could feel the warm, sticky blood covering the back of Stella's head, but she couldn't tear her gaze from the scene before her. Blood decorated the walls, the floor, the ceiling. Tissue she couldn't identify clung to the ceiling fan—what was left of it—and above it, a hole gaped wide like a massive mouth. Slowly the rain slipped inside and kissed her face.

The woman lay still, no longer trying to sit up. No longer moaning or crying or asking where her legs were. Her eyes were open as she slumped against what was left of the wall, staring up at the hole in the ceiling. Raindrops streaked rivers through the dirt, blood, and grime that covered her face. The tears of heaven washing away the woman's pain.

"Hello? Gina?"

Timmons's voice was rough. Anger? Frustration? She didn't know. She couldn't honestly say she cared, as she turned her head, only to be confronted by a woman's hand half-buried by wrappers of condoms. A left hand with purple nail varnish and a ring on its finger. Diamonds and sapphires. An engagement ring. A beautiful engagement ring, on an elegant-looking hand. But there was no thumb. No wrist. And nothing at all beyond.

"What do you need?" Timmons growled.

"A miracle," she whispered.

"How do you mean?"

"There were two of them, with bombs." She moved on autopilot, barely registering that she'd slipped Stella into the recovery position as she spoke. "There are a lot of people here."

"Dead?"

She couldn't stop herself glancing at the woman with her missing legs. "Oh, yes."

"Injured?"

"Many."

"Are you hurt?"

Was she? Physically she didn't think so. But her soul...that was a different story. "I'm okay."

"Look after yourself, then. We're on our way, Gina."

Gina sat for a moment just listening. The sounds of people crying in pain. The crunch of more broken glass beneath someone's shoes. Sirens in the distance. Ambulance? Police? Both? How many people had died? How many were dying? There were people around her now, dying, as she sat there doing nothing.

She was alive, she was breathing, and, most importantly, she wasn't hurt. And she wasn't panicking. *Maybe that'll kick in later. Maybe shock explains this numbness I feel right now. Can that happen? Does shock make you feel like you're looking at everything through someone else's eyes?*

She flexed her hands in front of her face, watching as each finger moved stiffly but obeyed commands from the brain in charge of it. Which wasn't her brain. She was fairly sure of that. But something was controlling her body as she slowly dragged herself to her hands and knees.

Cellophane crinkled beneath her palms, creating a sound she couldn't stop herself from focusing on. The high-pitched, almost static-like sound normally grated on her nerves, but today it felt like she'd never heard it before. Even though she knew she had. She rubbed two bits of it together to hear it again. It sounded false, fake, plastic. *That's because it is plastic, moron*, she told herself, but her brain still wasn't cooperating. It still insisted that she was a passenger along for the ride and that the body was functioning just fine without her, thank you very much.

The sensation—that distant feeling—reminded her of a film she'd watched years ago, *Being John Malkovich*, where people went through this tiny door into a tunnel and then found themselves inside the brain or the consciousness of the actor John Malkovich. They saw what he saw, did what he did, felt what he felt, but at first they had no control. They were simply voyeurs in his life. She felt the same way. She saw what her eyes saw, felt the glass cut into her knees through the denim of her jeans, but she had no control over anything. None.

Was this a new manifestation of her panic attacks?

To her left, a woman whimpered. Gina saw her own hand move forward, felt her legs move beneath her as she crawled towards the sound. She wouldn't give in to another panic attack. She couldn't. No, she didn't have to. She was stronger now. She was the one who could be in control. Just like the character John Cusack played. The puppeteer. Eventually he learned to control the body he inhabited. He learned to make John's body do everything he wanted, and eventually he controlled the mind too. All she had to do was the same.

She tried to focus on her breathing. If she could control pulling air into her lungs, then it was a start. Gina closed her eyes and concentrated on that one thing. Drawing air into her lungs. She put a hand to her belly and envisioned herself making that hand move by simply breathing. Once, then twice, until she shook off her daze and felt as though she were in control of her body again.

The soft moan drew her attention out of her own self again, and she moved quickly to the woman's side. Panic, shock, someone else in her head—whatever it was, it was done with now. She was in control and she was focused. Most importantly, she was focused on helping someone else.

The woman's blond-white hair was streaked with blood and shards of glass. Her lipstick was smeared, and her white jumper was quickly turning a deep claret. Blood bubbled on her lips, and her eyes looked glassy.

Gina grabbed at the first bit of fabric she could reach and pressed it against the wound in the woman's belly. "You're going to be all right. The ambulance is bound to be on its way by now."

The woman pushed at her hands.

"It's okay. I'm trying to help you. I'm sorry if this hurts, but I need to try and stop the bleeding."

"Too late," the woman whispered. Her breath caused the bubbles on her lips to pop and spatter blood across her cheek. "Help someone else, girlie." Her Irish accent was thick and lilted like a lullaby as she tried to shoo Gina away.

"Not a chance. I'm here and I'm helping you, so get used to the idea." She smiled down at the woman and saw that she was considerably older than Gina had first thought. Crinkles at the corners of her eyes spoke of the years she'd seen and laughed her way through. Middle age was well behind her, and Gina would have placed her in her late sixties, maybe even a little older. "I'm Gina. What's your name?"

"Pat."

"Nice to meet you, Pat. Now, hold still while I take a quick look at this wound, okay?"

Pat nodded.

Gina lifted the bloodstained satin, then Pat's jumper, before quickly pushing them all back in place. Blood gushed from the wound the moment she relieved the pressure. Bad. Very bad.

"How's it look?" Pat asked.

"I've patched up worse cuts on my nine-year-old when she jumped out of a tree."

Pat chuckled, then moaned. "You're not a very good liar, Gina."

Gina snorted. "Well then, it doesn't look great. I definitely think you need to see a doctor. Probably wants a stitch, maybe even two. Better?"

"Don't make me laugh. It hurts."

"Sorry." She smiled weakly. If help—of the trained medical variety—didn't get there soon, then it would be too late for Pat. Maybe it was already.

"You said the ambulance was coming."

Gina kept one hand pressed against Pat's middle and held her hand with the other. "Yes. My friend called before she...before she passed out." She glanced over at Stella, grateful and scared that she hadn't moved.

"Your friend's hurt?"

Gina nodded. "But she's a police officer. She called in the cavalry before she...before she gave in."

"Brave." Pat closed her eyes and grimaced, clearly fighting the pain she was in.

"Hmm. Something like that."

"You don't agree?"

"Oh, I think they're brave all right. I just worry."

"She's your friend. Of course you do."

"Yeah."

Pat opened her eyes and looked at Gina. It was a piercing look, a penetrating look, one that Gina knew was looking deep into her soul. "Oh. I see. Not just a friend."

Gina frowned. "No, Stella is just a friend. But her work partner is also my partner."

"Sounds like fun," Pat said and then coughed. More blood slipped from her lips and dribbled down her chin.

"Try to keep still. I'm sure help will be here any moment."

Pat nodded and closed her eyes again.

Gina wasn't sure what to do, but she was pretty sure that her closing her eyes and going to sleep wasn't a good idea. At least it always seemed not to be when they died in films and on the telly. "Stay awake, Pat. You need to stay with me. Tell me why you were in here today?"

"Probably same reason as you."

"You wanted to buy sexy lingerie for your girlfriend? Go, Pat."

Pat chuckled and moaned again. More blood trickled from the corner of her mouth. "In that case, not the same reason. I came for something for myself."

"Oh."

"Recently divorced. Usual old cliché, I suppose."

"Never too late to discover one's inner self, Pat." She winked.

Pat coughed again, and more blood dribbled down her chin. "I hope not." She squeezed Gina's hand in hers and tugged her closer. "I let too much time go by. Wasted too much. I didn't tell the people I loved that I loved them enough. I didn't enjoy life enough." Her voice faltered a moment, then returned with more strength than Gina thought she would have been capable of. "Where's my bag?"

"I don't know. What does it look like?"

"Brown leather, shoulder bag. Big."

Gina saw one a few feet away and stretched to grasp a handle without lifting the pressure from Pat's stomach. "This one?"

"Yes, that's it."

"Here you go."

"My purse. There's a picture."

"You want me to get it out for you?"

Pat nodded.

Gina unzipped the large bag using her foot to keep tension and make it a little easier to open. The purse was on top, and the flap popped open easily. The picture under the plastic cover was of a very young Pat and a soldier. The picture was badly faded. The miniskirt she wore and the mod haircut spoke of the late sixties, maybe early seventies. She couldn't be sure.

"Is this your husband?"

Pat shook her head. "No. He's the man I should have married. My George." She smiled and lay her head back down.

The wistful look on her face made Gina wonder about the pain she must have been in. It almost seemed like it had gone, as if whatever she was thinking about had taken it away from her.

"Why didn't you?"

"My father. The great Paddy O'Shea." She said his name with a sneer. Clearly not a great father-daughter relationship. "He wouldn't let me marry an Englishman. And certainly not a soldier. Murdering bastards, that's what he called 'em. Not his daughter, not over his dead body." She coughed up more blood. "Not a good Catholic family like we were."

"Oh. I see."

"Aye. I had to marry another good Catholic boy, even if I didn't love him and he didn't love me." Pat tapped the plastic. "But my George.

He loved me. Wanted to run away with me, he said. Said he'd go AWOL and everything to get me away from Ireland and the troubles."

"You refused?"

Pat nodded. "Couldn't. Didn't want to ruin his life." She laughed a bitter-sounding laugh. The movement caused her to cough up more blood.

"Please be careful, Pat. You need to keep still. Where the bloody hell is that ambulance? It must be coming by now."

Pat waved her hand in the air. "Too late for that now, Gina. Too late." She sucked in a gurgled breath.

Gina could feel tears wetting her own cheeks.

"Now, now. Enough of that, girlie." She smiled. "It's okay."

"No, it isn't, Pat."

"It is what it is, child. Life's funny like that." She tapped the picture again. "His name's George Boyne."

"That's unusual."

"There's a letter in there for him. I always said I'd find him and give it to him."

"Then you should definitely do that, Pat."

Pat closed her eyes again. "No time." She squeezed Gina's hand. "Find him for me. Find him and give him the letter."

"No." Gina shook her head. "You can do that, Pat. Just as soon as the ambulance gets here, we'll get you better, and then you can go find your George."

Pat shook her head again. "Find him for me." She wheezed, the Irish lilt shifting from lullaby soft to gutter harsh as she begged. "Please." Her grasp relaxed. "He deserves to know the truth." The strength in her arm faltered completely and fell from Gina's wrist. "About everything."

"Pat? What do you mean?" Gina grabbed at her hand again and shook her arm. "Pat?" She dropped her hand and slapped at her cheeks gently, trying to wake her. "Pat? Come on, now. Wake up and tell me more about this dishy soldier of yours."

Pat didn't move.

Gina lifted the cloth from her stomach, and the blood oozed slowly. No more gushing. No more pumping. The tension was gone from Pat's body, and Gina realised for the first time that she was kneeling in a pool of the other woman's blood.

Gina didn't know how long she'd been there but she had no intention of moving. She wouldn't leave Pat—she simply couldn't. She'd seemed so lonely that Gina couldn't bring herself to leave her all alone.

Instead, she stared at the picture of Pat and her soldier. How many years had she carried it with her? In her purse? Where a woman would normally keep a picture of her husband, her children...grandchildren even. Instead she'd carried his picture. Just since her divorce? Or longer? How many years had she dreamed of finding him again? Was it even something she could do? Did she want to? Was it something she should do?

Gina looked at Pat, her face relaxed in death as the pain of her injury was taken from her. Only the blood that marred her skin belied the fiction of a peaceful slumber. That and the pool of blood that surrounded them both, soaking into Gina's clothes.

Whoever she'd been in life, Pat hadn't deserved to die like this—terrified, in pain, and, for the most part, alone. From just the few moments they'd spent together, it had been so obvious that Pat had a wicked sense of humour and an adventurous spirit. She must have done, to be here in a sex shop at sixty or seventy or whatever.

She didn't deserve to die like this.

No one did.

CHAPTER 3

Kate blindly pulled up behind the string of cars already blocking the exit to the bus station. Nothing would be moving in or out of there for a good long time. Well, except the ambulances that were flying past at a rate of knots, ferrying the wounded to hospital.

A small flurry of snow drifted between the buildings, and a heavy clump slid from the roof of the bus shelter, landing in a sodden heap close to her feet. Snow in Norfolk was a rarity. When it fell, it was always in much lower volume than the rest of the country, and it didn't seem to last long. Except this year. Inches lay across the fields she passed daily. The surface had turned to an ice crust, reflecting the sun with blinding shafts of light.

She spotted Timmons in the middle of the walkway towards the main shops, next to the entrance to the supermarket, directing officers and first responders alike. She ran over to him.

"Sir," she said.

"Brannon, good. We've got a fuckin' mess here."

"What happened? There's absolute bullshit flying about. Some idiot's spreading a rumour this was a bomb going off." She kicked the soft snow from her boots. A habit she'd formed already in an attempt to remain on her feet in the winter conditions.

"Bullshit."

"Exactly what I said, sir."

"It was two of 'em."

Kate froze in midstep. "What?"

He turned to look at her. "Two bombs went off. Goodwin was on the scene when it happened. She's injured. I'm going to see her now." Timmons shrugged his massive shoulders and ran his fingers through what was left of his hair. "Gonna be a bloody nightmare, this."

"Bloody hell. Bad?"

He shrugged. "Don't know yet. When I spoke to her, she was slurring her words. Sounded pissed. Probably a head injury."

"Shouldn't she already be on her way to hospital, then, instead of waiting here for you to speak to her?" She didn't like the idea that the tough-as-nails DI would put Stella in jeopardy for a bit more information, but like herself, coppers did tend to have a one-track mind when it came to things like this. And Timmons might be her boss, but she wasn't afraid to stand up to him. She'd learned over the past couple of months that he respected that. Stella was her friend, and she clearly needed medical attention.

"I'm not holding her here, Sergeant. I'm going there now to make sure the bloody paramedics don't fanny about and get her to see the quacks as quick as fucking possible."

Kate stared; his thinning hair was wet and looked like he'd scraped his hands through it so many times it was ready to stand up on its own. His eyes were bloodshot, and he was breathing heavily. He clenched his fists over and over as he led her through the shopping centre and along the street.

"Sorry. I thought—"

"I know what you thought. But my officers mean more to me than that, Brannon. All of you."

She ducked her head. "Understood."

"Good. So, we've got two suicide bombers in a shopping area two weeks before Christmas. Two women, Asian, wearing burquas, who looked to be pregnant, walk into a sex shop and blow the fuckin' roof off."

"Fuck."

"Yeah."

"How many injured?"

"We'll find out in a minute. The boys from the counterterrorism unit will be taking the lead on this one."

"Sir, we don't need—"

"Yes, we do." He pointed to what was left of a row of shops. She knew that there'd been a shoe shop, a chemist, a card shop, and a clothes shop along the street next to the Ann Summers shop that was at the centre of the row. There wasn't a window left intact. Walls were crumbled in places, plaster hanging perilously in clumps, swinging on the wind. Kate held her breath, waiting for the clump to fall.

The wail of sirens, car alarms, and burglar alarms sounded a high-pitched chorus to a sickening melody of crying and screaming people. Paramedics, firefighters, and first responders of all kinds crawled over debris from one person to the next, offering assistance, comfort, and sometimes a shroud.

Knowing there was nothing more she could do for the fallen and the injured, she scuffed the toe of her boot in the glass. A blackened nut skittered away from her, pinging into a couple of ball bearings and a bent nail sticking out of a fragment of half-melted plastic.

"Shrapnel," he said. "They put them inside the vests to cause maximum damage when they...when they detonate."

Kate nodded. She knew that. They all did. Unfortunately.

Detective Constables Tom Brothers and Jimmy Powers stood together outside the front of the shop. Jimmy's face was ashen, verging towards the grey spectrum, and he seemed unable to tear his gaze from the floor.

Kate couldn't stop herself. She nodded in greeting to them both, even as she stared down at Jimmy's feet. Or, rather, at what was laid at Jimmy's feet.

A child's pushchair rested upside down on its front. Only one wheel was left, and it swung idly in the gentle wind. The canvas fabric of the chair was shredded and blown inside out. The arms and legs of the child that had been inside it protruded at sickening angles. Its clothes were torn, as was the little flesh she could make out. Bright-red blood pooled and cooled, forming a frozen pond around the sickening sight. Scarlet darkened to crimson and stood in stark contrast to the greying snow that clung to the stone paving slabs.

Her breath fogged as it left her lips in short, sharp gasps, and a cold that had nothing to do with the weather seeped into her soul.

Tom pointed to a dustbin that was mangled and dinted. "Puke over there if you got to."

Kate put her hand to her mouth and fought it, letting her head swing from side to side. She'd never been the weak woman on the force whose emotions got in the way of doing her duty. She'd never vomited at a crime scene. Never ducked out of a postmortem. She didn't intend to start now.

Tom clasped his hand on her shoulder and said softly, "It's okay, Kate. We both did."

She nodded, but still she fought it.

"Fuck's sake," Timmons muttered. "Do we have a name? Age?" he asked no one in particular.

"Not yet, sir," Tom said.

Timmons nodded towards the pushchair and then the other bodies on the pavement. "Brannon, get yourself to the hospital. Make sure Goodwin gets seen to. Quickly. The rest of us will be gathering witness statements and securing the scene while the CSIs do their thing. We'll be basically standing around with our thumbs up our arses on standby to help as needed with the investigation under the purview of the National Counterterrorism Network." He looked her in the eye. "If you can get statements from Goodwin and your girlfriend, that would be a bonus. She'll need to be checked over too, after all. Two birds, one stone and all that."

"Wait. Gina's here?"

"Bollocks," he said under his breath. "I thought you knew."

"Knew what?"

"Seems Gina and Stella were having a girly shopping day or some bollocks when this shitstorm hit."

"Oh my God." Kate's stomach threatened to reject her breakfast for the second time in less than a minute, and she was pretty sure her face had gone grey. All the blood in her body was rushing through her ears at that moment, so it must have done. "What happ...is she... where...where is she?"

Timmons wrapped a meaty hand around her arm and held her up. "When Stella called me, she passed out part way through. Gina talked to me. She's fine." He shook her gently. "Look at me, Kate. Look at me."

She tried to focus on what he was saying. Gina had spoken to him. That was good. Right?

"She was in Ann Summers when I spoke to her. She should still be there. They've only moved the critically injured so far."

Kate tried to swallow around the lump of pure fear that was lodged in her throat. "She...she wasn't injured?"

"No. She's fine. She was absolutely fine when I spoke to her. She got Stella into the recovery position, and she was moving around a little in there."

Relief washed over Kate, and the noise of the surrounding area came rushing back to her. The discordant sounds hit her full force, like a twenty-foot wave crashing over her head. "Okay. Okay, that's... that's good." She smiled in relief, then frowned as she remembered Timmons ordering her to take them both to the hospital. "Wait. Then why do I need to take her to the hospital?"

Timmons squinted at her. "Precaution. Purely precaution." He pulled her a little closer. "There may be minor cuts or bruises to be checked out. No doubt there was a lot of flying glass." He dipped his head to look her in the eye. "Cry now if you need to, but when you get to her, you need to hold your shit together. What went down in there... Well, I was fucking shitting myself when Stella was on the phone to me, Kate, so I can only imagine how Gina's feeling right now." He shook her gently. "Get me?"

Kate nodded, let out a long shuddering breath, and buried her face in her hands. And the tears fell. The sobbing began as Timmons wrapped his arms around her shoulders and held her.

She'd never cried in a man's arms before. Never cried on the job, or on the shoulder of her boss, but today she finally didn't give a shit. She truly didn't. Gina and Stella were what was important now, not the ridiculous fronts they all affected for the sake of the job. Gina and Stella had gone through something she couldn't even imagine, a horror she didn't *want* to imagine. And God alone knew how this was going to affect them for the rest of their lives. But at least they still had their lives.

Kate wanted to know how many had died, but she didn't think she could face the knowledge yet. She wanted to ask how many were injured, but she didn't want to know that either. Not yet. Later, her police brain would need the answers, but right now she wanted to just be Gina's girlfriend and help her through her emotions. Whatever Gina needed, Kate knew she would do.

"You're sure she's okay?" she whispered into Timmons's shoulder when her sobs subsided.

He nodded and pulled back a little. "Positive."

"Right. Okay. That's okay, then." The feeling of relief was palpable. Her lungs began to filter oxygen again, and the flood to her brain kickstarted it into gear. "Why were they in Ann Summers?"

Timmons frowned. "Shopping, I assume."

Kate frowned. "Right. But why? Why in there?"

He rolled his eyes. "Isn't that what women do on girly shopping trips?"

"No."

"Well, colour my delusions shattered." He turned her towards the debris-strewn entry to the shop. "Come on. Let's make sure they both get out of here now."

A mannequin in barely decent attire lay across the concrete slab—head missing, leg in half, and one arm reaching out towards her like it, too, was begging for her help. Racks of lingerie, sex toys, DVDs, and books were scattered across the shop floor and out onto the street.

"Bloody hell."

Kate crunched her way through the shop until she found Gina kneeling beside the body of an older woman and clutching a brown leather bag to herself. She was covered in blood. She was still, though. She didn't appear to be hurt anywhere. Well, not seriously, anyway. She just stared at the woman on the floor.

Kate approached her slowly. Like she would a frightened animal. "Gina, sweetheart, are you okay?"

Gina didn't look up, so Kate got a little closer. "Gina, baby, are you hurt?"

Gina shook her head. "Pat died."

Kate looked at the woman on the ground. "Is this Pat?"

Gina nodded.

Kate looked up at Timmons.

He shrugged and moved over to Stella. He bent down and touched his fingers to her neck. Nodding, he checked his watch. Counting off her pulse, no doubt.

"Gina, I'm sorry about Pat. Are you okay?"

Gina finally looked up at Kate and smiled softly, sadly. "Yes. I would like to go home, though. I didn't want to leave her alone, but I think...she's gone now, so I think she'll be okay now. Is that all right?"

Kate nodded. "We can leave anytime you want. But we need to go to the hospital first."

"Why? I don't want to go to the hospital. I'm fine. I just need a shower and some fresh clothes."

"I know. But Stella needs to get checked out. Boss's orders."

Gina glanced over at Stella. "Is she okay?"

Timmons offered Gina a gentle smile and nodded to Kate. "Like she said, boss's orders. For you too. Can't have you deciding we didn't take care of you at an incident and then suing us later. I've got my pension to think about."

Gina snorted. "Fine. But you better find me something else to wear." She motioned to her bloodstained jeans and jumper.

Kate didn't have the heart to mention the future that lay ahead for Gina's clothes. Timmons, it seemed, had no such compunction.

"No worries, Gina, that lot's all evidence now," he said. "Maybe Kate can get you a pair of those scrubs they all wear on casualty or something."

"But this is my favourite jumper."

Timmons looked her up and down. "You'll never get all that blood out of it anyway. Ex-wife used to say that white wine was good for getting stains out, but you could probably buy a new jumper with the amount you'd need to get rid of that lot."

Kate shook her head, trying to dislodge the image of Gina covered in blood, but it was no use. It wouldn't be until she got her out of there and into something clean and dry. She tried not to think about what could have happened. There were just too many ways today could have gone wrong. No, that wasn't right. It was wrong. All wrong. So wrong she couldn't even think straight. But it could also have been so much worse.

Gina was whole, and she was talking to her. Everything else they would deal with when it came up.

She had no doubt this would affect Gina in the future. How could it not? Kate knew it was going to affect *her,* so how could it not affect Gina too? Seeing that baby outside, so young and so completely innocent, struck down without thought or care. How could anyone think this was justified in any way, shape, or form? It wasn't. It was barbaric and cruel, and so entirely senseless. Such a waste.

Gina had fought so hard—worked so tirelessly to get herself back to some semblance of normal after Ally's attack, and now this. How was Gina supposed to deal with this too? How could any of them deal with this?

"Brannon? You okay there?"

Timmons's voice shocked her out of the desperate thoughts whirling around her head.

She caught his eye and dipped her head once, acknowledging that she was far from okay and thanking him for dragging her out of the whirlpool of unanswerable questions—the what-ifs and the could-have-beens.

This wasn't getting them anywhere. They'd be here all day at this rate, and she needed to get Gina away from here. She needed to get herself away from here. "Can you stand up?"

Gina laughed. It was a sad laugh that seemed hollow and unnaturally light as it floated out of the gaping hole in the roof like a helium balloon taking flight. Her gaze slid behind Kate and seemed fixed on something Kate didn't want to look at.

"I can." Gina's voice was thick and clumsy. Almost as if her tongue was suddenly swollen and too big for her mouth. She coughed and carried on. "I might need some help, though. My feet have gone to sleep."

Kate reached out and helped her stand slowly as the paramedics loaded Stella onto a backboard and lifted her onto a trolley. They were heading out of the door by the time Gina looked down her body and said, "Jesus, it's even worse than I thought."

"We'll get you cleaned up. Don't worry." Kate turned towards the door.

"I'm not worried." She reached up and touched her hand to Kate's temple. "You're here."

Kate smiled a smile she knew didn't reach her eyes. It said, "I'm always here". A smile that only Gina would ever see. "Whenever you need me."

"I know." She looked down at the woman on the floor again, and whispered something to her, but Kate couldn't make out the words. It sounded a little like "I'll find him for you", but that didn't make any sense.

Timmons acknowledged them leaving with a wave and a wiggle of his hand between his ear and his mouth. His sign to call him.

Kate nodded and led Gina back to the bus station and her car. She wanted to get to the hospital as close to Stella's arrival as possible.

She covered the passenger seat with a plastic sheet. This, too, would be brought in for forensic analysis. Not that she expected it to be revealing. The bombers were dead, and Gina had had no direct contact with them anyway. The most that sheets were going to tell them was who the blood belonged to.

"I really don't need to go to the hospital, you know. I'm fine."

Kate looked at her. She looked a little pale. Blood smears on her cheek added to the ghostly pallor, but her eyes looked clear, her gaze was focused, and her demeanour seemed far more normal than Kate had expected. If she didn't know any better, she wouldn't have suspected that Gina had been at the scene of a terror attack. Shock? Maybe. Would the reality of it set in later? Maybe. But right now, Gina did indeed seem to be handling everything better than Kate was.

"I'm sure you are, but our protocol is to have you checked over by a doctor," she said eventually, then offered what she hoped was a cheeky grin. "Like Timmons said, it's a safety thing so you can't sue, sweetheart." She winked at Gina. Just in case she wasn't sure she was joking.

"I would never."

Kate reached over and kissed her cheek. "I know. But we also need to collect your clothes for evidence. And that really needs to be done in a controlled environment. The hospital's as good a place to do that as the police station is. Maybe better. For you, anyway."

Gina glanced down at the plastic-covered seat. "At least I won't dirty your seats with that on there."

"I really wouldn't care if you did," Kate said earnestly. All she cared about was Gina being okay. She helped her into the car before getting in herself and pulled away from the scene slowly, not at all like her normal self, but fully aware that she was in shock. Add to the fact that she had to dodge a plethora of people running, ambulances pulling away, police cars blocking almost every inch of the roads, and CSIs suiting up in what appeared to be a staging area under the covered walkway.

A crowd was growing. An angry crowd. Circling the bus station and filling the road. People were whispering amongst themselves, calling out to people within the cordoned area. Demanding information. And hurling insults when it wasn't forthcoming. Kate wasn't looking forward to the fallout from this.

At the other side of the road, news crews were gathering. Reporters stood in front of cameras, making sure to get the bus station in the shot behind them as yet another ambulance tore away, lights flashing, sirens screaming, and Kate followed in its wake, hoping it was Stella's ride.

CHAPTER 4

Kate followed the ambulance but was quickly left behind. She had no lights or siren on her Mini, and Gina wasn't in need of emergency help. With everything else going on today, she didn't need to worry about her licence by breaking every traffic law there was. Never mind the icy road conditions to contend with.

"I need to get Sammy. I don't want her to see or hear about this. I don't want her having more nightmares because of this."

"I'll sort it. Will's looking after her. I'm sure he won't mind having her stay with him a bit longer."

"No, I'm sure he'd be fine with that. We just need to figure out what to tell Sammy why I'm not going to be home when I said. I don't want her to worry."

Kate glanced over. Gina was chewing her bottom lip.

"Do you think Stella would mind if we told Sammy she's in the hospital and we're staying with her a bit?" Gina asked eventually. "That she's banged her head or something? Something Sammy can relate to and won't scare her too much."

"She's had concussion before?"

Gina snorted. "I've been worried on more than one occasion that social services were going to think she was a battered child the number of times she's fallen out of trees or hurt herself one way or another."

"So no skateboard for Christmas?"

Gina closed her eyes and banged her head against the headrest. "Please tell me you didn't."

Kate grinned. "I didn't."

"Thank God. We'd have to take up permanent residence at the hospital if you did."

Kate sniggered as she reached the roundabout and took the second exit, joining the queue of traffic trying to get through the few roads left open around King's Lynn. It was bedlam. Pure, unadulterated chaos on the roads... Well, it would be if anyone was moving.

"We'd be quicker walking," Gina said.

"Not with your costume." She pointed to Gina's blood-soaked clothes. "You'd be accosted by plastic policemen in minutes."

"You so need to stop calling them that, Kate," Gina said with a grin.

"What do you want me to call our Police Community Support Officers instead?"

"How about PCSOs? Like Stella and Jimmy do."

"Pft," Kate mocked as she continually stole glances at Gina. She really was dealing with this remarkably well. Kate half expected her to be comatose or catatonic or something. In the past, panic attacks had been a dominant feature in Gina's coping strategy...or rather her non-coping strategy. This calm and collected Gina was a bit of a mystery.

"Are you sure you're okay?" Kate asked again.

"Why? Because I haven't fallen to pieces on you yet?"

"Well, yes." Kate chuckled a little, embarrassed to be so easily read.

"I really am. Believe it or not." She offered Kate a smile. "I had a really weird moment while I was in there, though, after Stella passed out and I'd hung up on your boss. He was really good, by the way."

"I'll not tell him that. He'll get a big head," Kate said with a gentle grin. "What happened?"

"Huh?"

"Weird moment."

"Oh, right, yeah. It was like... I'm not sure I can describe it. I was surrounded by this kind of silence. And it was like I was looking at everything through someone else's eyes."

"Like an out-of-body thing?"

"I suppose so. I mean, that actually does describe it pretty well." Gina crossed her arms over her chest and tucked her hands under her armpits. "It was weird, and felt like it lasted ages. But I really am okay now."

Kate peeped at her, trying to gauge if she was still in shock or if she really was coping with it all. *Time will tell, right?* "Okay. I'll take your word for it."

"I am sad, though."

"Yeah, it was... There's a lot of people hurt there."

"Yes but, specifically, I'm sad because of Pat."

Kate frowned. "The lady you were sitting with? The one who died?"

"Yes."

There was such sadness in Gina's voice that it was clear what a profound moment it had been for her.

"She told me she was in there to buy a vibrator because she was recently divorced."

"Wow. That...just... I mean...wow."

Gina giggled. "I know. She told me how her father made her marry the wrong man because he wouldn't let her marry the English soldier she was in love with."

"Why wouldn't he let her marry him? A soldier not good enough for him?"

"Definitely not. Especially as he was Irish Catholic and I assume the English soldier was anything but."

"Oo. You didn't cough up those details to start with."

"No. She showed me a picture of him. She still carries—carried—it in her purse all these years later." She reached into the bag and pulled out the purse and flipped it open to show Kate the faded picture.

"You brought her bag with you?"

Gina stared at the bag in her arms. "Oh my God. I'm so sorry." Her eyes were wide open. She clearly hadn't even thought about it. "You have to turn around. They'll need this to let her family know what's happened to her. They won't know who she is without this."

"It's okay. We can deal with it at the hospital. I can get it to Ruth or Len there."

"You sure? I don't want to cause any trouble."

"It's fine. I promise. I'll take care of it at the hospital."

"If we ever get there," Gina murmured.

"Quiet in the cheap seats," Kate said with a snigger. She put her hand on Gina's knee and squeezed gently. "It'll be fine. You have my word."

"Thank you." Gina slouched in her seat again. "I'm not sure I could face going back there right now."

"You don't have to." Kate inched forward towards the next roundabout. They were so close it should have taken less than two minutes to get parked up and inside the building. Instead it seemed like it was taking hours. "You okay?"

Gina nodded. "Just worrying about Sammy."

Kate fished in her pocket and handed over her mobile. "Go ahead and call. Might as well make the most of the travelling time."

"You sure?"

"Positive."

"Thanks," Gina said as she dialled the number at the campsite. "Will, it's Gina."

Kate listened in as they inched another few feet towards the roundabout.

"Yeah, could you do me a favour, please... Yeah, I know... Can you keep Sammy with you for the evening too? Oh no, a friend of ours has taken a...a fall, and we're taking her to the hospital to get checked out... Yes, sure, you can tell Sammy that, but please, please don't let her watch TV... No, I just don't want her to see the news, there was...an incident in Lynn today, and she knows I was going shopping there... Yeah, yeah, I'm fine... Really I am. I just don't know how long this will take, and I'd rather tell Sammy the details I want her to know when I see her and she can see me... Yeah, she can play on the Xbox with you." Gina rolled her eyes.

Kate knew this would lead to another amendment to Sammy's Christmas list.

"Of course...yeah, that's a good idea, Will. You know how much she loves pizza. Thank you...no, no, honestly, I really appreciate it. You're a really good friend, Will. We'll let you know as soon as we know anything. Thanks, bye."

"Xbox tournament and pizza. Sammy won't want us to pick her up."

"True. He said he'd make up a room in the hostel for her too, just in case we're really late."

"He's a good lad."

Gina nodded, handed back the phone, and stared out the window.

Kate concentrated on the miniscule movements in the traffic and slid the phone back into her pocket, content to sit in silence for a few moments. Moments turned to minutes, and finally they were at the front of the queue.

"She asked me to find him for her," Gina said eventually.

"I'm sorry, what?"

"Pat. She asked me to find George. She said she has a letter in here for him." Gina indicated the bag still on her lap.

Now Gina's goodbye comment made sense. "She gave it to you?"

"I suppose she did, in a way. She asked me to find him so that he would know the truth. She said he deserved to know the truth about everything that happened back then." She looked at Kate as they entered the roundabout and then joined another queue to exit it. "Will you help me find him?"

"Is that what you want to do?"

Gina nodded. "I think I have to. It was her last wish. Her last request."

"God, that's a morbid thought."

"Sorry," Gina said quietly.

"No, no. I didn't mean it like that. I understand why you want to do that. I really do."

"But...?"

"Maybe you should sleep on it before rushing in headlong."

"I don't—"

"Or at least shower," Kate suggested.

"Fine. That one I definitely agree with."

The car moved slowly but steadily until they cleared the pelican crossing and turned into the hospital grounds. It was surprisingly quiet in the car park, and Kate easily found a spot.

"I'll just grab a ticket." By the time she returned with her parking ticket, Gina stood beside the car, moving stiffly. "You okay? You're walking a bit like John Wayne." She grabbed her evidence bag and first aid kit from the boot of her car, stuck the ticket stub on her windscreen, and locked the car behind her.

"I feel like I fell off his horse," Gina quipped. "Then got flattened by it."

Kate frowned.

"When the bomb went off, Stella threw me to the ground and lay over me." She glanced down at her clothes. "Plus this is all drying, and it's stiff as a board."

Kate nodded and took hold of Gina's elbow to guide her.

"I know where I'm going, you know," Gina said with a small smile. "I've lost track of the number of times I've been here with Sammy."

"Somehow I can't imagine that little scamp of yours ever needing to come to a place like this." Sarcasm hung heavy on each word as Gina's lilting laughter peeled from her lips.

"You can bring her next time."

Kate nodded. Challenge accepted.

She led them through the automatic doors and quickly got Gina booked in. She flashed her badge to the receptionist. "Where's Detective Sergeant Stella Goodwin been taken?"

The woman looked up and scowled. "We don't give out information to—"

Kate lifted her badge up higher. "Goodwin's my partner. She saved this woman's life," she said, pointing to Gina. "Literally shielding her with her own body, and I know she's in here with a head injury. We tried to follow the ambulance away from the incident, but as I'm sure you can imagine, it was more than a little chaotic. Now, please, where is Stella Goodwin, and how is she doing?"

The receptionist sniffed and appeared to stare at the warrant card in Kate's hand like she was reading the print off it. She slipped her hand under the desk and a buzzer sounded. "Take a seat in the waiting room. I'll get a porter to show you through to her."

"A porter?"

"Yeah. The doctors and nurses are a bit busy right now. Treating people like your partner and those with even worse injuries." She nodded towards Gina. "They'll take a look at her as soon as they can. I'll let them know she's in with Ms Goodwin when they're ready."

"Thank you." Kate pushed open the door and held it open for Gina.

The porter arrived in less than a minute and led them to a family notification room. It was tiny. The chairs had been moved out, as had all other furniture, to make space for the gurney Stella lay on. Her face was pale. No, it was more grey and ashen than pale. There was a sickening pallor and rubbery look to her flesh that looked wholly unnatural. But her chest rose and fell with steady breaths, and the machine beside the bed announced the steady rhythm of her heart.

Kate crossed the tiny floor space and touched Stella's arm, needing to feel the warmth of her. Needing to convince herself that she wasn't cold, that the machine readings were real and not just a figment of her imagination. She let out a sigh of relief at the clammy heat of Stella's skin, then swallowed and took a good look at the room they were in.

A family notification room with a portable gurney in it instead of a real bed. There was a bathroom next door with a shower in it so Gina could clean up. Just as soon as Kate had collected her clothing.

As far as Kate was concerned, it was pretty fucking perfect.

"Do you have to go back to work soon?" Gina asked as she settled herself against the edge of Stella's bed.

There was nowhere to sit in the tiny room, and Kate knew they needed to get her out of those clothes as soon as possible so she could at least try to get a little bit comfortable. They were going to be here for a while.

"Probably. Timmons said the terrorism guys are taking over. Jimmy and Tom are at the scene, with the CSIs crawling all over the place already. There's not an awful lot for me to do right now, but no doubt there will be before long." Kate closed the blinds to the window that overlooked the tranquillity garden in the centre of the hospital. "It'll be all hands on deck before long: taking witness statements, following up whatever leads we find. If it's just two people going on a rampage, it's going to be wrapped up pretty quickly, as they're no longer a problem. If this is part of something else, something bigger, or if they have links to a terrorist group, then it could drag on and on for months, babe. We just don't know yet." She shrugged. "If there's something urgent, they'll call me, but I doubt that'll happen until I call Timmons."

"Why?"

"Technically I'm still working here."

"You are?"

"Technically."

"What do you mean, 'technically'?"

"My boss sent me with instructions to collect your clothes for forensic analysis. I need to get Stella's too. And I need to get your statements. All those things will take a good long time."

"They will?"

Kate nodded. *Nope, should take about half an hour if I crack on.* "Could take most of the day to get statements from witnesses and collect evidence in such a chaotic environment."

"I see." Gina nodded slowly, clearly not buying Kate's excuses. "Don't you want to be out there? I mean, not that I don't want you here, with me. God, I do. But you love your job. You love catching the bad guys and bringing them to justice. It's more than a job to you, Kate, it's you. It's what you do. But..."

"But...?" Kate encouraged.

"You're making excuses to not be there. Why?"

"I want to be here with you. Is that a bad thing?"

Gina shook her head. "Of course not, but is that really all it is?"

"I'm worried about you."

"I'm fine. I'm not even hurt."

"You've worked so hard with Jodi," Kate said, referring to Gina's counsellor. "You've seemed to be making so much progress, I'm worried this will...I don't know, put you backwards. Undo the work you've done."

"I get that. I was sort of expecting that myself. But it's weird. I don't feel like I can't deal with this. Don't get me wrong, it's horrific. That moment I was telling you about." She waited until Kate nodded. "I was staring at this pile of foil wrappers. Condoms. They must have been from this big bowl on the counter, but they were all over the floor in this pile." She swallowed hard. The muscles in her throat worked as she tried to call up the words. "There was this... There was a hand half-buried amongst those packets. Just a hand. A woman's left hand, with purple nail varnish and an engagement ring, and no woman attached to it. It was beyond surreal. I still don't think I've taken it in, Kate. I'm not sure you can...not sure I can, anyway. But I know that this is different than how I felt after Ally attacked me."

"How so?"

"Ally attacked me. Personally. She was someone I knew—had known for many, many years—and she could still...do that to me. She wanted to do that to me. As a person. What happened today was different. It wasn't a personal attack on me. I don't know the women who did this. I don't know why they did it. They didn't know me, they didn't target me specifically. It was just a case of anyone in that shop would do. Does that make sense?"

Kate pondered Gina's words. While they did make sense, and Kate could certainly see how it was making the situation tolerable—even better—for Gina, it made it so much worse for Kate. The randomness of it. The utter senselessness of the destruction, the violence, the sheer callousness and disregard for the sanctity of human life was almost more than she could take. But Gina hadn't seen the child in the pushchair outside on the street. She hadn't yet put it into the context of how it could have been Sammy walking down that road, of how it could have been her hand shorn off and half-buried in condom wrappers. She was still focused on examining the difference between the two events. And that was okay with Kate. Part of her hoped Gina never got to the stage where she could see Sammy in that crowd of destruction. Because Kate could barely see anything else.

She swallowed the bile that rose in her throat again and nodded. "That's really great, Gina. I'm so proud of you." And she was. She also knew that she'd be there when the shock wore off and Gina saw the rest of the picture.

"So why else don't you want to be out there?"

"Well, you see, we coppers are a bit of a territorial bunch, and this investigation is going to be massive on a scale Norfolk has never seen. A specialist counterterrorism team will be coming because we don't have the expertise or the number of bodies needed to do the amount of work involved. Officers, CSIs, doctors...God, all manner of people will be drafted in from all over. London, Birmingham, probably Leicester and Peterborough too."

"Why? They don't know the area."

"They don't, but we're a small rural police force. We have less than 1500 coppers, PCSOs, and specials across the whole county. If we pulled in every one of them and did nothing to cover every other crime or complaint in the county for the duration—which could be months— we still wouldn't have enough people to do what needs to be done. Do you know how many officers are involved in a major incident like this?"

Gina shook her head.

"The bombs on the London Underground, there were over two thousand people involved over almost six months of investigation."

"Six months. It didn't last that long."

Kate nodded. "Yes, it did. It was probably longer, actually."

"But the news, the media, it said it was resolved after a few weeks."

"I wish. Believe me. We all wish that were the case. Just because the media and the public move on to the next story doesn't mean our work is done. Far from it."

Gina nodded. "I understand. So the team that is going to do the investigating—the terrorism squad—won't they need you all the more?"

Kate nodded. "Yes. They won't know the area or the politics of the place, but that doesn't mean we enjoy acceding control to them." She chuckled. "Like I said, we're a territorial lot. And if I were in their shoes, I wouldn't like coming in like this either. They're a team that work together and know each other. They know each other's strengths and weaknesses and, most importantly, they know what they're looking for when it comes to terrorism. They spend months doing additional training for this stuff."

"So they really do know what they're doing?"

Kate nodded. "They really do."

Gina smiled. "But you guys don't like to admit that someone else knows more than you do."

Kate raised an eyebrow. "You saying I'm an egomanic?"

"If the mania fits, darling."

Kate put her hand to her chest, a pained expression on her face. "Thou woundeth me, my lady."

Gina chuckled, as Kate opened the bag she'd brought with her from the car and laid a large plastic drop cloth on what little floor space there was. Next she pulled on a pair of gloves, and her cheeks were flushed. "I'm really sorry, but I have to get your clothes."

"I know. I'll undress on the plastic and put them in the bags."

Kate's cheeks reddened further. "I'm really sorry, Gina, but I have to collect them from you as you remove them." She shook her head and lowered her gaze to the floor. "They're evidence. I have to preserve the chain of custody, in case they're needed in some way for the investigation."

Gina felt like a fool. She wished she'd known. She wished Kate had told her. Well, she had told her that she'd need to collect her clothes for evidence. She just hadn't specified that she'd need to watch her strip them off at the same time. This wasn't how she wanted Kate to see her naked for the first time. Yes, she was ready to move their relationship along, ready to take that next step—but not here! She was ready to let Kate see her, warts and all, she was sure of it. But not in the middle of a hospital room, with Stella unconscious on the bed not even five feet away. No, this wasn't what she'd wanted. Not even in her wildest imagination could she have come up with this as the scenario when Kate first looked at her body. And her scars.

She felt awkward, clumsy as she reached for the button on her jeans.

"I'm sorry."

Gina shook her head. "You're just doing your job."

"At your expense."

Gina's hands shook as she dropped the zipper and clasped the waistband. "It's okay." She pushed them down and clear of her legs, folded them neatly, and handed them to Kate, followed quickly by her socks and her coat. The easy parts. "This isn't how I pictured you seeing me for the first time."

A whisper of a smile graced Kate's lips. "Me neither."

"Good." Gina flexed her fingers and gripped the hem of her jumper. "Because that would be really perverse, Kate."

"How can I make this easier for you?" Kate asked quietly.

"Keep looking at me."

Kate chuckled. "Trust me, that's not a problem."

"I mean in my eyes."

Kate's smile widened. "Trust me, that's not a problem," she repeated.

Gina couldn't help but laugh with her. It eased the tension in the small room. "I'm nervous."

"I know. But you really don't have anything to be nervous about."

"And why's that?"

"Well, there are many reasons. Where would you like me to start?"

Gina squeezed the wool between her fingers. "Wherever you like."

"Well, reason one, you're beautiful. So, you don't need to be nervous that I will ever think anything different."

"I know that," Gina whispered. And she did. It had taken a long time for her to get to the place where she truly trusted Kate's words, but she did. She knew that the torture marks—the scars from a gutting knife— that Ally had left on her body wouldn't change the way Kate looked at her. Or what Kate felt for her.

"Good." Kate's voice was thick with emotion. She coughed. "Next reason, you really need a shower because you're covered in blood."

Gina laughed. "Not attractive?"

"Well, it's not the most, what's the word, *romantic*?"

"*Erotic*?"

Kate swallowed audibly. "I think I'll stick with *romantic*."

"Chicken."

Kate opened her eyes wide in a look of mock shock. "Whatever."

Gina laughed. "So my current attire isn't exactly floating your boat. That's what you're telling me?"

"Yes, ma'am."

"But I'm not going to be wearing it for long. That kind of negates that point."

"It would seem to, but for one other thing."

"What's that?"

"It's not conducive to that romantic mood I was trying to explain before I got interrupted."

"Ah, I see."

"Then there's the fact that you're in charge, so unless this constitutes a romantic setting for you—in which case I'd really have to worry about you—then you really don't have anything to worry about."

"All good points. But you missed one."

"I did?"

"Yes."

"What did I miss?"

"You missed the fact that I trust you." Gina took a deep breath and raised the garment over her head. She held it out to Kate. Her hands trembled, but inside she felt calmer than she thought she would. She'd expected to feel butterflies in her stomach with nerves, with fear. But the look in Kate's eyes made her feel beautiful. She'd expected to feel a battle going on inside her, a war between her desire to cover her body and her desire to let Kate see her. Instead, she felt desired and wanted to revel in the feeling. Gina had expected to feel exposed, maybe even a little intimidated, standing naked in front of a fully clothed Kate. Instead, she felt powerful. As though she'd finally reclaimed something she'd lost. "How do you do that?" she whispered.

"Do what?" Kate asked, as she folded the jumper and slipped it into a plastic bag, never dropping her gaze from Gina's, not even for a second.

"I'm stood here, covered in bloodstains, looking like I've been dragged through a hedge backwards, and half-naked, while you're still fully clothed. But you still look at me like I'm special."

"Oh, that." Kate dropped the sealed bag onto the chair with the rest of Gina's clothing. "That's easy. You are special." The look in Kate's eyes was all Gina needed to know that she meant every word. "Very special."

"I wish this were a romantic setting."

Kate smiled a little sadly. "Me too." Kate's cheeks flamed, and Gina knew her own were just as red. She could feel the heat all the way to the tips of her ears as Kate closed her eyes and chuckled silently, her body moving with each noiseless titter. Then she shook her head, opened another bag, and simply waited.

Gina dropped her gaze to the floor as she unhooked her bra and tossed it over to Kate. She turned to the side as she lowered her underwear. As quickly as she could, she donned the white Tyvek suit from the evidence bag that Kate had waiting for her. It wasn't the right time, or place, or setting. But that didn't seem to stop her body reacting while Kate busied herself collecting up the drop cloth and wrapping it into an evidence bag too.

"There's a bathroom with a shower in it next door," Kate said, pointing to her left and handing her a small hand towel. "I'm sorry. It's the best I could find. The other option appeared to be paper towels."

Gina took the towel and nodded. "I'll manage. It'll just be good to get the blood off me."

Kate smiled. "I understand. Take your time. Trying to get those suits back on if you're a little damp is a bit of a nightmare. But I'm afraid it's all I've got right now."

"Thanks."

"The doctors won't be here for a while. I'll get you a cup of tea when you're ready."

The water was hot and helped soothe her sore muscles as she stood under the powerful spray. She tried not to look down at her feet. She knew the water would be running away red and then pink as

Pat's blood sloughed from her body and flowed away, almost like she'd never been there. As though all evidence of her meeting with Gina were gone. And Gina let the water take her tears along with it.

She'd meant it when she'd told Kate that she didn't feel as bad about this as she had in the wake of Ally's attack. Immediately after that, just a few short weeks ago, she'd tried to pull away from Kate, convinced she would no longer be interested in a woman who was, without doubt, damaged goods. But Kate was going nowhere, and her steadfast refusal to let Gina pull away from her had been the biggest factor in her recovery from the attack.

Just as it would be now in the wake of this event.

It hadn't been a personal attack. It hadn't been directed at her. And she didn't know either perpetrator. But it was still horrific. She'd still seen things she wished she hadn't. The severed hand, Stella's injuries. The lady without her legs. Pat. And that's without even thinking about the ultimate fate she'd escaped.

She could have died in there.

What if she'd been stood in a different spot? Or at a different angle? Would she still be here, standing in a lukewarm shower, staring at a handful of antibacterial soap and wishing that Kate hadn't just seen her naked for the first time in a hospital room? Or would she still be lying on the floor in the Ann Summers shop while they collected evidence from her body.

From her cold, dead, body.

She didn't have time to shut off the water as she threw herself across the room, lifted the lid of the toilet, and emptied her stomach. Retch after heaving retch, she vented bile until there was nothing left.

As the cramps slowly began to subside, the sobs climbed up from her soul and clawed their way out of her mouth, choking her with their jagged edges and expanding girth. Each cry tore at her as it escaped, let loose upon the world, over and over until there was nothing left. Until the water ran cold across the tiled floor and pooled around her feet. Her skin pimpled with the chill, and the shaking in her hands eased to a tremor.

Her muscles protested as she crawled back under the cold spray and used handful after handful of antibacterial soap from the dispenser. There was nothing else available and Gina needed to wash it all away. She simply had to. The desire to be clean ran deeper than just needing to be free of Pat's blood, Stella's blood, and the shards of glass in her hair. What she really needed was to be free of the images in her head.

No water or soap would ever be strong enough for that.

Still Gina scrubbed every inch of her body. The strong scent of alcohol that came off the soap wasn't unpleasant, but it stung her nose, and made her eyes water a little.

Right now she needed a distraction. She needed something to think about that wasn't a half-buried hand or the ragged stump of blood and bone or the death mask of a stranger, and her mind latched on to whatever passing thought gripped it.

What was in that letter? What had Pat needed to explain to George? What truth did he deserve to know? Did he really need to know it now? After so many years, would it make a difference to him? Pat had certainly seemed to think it would. Would it affect others or just him? God, there were so many questions. So many things to think about. And if she did want to honour Pat's last request and find him, how would she go about it? She didn't exactly have a lot of information to go on. A name and the fact that he was a soldier who served in Northern Ireland, maybe fifty years ago.

"Maybe some people can find someone with only that, but personally I need an address and a phone number. Or better yet a Facebook account." She chuckled sadly to herself as she rinsed the last suds from her body. "I'll just have to ask Kate. This is what police do, after all. They find people. Some who don't want to be found, and with even less than this to go on." She turned off the water and grabbed the small towel. She held it up to examine it. Twelve inches by twelve inches of thin towelling fabric were all she had to dry her body enough to get back into a flimsy Tyvek suit without ripping it. "This should be fun." She started on her left shoulder. "In a kind of Krypton Factor sort of way."

CHAPTER 5

Kate's fingers itched under the nitril gloves as she placed items from Pat's handbag into separate evidence bags. One bag for her purse, a separate one for the cash. Cards, in yet another, and the picture of Pat as a young woman next to a man. The picture was faded—to only yellow and brown hues remaining—and the edges were worn smooth, like they'd been caressed many times over the years. On the back beautiful, careful handwriting had penned the words *George Xavier Boyne, Corporal.*

"Not your everyday garden-variety name, George. Wonder where that lot comes from." Over the years, Kate had learned names like that often had family significance, or one hell of a story behind them. She couldn't help but wonder at the story of Pat and George. Star-crossed lovers, from what Gina had said. The Romeo and Juliet of Belfast.

She smirked as the photo found its way into an evidence bag too, after she took a picture of it. The letter Gina had mentioned was there, sitting at the bottom, a brick that had hung around the poor woman's neck for God alone knew how many years. George Boyne. That's all it said on the outside of the envelope. Her handwriting was beautiful— smooth and flowing across the paper like a dancer across the floor.

Whilst many in her profession loved rifling through the private belongings of victims and perpetrators alike, Kate wasn't one of them. She hated invading the privacy of the victims she sought justice for. She could only bring herself to do it in the name of justice. A necessary evil in the pursuit of killers, crooks, and arseholes, in no particular order.

Gina had already told her that the contents of this letter were intensely private. A confession of some sort from one young lover to another. Yet her job still required her to read it to ascertain its investigative relevance. She couldn't take the word of a dead woman.

Kate checked on Stella, who was still sleeping, then used her finger to rip open the seal of the envelope. The contents slid easily into her palm, and she unfolded the pages with a deep sigh. It took her several minutes to read through the lengthy missive, and when she'd finished, she whistled as she folded the pages into another evidence bag and stacked them all together.

"Wow." She'd been right. There was nothing of any relevance to the investigation in the letter. Nothing. But the story—the history—on the pages was incredible. She'd heard many stories over the years: horror stories, sob stories, funny stories, unbelievable stories, and stories she wished were unbelievable. Pat's was a story she'd heard in a different way a hundred times over, but one that still broke her heart. "I'm surprised you're still going by your maiden name, Pat," she whispered to no one as she picked up her phone. "Not sure that old bastard deserved that much respect." Kate scrolled through her contacts and hit the button for the coroner's office.

"Too busy. Go away," Dr Ruth Anderson said as soon as she answered.

"I've got a time saver for you."

"Okay, I just found time."

"The lady who was killed in the Ann Summers shop."

"Which one? I've got multiple bodies from there. All women."

"Older woman, seventy-two, white hair."

"Yes."

"Her name's Patricia O'Shea. Birthday 20th of December."

"How do you know that?"

"I'm looking at her driver's licence."

"Why? Did you find it at the scene? I thought Timmons sent you home with Gina."

"No, he sent me to the hospital with Gina and Stella. Gina picked up the bag by mistake. She was in shock, you know."

"I'm sure. It must've been hell for her."

Kate thought about it and the way Gina had reacted. She didn't seem like it had been hell, even though it truly must've been. "I'm sure it was. We haven't really had a chance to talk about it yet. Anyway, I've bagged it for evidence, but I just thought if you had the ID, you could inform next of kin."

"Okay."

"I'll send you the picture of the driver's licence for verification."

"Thanks. I'll sort it out. Is Stella okay?"

"Cheers, Ruth. And I think so. I'm guessing a concussion at this point. She's seen the triage nurse but no doctor yet. They're absolutely run off their feet here. Did Timmons tell you? They were both in there, Ruth. When it blew up, Gina and Stella were both right there." Kate's voice caught in her throat, and she swallowed the sob before it could crawl past her lips.

"I know, my friend, I know. But they're both fine, right?"

Kate nodded, not trusting her voice.

"Right?" Ruth prompted.

"Yeah," she whispered. "They're okay."

"Then everything will work out. You'll all deal with this shit and move on. We all will. Don't let them win, Kate. Cry, scream, beat the shit out of that punch bag of yours, do whatever you have to, then get your head in the game and make sure this shit doesn't happen again. Make sure someone else doesn't have to live through this fucking nightmare."

"Easier said than done."

Ruth laughed bitterly. "Oh, I know. The face of terror may have changed, but it's not something new, is it?"

"No." Ruth was right. Isis, or Daesh, or whatever the hell they were supposed to call them now, weren't doing anything new. Britain had spent decades under the terrorist threat from the IRA. Bombs, shootings, kidnappings, beatings...same shit, just a different perp.

"Wanna hear the scuttlebutt going around about Stella?"

"Sure?"

"Apparently she got shot in the head."

Kate laughed. "Bollocks. There weren't any guns involved."

"Doesn't seem to matter. Her reputation as being your unit's badass has just overtaken yours, my friend."

"I'm gutted." Kate made sure that there was an adequate amount of sarcasm dripping from her retort.

Ruth laughed. "I'm sure you are. How's Gina holding up?"

"Pretty well, actually. Not sure it's hit her yet, to be honest, so I guess we'll just have to wait and see."

"Okay. Gotta run. Tell Gina I'm thinking of her."

"Will do." She ended the call and restacked the pile of evidence bags that were slipping off each other and heading for the floor.

"I believe you mentioned tea," Gina said as she re-entered the room.

"I did." Kate smiled. "Better?"

"Much."

"Okay, wait here and I'll be right back." The vending machine was closer than the cafe, but the coffee from it was little more than coloured water with more artificial sweetener than coffee in it. She didn't want to guess at what the tea was actually made of. The last time he'd tried it, Tom had reckoned it was gnat's piss, so she walked the five minutes to the cafe and back in order to get them decent brews. She didn't bring anything for Stella. As much as she knew Stella would complain if she woke up—probably including death threats—if she was suffering the concussion Kate suspected she was, the doctor needed to clear her before Kate was going to participate in feeding her.

Gina was sitting on the edge of Stella's bed when she returned, holding her hand and whispering softly to her. Stella's eyes were closed; a frown marred her face. Even in sleep, she was clearly in pain. Kate handed Gina the paper cup full of steaming liquid and sat down next to her.

"Has she woken up at all?"

Gina shook her head.

"Let's hope the doctor gets here soon, then."

"Yeah. Did you let them know who Pat was?" Gina asked and took a sip of her tea.

Kate nodded. "Yes, I phoned Ruth. She said to say hi, by the way. And that she's thinking of you."

Gina smiled. "That's nice of her."

"She is nice."

Gina raised an eyebrow. "Is she, now?"

Kate frowned. "Yeah, I've told you that before."

"I know." Gina's eyebrow was still hiked up.

Kate turned her head a little to the side, like she could gauge what was going through Gina's head better if she saw her from the side of her eye rather than straight on. Then it hit her. Like a plank. "Oh, no. Not like that." Kate held her hands out in surrender. "I mean, she is. I mean, I'm sure some people think she is, but not me."

"Not you?" Gina asked sceptically.

Kate nodded furiously. "Right. Not me."

Gina sipped more of her drink, eyes cast down.

"I swear."

Gina cleared her throat and peeked at her over the top of her drink. "I'm messing with you." She grinned widely. "Couldn't resist. Sorry."

She looked anything but sorry, but Kate was so happy to see her mischievous side that she simply leaned forward and kissed her lips gently. "I'll get you back for that one later."

"Really?"

Kate nodded and wondered if the look in her eye promised all the things she was thinking about. The things she'd been dreaming of doing to...and with Gina for weeks. If the blush on Gina's cheeks was anything to go by, it did.

"I smell coffee." Stella's croaky voice reached them from the bed.

"Hey, Stella. Glad you're still alive up there in the comfy chair." Kate sniggered and stood up so she could see Stella clearly.

"You call this hunk of steel comfy?"

"Trust me, it's better than the floor. At least you've got a blanket to keep you warm." She pointed her thumb over her shoulder. "All Gina's got on is a Tyvek suit."

Stella chuckled and grimaced. "You got nipples like chapel hat pegs, love?" Her words were slurred, but it didn't stop either of them understanding her.

"Now who's the bitch?" Gina retorted and crossed her arms over her breasts.

"I'll take that as a yes." Stella grinned and wrapped her fingers around Kate's hand. "Any chance you can turn off the lights? My fucking head's banging."

"No worries, Stella." The overhead light blinked out before she even moved from Stella's side. She looked over her shoulder, mouthed the words "thank you" to Gina, and offered her a smile. "That better?"

"Hmm." Stella's face seemed to relax a bit more. "Thanks." The slur made it sound more like "fanks" than anything else, but the tension around her eyes seemed to have eased.

Kate patted her hand and sat back down.

"Asleep again?" Gina whispered.

Kate nodded and picked her cup up off the windowsill. "Yeah." She checked her watch. Almost an hour since they'd been seen by the triage nurse. *Where the fuck was the doctor?*

"She'll be okay." Gina kept her voice quiet.

Kate smiled. "I know. She's tough as old hobnails, that one."

Gina chuckled softly. "Don't let her hear you say *old*."

Kate sniggered. "Only on purpose."

They let the quiet envelop them. The sound of soft breath and the gentle rustle of fabric as they breathed were only disturbed by the muted hum of the hospital running at full tilt outside the door.

"I don't know what to tell Sammy about all this."

Kate gulped down the mouthful of coffee she'd just taken. "What do you want to tell her?"

"Nothing." Gina laughed bitterly. "But that's not going to happen. Everyone in the village will know in no time, and it'll get back to her."

"So tell her the truth."

"She's nine!"

"And a lot tougher and stronger than probably both of us."

"I repeat, she's nine!"

Kate smiled, thinking of the tow-headed child who showed just how mischievous and childlike she was in one breath and then possessed a wisdom and strength beyond anything you had any right to expect from a kid her age. Her blue eyes, so like Gina's, would stare up at you innocently, then crinkle with a wicked grin as she ran off to another adventure, Merlin at her heels. Kate wrapped her arm around Gina's shoulders and tugged her in close.

"Tell her the truth, just the PG version of you living through an explosion. If she can see you're all right, she'll be okay."

"She'll have nightmares again."

"Probably. For a while. But we'll deal with that, and she'll get over them. She'll be okay."

"You really think so?"

Kate pressed a tender kiss to the side of Gina's head. "No doubt she'll demand having the last week off school to recover from the news. But other than attempting manipulation, she'll be fine."

"She calls it negotiation."

"She can call it whatever she likes, babe. It's manipulation, plain and simple."

Gina sighed. "I know."

"And I love her more for every bloody attempt she makes." She took hold of Gina's hand. "Sammy's a character, full of piss and vinegar, as my gran would've said. I can't make my mind up if she's going to end up a master criminal or a bloody good cop—"

"Maybe both."

"God help us all. But either way, life would not be the same without that kid of yours around." She leaned forward and kissed Gina's lips lightly. "And I happen to really like the life we're building right now."

"Negotiations and all?" Gina smirked, and Kate rolled her eyes.

"Negotiations and all."

"Thank you."

"No need to thank me." She gazed deep into Gina's eyes, wanting to make sure Gina heard her, and more importantly, believed her as she said, "I love you."

Gina laid her head on Kate's shoulder, snuggling as close as she could. "I love you too." She held her arms over her stomach as Kate wrapped her arm around her back and held her close.

"I know you're trying to steal my warmth."

"I never would."

Kate moved quickly; she took off her coat, wrapped it around Gina's shoulders, and tucked her back against her side in seconds. "Better?"

"Much."

"Good." She kissed the top of Gina's head. "So, while you were gone, I had a look through Pat's bag."

"I assumed you'd have to. Did you find the letter?"

Kate nodded.

"Did you open it?"

Kate nodded again.

"Well, I guess we can't give it to George now."

Kate smiled. "Well, when the investigation is over, perhaps we can give him the original, but not right now."

Gina nodded slowly and stared into her mug. "I guess it was a stupid idea to think I could try to find him and give it to him like she asked."

Kate held her breath. *Shit.* Now she felt like she had to help. "No, it wasn't. It was lovely to agree to do something for someone so badly hurt."

"She was dying, Kate. You can say it. I'm not going to fall apart on you."

"Okay. It was lovely of you to give a dying woman some peace in her final moments."

"But you think actually doing it's a stupid idea."

Danger. Danger! Beware girlfriends bearing that tone. Kate swallowed. "No. I'm not sure how realistic a goal it is, but I don't think it's stupid to want to try."

"Kate, you're a police officer. Of course you can find him."

Boom. That's the bit she didn't want to get pulled into. "He isn't someone we're investigating, and he won't be someone we investigate as part of this case. I can't use police resources to try and find him, Gina. That's an invasion of privacy and a violation of police ethics. Not to mention illegal. I could lose my job and face a prison term if I try to do something like that."

"You're joking?" Gina's face paled, and Kate shook her head. "Oh my God. I'm sorry. I didn't even think of that. I'm sorry."

"It's okay." Kate took hold of her hand and rubbed it between hers. "I'm sorry I can't do that for you."

"No, I don't want you to get into trouble. God. I'm so sorry."

"It's fine. Really."

"No, it's not. I just wish there was some way to try and find him."

Kate could see the tears welling in Gina's eyes. "Why is this so important to you?"

"Because I promised—"

"No, I mean right now. There's so much else going on. Why this? Why right now?"

Gina sniffed and looked down at the floor. "When I was in the shower, I kept thinking about what happened and how today could have ended up so different. If I'd been stood where Pat was instead of where Stella and I were...I'd still be there now. And it just kept going around and around in my head. I can't change what happened to Pat. I can't change what happened to anyone, and as awful as this will sound, I'm so fucking glad I was standing where I was today and not somewhere else." She swiped at the tears on her cheeks. "I'm so fucking happy that I'm still here, still alive, that Stella's going to be okay, because I know damn well she's gonna be. And I can't stop being happy about that, but I feel fucking awful for that."

"For being happy you're alive?"

She shrugged. "For being happy I wasn't in Pat's place."

"Ah," Kate whispered quietly. Survivor guilt was a powerfully destructive emotion. She'd seen people survive accidents only to go and self-destruct soon afterwards with pills and booze, with drugs and guilt. Was this need to find George, to give him Pat's letter, Gina's way of assuaging that guilt? Her way of apologising? Or simply her way of taking her mind off it all? Did it matter? It was a hell of a lot better than wallowing. "Well, we can. If you want to." She looked over at Stella again. A reflex that felt like it was becoming a habit.

"I don't understand. You just said you couldn't find him for me."

"No, I said I can't use police resources to find him for you. But anything that the public have access to is, well, public."

"Okay, but how does that help us?"

Kate smiled. "He has a pretty unusual name, sweetheart. An Internet search might bring something up. Give us a place to start."

"George Boyne? I didn't think that was so unusual."

"His middle name's Xavier."

"How do you know that?"

"It says so on the back of the photo."

"Oh, right. Well, okay. So, what do we do?"

"Are you sure you want to do this now? There's no rush."

"Now's good. Why are you stalling?"

"I just want to make sure you've got... I don't know how to put this diplomatically, so just bear with me, and don't get annoyed. Okay?"

Gina frowned but nodded for her to continue.

"Last time you went through something traumatic, you needed time to process what happened. To adjust and get used to it. It took me a long time to realise what was going on, because I wasn't thinking about the experience from a civilian perspective, just from my own. And that was wrong. I don't want to make the same mistake again. If you need time, I want to make sure you have it. If you need to talk, I'm here to listen... Or we can call Jodi, if that works better for you. Whatever you need."

Gina leant forward and kissed her cheek. "Thank you, but I'm fine. I really am." She sipped the last of her drink and tossed the cup into the wastepaper bin in the far corner of the room, pumping her fist when it landed dead centre of the receptacle. "I want to do all we can, as civilians, to try and find this guy and give him the letter Pat wrote for him. So teach me how to find people."

"You're sure?"

"Positive."

"Okay." Kate pulled her smartphone from her pocket and handed it to Gina. "Fire it up," she said with a smile.

Gina pressed the button.

"Open up a web browser, and we'll just try googling his name first off."

Gina's fingers flew over the keyboard, and they paused, waiting for the results. "I thought you said it was an unusual name. We've got tons of matches." Gina pointed at the screen.

"Less than a thousand. Trust me, that's a good result."

"Jesus. And I thought your job was so exciting."

Kate laughed. "Nope. Most of the time it's boring as hell."

"So how come you get hurt so much?"

Kate shrugged. She didn't, not really. Just bumps and scrapes mostly, just like everyone else. Except for the hulking great behemoth of a bloke who hit her a couple of weeks ago. And the sinking houseboat she got stuck in a couple of months back. The stitches and hypothermia hadn't been too much fun. "Just lucky I guess." She offered Gina a cheeky grin and pointed at the screen. "I'll bet any money that a lot of these hits are the same guy, because that really is an unusual name."

"So I just click on one and see if it's what we're after?"

"Yup."

Gina followed the top link and the Facebook page for a George X. Boyne popped up. He looked to be around eighteen or nineteen. "Not our guy."

"Nope. To have been Pat's lover, we're looking for someone in the early to midseventies, I'd expect. But this guy could be a relation. Families often recycle through the same names. Women call their babies after fathers or grandfathers. Even great-grandfathers sometimes. And names like George, James, William, John—well, they never seem to go out of fashion for long."

"So, do I message him?"

Kate blanched. "No. We try the other links first."

"But some of these are from years ago. I mean, look at this one. It's a newspaper article from five—no six—years ago."

"Follow it. When you're looking for older people, their web presence may well be historic, and places like Facebook and Twitter aren't where they tend to hang out."

"That's rather ageist, Detective Sergeant Brannon."

Kate chuckled. "Maybe. But unfortunately the figures speak for themselves. While not unheard of, people of the age we expect Mr Boyne to be are a tiny percentage of registered users on social media."

"Hmm. I still think you're being ageist."

"Well, I might be, but take a look at that." She pointed to the screen and a picture of a tall man in police uniform stared back at them. "Commissioner Charles Xavier Boyne on his retirement as the East of England Commissioner of the Independent Police Complaints Commission." She whistled.

"So he's a policeman?"

Kate shook her head. "No, the IPCC Commissioners are recruited from a nonpolicing background to ensure they're independent for the review."

"And he retired six years ago."

"Yes."

"So that would make him the right age."

"Approximately."

"So, how do we find him now?"

Kate laughed. "So eager. First we have to make sure he's the only one of these hits that fits the profile we're looking for. If there are others, then we'll need to investigate them a little more too. We need to reduce the investigative pool."

"We are if we just focus on him."

"But we may be wasting resources investigating him when it's a different George Boyne. While we're just clicking buttons on a screen, all we're wasting is a little time. If we focus on this guy, go and see him, and it turns out to be the wrong one, then we've wasted a lot more, and we're back to where we started."

"More boring police work?"

"Yup. I told you my job isn't all glitz and glamour."

"I didn't believe you until now."

"Thanks," Kate said with a chuckle. "So, the next link?"

The next link turned out to be the younger George Boyne on a skateboard, tagged in a picture on Instagram. The fourth took them back to the older George's independent review on a large child abuse case in Cambridge ten years ago. The next three all turned out to be other reports his commission published.

"I think this is Pat's George." Gina said.

"What makes you so sure?" Kate asked, having already arrived at that conclusion too.

"He looks like someone she'd like."

Kate snickered. "You only knew her for five minutes. How do you know what kind of man she'd like?"

Gina tipped her nose in the air haughtily. "I just do."

"Right," Kate responded. "Not sure that would stand up in court, sweetheart."

Gina pinched her arm. "Doesn't have to."

"Ow." Kate rubbed her arm.

"So how do we find out more about him?"

"What do you want to know?"

"I feel like I'm being schooled. Is this how you work with Gareth and Jimmy?"

Kate shook her head. "No, they've already done the basics at the academy and when they were in uniform."

Gina sighed. "Well, can we find out where he lives?"

"You can see if he's in the phone book."

"But I don't know which area to look in."

Kate pointed to the computer again. "Online phonebook has all listed numbers across the country. You don't need a specific directory for each district. You just put in a location, and it will do the rest."

"But I don't know the location."

"True. But we can start taking educated guesses."

"Such as?"

"Well, if he worked the IPCC in the east of England, then it would stand to reason that he lives or lived in the east of England. So we start with places like Bury St. Edmunds, Cambridge, Ipswich, Norwich, then work our way down."

"I didn't know that. Should you be teaching me this stuff?"

"I'm not teaching you anything that isn't in the public domain. You could probably find a YouTube tutorial that shows you all the same tips."

"The Internet really is a wonderful thing."

"In the right hands. In the wrong hands, it's a bloody nightmare."

"But there's no guarantee he's even in the phone book."

"Nope."

"So this might be a big waste of time?"

"Maybe."

"Is there any other choice?"

"We can look at the electoral register, but, again, without an area, we're shooting in the dark."

"Yes, but—"

"At least we'll know that he probably is registered to vote, while he might be ex-directory and not in the phone book."

"Yes."

"And given his job as the police complaints commissioner, he'd be daft not to be ex-directory. So we can use a website like 192.com to look through the electoral register."

Gina tapped away at the miniature keyboard and quickly pulled up the site. "Okay, name me some cities in the east of England."

"Peterborough."

Gina tapped the keyboard and waited for the site to tell her there were no records meeting her search criteria. Leicester. No records. Milton Keynes. Northampton. Bedford. Ipswich. All no records.

Kate could see Gina was getting frustrated. It was something she was used to. "Cambridge," Kate said. "Try Cambridge next."

Gina tapped the smartphone heavily and laughed loudly when the result came back. A single entry in a table. George X. Boyne. "We found him. We found him."

"Looks like it." Kate grinned at the exuberance on Gina's face. She looked so happy. Proud of herself.

"How do I get his address?"

"You have to register and pay to get the address."

"That's good."

"Why do you say that?"

"Well, it's been pretty damn easy to find out where this guy is. At least if you have to pay something and register your details, then they could track you if you turned out to be a crazy stalker."

"Ah, Gina. If only it were so easy."

Gina frowned.

"Well, the crazy stalker types, unfortunately, use fake details and usually a stolen credit or debit card for the transaction."

"That makes sense."

"Yup. Like I said, in the wrong hands, this is a nightmare."

Gina nodded like it was beginning to make sense to her too. The power of the Internet truly was a double-edged sword. Everything they knew, some criminal out there knew it too, and usually more of it. Give them a head start with knowledge, and sometimes they were impossible to catch. Other times, the police had the information, just too much to make heads or tails of it. Overloaded and buried in data. Damn Internet.

"I see what you mean now about not wasting other resources until we were sure it was the right man." Gina clicked the link to register and pay for his full details.

The amount was nominal. Barely worth thinking about for one person, and the details that came up once the card was charged were scary. At least they were to Kate. George Xavier Boyne's full address was now theirs. His telephone number and the names and ages of the other people living in the property with him were also there for them to see.

"Wow," Gina said.

"Yeah," Kate said with a lump in her throat. It had been a long time since she'd done a search like this. It was a lot easier now. Scary easy. The picture of the fifty yellow roses Gina had received popped into her mind. Fifty yellow roses, sender unknown.

Scary fucking world.

CHAPTER 6

The door opened, and the doctor walked in with a nurse behind him. The doctor was a tall guy, maybe six foot three, with a shock of blond hair held at the back of his head with a rubber band. A scruff of beard covered his lower face, but his eyes smiled despite the serious look on his countenance. "Stella Goodwin?"

Gina pointed to the bed.

He nodded and crossed the floor. "I'm Dr Gilad, this is Nurse Bell. Can you tell me what happened?" He peeled the wad of gauze away from the back of Stella's head.

She moaned and shifted under his hands.

"She was at the bomb site when the explosion occurred. She had her back to the blast. It looks like she got caught by some of the shrapnel flying around," Kate said.

"Do you know how far away she was from the blast?"

"No. Does it matter?"

"Yes. The further away she was, the less force the projectile would have carried—the lower the potential for serious issues."

"Sorry. All I can tell you was that she was in the shop. Gina, do you have any idea?"

Gina frowned, her face scrunched up in concentration. "Stella was trying to edge me towards the door, and they were by the counter, pretty much in the middle of the shop. Fifteen, maybe twenty feet away from them. But there were shelving units and clothing racks between them and us."

"Thank you," the doctor said. "Are you Georgina Temple?"

"Yes."

He nodded, and Nurse Bell closed the distance to her.

"I'm okay," Gina said. "Honest. Just a few bruises. The blood wasn't mine."

"Okay. Just let me take a quick look, and then you can be on your way," the nurse said.

"And I want an X-ray on this other patient as soon as you can," the doctor said.

The nurse nodded, then quickly concluded her examination and left the room.

"You think she has a skull fracture?" Kate asked quietly as she peered over his shoulder at Stella's wound. The gash was deep. So deep she could see the white bone beneath the thin layer of flesh at the back of her head. She couldn't make out any signs of damage to the bone, but that didn't mean anything.

"I want to rule it out. Yes."

Kate nodded.

"We'll get it taken care of. Don't worry." He slipped from the room.

Kate picked up her phone and dialled Timmons, never more grateful for the lowered restrictions on using mobile phones in hospitals.

"You still at the hospital?"

"Yes, sir."

"And?"

"The doctor's just been in. He's sending Stella for an X-ray to rule out a fractured skull."

"Right. How's she look?"

"She's in and out, sir. Mostly out, if truth be told."

"Bloody hell. And your girl?"

"She's okay. A few bruises, but now the blood's all washed off, she's fine."

"Right, that's good, at least."

"Yeah."

"Brannon, I need you to stay with her. With Stella. Don't leave her until we know she's okay."

Kate frowned. "You don't want me to come back to the scene?"

"Are ya deaf? I said stay with Stella. We've got bodies stood around here with nothing to do because the pricks from terrorism have got a bigger dick to swing right now. No point in you being here to help take measurements."

Kate chuckled. "But, sir, there's got to be something I can do."

"There is. Make sure Stella's all right."

Kate didn't answer. There was clearly more to this than she knew.

"She's important to me, Brannon."

Kate grinned and looked at Stella. "Understood, sir. Consider her under my personal protection." Kate gazed down at the stricken woman and hung up. This was gold. Pure, unadulterated gold.

"What's that evil grin for?" Gina asked.

"I've just been ordered, by my superior officer, to stay here and make sure Stella's okay, while our office takes part in one of the biggest investigations to date, because she's 'very important to him'." She curled her fingers in the air around the direct quote.

"Oo, Stella's been holding out on us."

"Looks like it." Kate rubbed her hands together gleefully as Gina's evil grin grew to rival her own. "I'm gonna enjoy this one."

"Oh, Kate, at least let her recover before you start taking the piss out of her."

"Of course I will. I'm not completely insensitive, you know."

Gina sniggered and grabbed her hand. She tugged on it until they stood close together again, leaning against the edge of Stella's bed. "Did he tell you any more about the investigation? You must be itching to be out there by now rather than stuck here with me."

"That's not true."

Gina raised her eyebrow.

"Okay, that's not entirely true."

Gina smiled.

"I love my job. I'm good at it. But I always want to be with you if I can be."

"It must be confusing. Wanting to be in two places at the same time."

Kate shrugged. "Not really. Most of the time it's not an issue. I mean, just a little while ago, I actually didn't want to go there. But now...right now, I don't know what's going on, and I don't like that feeling."

"So call Jimmy or Tom. Find out what's going on." She nodded to Stella. "I'll stay with her, and I promise not to let her know you know about her and Timmons."

"You sure?"

"Positive. Bring me back something to eat."

"You got it." Kate kissed Gina's cheek and closed the door behind her before Gina had a chance to change her mind.

She exited the main entrance and found an empty spot on a bench on the raised verge to sit down. It was wet from the melting snow, but she didn't care. Nor did she care that she'd no doubt look like she'd wet herself when she stood up in a while. Kate just wanted to take a load off and find out what was going on. Pulling her phone out of her pocket, she dialled Tom's number.

"Massage parlour, how may I direct your call?"

Kate burst out laughing. "Did you lose another bet?"

"When don't I?"

"Fair point. Well made, Detective Constable Brothers."

"So are you calling just to give me shit, or do you need something, Sarge?"

"Where are you?"

"Jessop's Photography Shop, next door but two to the main blast site, looking at the hole in the roof that collapsed about ten minutes ago."

"Very specific, thank you."

"Welcome. So...?"

"I just want an update on what you've got so far."

Tom sniggered. "You're still at the hospital, aren't you?"

"Yup."

"And Timmons is pissed off that the terrorism dudes have taken over."

"Yup."

"And you need little old me to fill in the blanks."

"Okay, I'll call Jimmy."

"Wait, wait, wait. There's no need to be like that."

Kate waited.

Tom sighed. "Nothing's been released to the press yet, but we think we've got pictures of the bombers."

"How?"

"The blast didn't take out the CCTV cameras server. We've got it all on tape. From the moment they walked in the doors until the second the blast destroyed the camera. Len Wild sent the footage straight over to Grimshaw in the tech lab. Fuckin' hell, that dude's scary with a computer."

"Do you have names?"

"Not yet. He's cleaning up the images before he can run them through facial recognition programs. He reckons he'll have an ID by the morning at the latest. But nothing so far."

"Who's heading up the task force?"

"Good question. Not sure we know yet. There's some woman here from Norwich who reckons she's the big cheese until the head honcho gets here from London. Apparently already en route."

"Who's the woman from Norwich?"

"One Chief Inspector Clare Green."

Kate groaned. "Fuck."

"Know her?"

"Yes," Kate said through gritted teeth. "Didn't know she'd made Chief Inspector, though."

"Oh, yeah. I forgot you came over from Norwich. What's she like?"

A fucking bitch who'll wander off with your girlfriend given half a chance. She didn't want to think about how close she and Clare had been. The woman had practically been her mentor when Kate started on the force. To know that she'd meant so little to her—that their friendship and their history had counted for nothing when it came to shagging Kate's then-girlfriend Melissa...well that just fucking stank. On a personal level. Professionally, Kate couldn't fault her. No matter how much she wished she could. "She's a decent copper. Good track record and knows how to play the game."

"Glad to hear that," Tom said. "At least knowing she's a human being will make this shit easier to deal with."

"Oh, I never said she was a human being, Tom. Just a decent copper. As a human being, I wouldn't trust her as far as I could throw her."

Tom cleared his throat. "Sounds like you know her well, Sarge."

"No. The problem was I didn't know her half as well as I thought I did."

"Ex?"

She laughed. "No. I thought she was a friend." She shook her head to clear it. Brooding about Clare and Melissa wasn't going to help her get the info she needed. "What's the count now, Tom?"

"Too much. Death toll's at twelve inside the shop and five outside. Injured at twenty-five. Mostly glass and shrapnel wounds, a few broken bones from people who were blown into walls or fell in the panic."

Kate gritted her teeth and asked for the piece of information that she already knew would haunt her. "The pushchair?"

"Two-year-old Gregory Walsh. His mum had just come out of the card shop, and they were going home. She's in hospital with shrapnel wounds. Lost a lot of blood. Touch and go, the paramedics said. She's on the critical list, and she doesn't even know about her son yet."

Kate whimpered. How do you tell a mother something like this? How do you look her in the eye and tell her that her little boy won't… can't…isn't…that he's dead? How do you even say those words? Never mind what you do after them. Kate pressed her thumbs into her eye sockets, hoping to push away the tears maybe just long enough to get through this conversation. It didn't work. They rolled down her cheeks while she sat listening to Tom breathe. She sniffed back a sob.

"It's okay, Kate." Tom's voice was soft. "Let it out."

She barked a harsh laugh. "I've never cried on the job before, Tom. This is the second time within one day."

"I saw Timmons crying when he pulled the blanket over the baby's body. We're human, Kate. If we don't cry on a day like this…well, it's time to pack it in then. Don't you think?"

She wiped her cheeks dry. "Yeah, you're probably right."

"Not probably. I am. Anyway, how's Stella doing?"

"Possible fractured skull. We'll know more after the X-ray comes back."

"Bollocks."

"Yeah."

"Well, other than that, I've got nothing to add, Sarge. Other than making sure the perps were acting alone, there's not a lot more we can do."

"And you think they were?"

"Acting alone?"

"Yeah."

"Yeah." He blew out loudly. "Maybe. I dunno. I mean, maybe that's just wishful thinking, but King's Lynn isn't exactly a bustling hive of Islamic or Muslim action, never mind radicals or extremists. I mean how many Muslims are even in King's Lynn? Less than a thousand?"

"Yeah, but you know as well as I do that tension has been rising. The last couple of years, there've been a string of incidents at the mosque. Racial slurs, graffiti; then there was that attack a few years back. It all builds, Tom."

"So you're saying focus on the mosque."

"No, I'm saying keep an open mind."

"I always do, Sarge."

She sniggered. "Yeah, about as open as a Yorkshireman's wallet."

"Now, Sarge. No need for racial abuse like that."

She shook her head. "Right. Thanks, Tom, and keep me informed, okay?"

"Got it, Sarge. You let us know how Stella's doing."

"Will do."

"And, you...you look after Gina too, okay?"

What was this? Body swap soppiness? "I will."

"And be kind to yourself, Sarge. This is off the fuckin' chart." And he was gone.

She slid her phone into her pocket and walked to the cafe. She got sandwiches and croissants for them both before heading back to Stella's room. It was empty when she got there. "Bugger." She closed the door and spotted the nurse who had seen to Gina earlier.

The nurse held her hands up to ward off the questions that she knew Kate was going to ask. "They've gone down to X-ray. Should be back in just a few minutes. Wait in there. Then you won't miss them." She pointed back to the room.

Kate smiled at her seeming omniscience. "You've worked here a while, then, I take it?"

"Feels like forever, except the place wasn't built until the fires of hell cooled a little."

Kate laughed. "Thanks, I needed that. Tell me honestly, what's going on with my friend? Is she going to be okay?"

The nurse's smile gentled. "It's always tricky with head injuries. Especially traumatic ones. The X-ray will tell us what we need to do next, but most likely it will just be rest. The best medicine for the brain is rest, relaxation, and time. She has a concussion, quite a bad one. Her head is going to hurt like hell for a while, but that will get better. If the skull is fractured, we may just have to give it time, or we may need to operate to fix it." She shrugged. "Until we get the result back, we just don't know. But don't worry. She's in good hands. I know he looks young, but Dr Gilad really is one of the best we've got here."

Kate smiled. "Thanks."

She reached over and squeezed Kate's arm. "She'll be okay."

"Yeah. Hard-headed. There was one more thing you could help me with, if you wouldn't mind."

"What's that?"

"Gina. She's stuck in that crappy little Tyvek suit and my coat, and it's getting cooler. I don't suppose you've got a set of scrubs she can use? They've got to be warmer than that paper get-up."

"Let me see what I can do for you," the nurse said with a chuckle and moved on.

Kate went back to the room and sat down to wait. Gazing again at the small mountain of evidence bags sitting in the corner of the room, she lifted the letter from the pile. Pat's neat handwriting stared back at her. She lifted the photograph off the pile too, her mind whirling before she quickly grabbed her phone and dialled Ruth's number.

"Yep."

"Did you get hold of the next of kin for Patricia O'Shea yet?"

"No. She's got a son, but he's over in Australia. Haven't been able to reach him yet. Might have to get one of their local officers to do the notification."

"Right. Okay, thanks."

"Why?"

"Gina was with her when she passed."

"Oh, I see." Ruth paused. "Want me to let the son know when he's informed?"

"Nah. Don't worry about it. Thanks, though."

"No problem. Now let me get back to work. I've got too much to do and not enough hands. Unless you want to come down and do an autopsy or two."

"No thanks. Bye, Doc."

Ruth sniggered and ended the call.

Kate read through the letter again. The poignancy, the bittersweet, the history in those few pages. Well, it wouldn't help the investigation at all. And it didn't sound like it would hurt them to hold on to the letter while Gina decided what she wanted to do about it. The idea of tampering with evidence felt alien to her. Difficult. She was the one who wouldn't use police resources to try and find George in the first place. The idea of keeping the letter out of evidence, no matter how little it would affect the outcome of the investigation, made her itch.

No, she couldn't do that. But she had the pictures of it. She could still use the letter, reprint it, and give the copy to George Boyne if Gina wanted to go and see him.

It made sense to her. Evidence wasn't tampered with, and Gina could still get the resolution she needed. She could still grant Pat's last request. As much as she'd tried to hide it, Kate could see that it had bothered Gina to not be able to do what the woman had asked of her. Well, it was a pretty good compromise as far as Kate could see.

CHAPTER 7

Gina followed behind the sleeping Stella while the porter wheeled her back into the room and clipped on the brakes of her bed. She smiled at the heavyset man as he winked at her and pulled the door closed behind him.

"Hey." Kate's voice was quiet as she leant against the windowsill.

"Hey. Have you been waiting long?" Gina stood next to her and leant back against the wall, casually letting their shoulders touch and absorbing the warmth of Kate's body through the paper suit, hoping it would ease a little of the ache that was starting to settle in her bones. Everything hurt.

"Not too long. How's she doing?" She nodded to Stella.

"She was really groggy when they were trying to get her into position. It's weird seeing Stella like that."

"Yeah, I know." Kate folded her arms over her chest. "I have gifts for you." Kate grinned.

Gina smiled widely in response. "Please tell me it's tea and cake."

Kate's smile faltered. "Sorry, no."

Gina chuckled and squeezed Kate's arm. "I was joking." She smiled as Kate let out a stuttered breath, seemingly relieved, but the look in her eyes... She was a million miles away. "You okay?"

Kate swallowed and shook her head.

"Tell me."

"I can't. Not right now."

Gina watched her closely. Her eyes were red-rimmed and puffy, her nose looked a little sore, and her cheeks were flushed. Clearly, Kate had been crying, but Gina wasn't going to make her talk if she didn't want to. There were things in Kate's job she couldn't say, and there had been more than a few times she had let Gina keep her thoughts and feelings to herself when she needed to. The least Gina could do was allow her the same courtesy. Kate would talk when she was ready. If she could. "What have you got, then?"

"Sandwiches, croissants, tea, and something warmer to wear."

Gina reached over and kissed her lips lightly. "You are a goddess."

Buffing her nails on her shirt, Kate said, "All in a day's work." She pointed to the chair. "I asked the nurse. She managed to scrounge up a pair of scrubs, and she's lent you her hoody. The socks, I'm afraid, are from the lost property box, but she swears they're clean, and I've got to admit they pass the sniff test—"

"The sniff test?"

Kate nodded.

"The *sniff* test?"

Kate folded her arms again. "Yes." She arched an eyebrow. "Don't tell me you've never conducted a sniff test."

Gina sniffed and tipped her nose in the air haughtily. "I never have."

"Right," she drawled. "Anyway, the best she could find for shoes was a pair of the surgical clogs they use, but she said they're really comfy, and they look like Crocs to me."

"Thank you." She gathered up the bundle and slipped into the bathroom to change. The scrubs were surprisingly soft, and the hoody was thick and roomy, like a big, woolly hug.

Kate smiled when she re-entered the room. "Better?"

I don't think I'll ever get tired of seeing that smile. "Much."

"Then this will make it better still." She pointed to the windowsill acting as a table, with the food and drinks she'd managed to find for them laid out. "I also called Will. He's still fine with Sammy. He said he's made up one of the rooms in the hostel for her to stay in if it gets too late. I spoke to her. She's fine with it. More than fine, actually. Said it was like camping. I told her if that's what she thinks camping's like, then she's never been and we really need to rectify that situation."

"You're waffling," Gina said as Kate took a breath.

"No, I'm not."

"Yes, you are. What's wrong?"

Kate shook her head. "Nothing's wrong. I just kind of made a decision, and I'm not sure if it's the right one or not."

"If you're not sure, doesn't that usually mean it's not the right one?"

"Maybe. But it could just be that I have no way of knowing what the consequences of it will be. And I don't like not knowing."

Gina smiled. "That's true. You are a bit of a control freak."

Kate's eyes opened wide, and her mouth dropped open a bit. "I am not!"

Gina laughed. "I beg to differ."

"You can beg all you like. It doesn't change the fact that you're wrong."

"No, she isn't," Stella's voice rasped the air as she spoke. Her eyes weren't open, but she smiled at them from her bed. "Tell me you brought me coffee."

"Nope. You're not allowed anything until we know what's going on with your head."

"It's still on my shoulders, isn't it?"

"Yes," Kate said while Gina giggled.

"Then it's fine. I want coffee."

"I'm afraid not," the doctor said from the open doorway. The young doctor looked even more harassed and exhausted than he had earlier, but his smile seemed genuine. "You have a concussion and a fractured skull. No coffee. You need to rest, not take a stimulant."

"But I can't sleep without coffee," Stella grumbled.

"A fractured skull?" Kate asked.

"I assure you, you can." The doctor shone his penlight into each pupil, making Stella hiss in pain. It didn't stop him carrying out his examination, making her grasp his fingers, push and pull on his hands, and so on. "And yes, to answer your question. There's clearly a skull fracture. It's a small, hairline fracture, but the swelling around it is increasing the pressure on the brain, which complicates that concussion a bit. We'll be keeping you in and will reassess in the morning. Right now, we're trying to find you a bed. A proper one. So hang tight, and we'll get you settled as soon as we can." He didn't give any of them a chance to argue with him or ask questions. He simply closed the door behind him and was gone.

"Chatty, isn't he?" Kate murmured to the closed door.

Stella waved a hand listlessly. "Fill me in," she demanded, her eyes still closed. One could easily assume she was asleep, except that there was a tension to her body that hadn't been there when she was unconscious.

"It can wait, Stella."

"Piss off." She opened her eyes and sat up a bit straighter. "I'm not dead. Now tell me what's going on. I was there, remember?"

"I remember," Kate said. "You took my girlfriend to a bombing."

"Fuck off, it was Little Miss Fancy Knickers' fault, not mine. She invited me."

"Hey! I think I'm offended!" Gina cried, smothering her laughter at Stella's outburst.

"You only think? Christ, I must be dying." She put a hand to her head. "I can't even offend civilians anymore."

"Fine, fine. Mock my concern all you like. But you know the boys are going to start bringing you johnnies for your desk, don't you?" Kate grinned smugly. Finally, someone else for them to torment. It might get them to forget about the snorkel they kept leaving on Kate's desk—a reminder that her car drowned when the harbour car park flooded. Or the crutch they kept propping over the back of her chair as a reminder of the time she got her leg trapped in the smouldering ruins of a boat sinking on the marshes. She didn't want to put money on it... She wasn't that daft, but a girl could hope.

Gina frowned at her as Stella groaned. "Johnnies? Why?"

"Because you two were in a sex shop when this happened. It's that or blow-up dolls, probably. And since they're a bunch of cheap bastards, condoms are cheaper...and easier to get hold of." Kate shrugged. "Police humour."

"Right," Gina said, drawing out the word to make it last at least five times as long as it needed to.

Stella sniggered and settled back against the pillows. "So?"

Kate sighed and slowly began to pick off the details she could. "Two bombers. We may have pictures of them—"

"That was fast."

"The bomb didn't destroy the camera server. It was in a different room, so we were able to get camera footage to Grimshaw. He's confident he'll ID them by morning."

Stella met Kate's gaze. "Casualties?"

Kate swallowed and glanced at Gina, clearly concerned about what she could and should say in front of her.

"I'll hear it on the news before long anyway, sweetheart. What you say won't leave the room. You have my word."

"Yeah, I know." She took a deep breath, steeling herself against the words she would have to say. "Seventeen dead and twenty-five injured as it stands."

Stella closed her eyes. "Critical injuries?"

Kate nodded. "Yes."

"What do you mean?" Gina asked.

"Critically injured victims who may still die yet as a result of their wounds," Stella said softly, her voice croaky and thick. "Please tell me there aren't any kids on the victim list."

Kate's head dropped to her chest, and she covered her eyes with one hand. Her shoulders shook as she fought her emotions.

The bedclothes rustled under Stella as she moved. "Fuck. Tell me." She wrapped a shaky hand around Kate's arm.

"Two-year-old, in a pushchair. Out shopping with his mum. She's in critical."

"Oh God!" Gina cried and wrapped her arms about her waist as Stella and Kate stared at each other. A plethora of details passed between them in that look, things Gina would never understand, and for that small mercy she would be eternally grateful. But she was a mother. And the pain that woman was suffering was the single worst pain she could possibly imagine.

Nothing—absolutely nothing—would ever hurt more than her daughter's pain. Worse...the mere thought of it sent her running out of the room and exiling her lunch.

She hung over the bowl, arms braced on the cistern, tears running in rivers down her cheeks. It was too much. There was just too much horror to take in, too many vile details that she didn't want to know and that she didn't want to remember. She couldn't. She knew that if she held on to this, it would paralyse her, entomb her, until she simply couldn't function. Gina refused to carry the burden of someone else's actions. Not again.

Slowly, wiping the tears from her eyes, Gina flushed the toilet and glanced at herself in the mirror over the sink. Her eyes were bloodshot and her skin pale. Her hair hung in damp strands as it continued to dry. She sucked in a deep breath, held it for a count of six, and blew out in a steady stream, taking each precious second to rebuild the defences around her heart, telling herself all the time that Sammy was just fine. She was okay, and nothing was going to happen to her precious little girl.

By the time she returned, Stella and Kate were quiet, watching her. No doubt waiting for her to say something. "Sorry," she murmured and stood next to Kate again.

Kate slipped her arm about her shoulders and kissed the side of her head. "You okay?"

Gina nodded. They all knew she was lying.

"Well, if I'm stuck here, you can tell me all about your questionable decision," Stella said.

"Bollocks."

"Yes, that's a questionable decision. Are you thinking of getting a pair or simply trying them out?"

"I'm getting that doctor back." Kate started for the door.

"Why?" Stella frowned.

"Because there's clearly more damage to your brain than he said."

"Funny." She laid her head back down on her pillow. "So, come on. Tell me what's going on."

Kate sighed. "Well it's about Pat—"

"Who's Pat?"

Gina frowned and listened as Kate quickly gave her the details of Pat's death and Stella's promise.

"You've read the letter?"

Kate nodded.

"Did you bag it first?"

"Of course."

"Okay. Then nothing problematic so far."

"I think we should give the letter to George. It was meant for him, and it won't change the investigation in any way if we do." Kate folded her arms across her chest.

Gina took in the stubborn set to her chin and wondered what would happen if Stella told her not to.

"Must be some letter," Stella said, a frown on her face. "I'd ask to read it, but since I'm currently seeing two of you, I don't think that would help matters. Read it to me."

Kate flicked her gaze to Gina, and Stella just nodded.

Kate picked up the letter and cleared her throat before she started to read. "My dearest, darling George: I have tried so many times to write this letter to you, to try and explain all that happened so many years ago, but I have never been able to convey all that I felt. Now I'm old enough to know that one can never truly expect to do that. Instead, all I can do is tell you the truth of what happened and hope you knew well enough the girl I was to be able to deduce the rest. The ways of the heart was not meant to be explained with words."

"She was so eloquent," Gina whispered.

"You asked me to run away with you, and I said no," Kate continued to read, her voice a little shaky, hoarse, and deeper than normal as the emotion took its toll on her vocal chords. "I said I wouldn't allow you to ruin your life by going AWOL for me. But I think you suspected, quite rightly, that there was much more to it than this. There were two things that you didn't know, and I couldn't find the strength to tell you back then. Both secrets I kept to save the lives of others—your life, dearest George, and that of our darling baby girl."

"Oh." Gina clasped her hands together and squeezed them between her knees. She could picture young Pat, tears streaming down her face, when she told her lover goodbye.

"It's starting to sound like an episode of EastEnders," Stella said.

"Do you want me to finish reading this or not?"

"Yes," Stella and Gina said at the same time.

"Right. Well, keep quiet and listen, then." She stared at them both and flexed the page in her hand. "Where do I start to explain those secrets? The day you asked me to marry you, to run away with you, was the happiest and saddest of my life at that time. Happiest because of how much I loved you—and you must believe me, George, I did love you with all my heart. But saddest because I knew my father would not allow us to wed. You were an Englishman, a soldier, a Protestant. Everything my father hated and stood against. He would have skinned me alive had he known we were lovers. And I truly dread to think of what he'd have done to you." Kate's voice petered off, and she cleared her throat before she carried on. "I said yes at first because it was what my heart wanted, even while my head told me it would never happen. Hence the sadness I felt. I knew that I wouldn't be able to see you again. I knew that my father would run you off, and when you started to talk of running away, of abandoning your post, I knew I couldn't let you do it. I knew that my father would hunt us both down and kill you. If not both of us. We'd spend the rest of our lives running, not just from the army after you deserted, but from my family and the army my father was a part of. The Irish Republican Army."

"Bloody hell," Stella said.

"Shush." Gina slapped her arm.

"Paddy O'Shea was not just a member of the IRA, George, he was one of their leaders. He plotted, and carried out, a number of attacks that led to the deaths of your fellow soldiers. He killed, have no doubt about it. My fears for you were not the delusions of a paranoid fantasy, they were very, very real. So I changed my mind, I gave in to my fear, and I told you no." Kate's voice cracked again, and the page shook in her hands. "The shortest engagement in history. Wasn't that what you said? Well, perhaps now you can understand why. I should never have gotten involved with you, George. I knew what my father was. I knew that before we met, and I kept it from you. For that, I'm sorry. I wish

I'd never had to lie to you, but it was a difficult time and a difficult position to be in. As much as I hated what he did, he was still my father, and I loved him. Then I loved you. I was too young to know what to do with the feelings I had. And too immature to know how to deal with being on both sides of the argument."

"Oh, she must have been so scared," Gina whispered.

"Shush," Stella told her.

"Bitch."

Kate cleared her throat.

"Sorry. Please carry on," Gina said.

"But by the time I realised what a mess I'd made of everything, it was too late. I didn't know it then, but I was already pregnant with your child. I know what you're thinking now, George. Had I known, would I have made a different choice? Would I have run away with you and taken our chances? I know, because those are questions I've asked myself a million times. Sitting in my bed at Mary Magdalene's Convent while our baby grew inside me, I thought of nothing else. When they came to take our baby away for adoption, I screamed and cried and wished I'd made any other choice than the one I did. But with time comes age, distance, and a little wisdom."

Tears dripped down Gina's cheeks. She couldn't imagine being without Sammy, and the thought of carrying her baby and then having it taken from her broke her heart.

"It was a different time back then," Stella said gently. Her face was still white as the sheet she was lay on, but her eyes looked a little clearer, brighter, more like the Stella Gina had come to know. "Women didn't have the choices they do now. Especially young, unmarried, pregnant ones."

"I know." Gina wiped the tears from her cheek. "It doesn't make it any less awful, though."

"No." Stella took hold of Gina's hand. "But maybe it gets better. Please continue, reader."

"Ha bloody ha." Kate lifted the page again. "I made the right choice, George. For all three of us. I made a choice that left you free to move on and live the life you deserved. Happy and healthy. I hope you've made the most of it, my darling." Her voice was thick, full of emotion and pity. "I hope you're married and surrounded by children and grandchildren now. I hope you had a long and fulfilling career. I hope you're sitting by the fire with a cup of tea, telling your wife about the Irish lass you once knew. I hope you'll be able to find our daughter. I hope you'll want to sit with her and tell her all about us and what we meant to each other. I hope you have the life I could have never given you."

Gina swiped at her tears again and noticed Stella surreptitiously doing the same.

"I never told anyone who the father of my baby was because I knew my da would kill you for having touched me. But our little girl was born on the 8th of July 1965. She weighed just 5 pounds and 12 ounces. Oh, she was a skinny little thing. But long. She had such long legs and perfect tiny little hands and feet. It was a marvel, George. I sat there the whole night just looking at her. I memorised every tiny, perfect fingernail, the way her skin smelled so sweet. I even tried to count every hair on her head, but there was just too much of it. We made a beautiful baby, George. Beautiful."

The page shook in Kate's hands. "Want me to read a bit?" Gina asked.

Kate shook her head and offered her a teary smile. "Perhaps this was the mistake I made. Some of the other girls didn't hold their babies before the nuns took them away. But I knew I had to hold mine. I had to hold her before I let her go, because I wasn't just holding our baby that night, George. I was holding you too. I didn't cry. I don't think I had any tears left by then. I'd spent so many months there, crying while I scrubbed sheets. There's been rather a lot in the media over the past few years about those places, and I have to admit that I was rather luckier than others seem to have been. Yes, we were made to work hard, but we weren't abused, as many reports said. We were shamed. But then we all knew we had done something to be ashamed of. In my case, several things. Most of all, I was ashamed of the way I'd treated you."

"Poor kid," Stella said as she tugged the blanket up her shoulders. "She'd done nothing wrong, but they made all those young women believe they had."

"Like you said, it was a different time," Kate pointed out.

"Doesn't make it any better, Kate." She sniffed. "Go on and finish it."

Kate nodded and carried on. "Our baby was adopted by an English couple, as so many children were back then. I called her Alison. I don't know if they kept that name, but that's what I called her. My little Alison O'Shea. I tried to find her. I went to the church to try to get the records of who adopted her, but I was told I couldn't have them without my father or husband's permission. Well, that was several years ago. It's probably changed by now, but then I got wondering about what kind of life she's had. If she's happy, would she even want to know me? If she's not happy, would she be angry at me letting her go into that life? Would she even know she was adopted? Many folks back then didn't talk about those things. There were so many questions, George. So many doubts and fears. I was paralysed by them. I'd spent so long regretting and questioning the choices I made back then that I didn't have the confidence in myself to make any more." Kate flipped the page over and carried on. "Maybe one day I will. Maybe, when I finally have the courage to find you, we can be friends and laugh at the fears of a stupid old woman. Who knows, maybe we can find her together. If you can ever forgive me. Yours sincerely, Pat."

All three of them had tears on their cheeks. Stella had her eyes closed again, but it didn't seem to slow her tears. "God, I told you. EastEnders."

Kate sniggered. "Nah. If it was, then they'd have been brother and sister to cap it all off."

"Fair point," Stella acknowledged. "And I agree. There is nothing in there that could possibly affect the investigation. Give it to the man it was intended for."

"But we're tampering with evidence," Kate said, clearly still uneasy. Gina could see it in her face.

"Then photocopy it, give him the copy, and submit the original into evidence, if it'll make you feel any better."

Kate nodded. "That's the way I was leaning."

"IRA, hey?" Stella shook her head against the pillow. "Well, she really didn't have much choice, did she? And you say you've found George Boyne?"

Kate nodded. "Pretty sure it's him."

"That was fast. Did you call in a favour?"

"No. All Google."

"You're joking?"

"Wish I was. It's been a long time since I've done a civ search." She whistled. "It might actually have been quicker than going through official channels."

"Bloody scary."

"Yeah."

"So when are you going to go and see him?" Stella smiled.

Gina was fascinated to watch the two of them bounce off each other. They understood each other in a way she never thought she could understand Kate. Their minds worked so similarly.

Kate shook her head. "Don't think that's a good idea."

"Course it is. How else are you going to give him his letter?"

"No, I think we should write to him first. Check if he is the right one and if he wants to know. If he doesn't and we just turn up on his doorstep, we could be opening a whole can of worms."

"Since when did you start doing sensitive?"

"Since I got me a girlfriend."

Stella smiled. "Fair point." She turned her head towards Gina. "And what do you think of the letter-writing plan?"

Gina shrugged. "If that's what Kate thinks is for the best." Personally, she just wanted to jump in the car, drive to Cambridge, and knock on his door. But she could see how that might cause problems.

"Besides, I don't have time right now to drive over to Cambridge," Kate said.

"Why not?" Stella looked at her.

Kate grinned evilly. "I'm under orders not to leave your side until we know you're going to be okay, because you're "very important"." She curled her fingers in the air.

Stella frowned and opened her eyes a slit. "What are you on about?"

Gina chuckled. "You might as well 'fess up, Stella. He made it really obvious."

Stella's frown deepened. "What am I supposed to be confessing to?"

"You and Timmons." Gina winked at her.

"What?" Stella sat bolt upright in her bed and grabbed at her head as she came to an upright position. "Ow, ow, ow, ow, ow. Don't make me do shit like that," she complained and lay back down gingerly. "Now what the hell are you talking about? Me and Timmons? There is no me and Timmons."

Kate grinned. "Really?"

"Really."

"Then our DI has me sitting here with you because he's got one hell of a crush on you, my friend."

"Piss off."

"Nope. I can't. I'm under orders."

"You're serious?"

"As a heart attack."

Stella's eyes were wide, her mouth was slack, and her cheeks looked a little more flushed than before. "Bollocks."

"Yup, I agree. I think that's the line he's thinking down, Sarge."

Gina watched as Stella swallowed, one hand over her stomach, the other resting on her forehead.

"Well, I suppose he's not a bad-looking bloke."

Kate laughed.

"But I don't do other cops."

"Why not?" Gina asked.

"There's only room for one ego like that in a relationship."

Kate sniggered.

"Isn't there, Gina?" Stella grinned wickedly.

Gina grinned and blew Kate a kiss. "Certainly is."

"Hey." Kate planted her hands on her hips. "I think I've just been insulted."

CHAPTER 8

Kate rolled over and slapped her hand at the infernal buzzing on her bedside table. It couldn't be eight o'clock already. Blessedly, the vibrating stopped. She glanced at the clock. The big red number mocked her sleep-deprived brain: 5:55 a.m. She'd finally managed to crawl into bed somewhere around four by the time she'd felt comfortable leaving Stella at the hospital, then had gotten Sammy and Gina settled in the spare room. She'd needed some time to let herself calm down and decompress a little.

"I set the alarm for eight." Her voice was hoarse as it scratched its way out of her throat, and the buzzing started again. "For fuck's sake," she cursed as she picked up her phone, pulled the charging cable out, and held it to her ear. "Yeah?" she growled, flopping back against her pillows and rubbing at her eyes as she listened.

"Good morning to you too, sunshine." Timmons sounded gruff, and Kate wondered briefly if he'd managed any sleep at all. Probably not.

"Sir."

"Did you get the statements and evidence?"

Kate nodded, then remembered he couldn't see her. "Yeah. I took the evidence bags down to the crime lab and signed them over to the duty officer. I have the statements recorded."

"Good. Then get your arse out of bed and get in here. Full team briefing in twenty."

"Twenty minutes?"

"Yes."

"Sir, it takes thirty to get there." She pushed the curtain aside and saw that more snow had fallen overnight. "Plus it's icy."

"Better get a move on, then."

Kate groaned and shoved the covers off her legs. "Where?" She pulled open the wardrobe, grabbed a pair of jeans and a fleece and tossed them onto the bed.

"Base incident room. Standing room only. We've got bodies coming in from all over, from both inside and outside of the county."

She grabbed clean underwear from the drawers and quickly changed while she was still on the phone, bra and jumper in her hands. "Right. I'll be there as soon as I can."

"Drive safe." He didn't say goodbye. Just shut off the connection.

Kate shook her head and finished dressing before she ran down the stairs as quickly and quietly as she could. After she scribbled a note for Gina and stuck it on the fridge with a big magnet, she let Merlin— the blue merle Border collie she'd adopted after her owner had been found murdered a couple of months ago—into the back garden to do her business.

She had her jacket on one shoulder, car keys in one hand, and an apple in the other as she let Merlin back in and pulled the back door closed behind her. She didn't remember being told there was a briefing last night when she spoke to Timmons and updated him on Stella's condition. But if she were a hundred per cent honest, at that point she was so exhausted she wasn't sure she could remember her own name. Two hours sleep later, she already knew today was gonna be a bitch.

The roads were surprisingly clear—the gritters had obviously been working overtime—and the thirty-minute journey was shaved a bit—or a lot—by Kate's admittedly heavy-footed driving skills. Speed limits were more like targets, after all. Besides, Kate was too busy trying to anticipate what would happen at the briefing. And, just as importantly, who would be there.

Bodies from all over the county. She already knew Clare was there. Did that mean Melissa would be too? Would she have to deal with the two of them together, or rather at the same time, since force gossip had confirmed that they had long since split up after the affair that had cost Kate and Melissa their relationship?

In the wake of everything that had happened yesterday...why was that the issue she couldn't get out of her head? Kate felt like a scratched record going over and over the same question, the same personal riddle, that she wouldn't have the answer to until it was right in front of her. She couldn't prepare herself. It was simply going to happen, or it wouldn't. Until then, she was just stuck on everything that had happened between the three of them. The pain of betrayal, the hurt of her shattered heart and—more fragile even—her shattered trust.

Kate still wasn't sure who she was angrier with—Melissa, for cheating on their relationship, or Clare and the betrayal of a friendship. No, it had been more than a friendship. Clare had been her mentor, her confidante, her greatest supporter, and her strongest ally. She'd been more like a sister than a friend. And Kate couldn't get past the thought that she'd be seeing her again soon. Maybe both of them.

Kate supposed it was a kind of coping strategy. One she'd seen in victims over the years. When the bad stuff was just too big, too awful, your mind focused on the little, pathetic, seemingly inconsequential details to try and get you through. She'd seen women scrubbing floors after being told their child had died in a car accident, because they simply couldn't face the prospect of their baby not coming home. She'd seen blokes pick up their keys and go to work upon learning their wife was dead, just focusing on the mundane, the everyday, the superficial, because everything else was just...too much.

So this was her scratched-record moment. Her fixation.

"I'd rather be thinking about Gina and Sammy, if it's all the same to you, brain," she muttered under her breath as she parked her car, flipped her hood over her head, and ran from her car to the door of King's Lynn police station. Late for the briefing...but only just.

She snuck into the incident room, shouldering her way through until she could see. At the front of the room, Timmons slouched against the wall behind him. His usual scruffy appearance had dropped to a new low. The jacket and tie of his well-worn brown suit had been discarded. Large sweat stains marred the creased shirt he wore, as did a greasy-looking splotch. Remnants of some hastily grabbed sustenance, no doubt. But it was the figure next to him she was staring at.

Chief Inspector Clare Green, in all her crisply starched, uniformed glory. Short, dark hair framed an almost elfin-looking face with small dark-rimmed glasses perched on her nose. There was more grey at the temples than Kate remembered, but it had been a while. Kate shook her head a little and focussed on what Clare was saying.

"The images from the CCTV footage we got off the server yesterday have been cleaned up and run through every database we've got." She pinned two photos to the board behind her. "Confirmed IDs as Nadia Ahmed and Saba Ayeshydi."

"Confirmed by?" a man's voice in the crowd asked.

"Yes, confirmed by their passports."

"They're both British nationals?" It was the same questioning voice that Kate didn't recognise.

"Yup."

"Bollocks."

"Yup."

"How old?"

"Ahmed was seventeen, and Ayeshydi was nineteen. No priors and they're not on any watch list that we know of, or, should I say, none that we have access to. We might get more info on that later." Clare took a deep breath. "Right now, all we know for sure is that these two girls walked into a shop almost two weeks before Christmas and blew themselves and the shop to pieces, taking with them seventeen innocent people and injuring twenty-five more. The tech lab has been over the fragments of the bomb they've found already, and it is clear— crystal fucking clear, people—that these were very sophisticated weapons. Now, while I wouldn't swear that there is no way on God's green earth that either of these two girls could have built them, it is highly unlikely. And it's fucking impossible that they didn't have help."

A murmur ran around the room.

"Which means they have links somewhere. We're now looking for anything on the cell they must have been involved with. We need to know who made those bombs, where they made them, and whether they have made any more." She nodded, reinforcing her words. "These weapons were sophisticated, and they had built-in fail-safes. The detonators were linked, so if one girl tried to pull out, the other would detonate her vest anyway. This is not a first-time bomb maker, lads and lasses. No bomb maker creating this kind of fail-safe is doing so for the first time and achieving this level of success."

"Is that why there were two bombers? Just to ensure this fail-safe?" a faceless voice in the crowd asked.

"That's our best guess at the moment," Clare said.

"Why did they target that particular shop? There were busier places on the High Street if they were going for maximum impact." Another voice from the crowd, a woman this time.

"We don't know yet. There must have been some reason. We have authority to search the homes of each girl. Maybe we'll find some information there."

"Are the CSIs in there already?" the woman asked again.

"No, the CSIs are all tied up on the High Street and recovering bodies at the moment. Detective Inspector Timmons and I are assigning teams of investigators to each property."

Timmons handed her a sheet of paper, and Kate saw Clare's eyebrow quirk before she cleared her throat and addressed them all again. "Team for Saba Ayeshydi's home: Detective Tom Brothers, Detective Jimmy Powers from Lynn—team up with Sergeant Martin Sanderson and Constable Roger Manners from Norwich." She held up a piece of paper, and a guy Kate recognised as Manners took it from her with a quick nod.

"Team for Nadia Ahmed's house: Detective Sergeant Kate Brannon, Detective Gareth Collier, from Lynn, with Sergeant Vinny Jackson and Constable Melissa Brown from Norwich." She found Kate in the audience. The look on her face was unreadable.

But Kate now knew what that quirked eyebrow was about.

Not only was Kate going to see Melissa, she was going to have to fucking work with her. Fantastic.

Clare quickly handed out more assignments once Vinny collected the address from her and made his way across the room to Kate. His smile was wide, but his eyes looked as haunted as everyone else's in the room.

He clasped her hand and pulled her into a quick hug, slapping her on the back. "It's good to see your ugly mug again, Kate. How's life in the sticks?"

"Ah, you know. Sliding along nicely. You?"

"Same old, same old."

"How's the wife?"

"Great. Yeah, just great. She's married to someone else now."

Bollocks. "Sorry to hear that, mate."

"Nah, it's for the best. As long as the kids don't start calling 'im Dad, it's all good, you know?"

She nodded and kept her mouth shut.

"Listen, I know things didn't end all that well with you and Mel, but—"

Kate waved a hand to quiet him. "It's fine. I can be professional, Vinny. You know me."

He nodded as Clare called for everyone's attention again. "That's it for now, folks. Crack on. When we know more, you'll know more."

Small groups began to form within the room and then quickly exited to their various tasks. Kate waited for Gareth and Mel to join them.

"Sarge," Gareth greeted her and nodded to Vinny, holding out his hand. "Gareth Collier."

Vinny gripped his hand and shook firmly. "Detective, nice to meet you."

Kate stared at Mel as she stared back. She hadn't changed. Her hair was still blond, her eyes were still blue, and she still had that dimple in her right cheek that showed even when she wasn't smiling. And she was still a bitch. Kate had no doubt about that.

Gareth cleared his throat and held his hand out to Mel. "Collier," he said. "Gareth."

"Mel Brown." She quickly shook his hand, but her gaze had barely left Kate's.

"Should we?" Vinny held his hand out towards the door and inclined his head.

Kate swallowed, clenched her jaw, and led them out of the room. She pointed to her Mini.

"Want a lift?" She spoke to Vinny but didn't look around. They'd either follow or not, and, quite frankly, she hoped not.

"That'd be great, Kate. Since we don't know the area like you do, it'd definitely make things easier." They all stopped when they reached the car and looked at it.

Kate shrugged, a smirk tugging at her lips. "You sure about that?" The Mini wasn't known for its generous backseat space or copious amounts of legroom. And the six-foot-three-inch frame Vinny boasted could definitely use more than she could supply.

To his credit, he tossed his head back and laughed. "Shotgun," he cried and scurried around the passenger side.

Collier scowled.

Kate refused to look at Mel.

Kate climbed in and pulled her seatbelt over her shoulder. "Gareth, you got your phone handy?"

"Yep."

"Plug in the address, will ya? I might know Lynn better than you do, Vinny, but that's not saying a lot."

Vinny laughed. "You mean you haven't got a map of this place in your head yet, Detective? Tut-tut."

"What can I say? I'm slacking." She gunned the engine to life and coaxed it out of the carpark. "Left or right?" she asked Collier.

"Right. Towards the Hardwick Industrial Estate. But take the first exit off the next roundabout instead of the second one. Vancouver Ave."

"Okay." She quickly steered them out onto the road and dodged around the road sweeper as it clung to the kerb, clearing the drains of litter, leaves, and other nefarious detritus. As she guided the car under the archway that stood sentry to London Road and the main thoroughfare of the town centre, she noted just how rundown this part of town was looking. It wasn't just that the streets were still dark and soaked in rain. It was the way the mid-December gloom had to war with the excessive use of Christmas lights, chipped paint on every building they passed, and the graffiti scrawled across metal boards that covered building after building. Widespread repossession, abandonment, and crime did nothing to help the situation.

At the roundabout, Vancouver Avenue was flanked by a billboard with the advertisement peeling off on one side and a bank of stunted trees on the other. Houses looked to be cramped and squashed together...until she was a little way down the road, anyway. Then it opened up into a wider, leafy suburb. She didn't remember ever being down there before, but it was surprisingly nice. "What are we looking for?"

"Extons Road. Should be just before the football grounds," Collier replied.

"King's Lynn Town?" Vinny asked.

"Yeah."

"Didn't even know Lynn had a football club," Kate mumbled.

Vinny chuckled. "Some would say they don't. They're not even a professional team."

"Hey, don't start on the Linnets!" Gareth moaned from the back seat. "Next right, Sarge."

Kate chuckled and turned on her indicator. She glanced through her rear-view mirror and caught Mel staring at her, a little Mona Lisa smile on her lips. It was a smile that Kate was familiar with, one that had proven beguiling when they'd first met. Kate turned back to the road. Not anymore.

"What number am I looking for?" Kate slowed as she entered the road and eased past a large gothic-styled building on the left that read *St. James' Clinic.*

"Sixty-one. Further up on the right." Collier pointed between the two seats.

Kate nodded and kept her eyes peeled for a parking spot. The road was filled with townhouses with big bay windows and high steps to front doors that were covered under brick archways. Wealthy Victorian in style, but perhaps not in actual age. Large sycamore trees lined the street. Cars were parked in driveways and along the kerb—some half mounting the pavement. She'd driven well past the house they were looking for before she found a place to park, and they had to backtrack on themselves. Kate led the way and cringed inwardly when Mel fell into step beside her.

"Hey." Mel's voice was quiet.

Kate half turned her head, almost looking before she caught herself, and stared at the broken paving slabs at her feet. She didn't answer.

Mel sighed. "Look, it's not my fault we've been stuck together like this, Kate. I can't change what happened, we've just got to deal with it."

Kate snorted. "We did deal with it. We split up. Nothing left to deal with."

"Really?"

Kate shrugged and opened the gate to number sixty-one.

"Then why can't you even talk to me like any other colleague?"

Kate hitched an eyebrow. "Because you're not."

She let go of the gate and let it swing into Mel's hand as she mounted the steps and rang the doorbell, leaving Mel in her wake. She turned back and looked over Mel's head. Vinny and Gareth were just stepping into the garden.

There were noises on the other side of the door, a scraping sound, followed by a series of shuffling footsteps.

"Hello?" a woman's voice called out.

"Hello. Is that Mrs Ahmed?"

"Who is it?"

"Mrs Ahmed, my name is Detective Sergeant Kate Brannon. Would you open the door, please so that I can speak to you? It's very important."

"My husband isn't home."

"That's okay, Mrs Ahmed. I need to speak to you too. It's about Nadia."

The door swung open. The woman was clothed in a traditional *shalwar kameez* and *dupatta* that was so often worn amongst conservative families. The loose-fitting trousers, baggy tunic, and headscarf hid much of the short woman, but her face belied her worry.

"Nadia? What has happened to Nadia?"

"May we come in, Mrs Ahmed?"

She looked around, seemingly unsure, but quickly nodded and stood aside to let them pass before leading them into the parlour at the front of the house. It was a well-lit room. The huge south-facing bay window let in every moment of the sun's journey across the sky and cast soft shadows from the furniture. The large fireplace was surrounded by a faux-marble mantle and antique-styled tiles, and knick-knacks littered the shelf. An ornate gold clock sat in the centre.

"Please tell me, what has happened to my Nadia? She did not come home last night. We are frantic with worry for her. He is out looking for her now."

Kate and Vinny exchanged glances, then Kate held her hand out to the sofa. She sat beside the woman when she followed Kate's cue. She held out to Mrs Ahmed a picture taken from the CCTV footage the day before. Before the cameras had been blown to smithereens and Norfolk was forever changed. Before an act of terror tore at the heart of a community that would always remember.

"Is this Nadia?" The image had been blown up and cropped to show just Nadia's face.

Mrs Ahmed took the page, smiled, and nodded. "Yes, that is my daughter. Where is she?"

"I'm very sorry to tell you this, Mrs Ahmed, but we believe Nadia is dead."

Mrs Ahmed's hands flew to her mouth, crumpling the page between her fingers. The wail that tore from her throat was a primal thing, an abject cry of pain and misery that no parent should have to suffer. "No, no, no, no, no, no, no. Not my little girl. No, no, no. What happened? Who did this to her? What happened?"

How do you say the words *she did it—Nadia. She's the murderer, not the victim.* How do you tell a distraught mother her child—her beloved child—has just taken the lives of seventeen innocent women and children? Children. Two-year-old Gregory Walsh. Kate clung to the image of his pushchair to help her. He was the one who deserved justice. He was the victim of this crime. Not Nadia. Not Mrs Ahmed. Gregory.

She swallowed the gullet-burning bile of revulsion and fortified herself with the antacids of justice and the unshakable need to make sure there were no more two-year-old Gregorys. Not on her watch. "This will be very difficult, Mrs Ahmed, but Nadia was in the town centre yesterday when the bomb went off."

"My baby! My baby! Killed by bombers!" She cast her face to the ceiling, hands clasped to her chest, as if in prayer, speaking words in what Kate assumed was some Arabic dialect.

"Mrs Ahmed, Nadia was one of the bombers."

The wailing ceased, and the woman stared at her.

The clock on the mantle shelf ticked loudly in the otherwise silent room. One second. Two. Three. Four. Kate counted, watched as the news was assimilated into Mrs Ahmed's new reality.

"What?" Her voice was little more than a whisper, almost lost against the tick of the second hand moving again. "What did you say?"

Kate licked her lips and steeled herself again. "Nadia was wearing one of the two bombs that were detonated in the town centre yesterday morning. My colleagues and I are here to inform you and to search your home." She pulled a second document from her pocket. "This is a warrant, granted by the magistrates, that allows us to search and remove from the premises anything that we think may aid in our investigation." She handed her a copy of the document. "Do you understand, Mrs Ahmed?"

The woman nodded and her mouth moved like she was talking, but no words came out.

"I'm sorry, I couldn't hear you. What was that?"

"Must call my husband," she whispered.

Kate nodded. "You go ahead, we'll get started."

"No. Not until my husband is here."

"I'm sorry, that's not how this works." She pointed to the warrant. "We don't need permission to do this. That gives us the right to conduct this search immediately." She tipped her head to Vinny. "Sergeant Jackson will start in this room."

Jackson nodded. They both knew he would spend less time searching the property and more time babysitting Mrs Ahmed, and then dealing with Mr Ahmed when he arrived, but those were the breaks sometimes.

Kate stood up and led the other two out of the room as Mrs Ahmed picked up her phone. Kate could hear her angry then tearful entreaties in the hallway as she sent Mel to search the rest of the downstairs and left Gareth to take the master bedroom they found. Given Mrs Ahmed's reaction, she didn't really expect to find a great deal through the rest of the house, but she was hopeful that there would be something in Nadia's room.

She sighed as she located Nadia's bedroom with only a little snooping around . There were posters on the wall, dirty clothes on the floor, and the bed was unmade. A desk in the corner was covered with notepads, textbooks, and pens. A laptop was on the bedside table, alongside a lamp, an alarm clock, and a jewellery tree; from each branch hung a bracelet, a necklace, a ring, or some earrings.

Just like every other seventeen-year-old's room.

She leafed through the pages of the notepads, reading what was in English and putting to one side all the ones that were filled with Arabic and would have to be taken away from translation. She bagged the laptop, and flipped the mattress. As a teen, she'd hidden plenty of things under her own mattress from her gran—magazines, books, her first copies of *Rubyfruit Jungle* and *Curious Wine*—the beginnings of her own journey into the woman she'd become.

And just like billions of other seventeen-year-olds before her, Nadia had hidden hers there too. The black Moleskine diary stared up at Kate. She leafed through the pages, only to be stymied by the

Arabic language again. So Kate bagged it and checked the rest of the wardrobes and drawers for anything else. She pulled posters away from the wall to check there was nothing on the back or hidden behind them before lifting the rug in the centre of the room and checking the floorboards. One seemed particularly loose, but when she pried it up, all Kate found was a mousetrap. Missing the bait.

She was almost finished with the room when Mel leant around the door. "How's it going?"

"Treasure trove."

"Really?" Mel stepped in and surveyed the bags of evidence Kate had collected.

"Yup." Kate added another bagged notebook to the small mountain she'd piled up. "As soon as I learn to read Arabic, I'm certain it will be."

Mel chuckled. "Ah, there's the Kate I've missed."

"Don't." Kate ground her teeth to stop herself continuing.

"What?" Mel frowned at her.

"Don't start." Kate ran her hand along the top of the wardrobe and felt something roll away from her fingers and down behind it. *Bollocks.* The wardrobe was big, fitted snugly into an alcove beside the chimney breast, made of solid wood, and bloody heavy. "Help me pull this out."

Mel stood at one side as she grabbed the other, and slowly they managed to ease it out of the alcove.

A door banged downstairs, and raised voices floated up to them.

"Sounds like Mr Ahmed's home," Mel said, grunting as they inched it out far enough for Kate to slide in behind it and pick up what had fallen: a small silver ball, about half a centimetre in diameter.

Mel groaned. "All that for nothing."

Kate shook her head. "The bombs were filled with nuts, nails, bolts, and ball bearings." She held the small sphere up to Mel. "Just like this one."

"Yeah, but you can get ball bearings in loads of things."

"True." She held it a little closer to her nose.

"What? Can you smell explosives on metal now?" Mel quipped.

"No. But it didn't hurt to rule it out." She bagged and labelled the ball bearing and turned slowly to make sure she hadn't missed anything else in the room. This was the place where they would start to find some answers.

Why two bombers? Surely one would have been enough? Where did they get the bomb? Why Ann Summers? Hell, why did they pick King's Lynn? There were bigger cities, better targets out there then this little rural town—not even a city.

Or was that the whole point? The true meaning of a seemingly random terror attack: It could literally be anywhere. Anyone. Anytime. There was no safety, because there was no safe place. Everything, everyone, everywhere was a target. In picking a place many people in the country didn't even know existed, they were making the boldest statement of all.

We are coming for all of you.

We can find you all.

Kate swallowed and picked up an armful of evidence bags.

Now she understood.

In a world where everything could change on a split second, there was no point in wasting a single second with what-ifs and maybes. After coming so close to losing Gina the day before...Kate knew what she wanted, what she needed.

Yeah. Now she understood.

CHAPTER 9

Gina woke to a skinny arm across her face and the hundred-decibel buzz saw that she also called Sammy next to her ear. They'd picked her up from the campsite and relieved Will of her care after midnight. Kate had offered to drop them home, but neither of them really wanted that. Yet, as much as she'd rather stay at Kate's than in her own home, sharing a bed with Sammy was getting old. For all of them. It wasn't her daughter she wanted to share a bed with.

She climbed out, careful not to wake Sammy, and wrapped her arms about herself. It was cold. She slipped into the bathroom, quickly ran through her morning routine, and grabbed the dressing gown Kate left hanging on the back of the door for her. It was thick, grey towelling, and it was just what she needed as she descended the stairs and put the kettle on to boil. She opened the fridge to get the milk and spotted a note stuck to the door with a large magnet.

Morning gorgeous,

Timmons called me before six a.m., had to go in. Not sure what time I'll be home, I'll text you later. Don't feel you have to rush off, though. Stay as long as you like. And, please, would you mind giving Merlin a walk? She looked at me like I was abusing her when I left this morning.

K x

"Looks like it's just you and me till Sammy wakes up, then," she said to Merlin. The grey and white dappled dog watched her intently and glanced towards the door. "Oh, right. Sorry."

Gina opened the back door to let her out, chafing her hands up and down her arms against the cold. Merlin quickly sniffed, circled, relieved, and then hopped back inside where she jumped onto her sofa, pushed off a cushion, and settled back down to sleep.

Gina shook her head and went to finish making her drink. Sammy still had a couple of days left until the end of the school year, but it was Sunday, and a long walk on the beach with the two of them sounded like a good idea. She glanced at the clock. Eight thirty in the morning. Sammy never slept this late. She was usually up before the sun... well, in the winter, at least. The result of the late night, no doubt. She smiled and enjoyed the quiet time before Hurricane Sammy arrived. There was something she needed to do.

She put her mug on the dining room table and gathered a notepad and pen from the bureau in Kate's living room. She sat down and tapped the pen to the top of the page. Trying to find the right words was difficult. She couldn't imagine how hard it must have been for Pat to write those beautiful words. A lump rose in her throat, and she swallowed it down before poising her pen to write.

Dear Mr Boyne,

Please excuse me writing to you like this, but I thought this might be better than a stranger turning up on your doorstep with a somewhat fantastical story. Please bear with me.

My name is Georgina Temple. I live on the North Norfolk coast with my daughter. I can assure you I don't want anything from you, and I'm not crazy. You don't know me, but yesterday I met a woman who I think may have.
Her name was Patricia O'Shea.
If that name means nothing to you, then please accept my apologies for intruding into your life and throw the letter away. If it does mean something to you, then I have something for you that Pat wanted me to give you.

Please let me know what you wish.

Yours sincerely,
Gina Temple.
Croo Cottage,
Station Road,
Docking.

Gina slid the note into an envelope, sealed it, and addressed the outside. She took a sip of her coffee, grimacing at the bitter brew that had long since cooled, and tipping it away. The kettle was set to boil again. There was nothing she hated more than microwave-heated coffee. It wasn't the perfect letter, but she hoped it would mean something to him. All she could do now was post it and wait.

Her phone pinged. She smiled when she saw it was a text from Kate, but the smile quickly turned to a frown.

Definitely going to be a late one today. No idea when I'll be home.

Want me to take care of Merlin?

She sent back before the phone in her hand rang.

"You could have just texted back," Gina said.

"I know. But I wanted to talk to you anyway."

"Then I'm very glad to hear your voice." Gina smiled. She could picture Kate's cheeks turning pink. "So, want me to take Merlin home with me? I know it's probably going to be manic for you right now."

"Thank you, and I would love for you to watch Merlin for me, but I was going to... Well, I thought maybe..."

Gina waited, but Kate wasn't forthcoming. "Come on, Kate. I know you'll need to get back to work, so you should just spit it out."

"I want you to move in with me."

Gina pulled the phone from her ear and stared at it, her brain struggling to comprehend simple English. Surely Kate hadn't just said that? She held the phone back in place and asked, "What?"

"I-I-I'd like you and Sammy to move in with me."

No, she hadn't misheard, she hadn't misunderstood. Kate was really asking her to move in with her daughter. To be a family. It was Gina's greatest fantasy come to life. There was nothing she'd wanted more since Kate had asked her for more than a weekend. Nothing. She just hadn't thought they were there yet. A couple of months was fast by anyone's timescale, and add to that the fact that she and Kate had done little more than kiss... Well, she had thought they still had a long way to go. She was ready to move their relationship to the next level. If she hadn't been sure of that before yesterday, she certainly was now. But moving in together... Was she ready for that? Was Sammy?

Who was she kidding? Sammy would love it. Besides having her new best friend, Kate, on tap, she'd have her own dog. What more could any Sammy want? What more could Gina want?

She ran through the list of things she'd need to organise to get them packed up and moved out of their old house. The house that still haunted her with memories of Ally holding her captive and torturing her. Gina had to be honest, the idea of never having to step foot in that hallway again was almost enough on its own to convince her to say yes. But the idea of being with Kate every moment she possibly could...of kissing her goodnight and good morning...of cooking for her...having Kate hold her just because...of watching Kate torment Sammy about giving Merlin too many pizza crusts or doing her homework before she got to watch cartoons. The promise of living that life—of building that life—together...was so much more than Gina had ever thought she could have. So much more than she'd ever expected...or allowed herself to dream of having.

She licked her lips, trying to wet them enough to whisper the word on the tip of her tongue. To tell Kate how much she'd love to spend every single day right there with her. Tears coursed down her cheeks as she licked again, mouthed the word, but couldn't give it any volume—

"I mean, just over Christmas, I guess."

What? What did she mean 'just over Christmas'? What about the life they were going to build together? Had she waited too long? Had her silence been perceived as a negative? Was Kate backtracking, or was this what she'd meant all along and Gina had misunderstood?

"I mean, Sammy's almost finished with school and stuff—"

"She…she still has a week left." Gina cleared her throat, roughened by the sharp edges of disappointment.

"Yeah, but you pass her school to and from work every day, so it won't make any difference to her. And I thought it would be nice to spend as much time as we could together over the holidays, but I know I'm going to be busy."

Kate stuttered through words that should have made Gina happy. Instead, they made her feel a little sad. *But that isn't Kate's fault,* Gina reminded herself. She didn't know what was going through Gina's head. *And she won't if you don't tell her.* She swallowed. *You haven't even slept with her yet. How could you possibly think she'd ask you to move in—permanently—if she thought she was asking you to permanently share a bed with Sammy the buzzsaw?*

"Especially with this case now," Kate continued. "There's, literally, a metric tonne of this shit to get through, and then there's the other thing with your place."

Gina was pretty sure she knew what Kate meant, but she didn't want to start guessing and get things wrong. She'd already done that today, and she didn't want to deal with any more misunderstandings. "What thing?"

"That you hate it. And I get why. It's full of bad memories, with Ally and everything. So I just thought we could have a nice Christmas at my place. As a, well, as a family, I guess." Her voice dropped. "If that's okay."

Gina swallowed her earlier disappointment and cleared her throat again. Her chest felt tight with a mixture of happiness at the thought of being a family—just the three of them—and disappointment that it was just for a short while. But their relationship was still so new, still raw. There was no need to rush it forward.

"That's more than okay with me." Then another thought occurred to her. What if this was some sort of test? A trial run, perhaps? Kate's way of testing the waters on this becoming a permanent arrangement? *Please let that be the case.*

"It is?"

"Of course it is."

"Okay. Well, let me know if you need me to pick anything up." The smile on her lips was so clear in her voice.

Gina grinned. "Kate?"

"Yes?"

"Sammy and I will need to pick up a tree."

"A tree?"

"Yes, a Christmas tree. It's looking a little Grinchy in here."

"Oh, right, yeah. Of course." Her voice dropped a little. "Do whatever you want."

"Whatever?"

"Yeah. I, well, I want—doesn't matter." Something muffled her voice as she said, "I'm coming now, Vinny." Then the line came clear again. "Okay, I've gotta go. Looking forward to seeing the place de-Grinchyfied."

"That's not a word."

"It's a good word. Ask Sammy." Then she was gone.

Heavy footsteps on the stairs drew Gina's attention, and Sammy shuffled into the room. "Morning, sunshine."

Sammy grunted and pulled herself into a chair.

Clearly she was still unhappy about everything Gina had had to tell her last night. She'd clung to Gina all night after they'd told her the truth of how Stella had been hurt. But at least she hadn't woken either of them, screaming from her nightmares. It was more than Gina had hoped for. Merlin appeared and sat beside Sammy, lovingly accepting the strokes and pats to her head. Every time Sammy stopped, she lifted her paw and tapped Sammy's knee to get her attention again, and Sammy slowly came around with a smile. It was a picture Gina could get used to. And she knew Sammy would be more than happy with the arrangement too.

"I slept very well, thank you, Sammy. How about you?"

Sammy stared at her through squinty eyes. "You're happy."

"I am."

"How comes?"

"Want to come Christmas tree shopping?"

Sammy eyes opened wide, and her lips curled into a smile. "Yeah." Then she frowned. "But we've already got a tree at home. Why'd we need anover one?"

"Another."

"Same difference."

Gina cocked her eyebrow. "Sammy, you're nine years old. You know how to speak properly. Constantly refusing to makes you sound stupid or lazy. You're neither. Talk properly if you expect me to respond. Otherwise, I'm just going to ignore you."

Sammy rolled her eyes. "Another tree," she said, perfectly articulating the *th* in the middle.

"Good. And it's not for our house. Kate says we can de-Grinchyfy her house."

"Cool. That's an awesome word." Sammy wiggled in her seat and held Merlin's paw when she set it on Sammy's thigh. "We're gonna be de-Grinchyfying, Merls. De-Grinchyfying."

"It's not a word."

"It's a good word. An awesome word. Kate used it, it must be."

"I swear, you two are more alike than you and I are."

"Me and Kate?"

"Yes." She grinned. "You're both trouble." She tickled Sammy's ribs until she giggled so hard she fell off the chair.

"Child abuse," she cried as Merlin licked her face.

"I'll give you child abuse." She tapped Sammy on the bottom as she lifted her to her feet and pushed her gently towards the stairs. "Go and get dressed while I make you breakfast. We've got a big day today."

"Okay." Sammy started up the stairs with Merlin at her heels.

"Oh, and Sammy?"

"Huh?" Sammy spun around to look at Gina.

"How would you feel about living here for the holidays?"

"Like, for reals?" She grinned gleefully and rubbed her hands together in excitement.

"Yes."

"Yay!" She ran up the stairs, screaming all the way.

"I'll take that as a yes, then."

Breakfast was a fast and animated affair, with Sammy's eagerness bubbling over. Merlin was restless in her presence, and Gina couldn't help but feel the same enthusiasm.

Packing their clothes and the gifts under their own tree took less than half an hour of running around to accomplish. The trip to the garden centre to pick out a tree took three times as long, and securing it to Gina's beat-up old Astra took almost as long again. She was grateful for the length of rope she had in the boot, but trying to tie the knots tight enough to keep the tree still was a different story. In the end, it was Sammy who managed to tie them. Gina didn't want to think about where she'd been practising her knot-tying skills. Some days you just had to roll with what life dished out and enjoy it the best you could.

Once the tree was back at Kate's house and sitting in its stand, they went to shop for decorations, buy food, and post the letter she had almost forgotten about in her excitement. Then they went to the beach to give Merlin—and Sammy—a good run. She felt so comfortable settling into Kate's house. It felt like they belonged there.

The tree sparkled and twinkled in the corner. She'd lit the wood burner and watched how the flames danced through the thick glass window. Sammy was curled on the sofa with Merlin, rubbing her tummy and staring idly at the TV screen as *The Santa Clause* flickered from one scene to the next. Gina just wished Kate were with them. She could imagine her arguing with Sammy about which reindeer or which elf was the best. Making them hot chocolate and raiding the cupboard for biscuits. Domestic bliss. All that was missing was Kate curled up on the sofa beside her.

She sighed. This was what she wanted.

The doorbell rang.

"Are you expecting anyone?" Gina asked Sammy with a smile.

"Nuh-uh. I'm nine. My friends are all in bed now."

"Good point. Must be for someone else, then."

The bell rang again.

"I guess I should get it, then." She pulled open the door and froze. Her brain short-circuited.

CHAPTER 10

Kate pushed open the door to the crime lab, with its graffiti-covered door—the result of someone a long time ago getting creative with a marker pen and declaring it the home of the CSIs. There were twenty-five CSIs that carried out the crime scene work for King's Lynn and the surrounding area. Usually they worked one of three shifts. Not today. Today all twenty-five of them were in the room, fighting for precious work space, test equipment, and the printer, which was spitting out reports on a scale to aid global warming.

Len Wild, a.k.a "Sarge"—a retired police officer now working as a civilian crime scene tech—was signing in every new piece of evidence as it came through the doors. The mammoth task of cataloguing, securing, preserving, and then analysing each and every single scrap of evidence was ultimately his responsibility. And one Kate didn't envy. He looked like he was drowning in paper.

He caught her eye as she strode into the room and nodded a quick greeting before focusing on his work again.

That was fine. She wasn't there to see Len. Not today. Right now she needed to see the resident self-proclaimed genius that was Simon Grimshaw. As ever, he looked like he'd just rolled out of bed, but his beard was a bit scraggier, his eyes a lot more bloodshot, and his temper worse than ever, as he bawled out a young tech who stood shaking under his caustic ire.

"Mr Grimshaw," Kate said, allowing the tech to scurry away like a bug fleeing being pinned to a board for dissection.

Grimshaw sighed. "Detective Sergeant Brannon. I know why you're here, and, quite simply, even I need longer than ten minutes to translate two hundred pages of handwritten Arabic." He held up the diary she was most interested in.

"Okay." She smiled. "How much longer?" She glanced at her watch.

"Tomorrow. I'm scanning the pages into the computer now, then I have to run the ORC over it. I'll get the first digital translation through later this evening. Then I'll need to go through and check for any anomalies, correct any ambiguities, and try to figure out anything that the computer can't decipher."

"Okay, so tomorrow morning, afternoon, end of the day? Which?"

"As early as I can, but until I see what the computer can't tackle, I won't really be able to tell you anything more definitive than that."

"Fair enough. When you get it through, send me the translation."

"Green said she gets it first. Then the NCTN team wants it."

Great. Pissing contest already. "Right. Well, if they get the originals, any chance I can get a copy? I mean, Stella was right there, Simon. Gina too. I spent nearly all night at the hospital with Stella to make sure she was okay, you know?"

He snorted. "Does that tactic work on anyone else?"

"Don't know, not used it before."

He chuckled. "Fine, I'll send you a copy."

"Thanks. Anything else I need to know?"

"Don't know. I'd say speak to the sarge. But he's pretty fucking swamped at the moment."

"No worries, Simon. Thanks." She turned and left him to it as her phone rang in her pocket. She pulled it out and groaned at Clare Green's number sullying her screen. *Bollocks.* She slid her finger across the screen to answer. "Yes, ma'am?"

"Incident room. Now." Then she was gone.

"Merry fuckin' Christmas to you to, ma'am." She stuffed the phone back in her pocket and headed for the door. At least being busy was keeping her mind off her early conversation with Gina. Or, rather, her earlier chickenshit moment with Gina. What happened to I-know-what-I-want-so-I'm-gonna-go-and-fucking-get-it? What happened to that shit? Simple. Silence. An uncomfortable, question-ridden, question-asking silence. And it had opened up a gulf in Kate's self-assured certainty that asking Gina to move in with her was the right thing to do.

She caught up with Vinny Jackson and Gareth as they pushed their way into the packed room.

"Okay, everyone, listen up," Clare shouted from the front of the room. Timmons sat on a chair, elbows on the table in front of him. He looked worse than earlier, but at least he was wearing a clean shirt now. "We've got good news and bad news, folks. So, I'll start at the bottom. New death toll is at twenty-one. We found two more bodies in the rubble, Lauren Walsh passed away an hour ago. Marian Jones just a few minutes ago. The families are being notified."

Silence filled the room. As the barbaric senselessness struck her again, Kate knew she wasn't the only one feeling it. Slowly the sorrow and despondency morphed into the determined anger that would allow them to do their jobs—to focus and do the dirty work that had to be done.

"I know, people, I know. Let's focus on the positives and see if we can bring their families some peace now. We have had some great results from our investigators at the perpetrators' houses." She pinned photos to a board behind her. "Evidence that one of the vests was stored in Nadia Ahmed's bedroom." She pointed to the picture of the ball bearing Kate had found. "Preliminary testing shows this has traces of explosives on it consistent with those used in yesterday's bombing."

A stilted cheer went around the room. Nothing new. Just more corroboration of who had blown themselves up. They already knew that. They'd seen it. They'd even found one or two body parts.

"DNA testing is going on to confirm identity, but we have visual confirmation of the photo from the CCTV footage by the girl's mother." She turned to Kate and Vinny. "Gut feeling, are the parents involved?"

Kate shook her head. "Definitely not the mother. She was shocked when we told her. Genuinely. I can't see her having any foreknowledge of this attack."

"Agreed," Vinny said. "The dad, though, I'm not as sure. The mother said he was out looking for his daughter when we got there because the girl hadn't come home. When he turned up, though, he said he'd been at the mosque. No mention of having been looking for Nadia."

"Miscommunication?" Clare asked.

Vinny shrugged. "Possibly, but his attitude didn't seem right for a bloke who'd just found out his daughter had blown herself and twenty-odd other people to bits. Certainly it wasn't consistent with his wife's reaction."

"Kate? Do you agree?"

"I was upstairs collecting evidence from the girl's room when Mr Ahmed arrived home. I didn't have as much contact with him, and not initial contact, but I would agree based on the little I did see."

"Okay, what do we know about Mr Ahmed, then?"

Gareth cleared his throat and straightened himself up. "Tariq Ahmed. Fifty-two-year-old male, moved to the UK in 1995 from Pakistan. Married in 1998 to Mishra Khan. Two children—well, one now. Nadia at seventeen was the oldest and Mohammed, eleven. He runs a market stall but used to own a clothes shop on the High Street."

"Where?" Clare asked the question that sat on the tip of Kate's tongue.

"Right where Ann Summers used to be." Gareth said, a smug smile painted across his lips.

"Boom!" Clare shouted. "And now we know why that shop was the specific target. Get Mr Ahmed in for questioning. Let's see if we can find out who his little girl's been hanging out with and what else he might know." She looked at Kate, Vinny, and Gareth. "Good work, people. Very, very good work. I hear we've got the girl's diary as well."

"Yes, ma'am. Hoping to get the translation back at some point tomorrow," Kate said.

"Excellent." She looked down at the other pages in her hand. "Saba Ayeshydi. Tell me what we've found?"

Kate clapped her hand over Gareth's shoulder. "Well done, mate. That was bloody good work."

The young detective beamed under her praise. "Thanks, Sarge."

"Saba Ayeshydi, nineteen, married to Ishman Ayeshydi, twenty-eight, haven't been able to find him to speak to him yet," Tom said. "But Ayeshydi's home is spotless. Literally not a hair in there. We think we've got her toothbrush for DNA comparison, but I couldn't be sure it wasn't a brand new one. It really looked like it hadn't been touched. Same with her hairbrush. I'd be very surprised if we don't find out that it's new as well, and the room's been emptied to discard any possible evidence she could have left behind."

"The husband?" Clare clarified.

Tom nodded, as did many others around the room. "It makes sense. For a start, I think he's the only one with access to go through the room like that. And if so, then why unless you have something to hide?"

"But surely he wouldn't be stupid enough to do something so suspicious?" Mel piped up.

Clare shot her down. "I've seen people do a lot more stupid things than empty a room."

Kate fought not to snigger. Clearly their breakup had been just as amicable as Mel and Kate's.

"Besides, while it looks suspicious, we can't lock people up for suspicious—"

"Unfortunately," a voice from the crowd said.

"Quite. But nonetheless, suspicion only allows us to ask questions. Find me the evidence we need to lock these people up, if they were the ones involved."

Murmurs of assent went around the room.

"Right, get me Tariq Ahmed in here and you lot," Clare said, pointing to Tom and his team. "Find me Ishman Ayeshydi."

The energy in the room rose as seventy officers set about their business.

"Kate!" Clare called.

Kate met her gaze questioningly.

"A moment." She indicated her head to the office just behind them.

Timmons was watching her, holding the door open as she nodded. She caught Vinny's eye and shrugged. He grinned and tapped the face of his watch as she pushed her way through the crowd.

"Ma'am. Sir," Kate greeted them as she stepped in. The closed door muffled some of the noise from the room beyond, but not all of it.

"That was good work from your team this morning, Kate."

"Thank you, ma'am." She stuffed her hands into the pockets of her jeans. "We were just doing our jobs."

Clare nodded. "I know, but still...well done."

"I'll pass that along to the rest of the team. They all did the same."

"Jesus, Brannon, it's colder than a witch's tit in 'ere. Want me to hold your handbags while you scratch each other's eyes out? Christ." Timmons said.

"Sir?" Kate stared at him, wide eyed and slack-jawed.

He looked at Clare. "Just get on with it."

Clare sighed. "Has it been... I mean, this morning, was it..."

"Fuck's sake. Brannon, it was my fuck-up sticking you with your ex-bird. Didn't know the history. Do you need a body swap? There's too much riding on this investigation to fuck it up because you're uncomfortable working with...well, someone who shit on ya. If you know what I mean?"

Kate did. In his own, completely politically incorrect way, Timmons was worried about her.

"It's been a difficult couple of days, and I know you must be worried about that lovely girl of yours. Being as she was there yesterday...not to mention Stella..." He glanced out of the corner of his eye.

Was he watching Clare's reaction? To what? Then she got it, and she bit her lip to avoid smirking at his little game. He was letting Clare know just how well her life was going for her now, in his own little way. Worried and protective. This was why she liked working for Timmons. She knew exactly where she stood with him, and she knew damn well he always had her back.

"I appreciate it, sir, I really do. It has been difficult, but I can be professional. A lot's changed since I left Norwich." She looked him directly in the eye. "Best move I ever made."

He grinned and winked at her. "Couldn't agree more." He lifted his head, and nodded towards the door. "Go and bring in Mr Ahmed. Let's see what he's got to say for himself."

CHAPTER 11

Gina stared, her mind barely able to comprehend what her eyes were seeing. A woman with dark, shoulder-length hair. Finely arched eyebrows twitched over the azure-blue eyes that stared back at her. There were more lines beside those eyes and more grey at the temples than Gina remembered from ten years ago. Even so, Gina couldn't have denied who was standing at Kate's door, no matter how much she might have wanted to. It was like looking at her older self in the mirror.

Alison Temple. Her mother.

"I'm sorry. I know this probably isn't the best time to come, but I just needed to see you were okay."

Alison... No that didn't feel right, but neither did thinking of this woman as her mother.

She wrung her hands together as she stood on the doorstep. "I just needed to see with my own eyes." She reached a hand forward, towards Gina's cheek, then let it drop as Gina jerked her head back and away from her like she was a snake about to strike. Alison's...her mother's...her face fell. "I'll go now." She turned.

Gina opened her mouth to speak, but she didn't know what to say. When she'd fallen pregnant, her father had ordered her to get an abortion. To have her baby—her Sammy—terminated. The woman in front of her had said nothing, done nothing. She hadn't tried to talk him around, but to be fair, she hadn't tried to talk Gina around to her father's position either. She'd simply sat silent as Gina's father had thrown her out of the house a decade ago. At seventeen, Gina had been all alone and pregnant, with no job, no prospects, and no clue what to do with herself. She hadn't seen either of her parents since.

It had been less than a week since Kate had met Alison during a case and Alison had asked about Gina. Less than a week since Gina had begun to think about her again, and the relationship they didn't have. The relationship they'd never had. Gina's anger at this woman's inaction when she'd most needed her had driven her to the decision to never allow Alison back into her life—into their lives. She didn't need the heartache that would come with the discussion they'd need to have, the memories they'd have to rake over.

Gina had enough to deal with, and she was more than happy with the way her life was going right now. She didn't need Alison Temple's complications to add to it.

Well, tonight she had the chance to get all those negative thoughts out of the way in one epic *fuck you* to the woman who had abandoned her.

But she hadn't done that. She hadn't told her where to go or slammed the door in her face, as she'd pictured herself doing so many times. No, she'd opened the door and let her speak. Why?

It was simple.

Pat.

Gina had listened to Kate read Pat's beautiful letter last night and wept for the heartbreaking decision she'd made with the best of intentions for everyone involved. She'd had no way of knowing if it was the right decision then and still hadn't when she had died. But she had loved that baby girl, and George, even if her actions had spoken to the contrary. It was so clear in every word she'd written. There had been no good choices for her to make, so she'd chosen the path where she saw the least harm, the lesser of the two evils she was presented with.

Kate had told her that Alison had fought her own demons in her marriage to Gina's father. Maybe silence was the lesser of her two evils. Would an explanation really hurt Gina any more at this point? Could anything her *mother* have to say for herself hurt more than her silence had a decade ago?

"Wait." Her voice was quiet, little more than a whisper, as her mother—no, Alison—started to walk away. She wouldn't call her *mother*. It just didn't feel right. There was too much unsaid to be able to think of her like that. Too many years had passed, too much pain still to be accounted for before she could accept this woman as her mother. She needed time to get her head around that. Time and an explanation she could understand. This wasn't the woman she'd grown up with, and Gina sure as shit wasn't the same little girl who had called her *mum*. This was Alison Temple. Not *mum*, not *mother—Alison*. It was a step forward to thinking of her as *bitch*, though.

Alison stopped and turned back, the look on her face as hopeful as any Gina had ever seen.

"Would you—" Gina's voice cracked and gave out. She coughed to clear it and tried again. "Would you like a cup of tea?"

Alison smiled and brushed a tear from her cheek. "I'd love one."

Gina held the door open and let her mother inside.

"Mum, who is it?" Sammy shouted from the front room, then appeared in the doorway. Her pyjama top was on inside out, and there was a ketchup stain in the middle of her chest. Her hair was slicked back, still wet on top, even though the ends had dried after her bath. "Mum? You okay?" She walked over and tucked her hand inside Gina's as Gina pulled her into her body and wrapped her arms around Sammy's skinny frame.

Sammy had never met her grandmother, and Gina couldn't for the life of her decide how to introduce her.

Tears were running down Alison's cheeks, tears of guilt, tears of pride, tears of all the years they'd lost—Gina didn't know. Maybe later she'd find out, but right now Sammy was her focus. She squatted down so she was at the same height as Sammy and nodded. "I'm good, kiddo." She cupped Sammy's cheek, and ruffled her hair. "This is Alison Temple." She turned a little to look at her.

Sammy followed her gaze. "That's our name."

Gina nodded and smiled at Sammy's wide-eyed stare. "That's because she's my mum."

Sammy spun to face Alison fully and looked at her like a bug under the microscope Kate had been showing her how to use. She leant close to Gina's ear and whispered loud enough for Alison to hear. "She looks like you but old."

Gina slapped her hand over Sammy's mouth as Alison barked out a laugh.

"I'm sorry." Gina said. "Sammy, apologise."

"What for?"

"For being rude."

Sammy frowned, clearly confused about what was rude in her statement. "I'm sorry for being rude."

Alison squatted down. "That's okay, Sammy. I don't think you meant to be rude. You just told the truth, didn't you?"

Sammy nodded and threw her mother a withering look.

Alison laughed again. "I'll bet you keep your mother on her toes, don't you?"

Sammy frowned. "She doesn't do ballet."

It was Alison's turn to frown.

"She watched a TV show with ballet dancers in and I had to explain dancing on pointe."

"Oh, I see. Well, what I meant was that you're a clever little girl who's full of fun."

Sammy grinned. "Yup. That's me."

Gina rubbed her hair. "Go and put your top on the right way, and brush your teeth. It's time for bed."

"But the film hasn't finished yet," Sammy complained.

"You can finish watching it in bed. Go on."

Sammy sighed heavily and trudged up the stairs.

Gina stood up and went to the kitchen.

"She's beautiful."

Gina smiled. "Thank you." She held up the kettle. "Do you want tea or something a bit stronger? I've got a bottle of wine in the fridge."

Alison smiled. "A glass of wine would be lovely. Thank you."

Gina opened a cupboard and pulled out two glasses. The white Marlborough was crisp and clean on her tongue as she led Alison into the living room and put the TV on mute. She didn't turn it off when Sammy was being allowed to watch TV in her room. That was a fatal mistake that led to Sammy watching action movies and staying up to all hours.

"So...?" Gina said.

"Yes. Where to start?"

Gina shrugged and sipped her wine. "I guess that's up to you. You're here."

Alison nodded. "Did Kate tell you? About your father?"

"Which part?"

"Where he is now?"

Gina nodded. "He's in prison."

"Did she tell you why?"

Gina nodded again. Kate had given her the details Alison had shared with her. Including the full list of Alison's injuries at the hands of the man Gina had called "Dad" for so long. "I'm sorry he did that to you."

Alison shrugged off the comment. "Not half as sorry as I am for what we did to you." She swiped at the tears again. "Sorry. You don't want a blubbering mess complaining about everything that happened."

Gina took a deep breath and let it out slowly. "If you'd come to see me a couple of months ago, I'd have told you where to go."

"I don't blame you." Alison put her glass on the coffee table and started to stand up.

"But a lot has changed in the last couple of months," Gina continued. "Yesterday I held the hand of a woman who was dying. She told me about a mistake she made and spent her entire life regretting because she didn't tell the truth. When she died, all she wanted was to set the record straight, but by then it was too late. She'd missed her chance." Gina sipped her drink, giving herself a moment to get her thoughts in order, to find the words she wasn't totally sure she felt, but she didn't want to regret not trying. "I don't want to die like that. I might not like the truth. I might get angry about it. I might not understand. But unless I know…" She shrugged and sat back in her chair. "I've changed a lot, and I want to know what happened. The good, the bad, and the ugly, as they say."

"You're sure?"

Gina nodded and sipped her drink.

"You might need more of that."

Gina smiled sadly. "Kate has a pretty well-stocked wine cupboard."

"She's a lovely woman, your Kate."

Gina couldn't stop the smile that spread over her lips. She didn't even want to try. "Yes, she is. I'm very lucky to have found her."

"She gets on with Sammy too?"

"They're like best pals." Gina finished her glass and put it on the table. "Now, stop stalling."

Alison smirked. "As patient as ever, I see."

Gina stared. She wasn't ready for that kind of banter, for that level of easy conversation that resulted in piss-taking and reminiscing. Gina wasn't anywhere near ready to face that, to accept that kind of relationship with Alison. That was a mother's privilege. Not Alison's. She hadn't earned it. Not yet, maybe not ever.

"Sorry that was out of line." Alison said, obviously seeing Gina's discomfort. She cleared her throat and started, "When I was a girl, my parents were very strict. Very controlling. But that wasn't unusual for the time. Far from it. They were older than most of my friends' parents and always a bit, I don't know, aloof, maybe. They didn't really mix with anyone else. Kept themselves to themselves, and there was never any family around. That was unusual. It was just the three of us. I found out after my mum died that it was because they couldn't have children. They adopted me and moved away from everyone who knew them to keep it a secret. My dad told me while I was helping him box up her things."

"I didn't know that." It was an aspect of Alison's history Gina had never known. Was it something Alison was ashamed of? Was that why she'd kept it a secret? Or was it simply a reflection of just how estranged they'd been as a family even when Gina had lived at home? She didn't remember ever really talking to Alison. Not the way some of her friends at school said they could tell their mums anything. Not the way the girls at work had done. They'd never had that kind of bond. She'd never sat at the dinner table and spoken to Alison the way Sammy talked to her. It made her realize just how amazing her relationship with Sammy was. And she vowed right there to make sure that it only ever got stronger. She never wanted to be faced with having this conversation with Sammy in twenty years. Never.

Alison shook her head. "Not something they ever talked about. When I found out like that, when my dad told me, it made me feel like they were ashamed. Keeping it a secret like that all those years." She sipped her own drink. "I think they were ashamed. Not having children was seen as a failure, especially for the woman. Back then women were wives and mothers. They weren't career women. They were born and raised to give birth to the next generation. Those unfortunates who couldn't were ashamed and saw themselves as less than the other women around them. I think my mother felt like that. That she'd failed my dad." She swallowed. "And I think my dad blamed her. He couldn't prove his mettle as a man because she didn't get pregnant."

"It might have been his fault, not hers."

Alison nodded. "We know that now, Gina. Back then..." She shook her head.

"But they went to all the trouble of adopting you."

"Yes."

"Why would they do that if they were ashamed of you? Or going to be ashamed of you?" She shook her head, not sure she could express exactly what she meant.

"No, I don't think they were ashamed of me. At least, I don't think that now. Back then I suppose I did. Now I just think they were ashamed of *how* they got me. Of what they had to go through to get the family they were supposed to have, that society expected them to have. That they couldn't have their own kids." She shrugged. "It made me feel a bit different, I guess. And my mum was already gone then, so

I couldn't talk to her about it. That and the fact that Dad never spoke of it again." She snorted a quick laugh. "I thought I'd imagined it until I was emptying the house when he died and found all the papers and my real birth certificate." She shook her head. "Anyway, where was I?"

"Just the three of you."

"Oh, right. Well, I wanted to be like all the other kids, going out and having fun. Like teenagers do. And I met your father. He was a little bit older than me, as you know, and he seemed so sophisticated, so grown up compared to all the other boys. Well, your grandfather forbade me from seeing him. I should have listened, but of course, I knew best. I told my dad that I was old enough to decide who I was going to see and that he couldn't control me anymore." She chuckled. "I was a stroppy teenager, and I got myself a good belting for that, just like every other stroppy teenager got at that time. He wasn't a cruel man, just a strict one. But then I didn't know the difference. I didn't like it, so I ran away with Howard. We got married, and before I knew it, I was pregnant."

Gina frowned. She knew her mother and father had been married for several years before she was born. "But—"

"I had a little boy."

Gina's mouth fell open, and her brain stuttered to a halt. She had no sibling. She'd grown up an only child and had never even really thought about having a brother or a sister. To find out there was one... that there was yet another secret kept from her... It was like she'd lived an entirely different life in the same house as her parents. Yes, there were things that, as a parent, she protected Sammy from, but they shared a home, a life, and what happened to them both affected them both. So they both dealt with it all. At a level Sammy could handle wherever possible, but the past few months had shown Gina that Sammy could handle way more than Gina wished she had to. Clearly her own parents had never shared that sentiment. "I have a brother?"

Alison shook her head. "No, he died while I was pregnant with you. He got tonsillitis. Not usually fatal to children, but he'd never been poorly before. Just the odd sniffle, you know, like children get. So they put him on penicillin." She sniffed. "We didn't know he was allergic to it. He came out in these big, black spots that swelled up. They thought it was meningitis, so they gave him more penicillin."

Gina plucked a tissue from the box and handed it to Alison.

"Thank you." She blew her nose. "It was the allergy that killed him, but they didn't know that then. They thought it might be something I could catch from him. They wouldn't let me in with him. He kept crying for me, and all I wanted to do was hold him, but they wouldn't let me in to see him. They didn't want to risk you too." Her shoulders shook with the heaving sobs as she held the tissue to her face and cried.

Gina put her glass on the table and moved to sit next to Alison. She wrapped her arms around her shoulders and held her as she wept. She held a woman weeping for her dead infant, her son, and as Gina offered her comfort, so many pieces fell into place. They tumbled into order as Gina remembered what little she could of her early childhood. The sad, almost vacant look on her mum's face in pictures of her as a little girl. Gina had always thought it was something she'd done wrong. Something wrong they saw in her. *How self-absorbed we are when we're young. Until our Galileo moment when we realise that the universe doesn't revolve around us.*

"It's so easy now to look back and know I was depressed," Alison continued slowly. Her words coming in fits and starts as she wiped at her face, and caught her breath. "I was grieving, and I should have gotten help, but I don't think the doctors knew all that much about depression back then. Not really. All I knew was that I couldn't be with my little boy when he died because I was pregnant. And I know it isn't rational, but I blamed you for it. It didn't help later when your father started to show his true colours."

"Later?"

Alison nodded slowly. "He wasn't always bad. He just got worse and worse. He wanted a son, you see. But after Michael died, I didn't want to have another baby. I couldn't face it. He blamed me for Michael's death. Told me I'd failed him as a wife." She laughed harshly. "As if that was the only thing I was good for. So, as much as he wanted it, I refused to give him what he craved most. My little rebellion, I guess. Anyway, he started to take it out on me in other ways."

"So he wasn't always violent?"

Alison shook her head. "Not at all. We were bad for each other, and instead of bringing us together, losing Michael tore us apart. In our grief, we brought out the worst in each other and couldn't find a way to change that. I'm not even sure your father wanted to." She wiped her nose.

Gina wasn't able to make sense of every new emotion that filled her only to be replaced moments later by a new one, one even more intense than before. Every scrap of information was pushing her closer and closer to emotional overload, and she knew it would take days, weeks, to process it all. There was no way she could do it all in one night. Instead, she decided that tonight, all she should do was listen and try to absorb what she could. The rest she'd deal with later. She made a mental note to call Jodi and make an appointment. Between the bombing and Alison's visit...maybe a little counselling session was in order. But that would wait until tomorrow, or Monday. Right now she had to get through the rest of this conversation. "Did you want to?"

She shrugged. "At one time, perhaps. But not for long, and not until it was far too late for he and I to ever make it work again."

"You wanted it to be over?"

Alison nodded. "For many years before it happened." She sighed. "I think if he were honest, he did too. Like I said, we were bad for each other. But that's not really what you need to know about. I'm here to see if there's anything we can change between us, or if that's too late too."

From everything Kate had told her about Alison showing up on her doorstep, Gina knew that this was the ending that Alison wanted. But was it what *she* wanted? The question was still so new to her—and the emotions still so raw—but there was something Alison hadn't yet touched on. Something Gina still had to know before she could even think about a future relationship with Alison, because it would impact on the most important person in Gina's life. She pulled away from Alison and slid across the sofa. "I suppose that depends."

"On what?"

"Did you want me to get rid of the baby?"

Alison frowned. "I wished you weren't pregnant."

The words struck Gina like a cannonball slamming into her chest and expelling the air from her lungs in one great gasp. She grabbed at the fabric covering her chest like it weighed too much and she had to be free of its constricting presence. It was too much. There could be no room for this woman in her life. Yes, it was good to know what had been behind the pitiful relationship they'd had while Gina was growing up. She was sure that would help her in the long-term… maybe. But there was no room in her life for anyone who wished her daughter had been terminated before she was even born. There was no way Gina was going to introduce someone to Sammy who had the potential to make her daughter feel bad about herself. There was already way too much of that in Sammy's life. Between Connie's death and the circumstances surrounding it—including Sammy believing for three godawful days that she was the one who had killed her—and Sammy's father's absence from her life because of his own poor parenting decisions that had led to that fateful morning on the marsh, well, Sammy had enough to deal with. Alison would not be another millstone about the child's neck. "So, yes—"

"No. That's not what I said or what I wanted."

"You said you wished I wasn't pregnant." Gina ran her fingers through her hair, like she wished she could grab the thoughts—those memories—and pull them from her brain. She could still see her father's face so clearly as he'd raised his hand and pointed to the door. "You're no child of mine", he'd screamed at her, spittle collected at the corner of his mouth. "My daughter wouldn't shame me or herself shagging every Tom, Dick, or Harry that fancied a look in her knickers." He'd spat at her. She could still feel the sticky mucus from his throat like it had burned her face and left its mark forever upon her skin. "Whore" had been the last word her father had ever screamed at her before she'd run.

Gina took a deep breath before she said, "What else could you possibly mean?"

"For me, getting pregnant imprisoned me in a marriage where I was never happy. If I hadn't had Michael, I'm not sure your dad and I would've lasted those first few years, and then, when I was pregnant with you, well, I came to associate pregnancy with being trapped, not with the wonder of having a beautiful child at the end of it. I didn't want you to get rid of the baby. But I wished you hadn't got trapped. Because that's what it was for me. I was seeing my own nightmares again in what you were going through, rather than trying to help you find your path through it."

Gina frowned. She couldn't imagine ever seeing the world from her own perspective, if Sammy needed her, but then she'd never suffered the devastating loss of a child. Her child. Her firstborn child. She'd never been stuck in a loveless marriage, abused, controlled, and seemingly despised by the person who should understand you most. She'd never been forced to face, day after day, the person she blamed for not being able to say goodbye to that child either. Would she have been able to put all that aside if she saw Sammy looking at the same possible future?

She had to be honest, with herself if no one else. And the truth was, she didn't know. She'd like to think that she would put Sammy and Sammy's needs first. In her heart of hearts, she was pretty sure she would. But she also accepted that she and Sammy were closer than she and Alison had ever been. A sad fact, but a fact nonetheless.

"You said you wanted the truth," Alison said quietly.

"Yes, I did."

"The truth is I was selfish. I was scared. I was lonely, and I only thought of myself and what I could face from one day to the next. Your father never hit you. I was confident he never would. He loved you."

"He had a funny way of showing it."

Alison nodded. "Yes, he did. But he loved you. He only wanted what was best for you. What *he* considered best for you, not necessarily what *you* considered best for you. His anger was always directed at me. And I had to make the decision daily whether I could take another beating for standing up to him, or if today was a day to keep my mouth shut and hope he'd sleep on the couch."

The tears welled in Gina's eyes. How different it all could have been if Alison's depression had been treated. How all their lives could have changed.

"I was very good at pushing his buttons."

Alison smiled. "You kept us on our toes."

Gina smiled. "Is that your way of telling me that Sammy's my own fault?" She couldn't help but let her smile broaden. Sammy was certainly full of mirth and merriment. Mischief followed her as faithfully as Merlin did.

"I wouldn't be so presumptuous. I've only met the little scamp for five minutes."

Gina chuckled. "You wouldn't be wrong. She can get herself dirty in a clean bath and I never, ever know what a letter brought home from school could be. A report card full of A's or expulsion. Either's possible."

Alison chuckled. "Then, yes. It's your own fault."

"I was never that bad."

Alison shrugged. "You had more to be fearful of than she does."

Gina mulled it over for a minute. Would she have been as mischievous as Sammy if she hadn't been terrified of going home to tell her mother and father what she'd done? Yes. Without a doubt. Suddenly she was more grateful than she ever imagined she could be for Sammy's naughtiness. As much as people would tell her it meant she was getting it all wrong, in her eyes she could see now she was getting something right. Her daughter didn't live in fear of her. To Gina, that suddenly meant more than anything else.

Fear had caused Gina to suffer panic attacks on and off since she was a teen. Had made her too scared to have a relationship, to have friends, to open up to people. Because she was always afraid of being rejected by them, just as she'd been rejected by her parents before she even understood what rejection was. So many tiny pieces of her own psyche and behaviour suddenly made sense. "I don't want to be scared anymore."

Alison shook her head. "You don't need to be. He can't hurt you."

"I wasn't afraid he'd hurt me."

Alison watched her. "Then what were you afraid of?"

"What had already happened."

"I don't understand."

"I told you I needed to know the truth, that knowing it was going to be painful. And it has been. Believe me. It truly has been. If words could inflict actual wounds, there'd be blood everywhere—"

"I'm sorry." Alison whispered, tears welling in her eyes again.

Gina waved the words away. "I asked for the truth. I can't and don't blame you for giving me what I asked for. But I guess I'm asking now if that's what you want. Do you want the truth? Even if it will hurt?"

Alison took a deep breath, clearly steeling herself for whatever Gina had to say. "Yes. I think we both deserve the truth."

Gina nodded, reached for her glass before she realised it was empty, and leant back in her chair again. "I was afraid of being rejected even further. I felt I was hanging on to my family by my fingernails. I knew neither of you wanted me there, but I had no idea why." She laughed bitterly. "At one stage, I thought you could see all the naughty thoughts in my head, and that was why you hated me." She swiped angrily at the tears running down her cheeks. "I was just a little kid, and I didn't know anything except I wasn't good enough to love. Not even for her own parents to love her. And that affects a child. Deeply."

"I'm so sorry."

Gina shook her head. "I understand why now. You were ill. I get that. But that doesn't change the effect it's had on me all these years. Until Kate, I never found anyone to love, because I didn't think anyone would stick around. I have panic attacks. I'm terrified still that Kate will find someone better and ditch me. And I'm most scared that one day my daughter will grow up and realise that she doesn't love me either. That I was a bad mum."

Alison shook her head. "No. I saw the way she looked at you. She adores you."

"She's nine. She adores anyone who feeds her."

"That's not true." Alison reached forward to take Gina's hand but stopped before she made contact. "You will have your ups and downs with her. She's your daughter, and there will be times when you'd gladly strangle her and times when she'll tell you venomously that she hates you. But you'll come through those because she loves you and you love her more than anything else in the world. And you will always, always, put her first. I can see that. And as much as I love you, and I truly do love you, I know that I can't say the same thing. I put myself first too many times."

"You were protecting yourself from being abused, Mum. I don't think—" Gina frowned as Alison's face paled and her eyes widened again. "What? What's wrong?"

"You called me 'Mum'."

Gina realised what she'd said, but she didn't know what had changed in her head to make the switch. "Sorry." Suddenly she wasn't looking at Alison Temple any more. She was looking at her mum, the woman who had brought her into the world, nurtured and loved her as best as she was able, despite being about as broken and downtrodden as a woman could be and still function. Hearing her admit how she'd failed Gina had softened her resolve to see her as a different woman, as Alison Temple. While the reasoning behind her silence was flawed logic, Gina could see that it was an extension of Alison's own pain, rather than a manifestation of Gina's predicament. When Alison—her mum—had spoken of Sammy, there had been nothing but warmth in her voice.

Was it enough for them to build a relationship on? Gina had no idea. But clearly her overwhelmed brain was telling her something. That it was ready to take a chance? She was too tired and too emotionally wrung out after everything she'd just learnt to make a decision tonight.

It could wait. One thing she was sure of was that they had time now. And a chance, if she was ready.

Alison shook her head quickly. "No, please don't be sorry. I just never really expected you to call me that again."

Gina smiled sadly. "What did you think I'd call you?"

Alison chuckled. "Maybe *bitch*."

"It crossed my mind when I first opened the door." Gina laughed.

"Good to know." She joined Gina in laughing, slowly at first, just a few chuckles, then more. Until they were both laughing loudly.

Gina pulled her into a tight hug, and the laughter turned to tears.

"You're keeping me awake." Sammy said from the doorway, her hands planted firmly on her hips, and a look of confusion on her face. "Why are you laughing and crying?"

"Because grown-ups are crazy, kiddo." Gina reached her hand out, and when Sammy stepped forward and took it, she pulled her into a hug too. "Didn't I tell you that?"

Sammy shook her head. "No. Kate told me that women are crazy. She didn't mention that it was all grown-ups."

Alison and Gina laughed again. It felt so good to laugh away the hurts and the truths she'd learnt in the last hour. She glanced up to the ceiling. She didn't know if she believed in God or in heaven; she'd never really formed a definitive answer. But she smiled up at the sky and offered a silent thank you to Pat. If not for meeting her, she wasn't sure she'd have been ready to listen to her mother. Not yet, anyway.

Now they had time. Time to heal and get to know each other.

Maybe even time to be a family.

CHAPTER 12

Kate parked her Mini on Vancouver Street for the second time that day and climbed out, Gareth at her heels as Vinny and Mel edged by, slowly looking for a second spot. They'd decided to bring Mel's car too, as four coppers and one potentially uncooperative witness-slash-prisoner in a Mini was just asking for trouble. She and Gareth waited well back from the view of the big bay window for Mel and Vinny, before leading them all to the door. There was a lot more noise coming from inside than there had been earlier. She checked her watch. Six fifteen in the evening.

She pushed the doorbell, and a few moments later, she was greeted by a scowling Tariq Ahmed.

"What do you want?" he sneered.

"Mr Ahmed, we have some questions we need you to answer." She stepped back a little to clear an exit from the building for him. "Would you come with us, please?"

He snorted at her. "My family has just sat down to dinner. I'm not going anywhere with you."

Family sat down to dinner? *Is it just me, or does that so not sound like a family in mourning?* "I'm very sorry to intrude, Mr Ahmed, but I'm afraid I must insist." She stepped closer, reading his body language. She knew what was coming.

"Go away." He gripped the door, clearly ready to slam it in her face. "Kaffir," he added and threw his shoulder into swinging the door closed.

Kate was ready and had her booted foot jammed against the plinth to stop the movement.

He growled in frustration and stepped forward to push her out of the way. As he cleared the doorway, Gareth and Vinny grabbed his arms, then tugged him past Kate and onto the garden path, twisting his arms behind him.

Children's faces appeared at the window, looking out at the scene, their shock and fear evident in the wide-eyed stares and fists stuck in their mouths.

Vinny spun Mr Ahmed around so he was facing Kate again.

She nodded towards the window. "Mr Ahmed, don't make your children watch you getting arrested. Please, calm down and come with us quietly to help us with our enquiries."

His lip curled contemptuously and his eyes narrowed. "I have nothing to say to you."

Kate sighed and nodded her head. "As you wish. Tariq Ahmed, you are under arrest on suspicion of conspiring with terrorists to commit murder. You do not have to say anything unless you wish to do so, but you may harm your defence if you do not mention, when questioned, something you later rely on in court. Anything you say can be used as evidence. Do you understand your rights as I have explained them to you?"

He threw his head back and worked his jaw. Kate could see it coming and dodged to the left, avoiding the mouthful of spit he hurled her way. The venom and hatred she could see in his eyes was more than enough to confirm his involvement to her. What kind of man could do that? Regardless of everyone else who died, his own daughter did too. Could he really have been involved in that? Surely no father would condemn his daughter to such a fate.

"Do you understand, Mr Ahmed?" She waited for him to nod his assent before turning and leading them out of the garden. Her Mini was parked closest, so Gareth and Vinny bundled him into the back, Gareth climbing in beside him while Vinny took the front passenger seat.

"Meet you back at the station," Mel said as she headed for her own vehicle.

"Right," Kate said to her back as she got into her car and pulled on her seatbelt, all the while wondering why Mel had even bothered coming along with them. Kate could have dealt with the situation just with Gareth and Vinny.

She shook her head, turned on the car, and pulled away from the kerb as an awkward silence filled the car.

It should have taken ten minutes to get back to the station, but the maze of closed roads around the town centre resulted in bumper-to-bumper traffic. So instead they sat, waiting. Waiting for the lights to turn green, then red, then green, and finally red again before they inched forward and through the junction. Then they waited as the car crawled towards the roundabout, all the while the silence growing thicker, heavier, darker until it was wrapped around them like a boa constrictor, crushing them. She could almost see it—the sinewy body wrapping around Ahmed's wiry frame and squeezing. His eyes bulged, and his breathing had become laboured under its weight. Silence could be as powerful a tool of interrogation as questioning sometimes.

By the time they arrived at the station and he'd been booked in, Clare and Timmons were waiting outside the interview room where Ahmed sat...waiting some more.

"Has he said anything?" Timmons asked.

"No, sir," Vinny said. "Spat at your main woman here, mind." Vinny clapped Kate on the shoulder. "She's got under his skin, just a bit, if you ask me."

"We didn't, but that's good to know, Vin," Clare said with a smirk to take the sting out of it.

Vinny just shrugged it off as Clare turned to look at Kate. "What do you think? You up to questioning him?"

Kate gave the question the proper consideration it needed. It would be tough going in there. No doubt about it. She was going to accuse him of planning the bombing that could have killed Gina, had seriously hurt Stella, and had cost the life of his own daughter and the lives of twenty-one innocent victims. Including Gregory Walsh. The proper consideration took less than half a second. "Without doubt."

Clare nodded. "Vinny, go in with her."

"Actually, ma'am, I think another female officer would be better," Kate said.

"Why?"

"I think it offends him. To be questioned by a woman. I think it will throw him off balance even more and increase our chances of getting an emotional outburst from him. And that's the only way he's going to give us anything."

Clare and Timmons exchanged looks.

"Good thinking," Timmons said and tapped her forehead with his knuckle. "I've got my eye on you, Brannon. You'll be after my job next."

Kate grinned. "Nah, I wouldn't want your office until it's been aired for a year or two at least." She chuckled as he threw back his head and laughed heartily. It sounded out of place, but at the same time it sounded right. When everything felt wrong, sometimes it was the tiny things that made the world slip back into shape.

"Okay, then, you and me," Clare said.

Kate shook her head again. "No, you have too high a rank. It shows him respect. It'll make him feel important to have someone so high up the chain in there. We need to make him feel insulted. I want a standard PC, someone who looks young, fresh-faced. Maybe even like they're on their first job."

"Belt and braces." Timmons stuck his hands in his pockets and nodded. "Brown fits that description pretty well. Looks young enough and only a PC, as requested."

Kate had to agree, and while she didn't like the idea of working with her closely, needs must. "She does."

Timmons seemed to watch her carefully before he spoke, "Right. Brown?"

"Here," Mel said as she slipped into the corridor, slightly out of breath.

"You and Brannon, interview room one." He pointed a finger at her. "Follow Brannon's lead, and do not screw this up."

Mel frowned but said, "Yes, sir."

Timmons pushed open the door to the video suite, holding it open for Clare. He looked at Kate. "Earpiece in for this one."

Kate nodded, slid into the video suite, grabbed one of the earpieces that would allow her to receive comments and direction from them, and picked up a second for Mel. "Do you have a photo pack ready?"

Timmons shook his head. "What do you want in it?"

Kate swallowed and told him what she needed, then watched his jaw clench.

"Jackson, Collier, get it sorted. Brown, you wait outside until they've got it all, then take the file into Brannon." Each of them nodded, and Gareth and Vinny set off to gather what she'd asked for.

"Is his brief here yet?" Kate asked. As he'd been arrested, they had to wait for his solicitor to arrive before they began questioning him.

Timmons nodded. "Five minutes ago."

"Then I'll go and start the tape while I wait for Mel."

Timmons grinned and tapped her forehead again. "You do that." He winked at her and let the door close behind her.

"Looks like you've fallen on your feet." Mel's voice had the hard edge of bitterness to it. "Do you have to blow him every day or just once a week to get him to treat you like that?"

"Excuse me?" Kate whirled around, glad she hadn't opened the door to the interview room yet.

"You heard me."

"I did. And at the risk of repeating myself, excuse me?"

Mel stared at her belligerently. Daring her to deny the accusation.

Well, Kate had no problem with that. "DI Timmons is the best DI I've ever worked with. Yeah, he's a bit politically incorrect. Yeah, he's a bit old school. But he's a copper who respects hard work and results. You bring him those, and he doesn't care who's doing the bringing."

"Bullshit."

"Believe what you like, Mel. But Timmons is a good bloke who respects his team and knows how to get the best out of us." She looked Mel up and down. "We don't have to perform sexual favours for him to try and improve our careers." She smiled sweetly. "How's that going for you, by the way?"

Mel's face darkened further. "Fuck off."

"No thanks. Like you said, I've landed on my feet here. Moving away from Norwich, away from you, was the best thing I've ever done."

"You bitch."

Kate shook her head sadly. "Maybe. But maybe it's something you should think about a bit. What do you want, Mel? I mean, you've fucked everything up at Norwich. Clare's moving up further and further, and you're still a PC. You've been in three years longer than I have, you passed your sergeant's exam two years before I did, but you're still on the bottom rung. Not even moved over to CID. You're stagnating there, and it's making you bitter and jealous. And you know what? That's fine by me. I don't have to deal with you beyond this task force. But maybe it should bother you." She grabbed hold of the door handle. "Now, do not fuck up this interview, or you will regret it."

"What will you do? Tell all your little friends that I hurt your feelings?"

Kate shook her head. "Timmons will bury your career. You'd be lucky if you get to be a PCSO by the time he'd be finished with you, and any hopes you have of advancement...forget it."

"Bullshit."

Kate shrugged. "Try it and see." She pushed open the door and closed it shut quietly behind her. She leant back against it, giving herself a moment to collect her thoughts. How had she ever been blinded by those blue eyes and that dimple? How could she have been so stupid not to see it before? All Mel cared about was herself, and it had never been clearer to Kate how close she'd come to ruining her own life with her ex. As painful as it had been, Mel sleeping with Clare had been the biggest favour either of them had ever done for Kate. It had taken off the blinkers and let her escape a relationship and a job that was getting her nowhere.

Now she had everything she had dreamed of: a job she truly loved—well, on most days—colleagues who cared for and respected her, and a boss who respected her for the job she did and the skill she'd shown. Who clearly cared for her well-being too. And that was before she even started to think about Gina, and Sammy, and Merlin. When she'd left

Norwich, her life had been empty. Now she was rich with love and fulfilment, and she was fucking proud of everything she'd achieved in just a few short months. *Bring on the next fucking year.*

She straightened up and crossed the room, taking a seat at the table, across from Ahmed and his solicitor. Pressing the button on the tape recorder, she waited for the loud beep to end before she spoke.

"It's Sunday, the thirteenth of December, the time is seven twenty-four p.m. I am Detective Sergeant Kate Brannon. Gentlemen, please identify yourselves for the tape."

"Mr Chris Oxford, solicitor," said the suited man next to Ahmed.

Ahmed stared at her belligerently.

"Mr Ahmed?"

He said nothing.

"Very well. For the record, also in the room is Mr Tariq Ahmed. We are still awaiting the arrival of a colleague, so we shall just wait a few moments, if that's okay with you, gentlemen?" Kate didn't require an answer. Not that she expected one anyway. Ahmed wasn't going to talk to her. Not yet.

It was ten minutes before Mel arrived, slid the file in front of Kate, and sat in the chair beside her.

Ahmed's sneer grew.

"For the tape, Police Constable Melissa Brown has entered the room at seven thirty-four p.m., and we are now ready to begin this interview. Mr Ahmed, at your home this evening, you were arrested on suspicion of conspiring with terrorists to commit murder. You were read your rights. You are still under caution at this time. Do you understand?"

He said nothing.

"Mr Ahmed, you must answer the question."

Nothing.

Kate looked at his solicitor. "Perhaps you should advise your client to answer the question so we can move on."

Oxford nodded and leant over to whisper in Ahmed's ear.

"No comment," Ahmed said.

It was a start. "Thank you. For the tape, that was Mr Ahmed's voice. This morning, my colleagues and I informed you of the death of your daughter in the bombing incident at the Ann Summers shop in King's Lynn town centre yesterday morning. Is that correct?"

"No comment."

"As part of our duties, we carried out a search of your property and found a number of items of interest to us." She slipped the picture of the ball bearing from the file and placed it on the table. "This is a picture of an item entered into evidence, reference AHVS1802. Do you recognise this item, Mr Ahmed?"

"No comment."

"It was found in your daughter's bedroom."

"No comment," he repeated with a smirk twisting his lips.

"On top of her wardrobe."

"No comment." He crossed his arms over his chest.

"Tests show that it has traces of explosives on it consistent with those used in yesterday's attack. Did you know your daughter was hiding a suicide vest in your house, Mr Ahmed?"

"No comment."

"Were you aware she had explosives in there while your other children slept in the same house?"

"No comment."

"Your son—your eleven-year-old son—sleeps in the room next to Nadia's, doesn't he?"

He frowned. "No comment."

"Lucky, lucky, lucky boy." Kate slipped the picture from the file that haunted her. She swallowed down the bile and emotion that rose again and would render her unable to do the job she needed to do as she turned the page and set it down in front of Tariq Ahmed. "This little boy wasn't quite so lucky."

Ahmed's jaw and throat worked as he swallowed back whatever words he wanted to spew at her. He sat back on his chair, pulling away from the image of Gregory's pushchair as much as he could. Oxford blanched, his colour draining at the sight, and he scribbled notes across his pad, clearly trying to distract himself from the image.

Kate knew it would never work. That picture would stay with him for the rest of his life.

"I'm showing Mr Ahmed KLHS80936, a picture of one of the victims of the bomb blast. Gregory Walsh was two years old, Mr Ahmed. His mother had been in the card shop next door, to buy Christmas cards for her family, when your daughter detonated the explosives that had been in your house. An innocent baby."

"My daughter was an innocent victim too. Not the monster who did this. I do not deserve this abuse. I have done nothing."

Kate placed a third picture on the table, the same one she'd shown Mrs Ahmed earlier. "KLHS003657, a picture from CCTV footage before the bomb went off. Is this your daughter, Mr Ahmed?"

"Yes. See? She was just a victim of this hideous crime too."

Kate set another picture down, the expanded view of the first picture showing Nadia Ahmed with her burqa held open to expose the modified suicide vest—the explosives, wires, and blocks of shrapnel taped to it all clearly visible. "KLHS098736, a picture showing the device and the individual wearing it. Is this your daughter, Mr Ahmed?"

"No comment."

She tapped the image. "Is this or is this not the same girl you just identified as your daughter in image KLHS003657?"

"No comment."

"Is it?" She let her voice rise, she wanted him to think she was getting frustrated with him and too emotional to think clearly. She wanted him to think he had the upper hand.

The growing smirk on his face let her know she was on the right track. "No comment."

She pulled another picture from the folder and placed it on the table. Then she waited until his gaze dropped from hers and fell to the page. He scraped the chair backwards and jumped to his feet, pointing at the picture and hurling a string of fast-paced Arabic at her until he landed against the room's back wall.

"KLHS078956, a picture of human remains from the blast site. Is this your daughter, Mr Ahmed?"

The picture was truly horrific, and Kate was eternally grateful she hadn't eaten anything all day. She knew she wouldn't have been able to keep it down if she had. All that remained of Nadia Ahmed was captured in that image: Her head, her left shoulder, and half of her arm had been severed from the rest of her body and blown clear. The rest of her body had been torn apart by the shrapnel strapped to her. The force of the explosion had made her own bone fragments into weapons dug out of bodies of the dead and injured alike.

"Please, Detective, you're upsetting my client." Oxford tried to cover the picture with his pad, but Kate pushed it away. No way was this bastard getting off that lightly.

"I'm sorry about that. If he will answer the question, we can move on."

Oxford stood up, rested his hand on Ahmed's shoulder, and spoke quietly to him.

She had no idea what he said to the man, and, frankly, she really didn't care. She wanted him to tell them what he knew, that was all. They could all have nightmares for the rest of their miserable fucking lives for all she cared. She knew she would. "Is this your daughter, Mr Ahmed?"

Oxford guided him back to his seat, hand still on his shoulder. "Please answer the detective's question and then she can remove that picture, Tariq."

"Yes." Ahmed's voice was a mere croak as he spoke. "Now get that out of my sight."

Kate picked up the picture so he was no longer faced with it, but she didn't put it away. She tapped the ball bearing picture again. "Do you know what this is, Mr Ahmed?"

He nodded.

"For the tape, please."

"Yes."

Kate waited.

"It's a ball bearing."

"And do you know why it was in your daughter's bedroom?"

"No comment."

Bollocks. "Did you know she was hiding this vest in there?" She pointed to the picture showing Nadia in the vest.

"No comment."

Okay, Plan B. "Very well, Mr Ahmed." She turned to Mel, but watched Ahmed out of the corner of her eye. "Have the other officers finished bringing in the rest of Mr Ahmed's family?"

Mel's eyes widened a little, but thankfully she played along. "I don't know, Sergeant. Would you like me to go and find out?"

Kate nodded. "Yes, if they're here, we'll go and talk to them. I'm sure Mrs Ahmed will have more to say when she sees this picture of her daughter." She laid the page in her hand back on the table as Mel stood and started for the door.

"No! Don't. My wife is a proper woman, not like you. She will—she cannot... She must not see this."

"Then save her from it," Kate said, ignoring the insult. "Tell me what you know about your daughter's plan to murder all these people."

"My daughter was no murderer. She was a soldier of Allah." He picked up the photo and held it to his lips. "She will live in heaven forever for her sacrifice."

"Her crime." Kate pushed the picture of Gregory to the front again.

"You and your pious know nothing. Judgements mean nothing in the face of our beliefs, our God. The flesh is weak, but faith, honour, sacrifice, they are eternal, and my sacrifice will be honoured amongst my people."

"Your sacrifice? It was your daughter who gave up her life. Hers. Not yours."

"My daughter, mine to command, mine to grant life, mine to grant death. I have given her the greatest gift she could have ever hoped for. I have granted her eternity at the Prophet's side. The greatest of gifts."

"Yours to command?" The words didn't make sense; at least Kate didn't want them to make sense. Because if they did, then it was even worse than she'd feared. Not only did Tariq Ahmed know his daughter was involved, he had condemned her to die with her victims. "You commanded her to do this?"

His lips twisted into a smile that approximated paternal pride, but how could that be? How could anyone be proud of what Nadia had done? Proud that he'd sent her to do that? How? Kate didn't think she could be any more sickened in this case than she had been when she'd seen that overturned pushchair. God, had she ever been wrong. She wanted to hold her hand to her mouth to make sure the vomit didn't escape, but she knew she couldn't show that kind of weakness in front of this man. So she sat still. She schooled her features into neutrality and prayed she could maintain her professionalism for as long as this interview lasted.

Oxford put his hand out as though he could halt the flow of words now that they'd begun. "I must advise my client—"

"I trusted her with the greatest gift a father can give his child." Ahmed ignored him. His gaze fixed on Kate as he bent over the desk, weight borne on his hands. He whispered, "Immortality."

"Immortality?" Kate's voice was shaky, and she only hoped it sounded more like anger than the revulsion she really felt. "She's dead. There is no immortality."

"Her name as a martyr will live on forever."

"Her name as a murderer will live on only as long as the media interest does."

He barked out a harsh laugh and flopped back into his chair again. "You know nothing of my culture, my religion."

"Then teach me."

"I would not waste my time."

Kate's hands shook in her lap, and she was glad she didn't have to try and stop them to put evidence before him. She had only one more card to play to get him to talk. But she had this bastard. All she needed now was to tie it up in a bloody bow and get the fuck away from him. "You commanded your daughter to don a suicide vest, yes or no?"

"It was Allah's will."

"Yes or no?"

"Yes."

She licked her lips and forced the next sentence into life. "You commanded your daughter, Nadia Ahmed, to go to a busy public area and detonate that device. Yes or no?"

"Yes."

"Did you know she was hiding the device in your house?"

"Yes."

"Did you build it?"

"No."

"Do you know who did build it?"

"No comment."

"Was it built by Saba Ayeshydi?"

"No comment."

"Was the bomb built by Ayeshydi's husband?"

"No comment."

"Did you target that shop specifically because it was the scene of your greatest failure?"

He said nothing...but a frown carved itself onto his face.

Aha. "It was where you used to have a clothes shop, wasn't it?"

"No comment." The creases across his forehead deepened, and his eyes narrowed to slits.

"Where you were forced into bankruptcy because you were a failure as a businessman, right?"

He ground his teeth and said nothing.

Bingo!

"I don't think this has anything to do with Allah. Not for you. You're too pathetic and bitter for that. You picked that shop because you couldn't face knowing it was there, thriving where you failed. You almost lost everything, didn't you, Tariq?"

He growled but held his tongue.

"You lost the business, your stock, the building. You almost lost your house too. Didn't you?" She shook her head slowly. "And now it was there, selling condoms, chocolate penises, and vibrators. How shameful. That was once your pride and joy. Then it was everything you hated, wasn't it, Tariq? That's why it had to go. Nothing to do with God or Allah or jihad. Just plain, old fashioned male ego. And you didn't even have the guts to do the deed yourself. Sent a child in to do your dirty work for you. Your own daughter. You spineless piece of shit."

He slapped his hands on the table. "How dare you? I gave everything I had to being a good member of society when I came here. Everything. I worked fourteen hours a day, went to mosque, prayed. But you, all of you, you're all racist. You all decided that my shop wasn't good enough for you. You stopped buying your clothes from me. You passed my shop without even looking inside, and I lost it all. You took it from me. Every one of you. You took my hard work and my effort and you threw it in my face." He dropped the page back on the table. "I am a proud man. A good man. I did not deserve the contempt you all showed me. So, yes, I sent my daughter to purify the site of the evil that contaminated it. It was my service to God, my sacrifice for the good of us all, and now my honour is restored."

Honour? Honour? Where was the honour in death? Where was the honour in murder? How could a person, any sane or reasonable person, condemn their own flesh and blood to death for the sake of a concept as fleeting and misconstrued as honour? There was nothing noble or worthy of admiration in this. There was nothing to respect in this act. Honour spoke of deeds of moral character, distinction, acts to be venerated. Kate saw nothing here worthy of reverence. Not by anyone. If this was honour, she'd take shame any day of the week. If this was what it took to maintain a man's dignity and pride, she'd take ignominy, humiliation, and scorn for the rest of her life.

Seeming to take her disgusted silence as her listening to his insane ramblings, he leant back in his chair and continued, "Nadia was glad to do this. She knew her duty to God, to her people, to me. She was glad to offer her life to Allah as a soldier."

Kate swallowed and let her ire settle so she could speak without screaming. "Who built the bomb?"

He said nothing.

She knew she wasn't going to get anything more out of him. Not tonight. She was surprised they'd gotten as much as they had, if she was honest. She was willing to bet that Ayeshydi's husband was the bomb maker. But there was one more question she had to ask. "Are there any more bombs out there?"

She'd been right. He didn't answer. But the taunting smile on his lips made her blood run cold.

Fuck.

Kate closed the door softly behind her before she bolted for the bathroom. Having had nothing to eat all day, the acid burned her throat as she hung her head over the toilet and tried to keep her hair out of the line of fire. She heard the door open and close, and then a hand rubbed her back. She half turned her head to see Clare stood to the left and slightly behind her.

"Sorry, ma'am," Kate said softly as another cramp gripped her stomach and she dry heaved over the bowl again.

"Don't be. I'm surprised I'm not hanging over the bowl next door." She tapped the divide between the cubicles, and Kate offered her a wan smile.

"Thanks."

"You did well in there. Got a lot more than I expected out of him."

"So much for religious zeal. It was nothing more than a way for him to get a personal revenge on all the wrongs *we've* done him."

Clare nodded. "Yup. The very definition of those in power using religion to their own ends. Everything that's wrong with every religion, all boiled down to one crazy sound bite."

"You're more cynical than you used to be." Kate stood up and backed out of the stall. She ran the tap in the sink and held her hand under it.

"Nah, I just don't need to hide it now I'm Chief Super."

Kate sniggered and swilled her mouth out.

Clare offered her a pack of mints. "Here, I've been passing these out all day."

"Cheers." Kate took one and popped it in her mouth. "So, what's next, Boss?"

Clare shrugged a little and leant back against the wall. "Until we find the husband or get any of that translated stuff back, nothing.

We've already searched every known address for each girl, and we're looking everywhere for Ishman Ayeshydi. Right now, I suggest we get some sleep and get ready for another long day tomorrow."

Kate agreed, but it didn't sit well with her. Ahmed hadn't admitted it, but the look on his face was enough to convince Kate that there were more bombs out there, waiting to be strapped to someone else's son or daughter and walked into a crowd. Or a church. Or a school. Or a mosque. How the fuck do you keep people safe when even those you're trying to protect could be the very ones trying to kill you? Or was that just another weapon in the arsenal of terror? The insipid little smile that makes you think there are more out there when really there aren't? Just to keep you guessing, just to keep you awake, and afraid. To keep you on edge. To make you paranoid about every little thing. *Well, it was fucking working.*

"It's been an absolute pleasure to see you work today, Kate. The one true bright spot in all this shit." Clare's voice sparkled with the hint of pride and the raw edge of sadness. "I know you've got no reason to believe me, but I am truly sorry for everything that happened. You deserved better from both of us, and you sure as shit deserved better than both of us."

She looked across the small room, and she could see genuine pain in Clare's eyes. "I do believe you."

Clare smiled. "You always were a good friend, Kate—"

Kate held up her hand to stop her. "I believe you're sorry, and you're right, I did deserve better... I do. But that doesn't mean I can forgive you for what you did. I looked up to you. I trusted you. Fuck, you were like a sister to me." She shook her head. "Mel cheating on me... Well, if I'm totally honest, I could see that coming. But you?" She looked away from Clare's gaze. "I never expected that from you."

"I'm sorry."

"I know." She pulled open the door. "Night, ma'am."

CHAPTER 13

Kate checked her watch as she turned off the engine and climbed out of her car. One thirty in the morning and she needed to be back at the station by seven. They were only two days into the investigation, and she was already exhausted. Gotta love a major incident on the run-up to Christmas. Just one more day and she would have had some time off, but God alone knew if she'd get it now. As for Christmas... well that was anyone's guess. She'd been looking forward to her time off over the Christmas period, the first one she'd not worked since joining the police force, and she was looking forward to spending every moment of it she could with Gina and Sammy. Maybe it would still happen. If they could get their hands on Ayeshydi. And find out if he was the bomb maker. And find out if there were any more bombs waiting to be detonated. Then...maybe. The paperwork would still be there if she had a day off.

She slid her key into the back door and let herself in.

"Hey." Gina's sleepy voice met her from the sofa, the twinkling lights of the Christmas tree that hadn't been there that morning illuminating the room like the tiny twinkling stars they were meant to represent.

"Jesus Christ." Kate put her hand to her chest, gasping for breath. "You scared the crap out of me."

"Sorry," she said quietly with a small shrug.

"It's okay. I knew you were here. I just didn't expect you to be here, here." She pointed to the sofa.

"Hi, Kate," another voice said from the smaller sofa.

Kate stared at Gina, then at Alison, then back to Gina. "Hey, Alison." She mouthed to Gina, *What's going on?*

Gina smiled and shook her head.

Kate hoped this meant something along the lines of "I'll tell you in a few minutes" and not "none of your bloody business". But she wasn't entirely sure.

"I should get going." Alison said. "Thank you for, well, for everything, Gina."

"You can't go," Gina said.

"I can't?"

"She can't?"

Kate and Alison had spoken at the same time.

Gina shook her head. "We've gone through two bottles of wine." She pointed to the empties on the coffee table. "You'll never get a taxi at this time of night. It's hard enough to get one in the daytime, never mind after midnight. They're all around the towns, not out in the sticks."

Kate rattled her keys. "I can give you a lift."

"Then she's got a problem getting back for her car in the morning," Gina said. "And no doubt you've got an early start, right?"

Kate nodded. "I need to leave here by six thirty."

"Ouch." Alison grimaced. "I don't mind the sofa." She smiled. "It was comfy enough before you got home."

Kate chuckled. She didn't really want to head back out to take Alison home, she just wanted to crawl into her bed and try to get rid of the thoughts of dead bodies, bastard fathers, and bombs careening around her mind.

But even those awful thoughts couldn't shift her mind away from the fact that Gina had been there. She had been in that shop when Nadia Ahmed and Saba Ayeshydi had pushed those buttons. She'd been at the heart of it when it all started. Stella was still in the hospital because they had both been in the shop. And that was something Kate couldn't get out of her head. She could have lost Gina before they even really got started.

She rubbed her eyes with her thumb and forefinger, and when she opened them again Gina was standing next to her.

"Hey, you okay?" Her blue eyes swam with concern, and she wrapped her hand around Kate's arm. "You look exhausted."

Kate smiled ruefully. "I am."

"Come on, then. Let's get you upstairs. You can show me where the spare bedding is for Mum."

Kate let Gina tug her towards the stairs. "Night, Alison."

"Night, Kate. Sorry for crashing."

Kate waved her hand. "No worries. Glad to see you two together." With a smile on her face, she followed Gina up the stairs. She tugged her into the third bedroom, empty but for the huge wardrobe, some drawers, and a bookcase jammed full of books. The room was too small to make a decent-sized bedroom, so Kate had never thought to set it up as one. She'd always intended for it to be an office of sorts. How many spare rooms did a single woman with no real friends and no visiting family need, after all? "There's an extra duvet in there." She pointed to the wardrobe. "And a couple of pillows, I think."

"Thanks." Gina pulled it open and quickly removed what Alison needed for her night on the sofa. "I'll just run these down to her, and then I'll be back." She nodded towards Kate's bedroom. "Can I come in when I come back up?"

Kate looked at her, startled, confused, shocked...turned on. *Was she...? Did she...? But I'm knackered.*

"I wanted to talk to you for a few minutes. Is that okay?"

Kate let out a relieved breath. "Of course." She chuckled. "I'll leave the door open."

Gina quickly kissed her cheek and disappeared down the stairs.

Kate stripped and changed into the long T-shirt and leggings she wore to bed and was brushing her teeth when Gina reappeared.

"She's asleep already."

Kate rinsed her mouth and put the brush back in the cup. Drying her hands on a towel, she said, "That was a surprise."

"You can say that again." Gina sat on the edge of Kate's bed. "We've had a long talk."

"Over wine?"

Gina nodded. "It made it a bit easier, I think. Both to say and to hear."

"And are you okay?" Kate sat next to her and wrapped an arm around her shoulders, pulling her gently against her body.

Gina snuggled into her side. "I think so. It's a lot to process. Did you know that my mum had another child before me?"

Kate shook her head. "You have a sibling?"

"No. He died."

Kate winced and kissed the top of Gina's head. "I'm so sorry."

Gina waved the comment away. Clearly she didn't want to talk about that right now. "I sent a letter to George Boyne."

"Wow. That was quick."

"I couldn't get it out of my mind, and I just had to do it. I feel better now that I've done what I can. It's up to him now."

"It gave you some peace?"

Gina nodded and lifted her head to look into Kate's eyes. "It really did. I feel like I've given Pat what I can without becoming a creepy stalker."

Kate nodded. "Good. And while we're on the subject of creepy stalkers, I got a call from Styall Prison today."

"Ally?"

Kate shook her head. "I'm sorry, sweetheart. They tossed her cell, and there's no sign of any contraband like a phone or anything like that. They've been monitoring her calls since you received the flowers, and they checked back the records. It doesn't look like she sent those roses."

"But—"

"We knew it was a long shot. I mean, fifty yellow roses, isn't really Ally's style, is it?"

Gina sighed. "I suppose not."

"She's more your fifty cockles kind of girl."

Gina laughed. "True. But that doesn't help us figure out who sent me fifty yellow roses."

"No, it doesn't. Do you still have the card that came with them? Maybe I can get in touch with the florist and see if they have a record of who sent them."

"I'm pretty sure it's still at home. I'll pick it up when I go to work tomorrow."

"Good. Has anything else arrived? I'd be thinking that if this person is serious, then something would turn up for Christmas."

"There wasn't anything there when we went to pack."

"Okay. Listen, do you want me to pop round instead? I know you hate going home with everything, and I could swing by from time to time, you know, to see if something turns up?" Kate didn't want to say explicitly that this was another reason she wanted Gina and Sammy to stay with her over the holidays. But it was. One of many reasons, but it was one that kept playing on Kate's mind. Having them both here, safe, would give her some more time to figure out who this mystery flower sender was and if it was a serious threat or just a harmless admirer. Gina had had more than enough to deal with from Ally and her attack, and now King's Lynn... She didn't need anything else to top it off.

"Thank you, that's very sweet, but you don't have to do that. You've got far too much on your plate with work already, and it's out of your way. I'm practically there when I'm at work anyway."

Kate yawned. "Sorry," she said.

"Don't be." Gina snuggled in tighter, and Kate wished they could just pull the duvet over them both and let slumber take them.

"You sure? I really don't mind."

Gina shook her head against Kate's shoulder. "No, honestly, I can handle it." She turned her head and kissed Kate's cheek. "Thank you. You make me feel very special."

Kate could feel her cheeks burning, and she hugged Gina tighter to her. She wanted to tell her she was special, very special, and turn to capture Gina's sweet lips with her own. But she knew she was too tired to follow through on those thoughts, and the desire just to hold Gina was equally strong. Just to hold her and feel the day melt away. "Tree looks good, by the way. Definitely isn't Grinchy in here anymore."

Gina laughed again. "No, it definitely isn't. Sammy had to make sure that Father Christmas would know to leave her presents here instead of taking them to our house. Sorry."

"Don't be. It looks great."

"It looks like the leftovers from a bad year at Blackpool's illuminations."

"Well, I wouldn't go that far." Kate chuckled. "But if you insist." That earned her an elbow to her ribs. "As much as I'm enjoying this, I'm falling asleep. I've got an early start in the morning."

Gina squeezed back. "I know. Sorry." She lifted her face to Kate's and pressed her lips gently to hers. Her fingers curled into Kate's hair, tugging her closer until Kate's lips parted and welcomed her tongue.

Kate moaned around the caress and tightened her grip on Gina's waist. Torn between pulling back and continuing, she couldn't make up her mind until Gina's fingers slid under the hem of her T-shirt. She gave herself over to Gina's gentle exploration. She quickly found herself on her back with Gina's pyjama-clad body on top of her as she slid her legs apart to accommodate her.

She tried to stifle the yawn that broke their gentle kiss, but couldn't.

Gina chuckled as her jaw cracked loudly.

"I'm sorry, Gina—"

Gina touched her fingertip to Kate's lips. "It's okay. I just wanted to say goodnight properly." She pushed her finger between Kate's lips and drew in a sharp breath when Kate took it between her teeth.

Moving quickly, Gina replaced her finger with her mouth and set about Kate's, with a passion that made Kate's head swim. Kate moaned, and finally Gina wrenched herself away, pushing up and off the bed as she did so.

"You're rather dangerous, Detective Sergeant Brannon."

"Me?" She pointed to her chest as Gina's eyes roamed the length of her prone body. She knew the old threadbare T-shirt and figure-hugging leggings left little to the imagination.

Gina nodded and took a deep breath. "Next time," she said with a glint in her eye and a wink.

Then she was gone, and Kate was left uncomfortably turned on and wondering exactly what would happen next time. And just how quickly it would come around.

CHAPTER 14

Kate had arrived early enough to get a coffee, a croissant, and a seat near the front of the room. She gobbled the sweet, chocolate-filled pastry and brushed crumbling flakes off her chest as Vinny Jackson walked in, Mel Brown at his side.

Vinny grinned at her and held his fisted hand out to her.

Kate stared at him, eyebrow hitched. "We're not American, *dude*. We don't fist-bump."

She smirked at him as he gave her a half shrug, picked up her empty hand, and bumped his fist to hers anyway.

"We do when you rock."

Kate threw him a questioning look.

"That interview last night. Ahmed." He clapped her on the shoulder and dropped into the seat next to her.

Mel sat on the other side of him, for which Kate was eternally grateful. After last night's confrontation before the interview, she didn't feel like being any closer to Mel than she had to be...and right now, even that was too close.

"Classic. They're going to be using that as a training case study before you know it."

"Piss off."

"I'm serious." He leant in closer to her and lowered his voice. "Green was talking with that dude from gold command after she sent you home last night. The Chief Constable. What's his name?"

"Frank Carter."

"Yeah, that's him."

"He was here last night?"

"Yeah, saw about half the interview in the video suite. Fuckin' creamin' his Y-fronts."

"Ew." Kate smacked his shoulder and held her coffee cup away from her as the contents threatened to spill onto her hand. "Shit. Don't make me spill my coffee. I need this."

"Don't abuse me, then,"

"Then don't go overboard with the brain farts, Vinny. I don't need that image in my head at stupid-o-fucking-clock in the morning." She sipped her drink. "I've already got enough in here to give me nightmares."

Vinny chuckled and glanced to the front of the room. "Yeah, I suppose that isn't the prettiest of pictures." He leant in closer as the room began to fill up, and someone tapped Mel to get her attention. "Seriously though...you okay?" He slid his eyes towards Mel. "I heard you had words."

Kate rolled her eyes. "She tell you that?"

Vinny shook his head. "Nah, I heard, literally. I was bringing in some of those images for your photo bombs. Sorry."

Kate shook her head and shrugged. "Is what it is."

"If it means anything to you, I agree with everything you said. She needs to make a fresh start somewhere. She's shit on her biscuit at Norwich. The PCs and sergeants don't trust her, and the higher ranks don't rate her. They know she's trying to shag her way up." He had the grace to grimace. "Sorry."

"It's not a secret."

"No, but that doesn't make it any better."

"No, but there are more important things to worry about right now."

"Fair point. Speaking of which," he whispered and pointed to the office door as Clare, Timmons, and four other men stepped out of the room.

"Ah, bollocks," Kate muttered. "Bigwigs." She looked around for Gareth, curious as to where her young shadow was. It was unusual for him to be late.

Vinny crossed his arms over his chest and slouched down in his chair. Kate drained the last of her cup and managed to toss it in the wastepaper bin in the corner without getting out of her seat. She'd have been impressed with herself if she'd thrown it. But she didn't.

She passed it to the young guy on her left and got him to do it for her. Delegation—comes with the promotion.

"All right, folks. Glad to see you all looking bright-eyed and bushy-tailed this fine December morning," A groan stuttered around the room at Clare's greeting. "Good news first, chaps and chapesses. The three people who were still on the critical list last night have been declared stable. The head of the ICU called a few minutes ago. They've still a long way to go, but the doctor says they're out of imminent danger now."

A round of applause filled the room. The relief was palpable, and Kate hadn't realised just how much the idea of further deaths had been playing on her mind.

Clare held up her hands to settle them down. "I know, I know. It's great news. On the other good news front, Len Wild over in the CSI office has informed us that all missing persons have now been accounted for, and the crime scene has been cleared of remains. No more nasty surprises, folks."

A quieter round of applause followed this announcement.

"We've also arrested and, as of twenty minutes ago, charged Tariq Ahmed with conspiracy to commit a terrorist act and conspiracy to commit twenty-one counts of first degree murder. The CPS is working on what other charges they can throw at the bastard while they're at it."

Kate hoped the Crown Prosecution Service managed to drum up a number of other charges, because those just weren't enough. Not even close.

"Now for the bad news. For those of you who haven't met my esteemed colleagues, I'd like to introduce you to some of the folks that the powers that be in gold command think can help us with this major incident—"

"You mean you're not God on high, ma'am?" a voice from the back of the room shouted.

"Only to you, soon-to-be-demoted PC Drake," Clare shot back without hesitation, and snickers flittered amongst the crowd.

"As I was saying, from MI5, we've got Lester Porter."

A tall fair-haired, clean-shaven, suited, middle-aged bloke stood up and inclined his head. Totally Mr Average. He would not have stood out in any crowd anywhere. Perfect spook. "Glad to be here."

Yeah, right.

"Zain Mallam, also MI5." Clare gestured to an Asian man who could have been anywhere from thirty to forty years of age.

He had a full, neatly trimmed beard, slicked-back hair, and an arrogance to his posture that immediately put Kate on edge. But when he spoke, his voice was quiet, calm. "Happy to help."

Clare then pointed to a stocky guy in a black tactical uniform. "The head of CTU from the MET, Commander Jack Dalton." Dalton touched his right hand to his forehead and tipped them a quick salute. "And Superintendent Marco Palmer, head of RCTU for the east of England." He copied Dalton's saluted greeting and leant back against the wall. "Mr Mallam, I'll let you brief the troops on our Mr Ayeshydi."

"Ma'am," Mallam said and stepped forward, nodding to the crowd. "Ishman Ayeshydi. Twenty-eight years old, and of Syrian descent. Born in Leicester, and by all accounts lived there almost all his life. Records indicate that Ayeshydi spent time in Libya at a training camp with the Libyan Islamic Fighting Group in 2011 and returned to the UK in 2014. We know that he had extensive weapons training while he was in Libya, but we also suspect that he spent time in other Arab countries, getting further training and cementing ties with other Islamic terror groups."

"Which ones?" Vinny asked.

"I'm not at liberty to say."

Vinny scoffed and whispered under his breath, "That MI5 code for 'we don't fucking know', right?"

Kate sniggered.

Mallam cleared his throat, took a sip of water from a bottle on the table behind him, and then carried on. "Passport control shows Ayeshydi leaving the UK last year, bound for Turkey. We all know that Turkey is the first stop to crossing into Syria to join with IS. We have intelligence that puts Ayeshydi in the video footage of two beheadings in Raqqa. He's wearing a scarf over his face, but our informant has confirmed it's him."

Porter passed pages out randomly around the room. Each officer looked from one image to the other before nodding and passing it down the line.

"We suspect he received further weapons training, including explosives training, while he was out there. It only makes sense. What we don't know is why three months ago he left Raqqa, crossing back into Turkey, and got on a flight home with his new wife Saba Ayeshydi in tow."

"Obviously, it was to bomb the shit out of us," a guy's voice called from the back of the room as the pictures reached Kate's hands.

The first was a picture taken off a driving licence. She could see the watermark across the face as she stared at the belligerent eyes glaring up at her. That look didn't prepare her for the one in the next image. Covered so that only the eyes showed, the figure was waving a sword over his shoulder like he was ready to drop it down on the neck of the hooded figure knelt at his feet. It was pretty much unrecognizable. If Kate hadn't been told they were the same man, she was certain she wouldn't have picked them out as such. She almost thought the eyes of the man in the beheading photo looked more like Mallam than the guy in the DVLA picture. The same cast to the thick eyebrows, the same set to the belligerent stare, the same arrogance radiated off the page. *Must be the angle, or something?*

"Among other things," Mallam conceded.

"What other things?" Kate asked as she passed the picture on to Vinny.

"If his aim was to set off one bomb in a shopping area in the run-up to Christmas...why didn't he strap the bomb to himself and claim the glory of his beliefs?"

"Cos he's a gutless bastard," Vinny said.

"Maybe," Mallam again conceded.

Bollocks.

"Stop pussyfooting about, Mallam, and spit it out," Clare interrupted. "We haven't got all day, you know?"

"Ma'am." He took another drink of his water. "We have intelligence that Ayeshydi is the bomb maker."

"Yes, I think I can safely say that we've all surmised that, Mr Mallam. What else?" Clare demanded. "Corroboration to share with us?"

"Nothing at this time."

"Are you fucking kidding me?" Clare shouted.

"Ma'am, I'm afraid the information is on a need-to-know basis."

"Are you saying I don't have clearance to know what you're talking about?" Clare's face was red, and her eyes bulged.

"No, ma'am. Not at this time. We will, of course, let you know should the situation change."

A collective gasp echoed around the room. To her right, Vinny whistled, and Kate rubbed her hand over her eyes. *Fuck.*

So much for sharing fucking intelligence.

The silence in the room stagnated as Clare and Timmons both glared at Mallam.

Kate could feel the heat from those stares like it was burning her skin. If looks could kill, Mallam would be cinders.

Vinny cleared his throat and asked, "Any idea where Ayeshydi might be?"

Mallam shook his head, his gaze not breaking Clare's.

"Was he under surveillance?" Tom asked.

"No." He finally looked away from Clare and out at the sea of angry faces all glaring at him as hatefully as Clare and Timmons were.

"Was he at least on the fucking watch list?" Jimmy demanded.

"Yes. Along with about…a thousand more people. We simply don't have the manpower to watch them all. We have to prioritise based on the intelligence we have available."

"Well, your intelligence failed this time, mate. And people died because of it." Tom was angrier than Kate had ever seen him. "One of our own is still in hospital because of your intelligence failure."

Mallam nodded and had the good sense to look abashed. Whether he felt it or not. "We've had cutbacks just as much as you have. You know what it's like out there."

A more understanding grumble circulated. They really did.

"Known associates we can try to pin down?" Kate asked.

Mallam looked at her for the first time and nodded. "Yes, he travelled with Shiraz Zaghba to and from Turkey. Zaghba, thirty-three years old, Pakistani descent. He has been on the radar for some time. We've had a number of anonymous reports raising concerns about his behaviour, beliefs, and expressed views in regards to IS, extremism, suicide bombings, and beheading infidels."

"Why hasn't he been picked up?"

"We have him under surveillance. The hope is that Ayeshydi will make contact and then we can scoop them both up at the same time."

"And if he doesn't?"

"We are working on other leads."

"Care to share what those might be?" Vinny asked.

"Need to know," Mallam said with as much confidence as someone who thought they might be about to get lynched.

He wasn't far wrong. A chorus of mimicked farting sounds were hurled his way, along with a string of curse words to make a sailor blush. Might have even been one or two new to Kate...but it was hard to tell amongst so many old favourites.

In the end, it was Clare who held up her hands to bring them all back to order. "All right, people, give him a break. He doesn't set the orders."

"Just another bloody 'yes' man for the fucking government," someone shouted.

"We're all frustrated, we're all angry, and, by God, we've all seen more than enough. But this is why they pay us those peanuts and promise us a glorious retirement, folks. Because we go out there and we do our jobs. We do everything we can to keep people safe and when we can't, we bring pieces of shit like this to justice."

"How do you expect us to do that without all the information? We're not fucking mind readers, ma'am."

"Wouldn't it be easy if we were," Clare responded with a sardonic smile. "We do the best we can with the information we have," she glared at Porter and Mallam, "and trust that our colleagues will divulge all the information we do need at the appropriate times."

More grumbling from the crowd.

"It's not perfect. I know that, and you know that. But you know what? Nothing is. This is what we've got, and this is what we have to deal with." She met the eye of every officer looking at her. "I believe in my people, I believe in you. Every single one of you. There is nowhere you won't look, no lead you won't chase down, and not a fucking rock you won't turn over until we have this bastard in our sweaty little hands."

A rousing chorus of *hell yeah*s and *too fucking right*s chased her words with enthusiasm.

"Sanderson, Manners, Brothers, and Powers, you're with Porter."

"Ma'am?" Martin Sanderson asked.

"Surveillance on Zaghba. We need to spell off the team that are watching his place at the moment. Twenty-four-seven eyes and ears. You four take the next shift. You'll have cover come in by five tonight."

Sanderson nodded, and Kate could practically hear Tom moaning. He hated surveillance.

"Brannon, Jackson, and Co., take Mr Mallam here to meet with your Mr Grimshaw, and see where we're up to with that diary you found. See if Nadia left any clues in there as to where the bombs were made or where Ayeshydi might be hanging out when he's not at home."

Kate nodded. So much better than surveillance. Even if she did have to work with Mel and Mallam. She looked around to see if she could see Gareth, but if he was there, he was hidden in the crowd.

Clare continued to hand out assignments and quickly the room emptied until Kate, Vinny, and Mel were the only ones left besides Timmons, Clare, Mallam, and the two guys from the counterterrorism unit.

"Looks like you're missing a body, DS Brannon." Timmons cocked his head to the side. "Where's the pretty boy?"

"Not sure, sir." She pulled her phone from her pocket to see if she had any word from him, but there was no message, no missed call. She flicked the screen in Timmons's direction and shrugged.

As he ground his teeth, Timmons's face darkened to a ruddy shade of puce Kate usually associated with long-term alcohol abuse. "Right, well, carry on, and I'll send the little bastard to you when I'm done with him."

She nodded, glad she wasn't going to be in Collier's shoes when he finally dragged his arse out of bed.

Mallam wandered over to them and held out his hand to Kate. "Zain Mallam."

She shook his hand. "Kate Brannon." She pointed to Vinny as she let go of his hand. "Vinny Jackson."

"Nice to meet ya." Mallam shook Vinny's hand.

"Likewise."

"And Mel Brown." Kate pointed to Mel as they shook hands.

"Pleasure." Mallam smiled at Mel.

Mel just nodded.

"So, you found the diary?" he asked Kate.

"Yes. It's all in Arabic, so it's down for translation." She led them out of the room and down into the bowels of the station where the crime lab lived.

"Maybe I can help with that," he offered.

Yeah, like I'd trust you to tell me what it said? Need to fucking know, right? "Sure, I'm sure Grimshaw will be glad of any help you could offer."

They surely all knew she was lying. Grimshaw was never glad of help. Now, she was the only one who knew that about him. But the others had to know she was lying because none of them would trust Mallam as far as they could throw him either. He'd already proved to them they couldn't. And Mallam... Well, he had to know, if only because he was a spook. They knew everything.

Except where a bomb was gonna be set off.

Or where their suspect was hiding.

Or anything relevant he could share.

On second thought, maybe he didn't know she was lying to his face.

CHAPTER 15

Gina parked her beat-up old Astra on the main road and unclipped her seatbelt. "Don't forget your PE kit," she reminded Sammy.

Sammy slapped her backpack and pushed open the rear door.

"Have you got your lunch?"

Sammy slapped the bag again, slung it over her shoulder, and slammed the door shut behind her.

Gina climbed out of the driver's side, grabbed hold of Sammy's hand, and led her down the gravel-covered road to Brancaster Primary School. The low brick wall was topped with an ornate iron railing and heavy black iron gates that were swung open to allow entry. Mums and other kids milled around the small playground.

There were thirty-seven children in the school, ranging in ages from nursery to eleven years old. And not a one of them walked up to Sammy to say hi as Gina walked her across the yard and straight up to Mrs Eastern—Sammy's class teacher and protector since the bullying had started. Wrongly blamed for most of the kids' fathers facing jail time, Sammy was bearing the brunt of their confusion, fear, and the misplaced anger of the parents of the village.

Sammy wasn't the one who enticed their fathers into smuggling drugs from overseas, storing them in oyster pots on the sea bed, and then bringing them ashore on demand. Nope. That had been Ally and Adam Robbins. Sammy's own father—Matt the Prat, as Gina called him—also sat in a prison cell waiting for his trial. In fact, his arse-covering had set off the chain reaction that had brought the village's fleet to a standstill and put all the fishermen either in prison or out of work.

That was why Sammy was getting the shit-covered end of the stick.

Because Matt was far more than a prat. He was a fucking idiot. A fucking drug-dealing, child-abandoning, moronic imbecile whose poor parenting decisions led Sammy to believe she'd killed Gina's best friend, Connie Wells. So, yeah...Matt was way more than just a prat.

"Morning, Gina," Mrs Eastern said. "Terrible business all this in Lynn, ain't it?"

Gina slapped her hands over Sammy's ears and pulled her in front of her body so she couldn't possibly read her lips as she said quietly, "Don't."

Mrs Eastern frowned, her eyes begging the question.

"I was there."

Mrs Eastern clasped her hands in front of her mouth.

"One of our friends is still in hospital with her injuries. Sammy knows, but we've downplayed it. She doesn't need anything else to worry about."

Mrs Eastern nodded vigorously. "Of course." She forced a smile to her lips and dropped her hands. "Are you coming to the nativity this afternoon?" She reached over and ruffled Sammy's hair. "Someone we both know is playing the Angel Gabriella and narrating the whole show." She winked at Sammy. "We've been working hard on those lines for a while now."

Sammy nodded and looked up at Gina. "Can Kate come and watch me too?"

Gina's heart clenched in her chest. "I'm sorry, sweetheart, but she can't. Kate's really busy. With Stella getting that bump on the head, she's got to do all of Stella's work too. I know she'd want to, though. More than anything else."

Sammy's head dropped, the disappointment evident in the droop to her shoulders. "'Kay."

Gina thought quickly. "She made me promise that I'd video it so we could all watch it together later when she got home. That's how disappointed she was that she wouldn't be able to come."

Sammy's head shot up, her braid bouncing about and whipping her in the face. She waved it back with an exaggerated swipe of her arm. "Really?"

"Absolutely." Gina crossed her finger over her heart. *Note to self: text Kate and tell her to be OTT about disappointment tonight.*

"Kate's so cool. Laters." Sammy skipped away.

Mrs Eastern sniggered. "Saved by the awesomeness that is a smartphone, huh?"

Gina sighed. "Oh yeah." She pulled her phone out of her pocket and quickly started typing.

It's Sammy's nativity play this afternoon. She was upset when I told her you wouldn't be able to come because you were so busy at work. I cheered her up telling her you begged me to video it to watch later. Sorry. You now have to show excessive amounts of enthusiasm or face the wrath of a sulking pre-teen. xx

There. Now she could forget about it...until one o'clock.

The rest of her journey to work was uneventful. The campsite and hostel were empty, and Will was checking the stock of gas bottles stored in the locked cage outside the information centre. An uncomfortable thought battered at Gina's brain. Gas bottles...open cage...explosions.

"Will, can we get the gas bottles stored in the barn?"

He frowned at her. The dark beanie hat on his head was sodden and slipped low over his eyes. The ever-present cigarette hung from his lips as he spoke around it, hiking up his pants when he stood up straight. "Well, yeah. But that's gonna be a ball-ache when we have to traipse up and down every time we sell one of them."

Gina nodded. No doubt it would be. With just the two of them working at the campsite now, if only one of them was around when they needed to go up to the barn for a bottle, they'd have to lock up the shop, carry the often heavy canister down, unlock the shop, sell the gas, then take the empty canister back up to await collection and refilling. Like Will said, ball-ache. But she really didn't like the idea of those flammable, explosive cans just sitting there. It had never sat well with her. After...well, now...she really couldn't stand the thought of it.

"I know, but it is safer. I think that has to be a priority right now. Not the work involved."

Will scowled but nodded. "I'll sort it."

She smiled at him. That was his stock answer. Anything she needed, anything that needed doing around the site, helping with Sammy... "You're a star, Will. Thanks."

He dipped his head, and she pushed open the door to the information centre. A quick look over the booking system showed her that they'd had only one departure that morning, so only one room needed to be changed over. Will would no doubt sort that when he was done with the gas bottles, leaving Gina free to trudge through the growing mountain of paperwork sitting on her desk. They weren't even open as a campsite now; how did the paperwork continue to breed? She grabbed the small stack of post and walked up the lane to her office.

She switched on the oil radiator, dumped the post on her desk, and decided coffee was in order before she settled down. Brandale Café was a busy spot all year round. This morning it was filled with various contractors who were working on the holiday homes that sat vacant through the winter. Orders for bacon baps, sausage butties, and tea you could stand a spoon in were yelled across the counter to a harried-looking woman. Gina stood to one side and waited for it to quiet down a bit.

"It's a bloody disgrace, I tell you," one builder said to another.

Gina craned her head to see if she recognised the speaker. She didn't.

"Do they know who did it?" the second builder asked as he stirred a fourth packet of sugar into his tea.

Did what? Gina frowned.

Builder One shook his head. "Be kids, probably. We all know what Mrs M was growing in that hothouse of hers." He mimed taking a puff off a cigarette. "Wacky-backy."

Mrs M, a.k.a. Mrs Maureen Mitchell, suffered from multiple sclerosis and grew marijuana in her greenhouse for her own medical consumption. It was a well-known local secret. Even Kate knew and wished Mrs M all the best with it. As long as she was only using it for herself...Kate had no problem. The poor woman was suffering enough.

The idea that some ignorant kids had broken in and damaged Mrs M's medical stash was appalling. The woman was ill.

"Yeah, but when I saw her this morning, Mrs M said there was no damage to those plants. Just every one of her roses had been de-headed, and the pots knocked over. Sounds personal to me, not like kids looking for a quick smoke."

Gina's attention spiked. Mrs M was also renowned for her roses. Her beautiful, fragrant, yellow-headed roses. She grew them to help cover the smell of the marijuana plants. She had dozens of rose bushes in the hothouse, growing blooms all year round. She said the colours made her feel better, sunnier, when she felt nothing but grey or black inside.

"Bastards," Builder One said again.

"Excuse me," Gina interrupted. "When was this?"

Builder Two looked her up and down, a grin twitched on his lips. "Few days ago, love. Maybe a week at most. She'd had a bad bout and had not been in there for a few days, so didn't see the damage until this morning."

"Has she called the police?"

He shook his head. "They've got bigger fish to fry right now then a few damaged plant pots, don't ya think?"

Gina nodded. Of course they did. But a horrid thought skittered through her mind, and she needed to figure out if it was possible or not. "Thanks." She straight-armed the door open and jogged the couple of hundred yards to her house. A small stack of mail sat on the mat. She scooped them up and tossed them on the kitchen table as she passed through. The flowers were still in the bin where she'd dumped them after learning they hadn't been a gift from Kate. Fifty yellow roses.

She just hoped she could find the card that had come with them. She pulled each stem from the bin bag, grateful that the flowers were the only thing in it.

The tiny scrap of card sat at the bottom, the white of it standing out against the black bin bag.

Missed you last night. How about tonight we make it special? The Victoria, 8pm? xx

The handwriting was a ridiculous scrawl, and there was nothing else on it. No shop logo, no address of the florist that sent or delivered the flowers. Not even the name of the shop. *Shit.*

Gina's first thought had been that Ally had sent them to her. A kind of sick 'thinking of you' kind of gesture to make sure Gina kept reliving the nightmare over and over again.

But Ally was in prison.

Fear skittered up Gina's spine, but just as quickly, she shut it down. Gina pulled in one deep breath after another and focused her mind, refusing to let it claim her. Ally was in prison, she couldn't hurt her anymore. And whoever was sending her flowers...well, they were just flowers, right? What was bad about flowers?

Maybe nothing at all. Maybe...something else entirely.

Grabbing her mail and stuffing it into her pocket along with the card, she jogged out of the house and down the village to Mrs M's house. She knocked on the door until she heard "just a minute" in a scratchy, slightly strangled sounding voice that Mrs M had on a bad day.

Gina forced her worry and frustration to be patient. She couldn't shout at a disabled person to hurry up because she needed information.

When Mrs M opened the door, Gina gasped. Always a frail looking woman, today she looked like she was about to break. Her thin frame was little more than skin and bones. The hand that curled around the control of her electric wheelchair was white knuckled and more gnarled than Gina could ever remember seeing. There was a sunken look to her eyes and cheeks that gave her an almost skeletal look, and it was a shock. Gina knew Mrs M to be a feisty, fiercely independent woman who refused to let her condition beat her. Who had stood up to those in the village time and again for whatever she bloody well felt like, including the right to graze her horses on the common land around the village—something that hadn't been popular with the locals...or the farmers...or the tourists avoiding the mounds of manure the little darlings had left on every footpath they could fine. But the Mrs M Gina was looking at today, wasn't the same woman. She looked beaten.

"Gina," Mrs M said with a tight smile. "Long time no see." She scooted her wheelchair back to let Gina inside, leading her to the front room.

Gina smirked. "Yeah. Sorry about that."

Mrs M shook her head a fraction. "I heard you've had a lot going on. I was going to come and see you, but..." She turned out a hand to indicate her chair. "I've been a bit tied up myself," she finished with a bitter laugh.

"I heard your greenhouse has been broken into. Are you okay?"

Mrs M nodded. "Pissed off, and I can't get in there because of the mess, so there's not a lot I can do about it at the moment. I'll have to wait until the next time Susie, my daughter, decides to make a trip up from London to get it sorted out in there."

"What do you mean?"

"There are broken plant pots all over the place so I can't get this thing in there." She tapped the arm of her wheelchair. The cumbersome piece of equipment did indeed take up a lot of room, and no doubt with her mobility impaired as it was, cleaning up the mess left by a vandal was a little beyond Mrs M's abilities right now.

"What did they take, Mrs M?"

"Just some roses, from what I can see. My cannabis plants are down at the far end of the greenhouse, so I can't get in there to check them, but they don't appear to have been touched from a distance."

"All your roses?"

Mrs M shook her head. "Doesn't look like it. I mean they've all been knocked over, so they'll no doubt be dead by now, but only the yellow ones seem to have been de-headed. Not the pinks, oranges, or reds. Bizarre." She shook her head sadly. "The yellows were my favourites, you know?"

Gina nodded. "Do you mind if I take a look? Maybe I could go and check things out better for you."

Mrs M's face seemed to light up, and she sat a little straighter in her chair. "Would you?"

"Of course." She needed to see for herself. Flowers might not mean anything. But stolen flowers...leaving damage in their wake...well, Gina was no expert, but that didn't sound too good.

"That would be wonderful, thank you."

Gina followed behind her wheelchair, through the house and out of the back door. There was a wide concrete path between the door and the greenhouse. Everything had been specially adapted to allow her to move freely between the two places. The garden was surrounded by a six-foot wooden fence all the way around, with clematis, climbing ivy, climbing roses, and laurel growing up and around it. It was a beautiful garden. Truly. Gina knew that during the summer now, Mrs M had a small army of gardeners to help her tend to it. But it had been her creation years ago. Now all she could work with—sometimes—were the plants she could grow in pots, on easy to reach benches, in the greenhouse.

Mrs M nodded towards the door. "Help yourself."

"How did they get in?" Gina asked.

"Must have climbed over the fence. The gate's padlocked and the security light is on a sensor. If it comes on, one of the neighbours is at the window, looking what's going on." She laughed bitterly. "I wish I were well enough to be up to giving them anything worth gossiping about."

Gina pushed open the frosted glass door and gasped. Shattered clay was strewn across the room, with soil spilled everywhere and the roots of the poor plants exposed.

"A mess, isn't it?" Mrs M's voice was quiet, almost cutting itself off as it vacated her lips.

Gina nodded, but made her way to the back of the twenty-foot long room to the plants she could see at the back on a shelf, covered by UV lamps and silver foil. It was a bizarre-looking set up, but Mrs M seemed to know what she was doing, and the plants were clearly thriving.

It was the roses Gina had needed to see. And now she knew. Without a doubt in her mind, this was where those fifty yellow roses had come from. There was one half-open bud left on the floor that she picked up and smelled. The fragrance was the same. Not a definitive test, not one that would stand up in court...but it was enough for Gina. "They're all fine, Mrs M. Do you need any of them?"

"To the left. The blacked-out section, there should be some dry hanging on a hook. If you could bring me a little of that, I would be very grateful."

Gina quickly located the dried vegetal matter, wrapped it in a plastic bag she saw on a shelf, and carried it out to Mrs M.

"Bless you, child." Mrs M laid the bag across her lap and turned her chair around.

"I feel terrible about your greenhouse. I'm not much good with plants, I manage to kill pretty much anything I've ever tried to grow, but would you let me send Will around this afternoon to at least clear up the greenhouse so you can get in and tend to the plants he can save for you?"

Mrs M shook her head. "You don't have to do that, Gina. I know you've got to have your work cut out for you over there. What with Connie gone and leaving it all so up in the air, and then that bloody Sarah and her merry band of idiots dropping you in the shit." She waved a hand—well, a little bit. "No, you don't have to do that."

"Honestly, Mrs M, I'd feel better if you did. We've closed most things down for the winter, and I've got Will doing mostly busy work right now. He spends as much time babysitting Sammy as doing anything else right now. He'd probably be glad of the variety. I know he hates being cooped up in the office or the information centre."

"You're sure?"

"Absolutely." It was the only way Gina could think to make it even slightly up to the woman. Those plants, her greenhouse, they'd been wrecked because of her.

"Why?" She led them back into the house and indicated a chair for Gina to sit on.

Gina debated what to tell her. Did she tell her the truth and risk others learning what was going on? Could she trust Mrs M to keep it to herself? Something told her she could, and it was her property that had been ransacked after all.

Gina dropped into the chair and sighed. "A few days ago, I was delivered a huge bouquet of roses. Yellow roses."

Mrs M watched her as she started to prepare the marijuana Gina had retrieved for her. "Do you mind?" She indicated her hands.

"Not at all."

Mrs M nodded and waited for Gina to carry on.

"There was a note that came with them, not signed with a name, but the message was one that could have come from my girlfriend, Kate. I thought the roses were from her."

"Could you pass me that packet of cigarette papers please, dear?" She pointed to a Rizla packet on the table beside Gina.

She handed it over.

"Thanks. Go on."

"When I thanked Kate for them, she told me she hadn't sent them."

"Secret admirer?"

Gina shook her head. "I'm the village pariah, Mrs M. They all blame me for everything that's gone wrong."

"What with the fishing fleet and the drugs and those bloody Robbinses?"

"Yes."

"Then they're even bigger nitwits than I ever thought."

Gina laughed. "Thanks, but that doesn't seem to matter to them. I'm still persona non grata. So no, no secret admirer. I thought at first it might have been some sort of sick message from Ally."

"Ah. Yes, I can see why you might think that. But not now, I take it?"

"No." She fished the card from her pocket and showed it to Mrs M. "Nothing to identify the florist or anything like that. I don't think they were bought."

"You think someone stole my roses to give them to you?"

"Yes."

"Did you recognise the person who delivered them?"

Gina concentrated and tried to pull up the memory of the delivery. She remembered staring at the huge array of blooms in a vase, with a small card protruding from the top. She remembered barely tearing her gaze from them as she'd scribbled her name on a piece of paper on a clipboard, but nothing about what was on the page. Nothing about what the delivery guy was wearing. Nothing about his face. All she was sure of was that it was a guy...maybe young...slim...maybe.

"I don't really remember seeing him. I was too focused on the flowers and how beautiful they were. And how thoughtful Kate was to send them to me." She rubbed her hands over her face. "I know, I know. I should pay more attention, but, I mean, why would you? Flowers are a lovely gesture—"

"And you're in a new relationship, and getting flowers from your girlfriend is not exactly a bad thing, is it?"

"Exactly."

"And now?"

"I'm worried about what they mean."

"It could be a secret admirer."

"The note doesn't read like someone who's trying to win my affections, it reads like someone who thinks they already have. Hence why I thought it was Kate."

"I see." She sprinkled dried leaves across the cigarette paper she thumbed from the pack. "I wasn't going to bother with the police. They have bigger things to worry about right now. But if this is a bigger thing than just a few broken plant pots, I'm happy to give them a call and wait. It's not like I'm going out anywhere."

Gina smiled sadly. "I understand, and I think you're right. There are bigger concerns. Would you mind if I took some pictures, though? Then I can show Kate and talk to her about this idea. See if she thinks this is something for her to bear in mind if...if..."

"If anything else happens?"

Gina swallowed. "Yeah."

"Go ahead."

"Thanks." Gina quickly went back to the greenhouse, phone in hand, and snapped off pictures from every angle of the room, panoramas to give Kate the full layout, close-ups of each broken pot, a footprint she found in the dirt, and smudges of greasy fingerprints on the glass. She had no idea if they would be of any use...but it couldn't hurt.

When she got back to the kitchen, a fog of cannabis-laden smoke filled the room. Mrs M's eyes had begun to take on the glassy look of relief. Gina didn't want to hang around. She was pretty sure she'd get high off the fumes before long.

"Mrs M, I'm sorry to have to ask for another favour, but would you mind keeping all that to yourself? I don't want the village gossiping about it and it getting back to Sammy. She's had a rough time lately, and I don't want her to worry about me if there's no reason to."

Mrs M took another pull on the joint and nodded, her body already seeming so much more relaxed than just a few minutes ago. "Of course, Gina. The little scamp doesn't need to be worried about things like that. How's she doing, anyway? I bet she's taking it hard, huh? Her dad going to prison."

Gina was grateful that the vast majority of Sammy's involvement wasn't public knowledge and wanted to ensure it stayed that way. "Yes, they were close. And I know she misses him."

"She'll bounce back. Kids always do."

"I'm sure." Gina put her hand on the door handle. "I'll send Will over as soon as he's finished what he's doing now. Shouldn't be too long."

Mrs M waved her hand, sending smoke curling in circles in the air. "No rush. I'm not going anywhere."

Except off to space, Gina thought as she let herself out of the house and made sure the door was shut tight behind her. She blinked rapidly, then rubbed at her eyes. The odour clung to her skin and clothes. There was no way she was going to Sammy's nativity play stinking like she'd been in some sort of drug party.

Shower. Change of clothes. Work. Send Will gardening…ish. Nativity play. Food. Not necessarily in that order. Her stomach growled.

Okay, definitely not in that order.

CHAPTER 16

"Simon, give me good news," Kate said as she sidled up to Grimshaw's workstation and peered over his shoulder.

"Three-quarters done. Come back this afternoon." He didn't even look up at her as he scribbled more notes across a legal pad.

"What happened to good news?"

"I said this afternoon, not tomorrow."

"Zain Mallam." He stepped forward, hand held out for Grimshaw to shake.

Grimshaw still didn't look up.

Mallam frowned, let his hand drop, and continued, "Perhaps I can be of use."

"I'm sure you can, if you all piss off and leave me to it."

Kate sniggered as Grimshaw scribbled some more. His handwriting was almost as unreadable as the Arabic he was deciphering, as far as Kate was concerned, and she wondered if he was using some sort of shorthand, or code...or a drunken spider.

"Mr Grimshaw, I'm sure I have skills that would be useful to you in translating the diary. I'm fluent in Urdu."

Grimshaw dropped his pen on top of the pad and looked up at them. He smiled sardonically at Kate and rolled his eyes. "How about Pascal, or Joomla, or Script? Fluent in any of those too?"

Mallam cleared his throat. "I'm sorry, I understood that you were translating the perpetrator's diary into English."

"Nah, I let the computer do that. Now I'm translating computer code into English."

"I see."

Kate wanted to laugh at the uncomfortable look on Mallam's face. *Prick.*

"Brannon, I'll fire this up to you as soon as I get it finished."

"I appreciate that. Any chance you could send me anything you've already done? Even if it's just a bit, it could help us to get a head start on all this material sooner rather than later."

Grimshaw crossed his arms over his chest and opened his mouth.

Kate knew he was going to tell her where to go. She leant in close to him, dropped her voice so only he could hear. "You heard we arrested Ahmed, right?"

He nodded.

"Bastard implied that there were more bombs out there. Nothing concrete. Nothing we can prove. Yet." She pulled back and saw the shock in his eyes and leant in again. "This is the best lead we have in trying to find out if there are more or if he's just trying to scare the shit out of me."

Grimshaw leant back in his chair, pulled in a huge lungful of air, and exhaled loudly through his mouth. "Dirty, Kate."

"True, Simon."

He stared at her. "How's Stella?"

"Being released today. Want me to pass on a message when I see her?"

"Yeah, tell her to get back here quick. Someone needs to put the reins back on you." He hunkered over his computer and clacked loudly at the keys. "I'll see what I can do," he said, dismissing them.

In Grimshaw code, that meant he'd just sent what he had to her e-mail address. Jackson and Mallam followed behind her as she walked out of the crime lab.

"He's hampering our investigation," Mallam said when they cleared the doors and pulled his phone from his pocket. "I could have his credentials revoked and him in custody—"

Kate pulled her own phone from her pocket, refreshed her e-mails, and showed Mallam the screen. "How is he hampering the investigation? He's already sent me the documents he's finished translating." She rolled her eyes at him. "I'll print these when we get back upstairs so we can all have a copy to start going through."

"I'd suggest we take a section each," Vinny added. "Get through it quicker."

"Good idea," Kate said, even though she knew she'd read every page. It was all well and good going over the material quickly when they were looking for a specific lead, but she knew it was an easy way for details to be missed. Little codes and references that got shorthanded and would mean something significant in the context of the whole diary, but nothing as part of a single page...those were the details she wanted to find. Those were the ones that could make all the difference.

Mallam grumbled the entire way back upstairs and was still grumbling after Kate had printed off copies for them all and handed them out. "For God's sake, shut up." She dropped the pages in front of him and tossed a marker pen at him. "We've got work to get on with."

Her phone pinged as she settled in at her desk and started on the first page—a text message from Gina telling her about the private nativity viewing she was going to get later. A smile slid onto her cheeks.

Wish I could be there in person. I'm sure she'll be brilliant. She's such a natural when it comes to drama, I don't know why the Oscars haven't started rolling in already. xx

She snickered as she pressed *send* then pulled the cap off her own highlighter pen. Vinny, Mel, and Mallam had their heads down, pens at work. Still there was no sign of Gareth. If he wasn't dead already, he would be when Timmons got done with him.

Dear Diary,

There was a new girl at college today, Saba. She's in the year above me, but she joined a group of us at lunchtime in the cafeteria. She knows a lot of people already. She is from a good family, and her husband has introduced her to everyone. I think she knows more people than I do.

Kate quickly checked the date of the page. Only three months ago. When Ayeshydi returned from Raqqa. She wondered where Saba had been before then.

She invited me to mosque with her, and to meet her husband. I think we will be good friends, Saba and I. Good friends.

The innocence of the girl in the page seemed so at odds with the image of the girl she'd seen on the CCTV footage. The girl displaying her vest and crying "for Allah" as she destroyed herself and twenty-one innocent people. Where did this girl go? When did this Nadia become that Nadia? And did it really only begin just a few short months ago?

Each page she read took Kate further and further into Nadia's life and into her mind and led her step-by-step down the journey from innocent Nadia to confused Nadia. Nadia, whose confusion was twisted into anger and then hatred, her innocent trust abused by those who should have nurtured it rather than betrayed it.

"She was in love with Ishman Ayeshydi," Vinny said, holding up one of his pages. "Says she knows she's going to hell for loving another woman's husband but can't help herself. Seems like he barely even notices her, but she would, and I quote, 'do anything for him'."

"Bastard," Mel cursed.

"When was that?" Mallam asked.

"A month ago."

"Anything yet on a location?"

"Nope," Vinny said.

Mel and Kate both shook their heads, and Mallam sighed.

"Fabulous."

Gareth Collier chose that moment to waltz through the doors of the station, and Timmons's voice rose above the din.

"My office. Now." His head and shoulders leant around the door frame and looked like they were hanging in mid-air. Collier blanched, and Timmons's face had gone puce. Again.

"Traffic," Vinny said, trying to guess what Collier's punishment was going to be.

Mallam shook his head. "Picking up body parts."

"They've already finished that lovely task." Kate turned another page. "Surveillance. I just hope I don't get stuck with it too."

Mel sniggered. "The joys of a rookie partner, hey?"

"Something like that." Kate carried on reading as the three of them swapped war stories about bad partners they'd had in the past. Kate didn't think it would be conducive to a good working relationship to say that Mel had been worse and gotten her into more punishment jobs than Collier had. So far, at least. She supposed he still had time, though.

Skimming page after page, Kate highlighted a few sections that might be of significance, but there was still nothing to give them any idea of a location to search. Until she got to the tenth page in her handful.

"Saba took me to the lock-up today," she read. "An old garage at the back of their house. It's covered in graffiti. Crude penises, and women with huge breasts, but there's a swastika on there too. Clearly the thugs who drew it all don't get what's offensive to Muslims, but still. They shouldn't deface property that isn't there. She said it was better not to clean it off, because leaving it there makes the kaffirs think he doesn't care, so they won't set fire to it. She had to pick up some stock. I don't know what stock, though. They don't sell things on the market like my dad does. I tried to ask her, but she just said it was his business and she just had to get the bag and take it to the mosque."

"Address?" Mallam asked.

"The Ayeshydi house is on Diamond Street," Vinny said as Kate jumped out of her seat and ran across the room to Timmons's office. She knocked on the door and didn't wait for a response. Collier was slouched in a chair, looking sullen, and Timmons's face was crimson, spittle collected at the corner of his mouth. She almost felt sorry for Gareth. Almost.

"Sir, we've got something," she said before he could start to berate her. "The diary mentions a lock-up that Ayeshydi has at the back of his house. An old garage where Saba took her one day. Apparently they kept stock there."

"What fucking stock?"

"Not a clue. As far as we know, he's unemployed and she was a student."

"Brilliant, Brannon." He looked at Collier. "If you bothered to fucking show up, you could learn a lot from an officer like her. Do not let me see you skulk in here late again, Collier. Now get out of my sight." He looked at Kate. "I take it you don't have a specific address for the lock-up."

"No, sir. But we have a description of the graffiti that covers it."

"Outstanding. Get over there, and get me a unit number." He picked up the phone. "I'll have a warrant ready for it by the time you get there." He pointed to Gareth as he slunk towards the door. "You. Don't fuck this up acting like a child who's had his legs slapped. Grow up and grow a pair."

Kate let her gaze drop. Now she did feel a bit sorry for Collier. Just a bit.

"Well? What are ya waiting for?" Timmons asked, and they both shuffled out of the room.

Vinny, Mallam, and Mel were all waiting for them. Mallam had his phone to his ear.

"Warrant'll be ready by the time we get there." She nodded in Mallam's direction and looked at Vinny, holding her hands up in question.

"Porter. They're calling in that Dalton dude from CTU."

Kate sighed. "So, not so much on the little look-around and see if this might be something, then?"

Vinny sniggered. "Go big or go home, Kate."

"Apparently."

Mallam turned back to them and slid his phone away. "Shall we, ladies?" He pointed to the door.

Vinny and Collier scowled at his sickeningly sweet grin.

"All units are mobilising."

Kate stepped through the door and fished her keys out of her pocket. "Yippee."

CHAPTER 17

"Hello, Reman Unit," the voice said.

"Hi, it's Gina Temple. Is Jodi available?"

"Let me see. Hold, please."

A panpipes version of "Nights in White Satin" stuttered through the earpiece, and Gina shuddered. Really? On a mental health ward phone line? It wasn't the choice of song...it was the bloody panpipes!

"Hello? Gina?"

"Hi, Jodi. Thanks for taking my call."

"No worries. You caught me between appointments. What can I do for you today?"

"I wondered if you had a slot I could steal."

"Having problems?"

"Well, it's been a busy few days."

"Indeed. I've got a ton of extra people to see after what happened in Lynn—"

"I was in Ann Summers when it happened," Gina said quietly.

Jodi was quiet for a moment. "This afternoon? Four o'clock?"

"Sammy will have finished school then."

"Bring her along. We've got a playroom she can hang out in. It's got a TV and some video games in there."

"You sure?"

"Positive. Half the staff brought kids in today. We've had to cancel days off and, well, trying to get childcare was becoming a hindrance to providing the support we needed to, so we've hired someone to watch all the kids in the playroom. Ages seven to twelve, all in one big, happy room."

"Sounds like hell."

"Meh. For some." She chuckled. "So, four?"

"See you then."

The screen on her phone said 12:02 p.m. when she rang off. Almost time to go to the school as it was. The day had gotten away from her. She hadn't even had a chance to open the mail, never mind get started on paying the bills, noting the invoices on the account spreadsheets, or looking at the bookings for the beginning of the new year. She wanted to figure out how much time off she could realistically take to spend with Sammy and Kate, doing nice things, fun things. Like lounging around on the sofa and throwing popcorn at each other while still in their pyjamas at three in the afternoon. Or walking Merlin on the beach at sunset and holding Kate's hand. Or kissing her. Or maybe even more...no, definitely even more. Not on the beach, but definitely more.

She grabbed the stack of mail and opened the first envelope. Telephone bill. Water bill. Invoice from the coal supplier, another from the plumber who'd serviced the boiler, and yet another from the guy who supplied the kindling they sold in the shop. Gina set each one to the side, carefully stacking them in date-payable order. She slid open the tab on the next envelope and pulled out a card. The picture showed a sad-looking dog with droopy eyes and a real hang-dog expression on its face. Gina smiled. They sometimes got thank-you cards from guests. Not as often as they got negative reviews on a certain review website, but enough to make her remember that there were still some nice people out there.

She opened the card and read.

Gina,

I know you're going through some difficult times at the moment. And I want you to know that I'll always be there for you. You know you can count on me. I think I've proven myself to you now. I've done so much for you. Time and again, I've been at your beck and call, and it's like you don't even see me. Like you don't even realise how much I do for you. You don't even realise I'm alive.

I know you think she's good for you. She isn't. Ever since she showed up, everything has gone wrong. Think about it, and you'll see I'm right. Before she showed up, your life was perfect. We would have been perfect. I'm so much better for you than she is, Gina, and it's time you started to wake up and realise that. It's time you stopped seeing her and started to see what's really good for you. Me.

All she's brought you is trouble.

We belong together, Gina. You know we do.

X

Gina shivered as she dropped the card to her desk and plucked from her pocket the scrap of card that had come with the flowers. The handwriting was the same. The same scrawling arrangement of capitals and lower-case letters that were not ordered correctly. The first three letters in a word capitals, before they slipped to lowercase. It was a bizarre mixture, and something about it niggled. It itched at the back of her mind. She'd seen something like that before…a long time ago. But where?

She picked up the envelope again. She turned it over and looked closely at it. The address was clearly written, but there was no stamp on it. No postmark. It had been hand delivered. She tried to remember if it had been at the bottom or the top of the pile when she'd picked it up earlier, but she couldn't recall.

"Fuck," she cursed her lack of attention to detail and wished she'd figured out earlier how important a little something like that could be, but it was too late for that now. A cold hand wrapped itself about her heart and squeezed. The panic was rising. Why did this cause her more fear than a fucking bomb going off right there in front of her? Why was this so much more terrifying? A severed woman's hand disturbed her less than a bunch of flowers. Pat's death didn't grab her like this card did. Why? What was wrong with her?

Gina rested her head on the edge of her desk and focused on her breathing. She didn't have time to have a panic attack now. She had to get to Sammy's nativity play. She had to be strong...for Sammy. The card, the flowers, the bomb... It could all wait till later. It could all wait for Jodi.

She stuffed everything into her bag, shut down her computer, slung the bag over her back, and headed for the door.

Will was in the barn, filling the trailer with various tools, buckets, bin bags, and the plant pots she'd told him to use over at Mrs M's. Scowling and muttering to himself under the sodden brim of his ever-present beanie, Will worked the cigarette between his lips as he straddled the quad bike and towed the gear outside. "Do you mind getting the door for me, G? Save me getting off again."

"No worries." Gina grabbed the big, heavy door and swung it shut behind him. "Thanks for this. Mrs M was going to wait for her daughter to come and tidy up, but she's got no idea when she'd be able to come up from London, and she couldn't get in there to get to her medicine."

"You mean her weed."

"It's medicine for her, Will. You know that."

Will grunted and blew smoke into the air. "Do know how long this'll take?"

"No worries. I'm heading over to the school now, then I've got an appointment in Lynn later, so I was going to take the rest of the day off. Why don't you call it a day when you're done at Mrs M's?"

He shook his head. "Can't afford to be taking a half day."

"I'll pay you a full day, Will. You're doing me a favour, after all."

He grunted again. "Tell Sammy she better smash it."

"Oh, no. She might take that literally."

He sniggered. "True. Better tell her to be good, then."

Gina laughed. "Why? She'll only ignore that. Oh, before I forget, was this delivered at the same time as the rest of the post, do you know?" She showed him the envelope.

He pursed his lips, giving it no more than a cursory glance. "I can't say as I noticed anything. Why?"

"No stamp. No postmark. It was hand delivered."

"Really?"

Gina nodded.

"Don't remember seeing anything."

"Did you notice anyone hanging around while you were around the gas cage?"

"Nah. Too busy humping bottles to pay attention to anyone else." He frowned. "Actually, I did see old Ed Sands hanging about for a bit. Looked like he was picking up pinecones, but I wasn't paying much mind to him."

Edward Sands—the farmer who owned the property next to the campsite she and Will were working on, the campsite Ed and his son Rupert had been wanting to buy before Connie Wells had died. And as far as Gina knew...still wanted to buy. She tried to conjure up a scenario in her mind that would have the seventy-year-old Ed Sands shimmying over a six-foot fence to ransack roses from Mrs M to send to her as some sort of...what? Mind game to get her to hand over a campsite that wasn't hers to hand over? Nah. That didn't make any sense. And his forty-something-year-old son Rupert would be more likely to bring the fence down than scale it. His excessive bulk did not lend itself well to feats of acrobatic cat burglary as far as she could tell.

Still, it was worth bearing in mind. Maybe. "Okay, thanks, Will."

He nodded, revved the engine, and set off for Mrs M's.

Gina walked to her car and set off for the school and an hour of mind-numbing religious regurgitation of the birth of Christ as told by children. And one Sammy Temple. She considered stopping by Mrs M's and seeing if she had any special cakes she could take with her. That would make it a bit more entertaining.

Ah well. At least it would keep her mind off cards and flowers and her mother for a while longer. Oh, and the bombing, of course.

CHAPTER 18

Mel sniggered. "Do we take the penis-covered garage on the left, or the boob-covered garage on the right?"

"Neither, the swastika-wielding garage in the middle is the one we're going for," Kate said, dialling Timmons's number. "Lock-up unit five, sir," she said when he answered.

"Got it. One second." She heard him talking on a different line, then come back to her with "you're good to go. Watch your back, Brannon."

"Sir." She looked around at the team about her.

Mallam leant against the gable end of the row of terraced houses that made up Diamond Street. A slew of two-up and two-down houses with little by the way of garden or parking space. The garages sat on land reclaimed when indoor toilets were invented...possibly only a few years ago, judging by the stench in the alleyway. Clustered around them were a dozen new faces. Well, helmet-covered faces, so Kate couldn't be sure what was underneath the heavy masks of the tactical squad of the counterterrorism unit.

But she did know it was Commander Jack Dalton and his team—every single one of them kitted out in black tactical gear and cradling their weapons more lovingly than their firstborn sons.

Kate met Dalton's fierce gaze and was supremely grateful she wasn't facing him down today. "Good to go, sir."

They didn't know if Ayeshydi was in the lock-up, they didn't know if he was armed...or even if this truly was his lock-up. Either way, CTU was taking their job of kicking down the door seriously. And Kate was happy to let them lead on this one. Something about this place was making the hair on the back of her neck stand on end.

Dalton drew himself up to his full height and waved his finger in a neat circle beside his head, silently commanding the eyes of every officer to fall on him. Without question they did. Silence settled amongst them—not that they'd been noisy before, but now it seemed even breathing was cut to the absolute minimum. He pointed at his own eyes, then sliced his arm through the air, separating his team in two, directing the left flank to take up positions to the left of the unit and the right flank to circle around the front of the street and take up positions to the right of the unit, moving in from one end—a standard pincer movement to trap any suspects that might flee the unit once they set the raid in motion.

One of his team had already scouted around the back, and there was no rear exit, simply the roller door at the front that appeared to be locked, the handle in the centre of the shutter and in the lower third portion seeming to be the only thing securing it.

Dalton moved closer. The only sound was his boots crunching on the ice beneath his feet. He and Palmer moved cautiously, but with surprising speed, covering the ground in what seemed like seconds. They ran fingertips along the edge of the shutter. They'd mentioned checking for tripwires or failsafe devices that would destroy the unit if not deactivated before entering. Just in case, the bomb squad was on standby... Well, Clare had them on speed dial. Was that what they were doing? They hadn't gone into the minute details, and having never served in a tactical unit, Kate was guessing. An educated guess...but still a guess.

When Palmer froze, his hands over his head by a few inches and on the right hand side of the roller door, Dalton seemed to find the same spot on the left at the same time.

"Green? You there?" Dalton's voice crackled over the airwave radio.

"Go ahead, Dalton."

"Suspect the unit to be rigged. Probably just an alarm, but let's play it safe. Requesting optical unit to get eyeballs on this before we open it up."

"Roger that. Optics are rolling to you. Hold position."

"Understood. Do you have an ETA on those optics? Position is exposed here. Repeat, position is exposed."

"ETA two minutes."

"Roger that. Waiting on optics."

Kate glanced up at the curtains twitching in the houses overlooking their positions. Dalton was right. They really were exposed. Ishman Ayeshydi's bedroom overlooked the unit that they were stood in front of. If he was in there...they were totally blown. He could be running down the front of the street in his birthday suit and they wouldn't know it. Not likely, granted, but still... She moved away from her position and across the alleyway to give her an angled view of the unit and most of the street in front too. At least of Ayeshydi's front door.

But a more disturbing thought emerged to displace the one she'd found a semblance of a solution to. Any one of the people looking out at Dalton and his men could be friends, confidantes, or brothers-in-arms with Ayeshydi. And on the phone to him right now, telling him what they were doing.

What if the garage was booby-trapped and not just alarmed—if it was rigged to explode ...who was to say it wasn't rigged with a remote detonator? Christ, her mind was running at a million miles a minute through quicksand, unable to keep up with each one, even as she slogged through the possibilities and the fear each one brought with it. *I'm fucking losing it.*

"Chief Inspector, this is...Brannon. Just had a thought: what if that thing's not just an alarm. What if it's booby-trapped with explosives?"

"One of the reasons we want to get an eyeball on it, Brannon." Dalton glanced at her over his shoulder. She could almost read the 'we're not fucking amateurs' look under his face shield.

"I see. But, what if...well, what if the explosives are set to detonate with a physical trigger or detonated remotely? Can they do that sort of thing?" She pointed to the windows while Dalton continued to stare at her. "Sorry, over," she said into her radio, and shrugged her hands in question at him.

He stared up at the windows again, then back at the garage door.

"Brannon, there's no way we can know without getting eyeballs on whatever's in there." Clare's voice sounded raspy, a little out of breath.

"Dalton, get your team to fall back to the standby positions until the situation has been assessed. Let's not give anyone an easy target, over."

"Roger, ma'am. Left flank falling back, over."

"Ma'am, right flank following, over."

Kate caught the look Mallam was shooting her as he looked up from his phone. His pursed lips, raised eyebrows, and slow nod spoke of a good impression. She was pleased... Even if he was a smug, untrustworthy bastard, it was still something to impress an MI5 spook, right?

A police car screeched to a halt at the entrance to the alleyway, and an officer tumbled out with a bag in his arms before it was even still. His boots crunched the snow, and his heavy breathing, puffing in great clouds between his lips, was the only loud sound echoing off the breeze block and steel wall that were the fronts of the garages. Even the wind had stopped speaking to them.

Then all hell broke loose.

CHAPTER 19

Kate's head ached. She lifted her hand to the back of it. The smell of copper, smoke, and something she didn't recognise filled the air around her, and it took her a moment to realise that there was blood on her hand. And a lump on the back of her head the size of an egg.

"What the fuck...?" she whispered and licked her lips. They were chapped and cracked, and she could taste blood on her tongue. She fought the desire to shake her head in order to clear it, suspecting that it would cause her more pain than relief if she did.

She tried to focus on something and make her eyes work properly again. Across the wide alleyway there was a wooden cross-beamed fence delineating the garden at the end of the row of terraced houses. Icicles hung from the wooden beam, and the weak winter sun filtered through the crystalline structure, casting the weakest of rainbows as the prism split the light. The colours seemed to dance on a breeze she hadn't felt earlier, and she couldn't help but wonder why she couldn't hear it. Or feel it cool her skin. All she could see were those two icicles, quaking.

A tiny bead of meltwater slipped down the side of the frozen column, trembled on the tip, then lost its battle with gravity and plummeted to earth. Kate followed it with her eyes, her head slumped forward just enough to remind her of the pain and nausea she was feeling. Concentration hadn't worked, so she closed her eyes and took a deep breath.

When she opened them again, she wished she hadn't.

Rubble and twisted sheet metal were strewn across the expanse of the alleyway. Windows had been blown in on the houses directly opposite Ayeshydi's unit. As for the unit itself...it was just a space in the row. The lock-ups on either side were half exposed to view, and the cars and junk that had been inside were smouldering or scattered.

A piece of paper fluttered in the breeze, and suddenly, as the ringing began to ease, the sounds began to filter back into Kate's world.

A car alarm sounded, shrill and persistent.

A scream. The pain in that voice was evident, but Kate couldn't have told God himself if it belonged to a man or a woman. There was a level of pain where gender stopped being perceptible. And that poor soul was already there.

She glanced down at her legs sprawled out in front of her, and she was surprised to find she was sitting on the ground, her back pressed against a brick wall. No bones sticking out anywhere they shouldn't be, no signs of blood, no pain...besides her head... So far, so good. She lifted her knees and slowly managed to get her feet under herself. Using the wall at her back, she pulled herself up to standing. Dizziness swamped her, and she had to fight the urge to lie back down on the ground and leave...whatever it was that had just happened to... whoever the fuck it should be that dealt with this sort of shit.

Then she remembered. It was her who dealt with this shit.

She tucked her chin against her chest and wrangled her nausea into something a little more manageable. Like the desire to puke. Big words just weren't cutting it for her right now.

A moan to her left stopped her focusing on her own discomfort and drew her to the plight of those around her instead.

Again, she wished it hadn't.

Suddenly, nausea was like a day at the seaside. With doughnuts and candy floss and donkey rides and fish and chips on the beach when the sun goes down. And it wasn't anything like what was left of the lock-ups and the back of Diamond Street.

A shiver ran up her spine as the screaming faltered, took a breath, then began again.

Gareth Collier lay ten feet away from her, hands clasped over his eyes, and that indistinct wail oozed from his soul as blood welled beneath his fingers.

She staggered over to him, almost falling over blocks of rubble piled haphazardly around them. When she wrapped her fingers about his wrists, his screaming grew louder.

"Gareth, it's me. It's okay. It's Kate. You're okay, you're okay." She rubbed a hand over his shoulder and down his upper arm, offering what comfort she could.

"Kate?"

"Yeah, it's me," she said quietly.

"Kate?" he asked again.

She cleared her throat. "Yeah, it's me," she repeated with much more volume.

"I can't see, Kate. I can't see anything."

What the...? "Well, there's some blood there, Gaz. Move your hands, and let me see what's going on."

"Don't call me Gaz." He lifted his hands gingerly from his face.

Kate swallowed. "Well, we need to find you a decent nickname, then." Both his eyelids were closed, but blood ran from them like tears.

"What's wrong with my name?"

"Well, it's not—I don't know—if you get a nickname, it means people like you. It's a respect thing. Like positive bullying. We only take the piss out of those we like and respect."

"You're full of shit, Sarge."

Maybe, but you're a lot calmer now, and I'll take that. "I'm gonna lift your eyelids a bit so I can see, all right?"

Gareth didn't agree...but he didn't disagree either. That was enough for Kate. Slowly she placed a thumb and forefinger of her left hand over his right eye, then used the thumb of her right hand to lift the lid. She could see grit, brick dust, and metal slivers. The white of his eye was bloodshot and blood covered, and she had no idea how extensive the damage to the pupil or the cornea was. But it was pretty fucking clear that it was badly damaged. She'd be surprised if he ever saw anything out of that eye again.

"Looks like you've got a bit of something in it, Gazza mate. Brick dust or something. Can't really tell in this light." No way was she going to tell him what she was only guessing at. "The medics'll wash it out, and we'll see what they have to say when they get here. I'm gonna take a look at the other one now. Okay?"

He grunted as she turned her attention to the left eye. The lid looked different to the right. There was more blood and some sort of clear fluid too. She frowned as she positioned her hands to lift the lid.

Then she turned her head and vomited on the ground beside them, heaving silently as the image of Gareth Collier's empty eyeball socket seared itself into her brain.

"Sarge?" Collier whispered. "You okay?"

She nodded, then remembered he couldn't see her. He'd probably never see her, or anything else, ever again. She choked back the sob even as the tears fell. "Yeah, I'm okay." Her voice cracked.

"You puked. I can smell it."

"Yeah, I...erm...I took a knock to the back of the head, kid. Probably a concussion."

"You sitting down?"

She smiled. He wasn't such a bad guy. She'd dreaded having to work with him after how badly he'd clashed with Tom and the way he'd conducted himself in the various other cases they'd worked together. But, really, he wasn't such a bad guy. Just immature. "Kneeling. I'll be all right. But, Gareth, your eye's...well..."

"It's okay, Sarge. There was something stuck in that one. A rod, metal or something, and I was stupid. I grabbed it and pulled it out." He held his hand out palm upwards. "The metal was hot and I dropped it somewhere, but...but..."

Kate wrapped her arms about his shoulders and leant against him, resting her head next to his. "Help'll be here soon, I'm sure." She turned her head just enough to catch sight of the metal spike Gareth had pulled from his own eye. The hot sharp point had severed what she was pretty sure was the optic nerve, and Gareth's eyeball clung to the shard. Blood and fluid dripped from the rent tissue, weeping its own twisted tears onto the snow. She looked up and spotted those two icicles again, glinting against the light. Kate needed to focus on something innocuous, something benign, if she hoped to keep it together. And she needed to keep it together. She stared at those tiny frozen shards, committed their sparkle and shimmer to memory, and breathed out slowly as she let that image stain the back of her eyelids.

"Have you called it in?" Gareth's voice was shaky and broken.

"Shit. No, I've got to—"

"Go on. I'm not going anywhere." He patted her arm gently, and she wrapped her hand around his, squeezing his fingers.

She pushed the button on her airwave set. "Sir, ma'am, this is Brannon at the rear alleyway of Diamond Street, and I'm declaring a major incident, we need help."

"Kate, it's Clare. What the fuck happened out there?"

"Ma'am, the lock-up... It was rigged to blow. Possibly a remote detonation, because everyone was falling back when it went off. We've got multiple casualties. We need paramedics, fire service, and a police cordon, ASAP."

"How many casualties, Kate?"

"I'll be back, Gareth." She stood up and started to walk towards the site of the explosion.

Commander Jack Dalton was on the ground, looking straight up at the sky. His hips and legs were three feet away from the rest of his body. A razor-sharp sheet of metal that had once been the door to Ayeshydi's lock-up had severed him in two with the force of the blast. Palmer lay face down, in one piece, but not moving. Kate held her fingers to his neck, checking for a pulse. There was none.

She kept scanning around for people, looking for any that were moving, any that were crying or calling for help. Fortunately there were more of them than those who weren't. She could see Vinny on his knees, holding a wad of cloth to Mel's shoulder while she struggled to her feet.

"Kate?" Clare's voice was shrill over the radio.

"Sorry, ma'am. I make it two dead and ten wounded in the alleyway. Unsure of wounded in the houses, but I suspect more. The windows have all been blown in."

"Fuck."

"Ma'am, can you get hold of Commissioner Collier? He's...well, Gareth's...injured."

A pause on the line and then she heard ringing from her own personal mobile phone. She answered quickly and just remembered to let go of the button on her airwave handset. Commissioner Collier was Gareth's father and the reason that young Collier had joined the force to begin with. Throughout his career, Gareth's driving force had been to make his family proud by getting as far, if not further, up in the ranks than his father had.

"Critical?" Timmons asked.

"No, sir, he'll live. But he's lost one eye, and the other's in bad shape. I'll be very surprised if he's not blind."

"Bloody hell. Where's Dalton? I've been trying to get him on the radio."

"Dead, sir. Palmer too. They were closest to the unit when it...when it exploded."

"Right. Everything's on its way, Brannon. I'm getting in my car now. Find out what's going on in those houses if you can."

"Sir."

"Wait. Are you hurt?"

"Knock on the head. I'll be fine."

"You sure?"

"Positive."

"Right. Be there in five."

Kate stepped over bricks and twisted metal until she stood beside Vinny and Mel. "Can you walk, Mel?"

"Yeah, if this tosser would let me the fuck up." She scowled at Vinny as he continued to hold a huge wad of something that looked like a coat over Mel's shoulder.

He ignored Mel and spoke directly to Kate. "How long until the troops come wading in?"

"Timmons said five minutes. I suspect less for the ambulances. I need to finish assessing the most critically injured." She turned and pointed to Gareth. "Any chance you two can move over and sit with Collier?"

Vinny narrowed his eyes. "Can't he come over here? I'm not keen on moving Mel. I don't want this wound to open up more."

"He's...he had shrapnel in an eye. When he pulled it out..." She pointed to her own eye and pulled her hand away quickly.

"Fuck." Mel staggered to her feet. "Not leaving the poor bastard on his own." She stumbled the twenty feet to Gareth's body, holding the coat over her shoulder as she went. Vinny blanched but followed, and Kate straightened up enough to walk around. She needed to know where to direct the medics when they arrived on scene.

She lurched forward, her headache making her unsteady as she went, but she put aside the thought that the bodies she was checking for pulses and open wounds were those of colleagues, people she'd been laughing and joking with not half an hour ago. Some she'd known for years, some just a couple of days, but every one of them, she knew. Kate couldn't think about that, though. She had to put that aside and deal with the task at hand.

Assessing the scene.

Using the clothes of the victims to cover the faces of those beyond help, she walked through the alleyway, leaving each victim where they had fallen.

By the time the first ambulance arrived, she'd found four dead bodies amongst the rubble and identified three that needed immediate attention. She directed the two paramedics to them. It was their call who they worked on first. She knew the third would be unlikely to make it to hospital, but there was little more she could do to help them with that as she was already giving him CPR. Fred Martin. Twenty-eight years old, father of three girls, all under five. The youngest only a few weeks old. Kate couldn't help but think about that baby and how she was probably going to grow up without any memories of her dad. Kate knew how that felt, and she wouldn't wish it on anyone. So she pictured her icicles and pounded on his chest harder. He wasn't going to die just because she didn't keep his heart pumping, too afraid to break a rib. Ribs would heal. Hearts wouldn't spontaneously start beating again.

Kate was entering her third cycle of reps when a pair of strong hands and a green coverall-clad figure pushed her away and took over. She nodded and teetered to the houses, first entering the one directly opposite the lock-up. The door hung off its hinges and glass from the windows crunched under her feet as she called out, "Hello? I'm a police officer. Does anyone need help in here?"

"Get out!" a man shouted, a thick Eastern European accent colouring his words. "Your fault! You!" He cradled a crying young girl in his arms, blood pouring from a gash in her belly.

Kate looked about the room and spotted the table in the middle of what looked to be a kitchen-cum-dining-room. She swept her arm across the surface, clearing it in one swipe. "Put her on here," she demanded, staring at him until he did. She grabbed a fist full of dishtowels from a hook where they hung and pressed them to the girl's belly, catching a glimpse of her intestines and the stench of sewage that could only mean part of the intestine was open. "Find me more towels."

The girl cried and wriggled as Kate pressed hard against the deep wound. "Hurts."

"I know, honey, I know. I'm sorry. But we'll get you some help now. One of those nice ambulance men is going to get you to the hospital, and they'll make this all better, okay?"

The girl nodded, and her father stepped back into the room, his arms full of heavy cloth. Kate nodded and grabbed a handful of fabric, discarded the claret-stained dishcloth, and replaced it in one seamless motion.

Kate looked the man in the eye. "There are paramedics outside. Tell them you have a child with a gut wound and a perforated intestine visible. Tell them she needs immediate evac."

He nodded but didn't move.

"Now! Go!" Kate screamed at him.

He jumped and tore out of the door. When she looked back at the girl, she was almost glad to see she'd passed out. She checked for a pulse and found it, weak and thready and growing fainter by the second. But for now, it was still there.

She couldn't have been more than seven or eight years old. Not even as old as Sammy. Kate shook her head and reached for another towel, ready to swap them out again. She didn't even want to guess at how much blood the kid had lost. However much was too much.

While Kate knew that Ayeshydi hadn't targeted this child, he would have known that she lived here. He may have even met her. She was his neighbour, after all. Yet now she was his victim, because there was no doubt in her mind that Ayeshydi had set this bomb off. Either he did it remotely or Palmer and Dalton had triggered something when they were searching it. Either way he was responsible for another four murders and God knew how many more injured today, including the sweet little girl dying on the table under Kate's hands.

"Come on, come on." She looked over her shoulder, desperate for someone, anyone, to come back in and take over. To do what Kate couldn't and save the child. "For fuck's sake, what's taking so long?" She swapped out another saturated towel and tried to ignore what it meant when blood didn't gush from the wound when she relieved the pressure. But she couldn't. "No, no, no, no. Don't you fucking die on me, kid. Don't you do that." She pressed her fingers to the girl's neck, then shifted them and pressed again. And again. And again. Finally, she found the tiny flutter of a heartbeat beneath her fingertips.

"Thank fuck," she whispered and looked up at the ceiling. Kate had never been a religious person. Never thought of herself as believing in much of anything beyond what she could see and deal with. Right now, she was ready to pray to whatever god there might be to keep this little girl alive.

Heavy footsteps pounded through the door behind her, and Kate glanced over her shoulder. She could have kissed the paramedic that ran in. He didn't bother to greet her, just took over, his partner right behind him. Between them, they got the girl on a stretcher, secured a dressing over her middle, and ran her out of the door. Within a minute, she was gone.

Kate never even learnt her name.

It was Timmons who pulled her to her feet. Kate didn't even remember sitting down on the glass-covered floor. It was Timmons who led her out of the back door and into a car, a foil blanket wrapped around her shoulders and a cup of something she hadn't even tasted in her hand.

She could see the fence from where she was sitting now. The wooden beam that her icicles had clung to—that she had clung to—weren't there anymore. A part of Kate wondered if they ever had been.

Questions bombarded her with every breath she took. *How the hell do you close your eyes after seeing all that? How do you get up in the morning and carry on?*

How did you sleep at night, knowing you caused all that?

She held her breath, wondering if it would make the questions stop. It didn't. So she closed her eyes and wondered what was going to happen next. And asked herself, more importantly, would she be able to cope with it?

CHAPTER 20

"So, let me get this straight," Jodi said. "You were more bothered about seeing your mum again, finding out the flowers were stolen, and getting this card than you were by being in the shop where a terrorist blew you all up?" Her voice spoke of her incredulity.

"Sounds a bit mad when you put it like that," Gina mumbled.

Jodi tipped her head to one side. A movement Gina had come to realise was Jodi's non-verbal way of saying "Ya think?"

"I see your point, I do. But that bomb wasn't anything to do with me. I was just in the wrong place at the wrong time. It literally could have been anyone. These flowers, the card...that's personal. It's addressed to me. It's someone who wants something from me. My mum, again, personal. Ally, personal. The bomb wasn't."

"Okay, I can see the point there. But don't you think it's also possible that you're in shock, Gina? That it hasn't really hit you yet? That maybe you're still processing what happened?"

Gina flung her hands up. "I thought you'd be pleased that I wasn't a gibbering wreck again."

Jodi chuckled. "Oh, I am. Believe me. But I am surprised. Gibbering wrecks are expected in these circumstances."

Gina smiled. "Fine. I'll try and work on my gibbering for next time."

"You do that. In the meantime, let's talk about your mum. What made you decide to let her in?"

"The bombing."

"How so?"

"Well, specifically Pat. I just couldn't stop thinking about her and how sad she was. How many regrets she seemed to have from not talking to George. It might not have made any difference to what happened in the end, but the not knowing...that was playing on my mind so much. After what Kate told me, everything my mum had told her about how my dad was... Well, I guess I needed to know. I think I've come to the conclusion that we're always going to regret something in life, and I'd rather regret something I've done or tried to do, rather than not and constantly wonder."

"I can understand that. And how do you feel about your mum now you've had a chance to hear what she had to say? Has it helped?"

"I...Well, I think I'm still trying to get my head around all of it. I can understand how she was depressed, or rather, that she was, and how difficult that must have made everything for her. And I can sympathise with her for it. But understanding it now doesn't really change anything that happened then. It doesn't make up for the fact that we had, at best, a strained relationship when I was growing up. It doesn't wash away the hurt or the years of being alone."

"No. Do you honestly think anything will?"

Gina shook her head. "I don't think that's possible."

"Do you wish it were?"

"Yes. I can see how growing up like that has...damaged me."

"I'm not sure I'd agree with that. Certainly growing up in the family you did has shaped you. But I'm not sure I'd agree that you're damaged, Gina. Certainly no more than anyone else is, anyway."

"Thanks, but I can see it. I can see how that negativity has affected my self-esteem. I can see how it's affected all my relationships, friendships."

"Not with Kate."

Gina smiled softly. "I think that's more about Kate than about me."

"Maybe. Or maybe you just needed the person to help you see beyond the hurt. I don't think she's the first person to see you. I just think she's the first person you've allowed to show you what they see when they look at you."

"Deep, Jodi." She tried to play off the thought-provoking insights as much as she could. Sometimes Jodi let her. Sometimes she didn't. Today she let it go.

"So, back to your mum, then. Do you think you can forge a relationship with her now?"

"I don't know if it's possible. Not now. So much has happened, so much hurt."

"Do you want to?"

Gina gave the question serious thought. Did she? What would it be like to have the kind of relationship where she could pick up the phone and call her mother? To ask for advice or to listen to each other complain about a shit day at work? To talk to about...things. Did she want that?

Who was she kidding? Of course she wanted that. She'd always wanted that. But it was a fantasy that had no bearing on reality. It was an "I wish", not a "could be" or even a "maybe". A fairy tale that she'd outgrown. Still, in an ideal world... "Yes, but like I said—"

Jodi held up her hand to quiet Gina. "To get over the past, you first have to accept that the past is over." She smiled. "No matter how many times you revisit it, analyse it, regret it, or sweat it...it's over. It can hurt you no more."

"Again with the deep."

"Not mine this time. Mandy Hule, I believe. I saw it on one of those memes on Facebook, but the truth of it stayed with me. If you want to move forward, Gina, let go of the past. It's doing you no favours, and it can only hurt you now if you let it."

"I guess."

"Just think about it. Remember your new philosophy. Regret what you did or tried to do...not what you didn't."

Gina rolled her eyes and refused to admit out loud that she agreed. And she would try. Her phone buzzed. "Sorry, I left it on in case there was a problem with Sammy."

"It's fine."

Gina glanced at the screen to see a missed call from Kate. And a second from DI Timmons. She frowned.

"Everything okay?"

"I don't know. It's Kate and her boss." She pressed the button to call Kate and mouthed "sorry" to Jodi. Jodi waved the apology away. After a moment, it went through to voicemail. She tried Timmons's number.

"Yeah?"

"Mr Timmons, this is Gina Temple, I've had a missed—"

"Thank God. Brannon's been chewing my ear off to get hold of you. She's on her way to Queen Elizabeth's."

"Why's she on her way to the hospital?" Gina's heart leapt into her throat, almost choking off the words. "What's happened to her?"

"Banged her head when the blast threw her into a wall—"

"What!" Gina was on her feet, pacing as she listened and tried to make sense of the words. But they didn't make sense. What blast? What wall? What the hell?

"Can't go into details, Miss Temple, but there was an explosion as my officers were carrying out their duties. Kate wasn't seriously hurt, but she's taken a knock to the head. I want her checked out. So she's on her way to the hospital to do just that. She refused to go unless we let you know. So now you know."

"Is she already at the hospital?"

"She's on her way there now. Maybe a few minutes away."

"Okay, thank you for letting me know."

"No problem." Gina pulled the phone away from her ear to disconnect when his voice called, "Miss Temple?"

"Yes?"

"Look after her."

"I will."

"And tell her I'll be in to check up on her later."

Gina smiled. "I will." The line was dead before she finished saying the words. She opened her mouth to speak, but Jodi cut her off.

"Go. By the time you get across the grounds, she'll be there and you can make sure she's okay."

"Thank you." She slapped her hand to her forehead. "Shit, Sammy."

"Leave her here for the time being. When you know what's going on with Kate, you can get her then." Jodi scribbled on a piece of paper and handed it to Gina. "Text me when you know. Sammy will be fine with the other kids for a bit."

Gina nodded. Not an ideal solution, but she didn't want to drag Sammy over there only for her to be traumatised seeing Kate badly hurt. "Thanks."

Adrenaline surged through her, pumping energy-giving blood to her muscles and fuelling her brain in a random series of thoughts that bounced from *please don't let her be badly hurt* to *I want to kill the son of a bitch who hurt her* and back again. Every second seemed to last at least an hour as she punched at the door releases to let her out of the building.

The Reman unit that housed the mental health facilities at the Queen Elizabeth Hospital was a three-minute walk from the main entrance of the accident and emergency ward. Or, as Gina found out, a two-minute run, when you're not very fit. No matter how much her lungs protested, she kept going. Every muscle-ripping step brought her closer to making sure Kate was okay. To seeing her face and holding her again and making sure she never, ever let go. Never. She wasn't ever leaving Kate's side.

Gasping for air, she tapped on the receptionist's window and managed a sputtered "Kate Brannon?"

"Are you related?"

"She's my partner."

The woman nodded and tapped on her keyboard. "Did you say *Brannon?*"

"Yes."

"I'm not showing—"

The ambulance bay doors opened, and Kate was wheeled in on a stretcher. "That's her!" Gina pointed over the woman's shoulder. Craning her head around, the woman nodded and buzzed the entry door. Gina yanked it open and ran after Kate, catching a glimpse of her just as the curtain was pulled shut behind her. Gina didn't hesitate for even a second as she slipped between the curtains and pushed her way to Kate's side, her hands finding Kate's arm instantly.

Kate jumped. "Bloody hell, how'd you get here before me? You okay?"

Gina nodded, her gaze scanning Kate for every bump and scrape. There was dust all over her. And blood. Lots and lots of blood. There was a raw graze on her chin, and her hands were covered in little scratches. No doubt under her clothes there would be bruises...just like the ones that covered Gina's body after the explosion two days ago, but otherwise, Kate didn't look any worse for wear.

Gina couldn't stop herself; she cradled Kate's face between her hands, bent forward, and captured her lips in a kiss. Just to be sure she was really there, really okay. The panic she'd been fighting tumbled down her cheeks as tears of relief fell at the solid feel of Kate beneath her fingertips, beneath her lips.

"I was with Jodi," she said quietly when she pulled back and swiped the tears from her face.

"Ah." Kate leant back against the bed. "Timmons finally get hold of you, then?"

"Yeah, he said—"

A throat being cleared behind them grabbed their attention. Kate blushed and murmured, "Sorry, Doc."

"No worries." He smirked as he stepped forward and bent over Kate. "I'll just finish my assessment so we can get on with important stuff, shall I?"

Gina turned to see the same doctor who had treated her and Stella just a couple of days ago.

Dr Gilad shone his penlight in Kate's eyes, made her follow his finger, touch her nose, squeeze his fingers, and do all the other crap they made you do when you'd smashed your head into a wall, and then he shoved the light back in his pocket. "You have a nasty lump on the back of your head, a mild concussion, and no doubt a headache. But otherwise, you are a very lucky lady."

Kate looked at him, and Gina tried to read her expression. There was a sadness to it, a resolution, but something else too, something Gina had never seen in Kate's eyes before. And she didn't know what to make of that.

"I know. Is there any news on the little girl?"

"Name?"

Kate shook her head. "I don't know. Stomach wound. Bowel perforation."

"Why the interest?"

"I was holding her guts in till the paramedics scooped her."

"That was you?"

Kate nodded. "Did she make it?"

"She's in surgery now. She lost a hell of a lot of blood. Last I heard, she'd had four units already, but the team is working on her. I don't know any more than that."

"Thank you. How old is she?"

"Six."

Kate closed her eyes. "Even younger than I thought."

"Yes, we were a little surprised. Her name is Anastacia Pekov, by the way. Now, you get some rest, I'll get a nurse in to clean those cuts and scrapes, then we can get you out of here. No reason your lady can't take care of you at home, and I can use this bed for someone who needs it." He winked at her. "Sound good to you?"

"Sounds perfect, Doc."

"Good. The nurse will bring some information on what to keep an eye out for with concussions and head injuries," he said to Gina. "But I really don't expect any problems. Rest. That's the best cure." He tapped his hand on the rail at the side of the bed and slipped out of the cubicle.

Gina reached for Kate and kissed her again. "Are you really okay?" She ran her hands up and down Kate's arms, over her shoulders and her back, and quickly over her legs. "Not hiding anything from me under those jeans?"

"Just my legs, I promise." Kate smirked. "Want me to show you?"

Gina's lips twitched into a smile. "Well, don't these all have to go into evidence, Detective?"

"That's a very good point, Miss Temple. Think you can scrounge me up a pair of scrubs?"

"Probably not, but Timmons is coming to check up on you soon. He'll have one of those paper suits for you, I'm sure."

Kate shuddered. "Gee, thanks." She ran her hands up Gina's arms. "You okay?"

She chuckled and nodded. "You scared the shit out of me."

"Sorry."

"Don't do that again."

"Hey, you got blown up first."

"Oh, so was this a taste of my own medicine, was it?" Gina couldn't keep her hands still. She had to touch Kate everywhere. She just had to.

"I was just doing my job. You've yet to tell me what you were up to in Ann Summers, by the way." Kate's eyebrow arched, and her smile was positively wicked.

Gina blushed. "You'll never know now."

"Evil."

"Knock, knock." A nurse pulled open the curtain and stepped inside. "Kate Brannon?"

"That's me," Kate said from the bed.

"Good. I hear you've got some scrapes and cuts that need cleaning and a concussion we can't do anything about. That sound about right?"

"Sounds like what the doctor said."

The nurse smiled, her white teeth standing out against her dark skin. "Good enough for me." She busied herself getting her station set up to Kate's left and pulled in a stool. She sat and looked over at Gina. "Do you want to get a coffee or something while I do this, love? Won't take many minutes."

"Actually, I think I'll go and get Sammy. She's hanging out with some other kids in a kind of temporary day care over at the Reman unit." She kissed Kate again and smiled. "Won't be long."

"Won't she get upset?" Kate waved a hand at her blood-covered clothes.

"I'll get you something to wear, girly," the nurse said. "Don't want your little girl all worried about her mama being hurt worse than she is if we don't have ta."

"Oh, she's not my—" Kate started.

"That would be great, thank you," Gina said, meeting Kate's startled gaze. As far as Gina was concerned, that was exactly where they were headed. Gina loved her, and Sammy loved her. The rest was just semantics.

"I love you," Kate whispered.

"Love you too." She kissed Kate's forehead. "Now, behave, or I'll tell Sammy you cried like a baby."

"Low blow, Temple."

The nurse snickered and started running cotton wool over the cuts on Kate's left hand. Kate hissed, and Gina pulled the curtain closed behind her.

"So, how old's your little girl?" the nurse asked as Gina started to move away, a smile stretching across her lips. Kate was whole and healthy, and everything was okay. Everything was perfectly okay.

CHAPTER 21

"Couldn't even let me get blown up and concussed without trying to copy me."

Stella Goodwin stood beside the curtain as the nurse left, a set of scrubs laid at the bottom of Kate's bed.

Kate grinned. "Well, it looked like a good way to get some time off. They've been working us like dogs since your little fireworks party."

"Fireworks? That the best you could do?"

Kate shrugged. "Concussion."

Stella sniggered, then sobered. "Seriously, kid, you okay?"

Stella was only ten years older than Kate, but in police terms, ten years was a lifetime, and being called 'kid' by someone you respected in a situation like this...that was like winning the jackpot.

"Yeah, I'm okay." She took a deep breath. "Did you hear about Collier?"

Stella nodded. "Have you heard the update?"

"Not heard anything since he was evacuated from the scene."

"The second eye had to be removed. The metal fragments were embedded so deep, they couldn't extract them safely. The eye was beyond saving."

"Poor bastard. How's he taken it?"

"Not come around yet. His dad's up there. I heard you ordered Chief Inspector Green to call him. Ballsy."

"Clare and I go back a long way."

"I heard that too. You okay?"

Kate shrugged. "I've had better weeks. Same as you."

Stella perched on the edge of Kate's bed. "You know where I am if you wanna talk."

Kate nodded.

"And when your head's right, we're going out and getting well and truly rat-arsed."

Kate let her head rest back against the pillows. "Good plan." She hoisted herself into a sitting position and swung her legs off the bed. "Gina'll be here with Sammy in a minute. I want to get out of these bloodstained clothes so I don't scare her."

"That kid saw a dead body with its face blown off. A few bloodstains aren't going to scare her."

Kate inclined her head. "It's a fair point you make, but still. I'd rather not add to the traumatisation of a minor if I can help it." She waved her hand at Stella. "Pull me up."

"What did your last slave die of?" Stella asked as she gripped her hand and tugged Kate to her feet.

"Insubordination."

Stella barked out a laugh. "At least the concussion's improved your sense of humour."

"It was classic to begin with." Kate pulled her jumper over her head, quickly followed by her T-shirt and jeans. Her underwear had survived stains, and her socks and boots...well, they were a necessity to getting home. The scrubs were clean, comfortable, and surprisingly warm for how thin they felt.

"I've got a spare jumper you can use." Stella handed one over. "It'll be a bit big on you, but it'll keep you warm till you get home at least."

"Are you escaping today?"

"Yup. Thought I'd try and cadge a lift with you since you're on a catch-and-release program."

"Funny." She tugged the woollen jumper over her head. Stella was right, it was too big. Stella's impressive bust required at least an extra two dress sizes to Kate's more modest bosom. But warm was warm, and fashion was just a state of mind. Or some shit like that. "I think we could convince Gina to drive us both. You can always try a guilt trip on her if she looks like complaining. She dragged you to the sex shop explosion after all."

Stella grinned wickedly. "So she did." She stroked her chin, looking like some kind of deranged Bond villain. "So she did."

The curtain was yanked back, and Timmons stared at them both. He frowned at Stella, shook his head, and gave Kate the up-and-down look of someone inspecting a specimen.

"Glad you're both here. Saves me an extra trip, or repeating myself."

"Sir? Wasn't expecting to see you here." Stella crossed her arms over her chest.

"I told Miss Temple I'd be over shortly to check up on everyone." He looked at Stella. "Glad you're all right, Goodwin. I've been worried about you."

Stella raised an eyebrow but didn't say anything.

He cleared his throat. "Right, I've had a word with your doctor, Brannon, and he's told me you need a good week to recover from this."

"A week! Sir, he's sending me home—" The look on Timmons's face shut her up.

"That's right. A week. Head injuries in the line of duty are nothing to be messed with." He leant forwards and spoke quietly. So quietly that Kate had to strain to hear him "Three days. That's what he said. You need three days to recover. So take the three days, then I need you and Goodwin chasing something for me. Something major fucking important."

"Sir, I can't..." He pushed a piece of paper and a mobile phone into her hand.

"Play along," he whispered. "I don't know who's listening." He straightened up.

She squinted at him, then nodded. "I can't lie around for thre—for a week doing nothing while there a fucking terrorist out there blowing the world up!"

"You will follow doctor's orders, Brannon, or you'll ride out this investigation behind a desk. Am I clear?"

"Crystal," she spat out through ground teeth.

He grinned and gave her a thumbs up. "That was good work out there today. Your warning gave those boys a few seconds to move back, and saved lives."

"Not enough lives."

"It never is. But if you hadn't thought it, hadn't said it...well, I've little doubt the whole CTU team would be dead now."

"What's the count?"

"Five dead. Six still critical, and three of those in surgery. Fifteen injured, including Brown, Collier, and you. Jackson was the lucky bastard out there today. Just a few bumps and scrapes."

"What about Mallam?"

"Unaccounted for."

"What?" Kate and Stella both said at the same time.

"Missing. The site is being searched. Do you remember where he was before the explosion?"

Kate tried to recall the scene. She remembered stepping back to the far wall so she could see the front of the street as well as get a view of the lock-up. She remembered the car and the officer running out with the optics kit bag. Vinny, Mel, and Gareth had been peering around the wall opposite her, watching the garages, watching the tactical team. Mallam had been behind them, leaning against the wall. Right in the spot that should have been out of the blast path, protected by the houses.

"He was about ten feet along the wall from where Jackson, Brown, and Collier were stood, but he had his back flat to the wall. He wasn't even looking at the CTU team. He was..." She closed her eyes and tried to picture exactly what he'd been doing. She'd only had a peripheral view of him, but he was doing something, looking at something in his hands. What was it...? Her eyes snapped open, and her jaw slackened.

Timmons's gaze bore into hers, silently begging her not to say what she now realised she'd seen. He tapped the phone he'd put in her hand and mouthed "later" to her. She nodded.

"He was what?" Timmons then prompted.

She licked her lips. "I'm not sure, sir. Everything's a bit blurry."

"The doctor said to expect that. Concussion can be like that, Brannon. Not to worry. We'll find him."

And then he was gone.

Stella stared at her, hands held out in question, her face asking *what the fuck?*

Kate didn't know where to begin. One thing was for sure, things were not what they seemed, and she was definitely going to need these three days to get her head straight and figure out what was going on.

She unfolded the piece of paper and held it out for Stella to read.

My number's programmed in the phone. Call me—and only me—
when you get home.

"The plot thickens," Stella said.

"You can say that again."

Stella opened her mouth.

"Don't."

"Well, don't you two look cosy?" Gina stepped up to Kate and kissed her on the lips. Sammy grabbed hold of the railing at the side of the bed and rested her chin on top of it. She didn't say a word. Stella ruffled Sammy's hair.

"You keeping your mum out of trouble?"

Sammy shrugged. Her eyes hadn't left Kate's face.

Kate did what came naturally to her. She took hold of Sammy's hand and tugged her close, hoisted her onto the bed, and tucked her against her body, arms wrapped tight around her. She kissed the top of her head and whispered, "I'm okay, kiddo." She held her hand out, little finger extended. "Pinky swear."

Sammy wrapped her little finger around Kate's, then turned in her embrace, tucking her face into Kate's neck and wrapping her arms around her as far as she could reach.

Gina clasped her hands in front of her mouth as she watched them, her brow furrowed as she visibly fought to keep her own emotion in check.

"I'm not crying." Sammy's voice was muffled against Kate's neck, but she could feel how wet her skin was.

"I know." She stroked Sammy's back, rubbing soothing circles until she was almost ready to fall asleep; the motion was hypnotic. Eventually Sammy pulled back and wiped her hands over her face and hair.

"Can we go home yet?"

"I've been ready for ages, kiddo. I was just waiting for you."

"I was waiting for you!" Sammy jumped off the bed. "Can we get something to eat? I'm starving."

Gina rolled her eyes. "What's new?"

"We're near my favourite pizza place." She wiggled her eyebrows comically.

"No."

"But I need food, Mum. I'm wasting away!" She grabbed Kate's hand as they made their way out of the hospital, waving at the nurse as they passed her.

"Not pizza again. You're going to end up looking like a pizza."

Sammy frowned as if she was trying to decide if that was a bad thing or not. Then she shrugged. "Okay, what about some nice, healthy chicken instead? KFC's only—"

"No junk food."

Sammy stopped mid-stride, tugging on Kate's hand. "That's abuse."

Kate urged her back into motion and across the road.

"Tell her, Kate."

"No can do." She dropped her voice to a conspiratorial whisper. "I'm just her girlfriend. She's your mum...and you're the kid." She shrugged. "That makes her the boss."

Sammy scowled. "Bumholes."

"Sammy!" Gina squawked.

Kate and Stella laughed loudly.

CHAPTER 22

Kate sat on the deep leather sofa, her feet tucked under her bottom, glass of water resting on the thick padded arm beside her, fingers wrapped loosely around it as she watched a tiny air bubble escape the bottom and rise to the top. She kept playing the last few seconds before the explosion over and over in her head.

Stella was sipping her coffee and flicking through her phone while Gina put Sammy to bed.

At least Kate's headache had begun to subside. The phone Timmons had given her stared accusingly at her from next to her water glass. Was there any way she could have warned the team sooner? Could she have saved their lives? Would Gareth still be able to see?

"Stop it." Stella didn't even look up from her phone.

"What?"

"I can hear the self-recrimination from here."

Kate laid her head back against the leather with a heavy sigh. "I can't help it. I should have thought about it sooner. I should have said something to the team sooner."

"Kate, you're a good detective, but you're not a counterterrorism officer. They were. They spent months, years even, training as firearms officers, counterterrorism officers, specialists. They were the ones who should have thought about it sooner. Not you. They were trained to think like terrorists to try and stop the bastards."

"But—"

"No, no buts." She shut off her phone and gave Kate her full attention. "As soon as you thought of the possibility that those bombs could be detonated remotely, what did you do?"

"Called it in."

"Did you think about it for a minute first? Worry you might look a dick if you were wrong before pulling your thumb out of your arse and doing the right thing?"

"No."

"Then you did everything you could. More than anyone else there, and whether you realise it or not, you saved lives today, Kate." She shook her head. "Trust me when I tell you that, right there, saving lives, is the very best you can hope for in a situation like this." She leant forward, elbows braced on her knees. "Because you sure as shit can't stop it." She hung her head. "For the last couple of days, literally all I've thought about was whether or not I could have done something or said something that would have saved even one person before they pushed those buttons. But I didn't. I didn't shout at them to stop, I didn't warn people who hadn't seen it. I didn't even try to talk to them. I just turned my back and tried to survive."

"That's not true," Gina said from the doorway between the living room and the kitchen. "You tried to get me out. You told me to go."

Stella laughed sardonically. "Didn't even manage to get you out safely, did I?"

"You still kept me safe." Gina crossed the room and sat next to her, taking her hand in her own. "You saved my life." She kissed her cheek and wrapped her arms around Stella's shoulders. "You did everything you could."

Stella pulled away, waving her hand in the air like she was swatting a fly. "Ah, don't listen to me waffling on. I don't know anything."

"Bullshit." Kate's voice was quiet, tired, but steady. "You're right, we both did everything we could in fucking awful situations. It was the best we could do, the most anyone would expect of us, but we both know it will never be enough. We can't bring back those men and women who died. We can't give those kids the lives they'll never have. We can't make Gareth see again. So you know what we're going to do instead?"

Stella and Gina both looked at her in silence.

"We're going to catch the fuckers who did it. And we're going to show them that they will never, ever fucking win. They want to make us too scared to live the lives we have. Not going to happen. They want us to question everything, ourselves, what we believe in, who we love, absolutely everything. Well, I'm not going to let them. They've taken enough, Stella. I will not give them my fear or my self-confidence. And you better not either." She pointed her finger at her. "Or you will have me to deal with."

A grin spread slowly over Stella's lips, and she clapped her hands together in a steady beat of applause, gradually increasing it. "You should think about politics when you've wiped terrorism off the map."

Kate screwed up her nose. "No, ta. There's enough politics in policing. I don't think I could take any more."

The knock at the door made Kate jump. She looked at Gina and asked, "Expecting any one?"

Gina shook her head. "I'll go see who it is." She pulled the door to the kitchen closed behind her.

Kate knew it was to make sure their voices didn't awaken Sammy or keep her awake. Not that much would wake her once she was asleep. Except maybe a bomb.

I shouldn't use that as a joke anymore. It's loses all the humour when it's a distinct possibility.

"So, what do you think that was all about with the DI?" Stella asked quietly.

"I wish I could say I don't know, but I think it might have to do with our so-called 'friendly' spook Zain Mallam."

Stella rolled her hand for Kate to continue.

"Timmons said he was unaccounted for, right?"

Stella nodded.

"Meaning?"

"Probably dead, given there was an explosion."

Kate shook her head. "Mallam was stood in the most sheltered spot possible, given where the blast came from. He had the wall of the terraced houses at his back between him and the garage. He was too far away for shrapnel to have caught him, unless it can go around corners, and the wall was still standing, so no chance of him being buried underneath it."

"So unaccounted for means what?"

Kate didn't want to say it, because she didn't want it to be true. "Missing? But why?"

"Good question, Goodwin," Timmons said from the doorway.

"Sir?" Kate started to stand, but he waved her back down and sat down heavily next to Stella. "I thought you were going to call."

"Yeah, decided it was best discussed face-to-face. Didn't expect you to start without me."

Stella smirked. "Don't worry. We didn't get very far. So, what's the story with this guy?"

Timmons scrubbed his hand over his face and raked his fingers through his hair. "Okay, so my gut was all hinky about this dude. His attitude in those meetings was just wrong. I get that there's a lot of arse covering going on, but he was giving us nothing. Literally nothing. Then he walks out in front of you all and gives you the entire life story of Ishman Ayeshydi. The only other person who might have known that info was Porter, but if he did, he wasn't giving us anything before that either."

Kate frowned. "Has the information been corroborated by any other source?"

"You mean other than the diary leading us to a lock-up that then exploded?"

"Fair point," she conceded.

He sighed. "So is yours, and to answer the question, no. Supposedly Porter's trying to 'find out more about Ayeshydi', but I'm not holding my breath that he's going to find us anything."

"Why?"

"I think they've got a problem with their intelligence network and they don't want anyone to know that."

"You think Mallam got lucky in what he gave us being borne out by the diary?"

He shook his head. "Too coincidental."

"Then what are you saying, sir?"

"Something that I can't make sense of right now. Just...I don't know...just keep an open mind, and look at everything with fresh eyes."

"We always do, sir."

"I know. Just... Grimshaw's going to be sending you some stuff when he can. The rest of the diary and some other things he's looking into. He wasn't happy with Mallam either. Apparently, he's finding sources I don't want to know about or else I'd have to kill myself, never mind him."

Kate furrowed her brow. "Surely even Grimshaw isn't mad enough to try and hack the security services."

"I'm sure he isn't." Timmons looked far from convinced.

What was the saying? Plausible deniability? Yeah, they didn't have that. "What do you suspect, sir?"

He looked Kate in the eye. "Tell me what you saw. What was he doing before the explosion?"

She swallowed. "He was standing in a safe area, not looking at the garage, or any of the team. He was looking at his phone. When I wondered about the remote detonation, he gave me this look." She tried to mimic the look of grudging respect Mallam had directed at her. "Then he looked back at his phone again, and it exploded."

The words hung heavy and pregnant in the air, slowly giving birth to the thoughts Kate had been trying to ignore since she'd remembered what she'd seen. One thought led to another until she wasn't sure which was real, which was imagination, and which was purely nightmare. No, that wasn't quite right. Every single thought belonged in the realm of nightmares. He was a security agent. He had been screened, thoroughly. By many people, many times over his career. Agents like him had to have been in order to pass security clearance. Those guys read top secret files like the morning paper. They had to be cleaner than clean. Even if they were bastards. It was part of the make-up that made them able to do the job they had to do. They had to be focused like lasers on getting the mission accomplished and nothing else.

"Sir, what if we're seeing bad where there's simply more going on than we're privy to?"

"Entirely possible, Brannon. Let's face it, Porter and Mallam gave us jack shit in the way of useful leads or intelligence. What are you thinking?"

"I don't know. Is it possible they were put there to see what we learnt, more than to give us anything?"

Timmons nodded. "Sure it is. But then why did he disappear? Why isn't he still gathering intelligence from us? We're learning more and more all the time."

"Porter's still with you."

"Porter's still with us."

"What's he said about Mallam?"

"Hasn't worked with him before, but he's heard a lot of good things about him. Up-and-coming young officer, from what he said. Given the current situation, security services have been trying to recruit more Muslims. Mallam was one of the first to sign up following the London bombings. Apparently, he's done a lot of work undercover since then, infiltrating mosques, staying close to fellas suspected of radicalising youngsters and recruiting for IS."

Kate's head was beginning to ache again.

Timmons stood up. "Get some rest, the pair of you. You look like shit."

Kate chuckled. "And you wonder why you're still single, sir?"

He snorted. "Nope, I know it's because I'm a grumpy old bastard with a buried six-pack and thinning hair." He tapped his belly and buttoned up the coat he hadn't even taken off. "Take the next day or so, read through the diary, and see what you find. Grimshaw's working on more stuff, so we'll see where we're at."

She stood up to walk him to the door, and Stella stood up too. "Any chance I can grab a lift with you, sir? Save Gina having to go out again or call a taxi."

"Of course." He dipped his head and strode purposefully out of the house.

"I'll be here by nine. Have the kettle on." Stella plucked her coat from the peg beside the front door.

Kate mimed kissy-faces at her as she slid it on her shoulders.

"Piss off." Then Stella slammed the door hut behind her.

Kate sniggered and walked slowly back to the front room, wondering where Gina was. Probably gone to bed. The stab of disappointment at the thought wasn't a surprise, though the intensity of it was. She didn't want to miss saying goodnight to Gina. She didn't want to leave the little things left unsaid. Those were the things people always said they wished they'd done differently when life went to shit. Well, life was pretty shit, and Kate was determined that she wasn't going to regret the details.

She climbed the stairs slowly so she didn't spill the glass of water she wanted to take up with her, the thumping in her head increasing with each step. The door to the spare room was closed tight. She sighed and decided to put her glass down and then see just how quietly she could open that door and whisper words Gina would probably not even hear.

But when she opened her own bedroom door, Gina was sitting on the bed, her back against the headboard, her knees raised in front of her, forearms resting on top of them. She looked so unsure of herself, sat in a long T-shirt and the loose cotton shorts she wore for bed.

Kate wasn't sure what was going on, but she didn't want to disturb the beautiful picture that was Gina on her bed.

Gina's jaw and throat worked until words slid quietly past her lips. "I know you're exhausted, and I know this is...well, I know we've not...I just...I don't expect anything...I mean with us..." She waved her hand between them, her voice laced with the threads of love and fear in equal measure. "I could've lost you today."

"You didn't."

"No." She held out her hand. "But I don't want to waste any more time."

Kate stepped forward, taking hold of Gina's hand as she set her glass down on the bedside table. She perched on the edge of the bed next to her, lacing their fingers together, then leant over and ghosted a whisper of a kiss onto Gina's lips. "I get it." And she did. In the past few days they'd come close to losing each other, and it had certainly helped Kate to realise exactly what she did and didn't want. Apparently, it had done the same for Gina too. "There is nothing I want more than to make love to you, so please, please don't think this is an excuse, but I have a headache."

Gina chuckled and threaded her fingers into Kate's hair. "Poor baby." She kissed the tip of her nose. "We've got plenty of time to get to that. Can I hold you tonight?" She looked so vulnerable, almost scared to ask for what she wanted, for what Kate wanted too.

"How about we hold each other?"

Gina's eyes shone in the light coming from the landing. "You get ready for bed, then. I'll just check on Sammy, and turn out the light when you're ready." She slipped off the bed and out of the room, Kate staring after her.

The hinge of the door to the spare room creaked, spurring Kate into action. A quick change of attire. Her face washed—gingerly—her teeth scrubbed vigorously. Within a couple of minutes, Kate was sitting on the edge of her bed. Waiting.

She didn't have to wait long.

Gina stood silhouetted in the doorway, hands braced against the wood either side of her. "You okay?"

"Yea—" Kate's voice squeaked. She cleared her throat and tried again. "Yeah."

Gina's arm moved, and the light disappeared. Only the sliver of moonlight crept through the cracks in the curtains and danced across the carpet, turning everything to shadow. Soft footsteps across the carpet approached, and the gentle shifting of the mattress under Gina's weight alerted Kate to her every movement.

"Are you in?" Gina whispered, and the bedclothes rustled.

"One sec." Kate scooted around until she was under the duvet, laid flat on her back, with the covers pulled up to her chin. The mattress dipped, and Kate jumped at the soft touch of Gina's fingers finding her arm.

"Sorry." She started to pull back.

Kate grasped her hand, desperate to maintain the contact. "Just startled. Don't go." The words had barely left her mouth when Gina tugged on Kate's arm to give her space to settle her head on Kate's shoulder. She wrapped one arm about Kate's waist and slithered her leg over Kate's thigh, pinning her to the bed. And Kate had never been so thrilled to be unable to move. Tightening her arm about Gina's shoulder, she pressed a kiss against Gina's hair and sighed, content for the first time in...as long as she could remember.

This was what she'd needed. Intimacy. Something she had sought and thought she'd found with Mel. But the first time she'd held Mel in her arms like this...it hadn't felt anything like the way she felt now. She breathed in the apple fragrance of Gina's shampoo, the coconut body lotion she used, and the lingering scent underneath it that was Gina and Gina alone.

It was the first time she'd hold Gina through the night. And the last time she'd get to experience this first flush of intimacy. Because there would never be anyone else for her. Not now.

"I won't," Gina whispered and dropped a kiss on the hollow between Kate's collarbones, right at the bottom of her throat.

Kate frowned. "You won't what?"

"Go." She lifted her head, and Kate sought her eyes in the dark, wishing she could see Gina's face. "You said not to go."

"Oh, right." Kate laughed with relief. "So I did."

Gina's weight shifted on her body, and Kate felt her breath against her lips just before Gina captured them. It was a sweet kiss, a gentle kiss, one that was more promise than passion. A kiss that was perfect.

"I'm never going anywhere."

CHAPTER 23

"Morning," Gina whispered, and Kate stirred beneath her.

A smile danced on Kate's lips as she turned her head. "Morning." She squeezed Gina's shoulders.

"How are you feeling this morning?"

"A little stiff, a lot sore, but the headache's gone, thank God."

"Good." Gina caressed her waist, her fingertips finding the velvety skin of her hip where her sleep shirt had ridden up during the night. She traced a lazy pattern and marvelled at how comfortable it felt to wake up like this. Like it was how they woke up every morning. *Well, it damn well should be. It will be.*

"You?"

"I'm good." She kissed Kate's chin, then put her head back down on her shoulder. There was something else they needed to talk about, but not right now. She didn't want the discussion of something…unpleasant to tarnish a place where she wanted only beautiful memories. Besides, there wasn't time. So Gina sighed and said, "Sammy will be up soon, but remind me in a bit when she's out playing to tell you about some stuff I found out yesterday."

"Everything okay?" Kate was frowning when Gina looked up again, her head lifted as high as she could.

"It's about the roses."

"Oh." Kate looked relieved and dropped her head back to her pillow.

"What did you think I wanted to talk about?"

Kate shrugged and ran her fingers up and down Gina's arm. "Maybe this."

"Really?"

Kate didn't say anything, just continued to stroke Gina's arm and stare up at the ceiling.

Gina propped herself up on her elbow. "Look at me." She waited until Kate was watching her closely. "I love you. I want you. I want to be with you in every way, for every day of my life." She ran her fingers over Kate's belly. "I know this has been a really weird start to our relationship, and I'm sorry if I worried you when I said I needed to tell you something. But please believe me when I tell you that there is nowhere else I want to be right now, and I wish we could stay here all day."

Kate's eyes sparkled in the early-morning light, and Gina knew they were both feeling the emotional aftermath of yesterday. She needed to break the tension, or they were both likely to end up crying.

Gina decided to let her naughty self out a little and let her explore. She slid her hand up the centre of Kate's tummy towards her ribs. "And one day, very, very soon, I intend to make you believe that."

Kate's breath hitched as Gina traced the line of one rib up to her breastbone and then let the sides of her fingers graze the inner flesh of Kate's breasts. She licked her lips and tussled with her own conscience. She hadn't been kidding. Sammy would be up any minute, and that was not how she wanted to start the day. But the need to touch Kate was so strong. She wanted to lift that shirt and run her tongue across her skin, taste her, devour her. She wanted to run her fingertips a little further to the left and feel the nipple she could see had hardened under the fabric. She wanted to memorise the texture with her lips.

"I believe you," Kate groaned. "You have to stop looking at me like that."

"I don't want to."

"Mum!"

Gina let her head drop to Kate's chest, her hand still resting on her breastbone. "Would it be wrong to string her up right now?"

"No. Extenuating circumstances."

"Good to know."

"Mum!"

Kate tapped her wrist and started to sit up, hindered dramatically by Gina's body still draped across her. She laughed, but finally managed to roll Gina onto her back so she could sit up as Sammy threw open the door.

"Whatchya doin' in here?" Sammy had her hands on her hips, feet set apart, and a frown on her face. "I woke up and didn't know where you were."

"I got sick of your snoring."

"Kate snores."

"I do not!"

"No, she doesn't." Kate and Gina said at the same time. "Besides, Kate's got a bigger bed."

Sammy studied it closely, then shrugged and jumped on it with a running leap, landing between the two of them on her back. She folded her hands behind her head and stared up at the ceiling. "You need a TV in here." She wriggled her bum around and nodded appreciatively. "Nice."

Kate sniggered. "Glad you approve. Breakfast?"

"You're gonna cook breakfast?"

She reached over and tickled Sammy's ribs. "Coco Pops don't require cooking. I can cope with them."

That made her giggle, and she tried to push Kate's hands away. Finally escaping, she broke for the stairs. "I'll let Merlin out."

"Put your slippers on if you're going outside!" Gina shouted after her, not sure if she could be heard over the heavy pounding of Sammy's feet. She grabbed Kate's hand. "You okay?"

"Are we going to tell her? About us?"

"She knows you're my girlfriend." Gina cocked her head. "What else would you like me to tell her?" She smirked as Kate blushed.

"I mean, I guess if last night was just...you know...if it was just last night, then I guess...I mean she's only nine, so..."

Gina sat up and turned, giving Kate her full attention. "Last night wasn't just last night. I'd sleep in here with you every night, if you'll have me."

Kate whimpered at the double entendre but didn't say anything.

"I meant every word, Kate." She took hold of her hand and kissed her knuckles. "I know you asked us to stay for Christmas, and I und—"

"I only said Christmas because I was too gutless to ask for what I really wanted."

Gina visibly swallowed. "And what was that?"

"I want you here. With me. Every day. Both of you. I want to wake up with you and go to sleep beside you and argue about who's helping Sammy with her homework or picking her up from school. I don't want you to go back to your house. I don't want this to be my house. I want it to be ours." She surged forward and pressed her mouth to Gina's.

Gina pulled back ever so slightly and whispered, "I haven't brushed my teeth yet."

"I really couldn't care less." Then her lips were on Gina's in a bruising kiss that had Gina moaning breathlessly as Kate pushed her onto her back and trailed a hand up her side.

"Kate! Merlin spilled the milk again!"

Kate growled as she broke this kiss and rolled off Gina's body. "Shouldn't she be in school today?"

"I've decided to keep her home. After everything that's happened and how she was last night with you, I just want to keep an eye on her for a few days."

"You're a really good mum."

"Hmm. Tell her that the next time she accuses me of abuse for not giving her junk food."

"I will." She pressed her lips to Gina's again.

"Kate! It's dribbling on the floor!"

Kate broke the kiss and shouted, "Coming" as she stood up.

Gina sniggered. "Welcome to the Temple family," she said as Kate reached the door.

Kate looked back over her shoulder. "The Brannon-Temple family." Then she was gone, and Gina stared up at the ceiling again, grinning.

"Brannon-Temple, huh?" She mulled it over for a minute. "I think I could get used to that."

"Mum, the postman's been," Sammy yelled up the stairs as Gina wrapped a towel around her body.

"Okay. Pop it on the table for Kate. She'll open it when she gets back from the shops." Merlin's milk spillage hadn't left them enough for breakfast.

Sammy appeared in the bathroom doorway with Merlin beside her. "Does Kate have to go to work today?" She handed the post envelopes to Gina. "There's one for you."

"Oh, thanks." Gina riffled through until she found the handwritten envelope addressed to her. "And no. She's going to stay home for a couple of days." She slid her finger under the gummed flap and pulled out the page inside.

"Cool. What're we doing today?"

"Well, since you're staying home from school now, I thought we could spend some time together. What would you like to do?" She unfolded the page and scanned for the name at the bottom. George Boyne. "Bloody hell."

"Mum! You have to put a pound in the swear tin."

"Right," she agreed without listening to Sammy. She was too busy trying to read the words across the paper.

Dear Miss Temple,

Thank you for your letter. Patricia O'Shea is indeed a name I am familiar with. From a considerable time ago, but, yes, I knew her. I don't know what she could possibly have for me after all this time, but I am willing to meet with you, as I am curious. I hope you might be able to tell me what has happened to my old friend.

I realise this is short notice, but as my curiosity is piqued, I would like to get some answers quickly. If you don't mind. I'll be travelling to Norwich on the 16th for work purposes and wonder if it would be possible for us to meet then. I am staying at Morston Hall, near Holt, and have taken the liberty of reserving a table for dinner for us. They seat at 7.15pm. If you can't make it, please call me and we can arrange an alternative.

Yours curiously,
George Boyne.

"You're not even listening to me." Sammy's voice broke through her concentration.

"I'm sorry, Sammy. I was reading. What did you want?"

Sammy tutted and rolled her eyes. "I said can we go and see Grandma today."

Gina wasn't sure how she felt about how quickly Sammy had taken to Alison, but she smiled anyway. Sammy didn't need to know how mixed her feelings were on the subject of her own mother. "Why don't you give her a call and see if she wants to come to the beach with us and Merlin? We can go down to see the seals, if you like, and that'll give Kate some time to rest after yesterday."

"Mum," Sammy's voice was small, and she sounded so much younger than the brash nine-year-old that normally ran her ragged. "Is Kate gonna die?"

Gina's eyes widened, and her jaw dropped. "No! God, no! Why on earth would you think something like that?"

Sammy scuffed her toe on the carpet and shrugged.

"Talk to me." Gina wrapped her hands around Sammy's waist. "Come on, what made you think that?"

"She was blowed up."

"Blown."

Sammy sighed aggrievedly. "Blown."

"Yes, Kate was in an accident at work, but she's fine. She's not going to die. She's going to be with us for a long, long time."

Sammy scrutinised her closely, seemingly watching her every muscle twitch and tic for signs of deception, her eyes narrowed, her lips pursed, and her head cocked to one side. She was a human lie detector. She held out her hand, little finger up straight. "Pinky swear?" It was Sammy's most solemn oath.

Gina hooked her little finger around Sammy's. "Pinky swear." Now was as good a time as any, right? "So, while we're talking about Kate, how would you feel about you and me moving in here with her?"

"We already 'scussed this."

"Discussed."

"Well, we already did. I said yes."

"What if we weren't just talking about living here for Christmas? What if we moved in with Kate forever?"

Sammy's eyes widened. "I've got my own dog!" She started dancing around in place. Well, *dancing* might have been a generous term for the form of bum wiggling and arm waving that was going on, but still, Sammy was happy with her form of self-expression, so Gina was happy to roll with it.

Just as Gina had suspected, Sammy's world was easily made a wonderful place. "Very true," Gina said, "but there's something else too."

Sammy stopped 'dancing' and put her hands on her hips. "What?"

"It's about the sleeping situation—"

"You can't make me sleep on the washing line. I Googled it, it's abuse." She wagged her finger in Gina's face.

Gina had once threatened this in the wake of a particularly, no, *spectacularly* bad night trying to sleep next to the snoring that seemed to reverberate from the fires of hell and emanate from her little girl's mouth. The threat might have been a slight error in judgement, looking back now, but at the time, it had seemed entirely logical.

"No, I wasn't thinking of that as a solution." She grasped the wagging finger, lest she lose an eye to it. "I was thinking that since Kate's my girlfriend, I'd sleep with her."

"Like last night?"

"Hm," Gina mumbled, thinking more about the promising morning than the night before.

"Okay. Can Merlin sleep wiv me then? I worry that she gets lonely."

Right, Merlin gets lonely. "If she wants to." Gina wasn't convinced that the dog would voluntarily sleep with Sammy, but she didn't want to crush the child. She'd have plenty of boyfriends, or girlfriends, in the future who would do that. On second thought, no she wouldn't. There would be no boyfriends touching her little girl!

Sammy dropped to her knees next to Merlin, wrapped her arms around the dog's neck, and dropped kisses on her head. "You can sleep wiv me now, Merlin. You don't need to be all on your own anymore." Sammy threw Gina an impish look. "If Kate's your girlfriend, does that mean you wanna sleep wiv her so you can do sexy-times?"

Pulled out of her nightmarish daydream of Sammy getting a boyfriend and growing up, Gina found herself pushed straight into her real-life nightmare of Sammy asking about sex. *Shit, when did she learn about sexy-times?*

"Erm, what do you know about sexy-tim—about making love?"

Sammy shrugged. "Dad used to have the woman from the pub stay over sometimes for sexy-times. She made lots of noise, and it made it hard to get to sleep sometimes, but Dad was always happy in the morning, and she looked funny with sticky-up hair, and her lipstick was all over her face." She giggled and put her hand over her mouth. "And she didn't have no cloves on."

"Clothes."

"Fine, clothes."

"Okay, is that all?"

Sammy shook her head. "Simon Parker at school says his mum has sexy-times wiv the milkman, and the coal man, and the butcher, to keep the bills down. But when Patty Smith asked him what sexy-times was, he said it was kissing and hand-holding. But I don't think that's right, cos kissing and hand-holding wouldn't make the pub lady make all that racket. And when I held Dad's hand, he wasn't happy in the morning like he was after sexy-times. So it must be different. And John Carter said his dad called it bonkin' and that that was where 'im and 'is brother came from. And that don't sound like kissing to me. What's bonkin'?"

She's nine! I shouldn't need to cover the birds and the bees yet! Gina tugged Sammy to sit on her knee. *This'll be easier if I can't see her eyes. Maybe.* She swallowed. "'Bonking' is a terrible name for something that can be very lovely." She licked her lips. "When two people love each other very much, they want to show each other how much by making love. Kissing is part of it, and hand-holding, but you're right, there is more to it. Sometimes, when a man and a woman make love, they can make a baby."

Sammy twisted around in Gina's lap to look at her curiously. "How?"

Technical or fluffy?

"Does it happen when a penis kisses a gyna?"

What? I mean...what? "A gyna?"

"Yeah...you know..." Sammy pointed between her legs. "A gyna."

Technical it is then. "A vagina. And who told you about penises and gyn—vaginas?"

"Kiera Walsh's mummy and daddy are having a new baby, and they told her that when her daddy's penis kissed her mummy's gyn—vagina it made a baby."

Well...how much more detail did she need at nine? "There's a bit more involved, but, essentially, yes. That's what happens when a man and a woman make love and make a baby."

Sammy frowned. "Does that mean you and Kate are going to make babies? But you're both ladies, so where do you get the penis from?"

A peal of laughter from the doorway caught Gina's attention, and she turned her head to see Kate leaning against the door. Her eyes were wide, but there was a huge smile on her face and her eyebrows were almost at her hairline. "Been there long?"

"Long enough for this to be educational." She held up the bottle of milk. "Ready for some Coco Pops, squirt, or do you need more time with your mum?"

"Yay! I'm starving." Sammy hopped off Gina's lap and sidled past Kate, grabbing the milk bottle as she went. She ran back down the stairs with her ever-present shadow, Merlin, at her heels.

"Be careful with that one. Don't let Merlin near it."

"I won't."

Kate crossed her now-empty arms across her chest, smirking. And Gina focused on that little grin to stop herself thinking about how she was only wearing a towel. It didn't work. So she tried to focus on the fact that Kate had seen her wearing less than the towel only a few short days ago. That didn't seem to matter either. A mix of nervousness and excitement settled in her belly.

"Well, it's been a while, but she certainly knows how to get down to brass tacks."

A cushion from the bed made a handy projectile. Gina threw it at her, the towel slipping about her breasts as she did. She caught it before exposing herself, but not before Kate started laughing.

And then started running down the stairs.

When Gina was dressed, she trotted down the stairs and overheard Sammy and Kate talking.

"So, you're okay with me being your mum's girlfriend?"

"Yup." Her spoon clattered into her bowl. "Does that mean I have to call you *mum* too?"

"Erm, no, you can just call me Kate, just like now."

"Hm." The spoon clanked again. "Oh, I was supposed to see if Grandma wants to go to the beach wiv us."

"Then give her a call."

The raucous scraping of wood against tiles was followed by the heavy slap of feet as Sammy ran into the other room. Gina could hear her speaking within seconds and took her seat at the table next to a slightly shell-shocked-looking Kate.

"Still want us to move in?"

Kate sniggered. "It was worth it for the gyna-kissing conversation I overheard."

"Stop, or you won't be kissing any gynas anytime soon." Gina covered her mouth with her hand as soon as the words were out, and she stared at an equally surprised-looking Kate. "I didn't say that." Gina's face burned. "You did not hear that."

"I most certainly did." Kate wrapped her hands around Gina's waist and pulled her close. "And I'm looking forward to it," she whispered into her ear, then kissed it and pulled back.

"Oh God." She buried her face in her hands and ignored the wickedly sexy laugh that bubbled from Kate's throat. She slapped the letter from George on the table to distract them both. "Here, read that, and stop laughing at me," she said with a pout.

"Gran said yes. Do you want her to pick us up or meet her there?" Sammy yelled through the doorway.

Gina leant her cheek on her hand. "If she doesn't mind picking us up, that would be great." She heard Sammy convey this to Alison and turned back to Kate.

"Are you happy to go and meet him?"

"Yes. I can give him the letter, and it's over and done with, then."

"Then you should go."

"Will you come with me?"

"What about Sammy?"

"I'll find a babysitter."

"Then I'd love to."

"I'll let George know I won't be alone."

"Good plan." She handed the letter back to Gina. "Speaking of plans, what's the young madam organising through there?"

"Ah, trip to Brancaster Beach with my mother. I thought we could take Merlin with us and see if I can tire them both out."

"Merlin and your mum?"

"Funny."

"I try."

"Try harder."

"Ouch." Kate sipped at a glass of orange juice and offered some to Gina. She shook her head.

"I thought it would give me and Mum a chance to talk a bit more and give you some time to rest, or whatever it is you need to do after Timmons's visit last night."

"It's just a bit of reading." She checked the clock on the cooker. "Eight forty. Stella said she'd be here about nine to get started with it."

"Okay, well, we'll get out of your hair as soon as Mum gets here."

"You don't have to go out, you know?"

"I know. But I need to check on things at the campsite, and I need to try and get rid of some of that child's energy."

"What about the stuff you said we needed to talk about? The flowers."

"It'll still be there later, when Sammy's in bed."

"You sure?"

Gina was sure she didn't want to talk about it if she didn't have to. "Positive." She smiled and turned as the doorbell rang.

"I'll get it." Sammy ran through the room and opened the front door as Gina walked up behind her and put her hands on her shoulders.

"Mum! That was quick."

"I was on my way out already when Sammy called."

"Oh, we've interrupted your plans. I'm sorry."

Alison held up her hand and waved away her apology. "No, I'd much rather spend the day with you two than fighting my way around the supermarket. I'll order online and get it delivered. Much easier."

"Well, in that case, good plan."

"And great timing." She smiled over at Kate. "Hi, you okay?"

Kate nodded. "Hard-headed, Alison."

"I'm sure. I'm glad you're okay, though." Alison frowned at Gina. "You look...excited. What's happened?"

Gina giggled. "I'm going to a fancy dinner tomorrow."

"Oo. Night out, ladies?"

"Hm, something like that." She winked at Kate and handed Sammy her coat. "I'll tell you all about it while we're walking on the beach. Sammy, get Merlin's lead and her ball."

"Sounds intriguing." Alison said as Sammy scampered away.

"It is."

"Mum, can I have a jam butty before we go?" Sammy yelled from the front room.

Gina closed her eyes and shook her head. "You've literally just had your breakfast. You can wait till lunchtime."

"But I'm hungry. I'm wasting away."

Alison and Kate both tried to stifle their laughter, and Gina raised her eyebrow at the very poor attempt. "You're not wasting away. You're eating me out of house and home. Get a bag of crisps. You can eat them in the car."

"Yes." Sammy fist-pumped the air. "And that's how you conduct a negotiation."

Laughter filled the room, and Gina put her head in her hands. "Bloody kid'll be the death of me one day."

Alison wrapped an arm around her shoulder. "But at least she'll make it fun getting there."

Brancaster Beach was deserted. The white sand stretched as far as the eye could see, meeting the sky at the horizon in one direction and the sea in the other. The low-hanging winter sun glistened off the water and reflected back at them. Soft snow clung to the marram grasses in the dunes and the rocks that held back the sands at the beach's entrance. Clouds billowed in the sky, heavily pregnant with more snow just waiting for the right moment to cast their frozen offspring to the earth.

Turning left at the clubhouse and away from the site of Kate's last case, Gina slipped a pair of sunglasses over her eyes and launched the ball for Merlin and Sammy to chase. Sammy was, in Gina's opinion, far too interested in Kate's Skeleton case, and she was determined to steer her away from the old bunker where the remains had been found. And the police tape that fluttered in the wind as a morbid reminder.

"So, this stranger wants you to meet him tomorrow for dinner in a swanky restaurant to talk about a woman you knew for five minutes before she died. Is that the long and short of it?"

Gina smiled at Alison's succinct summary of the situation. "You forgot about the letter I'm going to give him, that I can't give him the real one of, just a copy, because the real one's evidence."

"Oh, yes. Sorry I missed those crucial details," she said.

Gina turned her head and caught the smirk on her mother's lips. It was jarring for her. This Alison was so different to the woman she'd grown up with. She had a sense of humour that Gina recognised in herself but had never seen in her mother before. Trying to reconcile the two women in her head was going to take some time. But she wanted to take the time to do that. And as Jodi had said, the only way she could move on was to let go. She had to get to know Alison as she was, not as Gina expected her to be. She smiled as she responded, "Exactly. Crucial."

"So what are you going to do with Sammy?"

"Well, I was going to ask you if you wanted to spend the evening with—"

"I'd love to."

Gina grinned. "Thought you might, but I don't want you to think that I've only asked you here today—"

"To butter me up?" Her mum laughed.

"Something like that."

"No, I don't. And I'd love to look after Sammy. I can't tell you how happy it makes me that you'd ask." She turned away and tried to hide the fact that she was sweeping tears from her cheek. "Thank you." Her voice was thick and raw with emotion.

"No, no, no. Thank you." Merlin deposited the ball at Gina's feet, and she launched it towards the water again. "You've no idea how hard it is to find a babysitter for that little monster." She called out loud enough for Sammy to hear.

Her daughter turned around with an offended look.

"A monster? Sammy?" her mum piped up, playing along. "Never. She's an angel."

Sammy grinned and threw Gina a 'see-I-told-you-so' look before running after Merlin again.

Alison touched Gina's arm. "If you want, she could stay overnight. If you and Kate want..." she faltered, her cheeks turning red. "Well, if you'd like some time alone together. Just the two of you."

Gina knew her cheeks had turned just as red as her mother's, but she was a grown-up now, and it wasn't exactly a shock to Alison—her mother—that she'd have a sex life. Alison knew Kate was her girlfriend after all. And as far as she knew, they were sleeping together while Gina was staying at Kate's. While she didn't seem totally comfortable with discussing Gina's sex life, Gina was pretty sure it was more about the newness of the situation than anything else. She hoped. "Kate and I...we, erm... Well we haven't been together very long."

Her mum nodded. "When she came to see me about the embezzlement she was investigating at Brancombe House, I looked her up."

Gina laughed a little incredulous. "You Google-stalked my girlfriend?"

Alison blushed but nodded with a big, unrepentant grin on her face. "Yup. I like to do my homework."

Gina remembered all the times her mother had tried to drill into her brain that knowledge was paramount to making good decisions in life. The more one knew, the more one learnt, and the better able they were to cope with the curve balls life inevitably flung at everyone. Often with a catapult.

"I remember that about you." Gina smiled tentatively. "It's nice to know that some of my memories were of the real you, not the you that you had to pretend to be to protect yourself." She frowned. "I'm not even sure that made sense."

"It did." She chuckled and slipped her hand around Gina's arm. "Is this okay?" She squeezed Gina's arm to indicate the subject of her question and carried on when Gina nodded. "To be honest with you, Gina, I didn't know how much of me was me back then. So I guess it makes sense that you're questioning your memories now. Depression is a horrible thing. People describe it as this black hole or a cancer of the emotions, but that isn't how I remember it." She went quiet, staring out to sea as they walked arm in arm.

"How would you describe it?"

"Numbness, maybe." She shrugged and pulled in a deep breath. "On other days, it was like I was watching the world from behind a glass brick. You know those thick glass bricks they make obscure walls out of?"

Gina nodded.

"It was like I was encased in a tube made of them. I could see and hear everything, but it was too far away to reach me. I couldn't feel anything the way I was supposed to. The way I wanted to. Good or bad."

"Sounds like you were protecting yourself." She sniffed. "Like you'd wrapped yourself in bubble wrap."

"I hadn't thought of it like that, but maybe you're right. Maybe it was bubble wrap rather than those heavy unyielding bricks."

"Bubble wrap moves."

"It does."

Gina smirked. "And it's a lot more fun to pop."

"That it is."

They walked in silence for a few minutes, the tide drawing in and ebbing away in a constant rhythm that soothed Gina's thoughts and washed away the pain of memories she wished she didn't have. If only for a little while.

"So, what did you find out about Kate, then?"

"Oh, right. That's where we were up to." She squeezed Gina's arm again. "Sorry."

"No need to apologise."

"Okay. Well, I found out that she was recently promoted and moved to the King's Lynn area in September for the job. She's a detective, she's smart, she's beautiful, and she has fantastic taste in women."

Gina laughed. "Google told you all that?"

"Yup. It's the font of all knowledge."

"Really?"

"No. Not at all. Did you two meet when she moved up here, or did she move here to be closer to you?"

"Neither. We met when she was investigating Connie's death in October."

Alison's eyebrows rose as looked at Gina. "You only met then?"

Gina nodded.

"And you live together already?"

Gina laughed and shook her head. "No, Sammy and I are staying with her over Christmas, that's all. It's not... Well it wasn't supposed to be a permanent thing." She quirked her lips into a half smile.

"But it is now."

It wasn't a question, so Gina didn't answer. She guessed it was written clearly all over her face. "We're...well, with everything that's happened in the last few days, I suppose we've both come to the conclusion that we know what we want. Sammy's happy and loves Kate to bits already, so why wait? If nothing else, the past few months have proved that we never know what's around the corner and I don't... Well, I waited so long to find her that I don't want to waste any more time." She sighed. "Even if it is complicated."

Alison frowned. "Sweetheart, you're living together, and Sammy's happy. It can't be that complicated. So what's the issue?"

"Like I said, it's complicated."

"Pft." Alison dropped Gina's gaze and looked out across the water. "That's what I used to tell people about your father when they asked why I wouldn't leave him."

"What?" Gina wasn't sure she understood what her mum was suggesting.

Alison didn't say anything. She didn't need to. The look on her face clearly asked the question that she must have heard herself a million times over the years, as she'd hidden the latest bruise to her collection, made the newest excuse for the black eye or split lip, explained away the slightly crooked nose that had been straight the day before.

"You've got to be joking?" Now Gina was damn sure she didn't like what her mother was asking.

Alison just waited.

The implication and the suspicion grated on Gina and drove her instinct to protect Kate into overdrive. Kate would never, ever hurt her in any way. Gina was beyond certain of that fact. That anyone, no matter who they were, could even think anything differently hurt. She felt the wound of it already festering in the nascent relationship with her mother and knew that if left unchecked, it would render any effort between them irredeemable. She had to challenge her mother's unspoken question and shut it down. Her own discomfort—or the discomfort that her mother would feel as a result—was inconsequential in the face of this shred of information. Alison wanted to hear what complicated was? Well, so be it. Embarrassment was far better than Alison looking at Kate and wondering if she beat her.

"Unbelievable." Gina growled into the wind and just hoped it reached Alison's ears and she wouldn't have to repeat herself. "No, it's not *that* kind of complicated. Kate is not like that. She would never hurt me. She is the most protective and loving woman I've ever met. She saved my life, literally, when Ally Robbins was trying to carve a noughts and crosses board on my skin. She holds Sammy when she wakes up screaming in the middle of the night because she still sees the face of my best friend after it had been blown off by a sniper rifle. She found me a counsellor to help me work through the panic attacks and issues I have since the attack. Does that sound like a woman who would lay a hand on me or my child in anger?"

"No," her mum said quietly. "She sounds as wonderful as I thought she was."

"She is."

"Then why's it so complicated?"

"Because of me. Because I'm fucked up. Me."

Alison frowned. "I don't understand."

"Ally...she..."

"Wait, were you and Ally Robbins together? Is that why it's complicated? You still have feelings for her?"

"What? Are you insane?" She stopped and turned to face her mother. "I was never involved with Ally Robbins. She wanted information about Matt the Prat. Sammy's bloody father. She cut me to bits. I have scars all over my back, but those are these easy ones. I can't even see how bad they are. It's the ones on my stomach and breasts that make this so fucking complicated. They're the ones that have fucked me up."

Her mum's frown deepened. "Kate reacted badly to them?"

Gina shook her head. "I react badly to them." The wind stung her cheeks as tears wet a path to the corner of her mouth. "They're so ugly, Mum. I love her, and I want her. God, how I want her. But I find it hard to put them out of my mind. I'm trying, I'm really trying, and I'm getting there. But I still have this question hanging over me... over us: how can I expect Kate to find me attractive when I feel like Frankenstein's monster?"

Her mum laughed. "That's ridiculous."

It was Gina's turn to frown. "Excuse me?"

"Kate looks at you like she wants to eat you." She screwed up her face and closed her eyes. "Probably not the correct choice of phrase considering...well...you know."

Gina stared at her, wide-eyed and not sure what to expect to come out of Alison's mouth next.

"If I'm hearing you right, you're telling me that you live with the woman you love, but you've not slept with her—"

"I have slept with her."

"You said—"

Gina waved her question away and carried on, "Last night, after we came home from the hospital, I didn't want to be away from her. Even sleeping in the spare room with Sammy felt like it was too far away from her."

"I see. So you slept as in sleeping, not as in a euphemism for sex."

Again it wasn't a question, but still Gina nodded.

"Okay, so you've not had sex with her, despite the fact that the woman clearly adores you, because you're worried about a few marks on your chest. Is that the long and short of it?"

Her mother always did have a way of distilling an issue down to the finer points. Quickly. Apparently her childhood memories of this talent of her mother's were correct. It had certainly annoyed her on more than one occasion as a child.

"Then you're right. You are fucked up."

"Excuse me?"

"You heard me."

Gina stood still and faced her mother, her fists balled on her hips. "What is this? You waltz back into my life after a decade, after throwing me out, and think you have the right to criticize the way I'm living it?"

Her mother stopped and faced her.

"You think that you can pick apart my choices and feelings? I don't think so."

"You don't want me to criticize? Then stop feeling sorry for yourself and uncomplicate the situation."

"It's not that easy."

Alison smiled sadly. "Nothing ever is, Gina. I spent years telling myself your dad was complicated. That his feelings were so complicated they excused his actions. But it wasn't complicated at all. It was really amazingly simple." She put her hands on her hips, mirroring Gina's pose. "He was an arsehole. He was a bully. I told myself the situation with you was equally complicated. But that too was really simple. I was selfish. I was too wrapped up in my own pain to see what I was doing to you. Don't make my mistake."

"What are you talking about?"

"Don't be so wrapped up in what you see on your chest that you don't see what Kate sees in you."

Her arms flew over her chest. "I know she doesn't see it the same way."

"Good. Then don't you think it's time you, well, made a woman out of your woman?"

Gina frowned.

"Tomorrow. Take the time to enjoy a few hours alone together, Gina. Just the two of you. Go to your dinner with this man and I'll look after Sammy. Then you can just spend the rest of the night together. You already said that she's been told to take a few days off. So it's the perfect opportunity, isn't it?"

The two of them, alone. No interruptions from Sammy or work. No bad memories being triggered by being in the same house as she was attacked in. Or worrying because Sammy was in the next room. It was perfect. And as much as she knew she was as ready as she was going to get, it was terrifying.

But Gina acknowledged that she was ready. Physically, she'd been ready since the moment she'd met Kate. She was a gorgeous woman, who had proved to be nothing short of perfect for her. Gina hadn't stood a chance against falling in love. The trip to Ann Summers had been her symbolic stepping forward to grab their sexual relationship with both hands and revel in it. Of course, that hadn't exactly gone to plan, and everything that had happened in its wake—Kate watching her disrobe in the hospital, Pat's death, Stella's injury, the second explosion—had put that desire on hold. Sleeping in Kate's arms last night and waking up with her that morning had brought them all very much back to the forefront of Gina's mind. And other parts of her anatomy were beginning to make themselves known.

Yeah, it was time.

She smiled at her mother. At her *mother*. "Does this feel as weird to you as it does to me?"

"What? Encouraging my daughter into seducing another woman?"

Gina snickered. "Yeah."

"Just a bit."

Gina let her hands drop from her hips, but not before she recognised the similarity of their stance. Nor how often she saw the same pose from Sammy. Three generations of that same hands-on-hips-fierce-warrior posture right there.

"It feels good as well, though."

Gina cocked an eyebrow. "You thought we needed a chat about the birds and the bees?"

"No, I meant the frankness, the openness. If we want to have a real relationship in the future, we can't pretend to be anything but who we really are, right?"

Gina nodded.

"This is who I am, Gina. Warts and all." She tilted her head to the side. "Think you can handle that?"

Gina smirked. "It might take me a little while, but, yeah. I can handle you."

"Good." She shrugged and slipped her hand back around Gina's arm as they started walking again.

Sammy and Merlin were rolling around on the sand, tussling for the ball. Gina rolled her eyes but decided to ignore it. Clothes could be washed, Sammy could be hosed off, and Merlin...well, that was up to Kate.

"I can't believe you said I was fucked up."

Alison sniggered. "Didn't remember that side of me, huh?"

"I'm not sure that side of you existed a decade ago."

"It did. She was just tucked away in bubble wrap."

Gina snorted. "Well, wherever she was. I'm glad she's getting an airing now. Besides, it's good to know Sammy didn't come from the cabbage patch after all."

"You think…" Her voice trailed off as they both seemed to realise what Gina had said, and, more importantly, just how much she meant it. Gina saw flashes of both herself and Sammy in Alison. It was both scary and comforting.

"Should I be scared?"

Gina squinted as the sun broke through the clouds for a moment and shone brightly. "Of what?"

"What else I'm going to discover under the bubble wrap, if I'm going to end up like that little urchin?"

They both laughed before Gina said, "Maybe. Kate's not decided yet if she's going to end up a master criminal or a bloody good police officer. I suspect there a distinct possibility she could do both. At the same time." She pointed to where Sammy clambered to her feet and ran, splashing through the tidal puddles formed in the depressions of the sand. "Still okay about looking after her?"

"Positive." Alison's smile spread to a grin. "I can't wait to find out what secrets the little scamp has to tell about you."

Gina groaned and spread her arms wide. "World, swallow me now."

CHAPTER 24

Kate hummed along to a classic Elkie Brookes track on the radio, just hitting the chorus and wailing "Pearl's a singer" when Stella tapped on the patio door window at the back of the house. She was grinning and offering Kate a thumbs up for what was undoubtedly a spirited, if somewhat off-key, performance.

"Bollocks," Kate whispered under her breath as she opened the door. "Come in." She waved Stella in and waited for the piss-taking to start. It wouldn't take long.

"Thank God I got here before you made it rain."

Not long at all. "And to think, I almost missed you."

"Aw, thanks, babes." Stella squeezed Kate's shoulders, pecked her on the cheek noisily, and brushed past her into the room. She dumped her bag on the table and massaged her shoulder like it was aching.

"You okay?" Kate asked as she rubbed the spot on her cheek where Stella had kissed her, convinced she left drool there on purpose, and headed for the kitchen.

"Yeah, just still a bit stiff from the other day." She grimaced. "I guess I'm not as young as I used to be."

Kate sympathised. She was feeling more than a few aches and pains herself today. But Stella wouldn't appreciate a fuss any more than she would. She would, however, appreciate... "Coffee?"

"Only if you want to stay alive. Three days in the bloody hospital and not a decent coffee to be had. I've days of caffeine loss to make up for." Stella stood up and followed her into the kitchen. "Where's Gina and the precocious...I mean *precious* kid? Not left you already, have they?"

"Walking Merlin on the beach with Gina's mum."

"So we've got the house to ourselves. I can swear to my heart's content and not worry I'm going to get myself strung up for teaching Sammy any new ones." She snickered. "Again."

"Yeah, she's found a creative way around that one, by the way."

"What's that? And I didn't mean to call her dad an arsehole."

Kate waved the comment away as she spooned coffee into cups and waited for the kettle to boil. "Matt *is* an arsehole."

"Yeah, but he's still her dad. So what's she come up with as a creative alternative, then?"

"*Bumholes.*"

Stella chortled loudly. "I love that kid."

"You and me both." Kate froze as she picked up the kettle, realising just how true that was. God, those Temple women just wormed their way right into the heart of a woman.

"You gonna pour, or just carry on with your weird calisthenics program?"

"Sorry." She shook her head and poured water into the two cups before handing one to Stella. Pointing to the chairs at the table, she sipped and then took a seat. "What've you got there, then?" She tipped her head to the bag Stella had deposited a few minutes ago.

"A bag."

Kate nodded slowly. "So that's the level for the day, is it? Okay, Mrs Pedantic...what's in the bag?"

Stella grinned and then screwed up her face. "I couldn't sleep last night, so I started doing a bit of research to get us started." She pulled the bag over, unzipped it, and then pulled out the contents: her laptop, a legal pad covered in some sort of hieroglyphics, some sticky notes, a few pens, and a rolled-up A3 chart pad. She unrolled the pad, pushed the computer out of the way, and started to lay the pages of the large pad out side by side. Down the centre was a single straight black line transecting one page, then another, and then another. Cutting through it at irregular intervals were short vertical marks with a time and a brief description under or above it. Sometimes with pictures taped to thickish paper.

"Timeline." Kate squinted at the sequence of events and whistled. "You've been busy." On the chronicle was everything Stella knew of the operation, from the moment she'd walked into Ann Summers to now. Including from when Mallam and Porter arrived from London and from when Kate had found Nadia's diary to when Grimshaw e-mailed her the first translated pages and then to the explosion in the Diamond Street lock-ups. The time of death and name of each victim was written in a different colour along the timeline. So they could never bloody well forget why they were doing this. Not that Kate ever could.

"Told you, I couldn't sleep."

"You didn't say you'd been up all night." Kate held down the corner of one page so she could make out the approximation of handwriting on the paper. It wasn't unusual for coppers to have bad handwriting, but this was on a level with the notoriously bad doctor scrawl.

Stella shrugged off her coat and sat down next to Kate. "Slept too much in the hospital, probably."

The dark circles under her eyes told Kate a different tale. Had Stella been Gina, Kate knew she would have asked a few more questions and would have tried to draw her out to talk about what was clearly bothering her. But Stella wasn't Gina, and she wouldn't respond well to probing—no matter how gently—into her psyche. She covered Stella's hand with her own and squeezed gently. "If you ever want to go down to the gym with me and beat seven shades of shit out of a punch bag," she said and prodded her own chest with her thumb, "just let me know."

That was how they learnt to deal with shit.

Kate tapped the pad. "And what's this? I can't read this crap you call handwriting."

Stella cocked an eyebrow. "Don't even start, I've seen that mess you call a notebook. Most of those aren't even words, Kate."

"So are."

Stella sniggered. "You sound just like Sammy when you do that."

Kate smiled. "She copied me."

Stella looked unimpressed. "Kids do that." Pointing to the pad, she said, "Since we're now uncertain of Mallam's motives, I decided that we needed to re-examine each piece of evidence and intelligence he brought and for which we have no other corroboration."

"Good plan."

"The biggest section of this seems to be what we know about Ayeshydi. What did he tell you about him again?"

Kate looked at her. Stella had never asked her to rehash intelligence just for the sake of it. Had the head injury affected how her brain—

"I wasn't at the meeting when Mallam briefed you all about him. I need to know what you know so we can cross reference how truthful he might have been about Ayeshydi's history, if nothing else."

Kate felt a sense of relief that she hadn't expected. Stella was a colleague, and she was quickly becoming a very good friend too.

"Right, sorry. So, in a nutshell, he told us that Ishman Ayeshydi was twenty-eight, of Syrian descent. But Ishman was born in Leicester and raised in the UK, then went to train with the Libyan Islamic Fighting Group in 2011. He came back to the UK in 2014. He had extensive weapons training in Libya at that time. They also suspect he went other places while he was there but never specified where. He's been back for further training since then, they suspect."

"Where? Libya again?"

"No. Apparently, passport control shows Ayeshydi leaving the UK, bound for Turkey. And like we both know, Turkey's the number one crossing into IS-occupied Syria. Mallam said they could prove Ayeshydi was in the video footage of two beheadings in Raqqa and that they suspected he was trained to use the explosives out there."

"Do you have those dates?"

Kate frowned, trying to recall if Mallam had said when that was exactly. He hadn't. She shook her head. "He didn't give us that bit."

"Okay. That'll make it trickier, but I've got a friend who works for HMRC over at Manchester Airport. If he came in through there, she might be able to corroborate this part of the story and get us those dates at the same time." Stella picked up her phone. "Damn it, I've not got enough signal in here."

"Backyard's best."

Stella rolled her eyes and headed outside.

Kate continued to study the timeline, but she wasn't really seeing it. She was thinking about all the other things Mallam had told them and exactly what he'd left out. Why hadn't she picked up on that? He'd given them info, but it had all been so vague. She spotted a sheaf of pages stapled together. A copy of the CV for one Zain Mallam.

Good student, fluent in five languages, excelled at something called 'asset manipulation' while in training. Kate didn't really want to think about what that particular phrase meant, but once she'd read it, it was hard not to. Asset manipulation. Getting people to do what you wanted them to do. And Kate was willing to bet that that wasn't always what those people wanted to do. Nor in their best interests. She pictured Mallam. He must have been hiding some serious charm to have excelled at asset manipulation. Kate doubted he could have charmed a cup of tea out of her.

She read on. A levels in sociology, politics, psychology, and law. Degree in law. Master's degree, then a PhD in criminology. Out of education for less than a month when he signed up for a career in the security services. She checked the dates: First contact from Mallam, 9th of July 2005. Two days after the London bombing that had targeted the public transport system. Fifty-two people killed and almost eight hundred injured, by four individuals. The impetus for a young, patriotic Zain Mallam to stand up and defend his country, his people.

It didn't seem possible that a guy who took on this job under such circumstances would now turn against it. He was clearly a guy with a lot more experience and mettle than Kate had given him credit for. So where was he? Where was Zain Mallam?

"Carly said she'll see what she can dig up, but based on the fact we don't have a date to work with, it might take her a bit of time for the searches to come back. She'll call me back when she finds something." Stella stood behind Kate and looked over her shoulders. "Anything interesting in there?"

Kate shrugged. "Interesting, yes. But it raises more questions than it answers. I mean, this guy signed up to stop terrorists in the wake of seven-seven. Why the hell would he be involved with a bombing like this?"

Stella sat down. "Seven-seven was a long time ago now, Kate. A lot's changed since 2005."

"True. But..." She stared at the pictures on the table and scrabbled through them, trying to find the one she wanted. She grinned triumphantly when she slapped it down in front of Stella.

Stella straightened the picture so she could see it head on. "A picture of Zain Mallam. And?"

"By 2005, Zain Mallam had worked through his degree, his master's, and his PhD. So that had to make him, what? Twenty-five, twenty-six by that time?"

"Something like that. So?"

"In 2005. Over a decade ago. He's got to be pushing forty. Right?"

Stella nodded.

Kate tapped the image. "How old does that guy look to you?"

Stella picked up the piece of paper and studied it intently. "Thirty, maybe. But that could just be the picture."

"Trust me, it's not. It's a very good likeness."

"So, you think that this isn't Zain Mallam? Is that what you're telling me?"

"That guy looks closer to twenty-five than forty."

"So, he could just have very good genes. Some lucky bastards do."

Kate had to concede that possibility, but still... "The pictures we have of Ayeshydi came from Mallam. Even if he is just a lucky bastard with good genes, you're the one who said we needed to corroborate all evidence he gave us." She fished through the pile of papers and pulled out the picture Mallam had handed out of Ishman Ayeshydi. The full beard didn't hide the crinkle of crow's feet at his eyes. "He look twenty-eight to you?"

"I'll make a call to the DVLA see if I can dredge up a picture of them both off their database."

"We don't have a warrant." Kate said.

"He's...a friend."

"A friend?" Kate asked.

Stella's answering smirk was rather lewd in Kate's opinion, but whatever.

"Right." She waved Stella off as she stepped back outside to get signal again. Kate returned to staring at the pictures and Mallam's CV, and increasingly, her off-the-wall theory was making sense to her. But that begged far more questions than it answered. Chief among them—if that wasn't Mallam...who the hell was it? And where was the real Zain Mallam?

"Curiouser and curiouser, said Alice," Kate whispered to herself. The landline rang from its cradle on the kitchen worktop, and Kate answered it absentmindedly. "Hello."

"Gina?" the voice asked.

"No, I'm afraid Gina's not here. Can I help?"

"Where is she?"

"Who is this?"

"None of your fucking business. Where is she?"

"Listen, pal, if you're not prepared to tell me who you are, then I'm not prepared to stand here and listen to you swear at me. So?"

"Fuck you, whore bitch, she's mine!"

The loud bang resonated down the line and reverberated in Kate's ear. "Nice talking to you too, mate."

"Who're you talking to?" Stella asked.

Kate jumped and whirled around, handset still in her hand. "Someone for Gina."

"And?"

"He called me, and I quote, 'a fucking whore bitch', and apparently Gina's his."

Stella's jaw slackened, and her lips popped open in a perfect circle. She gripped the back of the dining room chair, then rested her forearms on it and her weight over it. "Well, I guess that rules Ally out of the equation."

Kate grumbled but had to agree. The woman's cell had already been searched, her calls were being monitored, and she was in prison.

The chances of her being able to orchestrate something like this and get a guy in to help her were, realistically...slim to none.

"Has Gina had any other contact since the flowers?"

Kate shook her head, then stopped. "She said there was something she needed to talk to me about, later after Sammy went to bed."

"So maybe."

"Maybe," Kate conceded.

"Call and ask her?"

"She's out with her mum and Sammy. I don't want to worry her."

"So you'll worry instead? That's logical." Stella might gripe about it, but they both knew she'd do the same if it were the other way around and Stella's girlfriend, or rather boyfriend, was being stalked.

"I'll talk to her as soon as she gets in."

Stella shook her head and held up her hands, palms outward like she was surrendering. "Your girlfriend, kid."

"Not according to the guy on the phone."

"Yeah, well, I happen to think Gina has a say in it myself, and she's definitely chosen you."

Kate's cheeks burned, and she desperately tried not to think about Gina. She had to concentrate on work...stuff. There was tons of that to do. She scrubbed her hand over her face, then ran her fingers through her hair. "Come on, let's get this done before she gets back with Sammy and the dog." She tossed a sheaf of papers to Stella. "I printed each of us a copy of the full diary. I know how you like to scribble all over yours. Grimshaw e-mailed it to me last night, and apparently, the file has been corrupted, so he can't hand it over to anyone else until it's gone through the matrix again."

"Will he get in trouble for that?"

Kate barked a short laugh. "They'd have to prove he was lying first. And I don't know about you, but that guy scares me." She shivered. There was something a little unsavoury, a little unwholesome about the scruffy genius of a crime tech. There was no doubting his brilliance. It was just the...personality...that went with it. And the arrogance of the man. But didn't they say, the higher the IQ the lower the EQ? Well, the man had a 160 IQ. It said more than enough to Kate.

"Are we sure we should be keeping this—whatever it is we're actually doing—to ourselves?"

Kate sighed. "Good question."

"And the good answer?"

"I don't have one. Officially we're both off duty right now, but officially or unofficially, it doesn't really matter. Something is off here. Someone tipped off Ayeshydi that we were at the lock-up. It's the only thing that makes sense. There's no way the CTU team triggered it. They were moving away from the unit when it exploded. It had to have been detonated remotely. So, either one of the neighbours called Ayeshydi and warned him, not knowing that they'd be in the line of whatever measures he had in place to take care of it all, or someone else did. If it was someone else, but not Mallam, then who the hell was it? And let's not forget the fact that Mallam is missing. He was stood in the safest possible place, looking away from the blast site, at his phone, and is now nowhere to be seen. You don't believe in coincidences, Stella. Just the same as me."

"You're right, I don't. But if it was Mallam that tipped off Ayeshydi, then why?"

"I don't know. Maybe there's a link between them somewhere, and if we find that, we'll figure out what's going on here." She rapped her knuckles on the table. "So let's get back to work."

Stella scrunched up her nose and picked up her stack of paper, discretely nudging her coffee cup towards Kate.

Kate bit her lip and ignored the blatant though silent demand for another brew.

Stella faked a cough and nudged it closer still.

Kate sniffed and continued to ignore the juvenile behaviour.

One more cough and Stella managed to tip the cup over.

Kate was very grateful she'd already drained it down to the scratched porcelain of the mug's interior.

"More coffee, Stella?" Kate picked up the cup and strode to the kettle.

"Well, only if you're making one."

"Child." Kate spooned coffee into their mugs.

Kate ran her fingers through her hair, rubbed at her tired eyes, and sighed in frustration. Every page left her feeling unsatisfied as she got closer to reading the last page of Nadia Ahmed's diary. The young girl was hopelessly in love with Ayeshydi and twisted with guilt at falling for her best friend's husband. Add to the mix a father with more than a few issues of his own, and she was the perfect target for someone to brainwash, to groom, radicalise—whatever the hell you want to call it, those bastards did it to her. The pair of them prepared her to do things that were so far removed from her normal moral compass that Kate was almost ready to accept Mrs Ahmed's statement had a grain of truth to it—Nadia was a victim of the true terrorists too. Almost. In the end, she had still made that final decision, she'd still pushed the button, and she'd still killed too many innocent people to garner Kate's true sympathies. Because the girl she discovered in the diary, the one at the start, she didn't exist by the time Nadia Ahmed had walked into the Ann Summers shop on the 12th of December.

At the beginning of the diary, Nadia had been a normal, slightly naive seventeen-year-old girl, but she wasn't a radical extremist. She didn't sit writing in her diary night after night about the ills of the world. Nor did she pontificate over the injustices heaped upon her people. She moaned about her homework, about chores, about having to go to mosque. Complained about the clothes she was wearing, wanting to dress more like the other kids at school. The other British kids, rather than the other Asian kids. She wanted to wear jeans and get her ears pierced and leave her headscarf at home.

She wasn't born a time bomb waiting to go off. No, Nadia Ahmed had been crafted into one by men she trusted, men she loved and who she thought loved her.

"Anything?" Kate asked.

Stella shook her head. "Just the lock-up that you already blew up."

"Funny. Heard anything from either of your friends yet?"

"I wouldn't still be sat here reading if I had."

Kate nodded. "Just checking."

They sniggered, but neither bothered to look up.

There were still a few pages left to read. But Kate found herself wondering what Saba Ayeshydi was like. Was she as naive as Nadia had been? Had she been coerced into this plot by her husband? Other family members? Or was she more extreme in her views than Nadia? Had she contributed to Nadia's brainwashing alongside her husband? Did she know how Nadia felt about Ishman? There were just so many questions and too few answers. And they were getting nowhere.

Kate stretched her back out, swinging her arms over her head and arching over the back of the chair with a loud, satisfied groan. Rolling her head in circles, she asked, "What time is it, anyway?"

Stella glanced over her shoulder at the clock on the oven. "Nearly half five."

"Really?" Kate twisted to look at the clock herself. "Jesus. Wonder where Gina and Sammy are? I thought they would have been home hours ago."

"Probably run off to the circus."

"I'd tell you not to give up your day job to pursue a comedy career, but given how you can get blown up on your days off, it still might be a better option for you."

"For that, you can make me another brew." She pushed her cup across the table, looking for her sixth cup of coffee. It was thirsty work, reading all this teenage angst.

The back door was jostled open, and Sammy and Merlin came tearing in a shower of sand, water drops, and noise in their wake. Merlin danced in circles around Kate's legs, begging for attention, while Sammy dumped a carrier bag on the counter and ran over to Kate, wrapping her arms around her waist and clutching her tight.

"Hiya, Kate," Sammy said.

Kate heard the distinct sound of a kiss against her side.

Then Sammy was gone, following Merlin and tossing a ball for her to catch. *So that's how kids greet you when they get home.* It was nice. It was a surprise, but it was definitely nice. She glanced over her shoulder in time to see Gina grinning at her, and Kate couldn't help but wonder if she was going to get a kiss off another Temple woman.

The wondering didn't last long as Gina carried an armful of bags in with her, dumped them on the kitchen counter, and stood on her tiptoes to kiss Kate's lips, quick and chaste.

"Hiya, Kate," she mimicked Sammy's words and her voice.

Stella sniggered, her eyes purposefully glued to the pages in front of her.

Kate grabbed a dish towel and flung it at Stella's head, smirking when it hit the target.

"Hey."

Kate dipped her head for another quick kiss, enjoying for just a moment the sweet connection and the softness of Gina's lips.

Gina patted her on the arm and moved away a little, clearing her throat as she went. "I hoped you'd still be here. I brought dinner. There's plenty. Can I tempt you to roast chicken, mashed potatoes, and veggies?"

"Oh, thanks, but I usually don't eat late."

Gina frowned. "But it's not even six yet? What time do you eat?"

"Well, before eight, if I can."

"Well, this will be ready by half six, plenty of time."

"Half six? But how do you roast a chicken in less than an hour?"

Gina laughed, head thrown back in abandon. "I buy it ready roasted." She fished in a bag and pulled out the whole cooked chicken as Alison strolled through the doors, shopping bags hanging on her arm.

Kate pulled more cups from the cupboard. Looked like it had been a positive day for Alison and Gina. "Did you buy the whole shop?" She waved the mug in her hand towards all the bags. "This can't all be for one meal, surely."

"No, but since there's a human dustbin living here now, we need items to fill it with, or it has a tendency to moan." She pointed in Sammy's direction.

"Bloody hell. Sammy, you're going on rations!"

"What's rations?"

"Shush," Gina told Kate, prodding her shoulder. "She's teasing, Sammy. Go and get your homework. You can do your times tables with Grandma while Kate and Stella clean up their mess and I make tea."

"But..."

Gina lifted an eyebrow.

Sammy's mouth clicked closed, her head dropped to her chest, and she climbed the stairs like she was climbing the gallows.

Alison whistled. "Wish I'd known that trick with you."

"Glad you didn't," Gina said and began to unpack the shopping, securing places for things that Kate had never had in her cupboards before, like tins of kidney beans and soup, and packets of lentils. *Kids need lentils?* Frozen bags of French fries disappeared with vegetables into the large freezer she'd never put anything into besides pizzas and the occasional beer that needed chilling quickly.

"You okay?" Gina bumped her on the shoulder.

Kate looked up from the label of the peanut butter jar she was holding. "Oh yeah. But there's something I need to talk to you about too. Can we, erm, go outside for a few minutes while Sammy's with your mum? Would that be okay?"

Concern coloured Gina's face, but she nodded and followed Kate through the back door and down to the end of the small garden. She leant against the four-foot fence, looking out at the dark, empty sky. Lit from behind, it was hard to tell what Gina was thinking, but Kate could guess that she was worried and didn't want to drag this out.

"I had a phone call this morning. Someone asking for you, a guy, young-sounding, but over the phone, that can be deceptive. When I wouldn't tell him where you were, he got quite nasty. Called me the usual string of names that come out of these kinds of things and told me that you were his."

Gina's hands flew to her mouth, and her eyes widened. "Oh God."

"Has he been in touch before? Since the flowers, I mean."

"That's what I wanted to talk to you about later. I've got some stuff to show you and some to tell you. But I didn't think... How does he know your number?"

"More basic than that, Gina, how does he know that you're here? Who have you told that you're living here?"

"Just my mum today, but she's been with me the whole time. And you said it was a guy on the phone."

"It was. There wasn't a distorted voice. Or, at least, not one I could detect. Tell me what's happened."

Gina quickly told her all about the notecard that came with the flowers, about Mrs M's roses, and the greetings card that had been delivered. Kate's frown deepened with every word—as did her uneasiness. Whoever it was knew a lot about Gina. They had to. But more importantly, from what the card said, Gina also knew him. Kate considered everything she knew about stalkers and was surprised to find that it was shockingly little. That needed to change. One thing was abundantly clear, though. This guy wasn't going anywhere. He was a part of Gina's life, probably on the periphery of it. But he had some sort of relationship with her already. One that he considered much bigger in his head. And he saw Kate as a threat. While he wasn't overtly threatening, the content of the card implied it. The real question was who was he threatening? Gina or Kate?

"Kate?"

She shook her head, jostling her thoughts back to Gina. "Sorry, miles away there."

"What were you thinking?"

"That we need to talk about this a lot more and that I want to bring Stella in on it all too."

"Okay."

"I also need you to tell me, immediately, when you get something else delivered."

Gina swallowed. "You said 'when' not 'if'."

Kate nodded. "I think it's only a matter of time before he contacts you again."

"Why is he doing this? What does he want?"

Kate wrapped her arms around Gina and pulled her in to a tight hug. "You." She kissed the side of her head. "What he wants is you. Why he wants you—well, I can think of a couple of million reasons off the top of my head, but we don't have time for all that. The top and bottom of it is that stalkers believe they already have a relationship with the object of their affections. It's a delusion, but he believes you're already his."

"He's crazy."

"Not necessarily. I need to do some research and talk to a few people. Probably to Jodi. But I don't think they're all whack jobs."

Gina's arms squeezed her waist. "Helpful."

"Do my best."

Gina shivered.

"Come on, let's get back inside. It's too cold out here, and you've promised the locusts in there food." She twitched her thumb over her shoulder, then led Gina back into the house. Before they crossed the threshold, Kate kissed her cheek and whispered, "We can talk more later." Then she let Gina go.

Stella looked at her questioningly.

Kate started picking up the papers that Stella had already cleared into a neat pile, the top pages face down so that nothing was on show. "I think we should move this stuff to the spare room, Stells. Can you grab that pile for me?" She indicated the second pile and led Stella upstairs.

"What's going on?" Stella asked as soon as the door was closed behind them.

Kate didn't hesitate. Her explanation was brief and stuck to the facts. It was the only way Kate knew how to deal with things she didn't like, with things that scared her—succinct, factual, and to the point.

"Not a half-bad investigative job for a civilian," Stella said. "Shame she can't remember what the delivery guy looked like. I'd put money on it that it was him."

"Agreed." It had occurred to Kate too. "Something tells me that this guy would want to see Gina's face when she'd received his gift. One he clearly worked hard to obtain for her."

"Want me to do some digging around?"

Kate nodded. "I'll put together a list of males in her life."

"Kate, we both know that while this guy thinks he has a relationship with her, it could be someone who's stayed on the campsite as a guest or something. Someone she served in the shop, even just one time."

"I know that's possible, but that line about everything he does for her and how she acts like he doesn't exist makes me think that there's more of a connection, that it's more personal than that. That she's had more interaction than simply selling him tickets to a tourist attraction in the area."

"Good point, but I'm still not sure how that helps us. I mean, working where she does, with the public, there's just so many possibilities. Regular customer, someone in the village, someone who worked there in the past. I mean she's worked there for years, Kate."

"I know, and it's just too many people."

"Has she noticed anyone hanging around lately?"

"Not sure. We'll have to ask her, but not in front of Sammy."

Stella nodded. "I'll get those cards in to Len tomorrow and see if he can get any prints off them. Probably not on the flowers card, but you never know."

Kate agreed. They both knew it was unlikely that they'd get prints, but it didn't hurt to try, and if they didn't, they had no chance whatsoever to get the easy answer.

"With all the evidence they're processing at the moment, though, this won't be a priority."

"I know." Kate sighed heavily. "It can't be. Resources are tied up on far more important things right now."

"Doesn't stop you feeling like this is the most important, does it?"

Kate smirked at Stella's telling question. "Nope."

Stella rubbed Kate's bicep. "Don't worry. We'll find out who this prick is and find Ayeshydi...and Mallam. All at the same time." She shimmied her shoulders and puffed out her chest a little. "Just let me dig out my superheroine knickers, and we'll get right to it."

Kate chuckled. "Maybe we should have dinner first."

"Bitch."

CHAPTER 25

Stella's phone pinged with an incoming e-mail as Gina served them dishes of sherry trifle—thick whipped cream, set custard, and fruit jelly laced with heady booze.

"Mmm," Kate murmured in pleasure as the first splash of cream and alcohol hit her tongue.

Stella frowned at her phone, looked up quickly at Kate, and then handed the phone over. "From my friend at the Driver and Vehicle Licensing Agency. Look, that's Ishman Ayeshydi."

Kate stared at the image for a second. Then she squinted and looked closer, bending her head over the screen. "The DVLA gave you this? Seriously, that's Ayeshydi?"

Stella nodded.

Kate frowned and looked again. She needed to be certain of what she was seeing. It was too incredible. Too ridiculous. Too...wrong. "No, that's...but it's—fuck!"

"Kate!" Sammy yelled, eyes wide.

"Sorry, kiddo, sorry." Kate jumped to her feet, covered her hands over Sammy's cheeks, and kissed her head. "Never, ever repeat that word." She looked up at Gina. "Sorry."

Gina shook her head. "Don't worry, I've heard her say it before now. Go—do what you've got to do." Gina picked up her bowl. "I'll keep this safe till you get back."

"Thanks." Kate shrugged into her coat and slipped her feet into her shoes, not bothering with the laces. She kissed Gina's cheek and whispered, "Don't wait up for me. I might be a while."

Stella was out of the door behind her, car keys in hand. "I'll drive, you try Timmons."

Kate nodded and did as she was told. His phone went straight to voicemail. "Shit. Let's just hope he's at the station." She looked at the picture Stella had shared with her. "I knew there was something wrong with this shit, but Christ. How does an MI5 agent get replaced with a terrorist?"

"What if he wasn't replaced? What if he's simply both individuals?" Stella shoved her phone into Kate's hand. "Look at the second picture. That's Zain Mallam's driver's licence."

"Nah, they do tons and tons of screening to get into MI5. Surely they'd know if he had an alter ego like this shithead."

"They also do tons and tons of training for operatives. And undercover work."

Bollocks. "Ishman Ayeshydi is his undercover identity?" Pieces began to slip into place like the tumblers in a lock, but still, it stuck. "If that's true, then why did he let the lock-up explode and kill so many police officers? If he's Ayeshydi, it was his lock-up and his bombs. Why let that happen?"

"Maybe he didn't."

"He was on his phone, and now he's missing. We already agreed we don't believe in coincidences."

"True, but all I'm saying is, MI5 have given us diddly, and we know they're not above letting crimes go ahead if it helps them get closer to an objective they have further down the road. A few dead here in Lynn to stop a bigger attack later. Would MI5 let something like that happen to preserve an undercover agent in order to take down more criminals later? I believe they would."

Kate had to admire the logic...and the cold-blooded ruthlessness that would be required to make that call if it were true. A big if, as far as Kate was concerned. Too many twists and turns. Too many angles. People weren't generally all that clever. And most often they weren't half as clever as they thought they were. More often than not, cases were simple, and perpetrators were easily identifiable. Motives were easy to figure out and understand. Evidence was usually pretty easy to find, often the issue being an overabundance rather than a lack, and interpretation was the most difficult part of a case.

Most rapes were perpetrated by someone the victim knew. Most murders were committed by the spouse. Most children were killed or hurt by a family member.

Not always. But most of the time. So, most of the time, they played the percentages.

The percentages in their scenario told them that acts of terror were carried out by Islamic extremists, end of story. They didn't touch on potentially rogue MI5 agents or the girl's father having a personal motivation for winding her up and setting her off—quite literally—in one direction. Stella could be right just as easily as she could be wrong. Or they could both be wrong, and there was even more going on than they could even begin to fathom.

The station looked quieter than Kate had seen it since the bomb had gone off at Ann Summers. Only three-quarters full at seven o'clock in the evening. Plenty of parking spaces. She spotted Timmons's car and pointed it out to Stella.

She nodded and parked up.

Kate's boot heels cracked on the tile floor of the station as they hurried down corridor after corridor and up a flight of stairs. With her heart pounding with adrenaline, as well as the exertion of taking the stairs two at a time, Kate pushed open the squad room door. Timmons's office was at the back end of the room, door firmly closed, blinds drawn.

She and Stella were practically running across the room. Kate rapped her knuckles against the wood and pushed the door open. Porter and Green turned to look at them.

Timmons stood, leaning on his desk, his face paler than before, which made his cheeks look even more ruddy than usual. He had one hand raised, his finger pointed and his mouth open like he was in midsentence...or maybe midword.

"I thought I told you two I didn't want to see you here!"

"Yes, sir. But this can't wait." Stella slammed the door closed behind her. She glanced around, then crossed to his desk and grabbed a pad and a pen.

Kate glanced over her shoulder before she opened her images and put the picture of Ayeshydi/Mallam on the desk. "This is Ishman Ayeshydi." She flipped to next picture. "And Zain Mallam."

"Bollocks!" Timmons shouted.

Porter and Clare rounded the desk to look at the picture.

"You're sure?"

"Positive, sir. Uncontaminated source."

"Fuck." He pinned Porter with a look. "What the fuck is going on here?"

"I'm as shocked as—"

"Bullshit."

"I've never worked with him before."

"Right. But when you asked for the information I requested, shouldn't you have been sent an ID too?" Timmons leant closer to him. "Isn't that a standard on an agent's file these days?"

Porter squirmed.

They all took that as confirmation.

"Did you know beforehand that he wasn't who he was supposed to be?"

"He is who he's supposed to be."

"Explain."

"I can't."

"I said explain," Timmons snarled.

"You don't have clearance."

"I do!"

Porter shook his head and chuckled. "No, sir, you really don't."

Timmons tried again. "Every one of us signed the Official Secrets Act when we became police officers. As far as I'm concerned, everything on the job is top secret."

Porter stood up. "You don't have clearance."

Clare blocked the door so he couldn't leave. "Ishman Ayeshydi is his undercover ID. Correct?"

Porter stared at her in silence, his eyes burning holes through hers.

"I'll take that as a yes."

"Should've taken a bet on that," Stella said under her breath.

"An undercover operative?" Timmons asked incredulously. "In King's Lynn? I hate to break it to you, but Lynn isn't exactly a hotbed of dissidents and extremists."

Kate almost wanted to point out that that didn't seem to be the case since they'd had two explosions in three days, but it wasn't really the right time to butt in.

Clare shook her head. "I'm guessing he didn't start out here. Probably a major city. London?"

"I'm not a suspect for you to interrogate."

"London. Okay, so he followed a cell here? I know there've been rumblings that a major attack was expected in London. It was brought up in one of the gold command meetings on Sunday. There were four targets mentioned: MI5 HQ, New Scotland Yard, Westminster, and Westminster Abbey. Is this what he was working on?"

Porter didn't answer, his hands clenched into fists, and Kate wondered just how much more Clare knew that they weren't privy to. It seemed the higher ranks of gold command had suppressed a number of details that could have helped them in their investigation. Or even—heaven forbid—could have helped them to save lives. For fuck's sake, when were they going to realise that they were all on the same side? That Kate and her colleagues were not the enemy, and treating them as such had only put more people at risk.

"Just so you know," Clare said, "every question you evade or refuse to answer screams an affirmative response. You do realise that, don't you?"

He said nothing.

Clare smirked. "There was an intelligence report mentioned by gold command yesterday about training targets. They suggested that King's Lynn was one such target. Is that why Mallam was posing as Ayeshydi here?"

"You don't have clearance."

"He knew the bomb was going to be detonated in a shopping centre in the run-up to Christmas, and he let it happen." Clare prodded him in the chest. "That makes him a murderer."

Porter shook his head. "No."

Clare frowned.

"He's not a murderer."

Clare's eyes opened wider. "He wasn't the cell leader. He didn't know the details of the target, did he?"

Porter said nothing.

"So he wasn't the bomb builder?"

"You don't have clearance."

"Who built the bombs?" Kate asked.

Porter said nothing, nor did his gaze flicker from Clare.

"Saba?"

Porter's lips twitched. "You don't have clearance."

"Christ." Clare ran her fingers through her short, blond hair, her eyes flitting from side to side.

A habit Kate remembered well from their early days working together, when Clare had been her sergeant. She always ran through her memory like she was reading a book, her eyes twitching from left to right as she went over one memory at a time.

"The intel Mallam gave us was all correct. He just didn't state which Ayeshydi was the bomb builder. He went to the training camp in Raqqa as Ayeshydi. That's where he was married to Saba. She was the bomb builder."

"You don't have clearance, ma'am." The touch of respect that crept into Porter's voice told everyone in the room that Clare was right.

"For fuck's sake," Timmons said.

"So why did she blow herself up?" Stella asked. "That doesn't make sense. You don't take out your weapons expert."

Clare nodded. "The cell doesn't, but an undercover operative does if he has no other choice."

Kate frowned. She didn't like where Clare's thoughts were taking them now, but Porter wasn't correcting her. He wasn't denying it.

"Ma'am?"

"Did Mallam know that her plan was to go with Nadia?"

"You don't have—"

"Clearance, yes, I know. So Mallam knew she would be there when Nadia was sent to blow herself up. Saba wasn't supposed to detonate her bomb. She was going to walk away from it, and given that there was no CCTV footage afterwards, we'd assume she was obliterated in the explosion. Takes her right off the radar." Clare crossed her arms over her chest. "But they weren't a hundred per cent on Nadia, were they?"

Porter said nothing.

"So Saba rigged her own detonator to blow Nadia's vest, in the event that Nadia backed out at the last minute?"

"You don't have clearance."

"Coldhearted bitch," Stella said.

Porter turned his head to meet Stella's gaze, but he said nothing.

"What went wrong? Both vests blew, so did she get her wiring wrong?" Timmons asked.

"No," Porter said quietly.

"Mallam happened." Clare frowned. "I'm guessing Saba wouldn't tell him when or where the attack was going to happen, and she would know if he sabotaged the vests to prevent them from exploding. Then she could just fix it and carry on with the plan, and he'd have blown his cover. Instead he sabotaged the detonators."

"You don't have—"

Stella waved a hand to stop him.

"How?" Timmons frowned.

"The explosives experts said that either detonator would cause both bombs to explode. Both, not just Nadia's. It was the only way he could make sure that Saba wouldn't detonate any of the other devices. Correct?"

Porter ran his fingers through his blond hair. "You don't have clearance."

"He could have turned them in. He could have made an anonymous call and had the explosives found before they were used," Clare said.

Porter shook his head.

"Of course he could!" Clare's voice rose. "All those people died." Clare was furious. Raking her hands through her hair, she glared at Porter.

He didn't even blink.

"Was maintaining his cover so much more important than their lives?"

"You don't have clearance." His voice was sad.

Did he regret the choice that had been made? Would he have chosen a different path if it had been his choice? Did it matter when it was already done?

"Is that where he is now? Maintaining his cover?" Timmons demanded.

"You don't have clearance."

"For fuck's sake!" Timmons threw up his hands and dropped heavily into his chair, running his hands through his thinning hair in frustration.

"Mr Porter, can we assume from all this that the four targets Chief Inspector Green mentioned are correct and that Saba Ayeshydi had built the bombs for them?" Kate asked.

He turned and looked at her for the first time, but he didn't say anything.

"They were in the lock-up, her lock-up, her bomb factory, if you like, and Mallam didn't know where it was?"

"You don't have clearance."

"Bloody hell." Stella shook her head. "He should have warned them the bombs were built. He could have saved all their lives just by letting the bomb squad go in first."

Kate shook her head. "He didn't know, did he?"

Porter said nothing.

"He was on his phone when it blew up," Kate said. "To you?"

"No."

"Then what?"

"Shit." Timmons sat up straight and riffled through his desk, waving a sheet of paper when he found what he was looking for. "Initial report from the explosives team. There were fragments of a device in the wreckage, of a timer, like some sort of self-destruct button that had to be reset. They reckoned every twenty-four hours, or it would activate and blow up after sixty minutes without a code."

"You can make shit like that?" Kate asked. "Seriously?"

"Apparently." Timmons slapped the page back to his desk. "Did Mallam know about that?"

"You don't have clearance."

"Bollocks." Timmons slumped back in his chair again. "He was trying to shut it down. What did he do? Make a clone of Saba's phone or something?"

Porter said nothing.

"He gave those men no warning." Green glared at him.

Porter's head dropped a little. Shame, guilt, it didn't matter. They were all still dead.

"He couldn't," Kate said as the final tumblers slid into place and a door to a secret she wished she didn't know opened up before her.

"Why not?" Clare demanded as all eyes turned to Kate.

"His cover. He needs to maintain it to go back in and infiltrate the rest of the cell. With Saba and Ahmed out of the picture now, he's the bomb maker they need. They'll contact him to make the new explosives. Letting it go off like that, the casualties, they'll never question his loyalty now. They'll hail him a hero when he tells them he made the bombs that took out police officers. If he tells them he detonated it when they were there…he'll be…he'll be revered. It's his ticket into the big leagues."

"You don't have clearance."

Kate felt sick. Jack Dalton, Marco Palmer, Fred Martin, and so many others were dead. Fred's little kids would grow up without a father. Gareth was blind all so that this arsehole could get a leg up in the ranks of the fucking extremists!

"We're meant to protect people." Kate's voice was quiet, cracking in places as she spoke. "We're supposed to be the good guys, the ones who stop the bad guys." She wiped at the tears of frustration and bitter disappointment that clung to her lashes. "To stop women and children from being slaughtered." She stepped up to him. "Have you ever been at an explosion?"

Porter didn't move. "No."

"Then let me explain to you what it's like to hold a little girl's guts in her body while she's bleeding to death right in front of you." Her voice was rising quickly. "It's hell, Mr Porter. Seeing one of your friend's eyes skewered on a metal spike like a cherry tomato on a fucking kebab. Puts you right off your dinner. As for Dalton, well, he'll look normal enough when they stitch the halves back together. His family could have an open casket at his funeral, at least."

Stella wrapped a hand around Kate's arm, stopping her from advancing, but not holding her back.

"Children died."

"And if they set off bombs in MI5 HQ, New Scotland Yard, Westminster, and Westminster Abbey, how many do you think would die, Detective Brannon?" Porter didn't even flinch under her words. Not even a flicker of conscience. "How many would you sacrifice there to save your friend's eyesight? To stop you seeing a little girl's guts in your hands?" He bent his head towards her. "How many lives do you think Commander Dalton or Superintendent Palmer would sacrifice to have their own lives back?"

She stared at him, but she didn't answer. They both knew the answer was none.

"We do a dangerous job in dangerous times, Detective Brannon. We do so accepting the risks and knowing that there will be difficult choices to make." He slapped his chest. "I'm prepared to make them. Zain Mallam made them. And he will make them again. He will do what needs to be done to make this country a little bit safer."

"You think it's safer with all those people dead."

"I know it's safer with a sociopath like Saba Ayeshydi off the playing field. I know it's safer with Tariq Ahmed behind bars and that cache of explosives destroyed. And I damn well know we're safer with Zain Mallam out there risking his life to bring in other terrorists." He pointed his finger in her face. The muscles in his jaw bunched and flexed as he worked to spit out words that Kate knew could never justify his decision in her eyes. "You don't know what we're dealing with out there, pissing around in your little pond. You don't even know what's going on right under your nose. So don't give me all this crap." His nostrils flared, and anger emanated from him like a heat rising from a tarmac road in a heat wave. Kate leant back, hoping to prevent any scorch marks. "I've put my life on the line more times than you could count to make sure you can sleep safe in your bed at night. We don't ask for thanks. We don't ask for rewards. We don't even get recognition for what we do. But I will not take your disrespect either." He dropped his hand and backed off.

"Yes, this operation cost us. It cost us a lot. But I guarantee you it has also saved lives. If they'd detonated a bomb in Westminster Abbey...do you have any idea how many people would have been killed or injured there? Not just politicians, but schoolkids on day trips, tourists." He shook his head sadly. "I understand that this is a hard pill to swallow for you, but, believe me, this is a win. This is what success looks like in a country at war with extremists." He laughed bitterly. "Whoever said that success was beautiful was a liar. It's dead bodies and lies. It's sleepless nights and a drinking problem, if you're lucky. And if you're not..." He screwed his face up and dropped onto the bench seat at the back of the hut. "If you're not, then perhaps you're the lucky one after all." He held his hand up and offered them all a salute.

Kate wanted to slap that condescending look off his face and ram his words down his throat, and she was pretty sure she wasn't the only one. Stella's fingers flexed against her arm. Waves of anger rolled in Kate's guts, and she wanted to scream at him, to open her mouth at the futility of every word he spoke. The futility of it all. The deaths, the investigation, the time, the money, the endless, ceaseless, and relentless images of dismembered bodies that streamed through her head like a song on repeat. Over and over and over again. And every single one could have been avoided. Every single one could have been stopped before it happened. But they—the powers that be, those fucking arses in their ivory fucking towers—had decided that they didn't matter. That two-year-old Gregory Walsh didn't matter. That six-year-old Anastacia Pekov didn't matter. Dalton, Palmer, Gina,

Stella, Gareth...none of them fucking mattered, because they were just names to them. To him.

None of them mattered.

She looked at his smug face. Arrogant, thinking he was so superior, that his reasoning, as logical as it might be, made their actions—their life costing actions—forgivable. Understandable. Maybe even acceptable.

It didn't.

"Mr Porter, I don't know where you come from, but where I grew up, we learnt a few things. One was that life, any life, is precious. The other was that any action that cost the loss of it is a sin. You might think that these lives were worth less than those of people in London, but I don't. And I certainly don't consider this a success." She shook off Stella's arm and advanced on him. "This might be a stepping stone in a bigger battle, but people died. People have suffered in ways you cannot even begin to imagine, and will continue to do so every day, for the rest of their lives." She stood over him. "I hope that one day you'll understand what that means, but somehow I doubt it."

She turned on her heel and stalked out of the office, pushing away hands that tried to reach for her as she went.

CHAPTER 26

The brandy burned the back of Kate's throat as she swallowed and slapped the glass back on the bar, signalling for another. She didn't know exactly where she was, other than it was the first pub she came to when she walked out of the King's Lynn police station and that it was a dive. The kind of place where you were glad the lights were so low so you couldn't see that rats scurrying across the dance floor. Or someone else's lipstick on the glass you were drinking out of. As long as it served alcohol, Kate didn't care. What was the fucking point?

The stool next to her was pulled away from the bar, and a heavy form sat down on it.

She half turned away, hoping that whoever it was didn't expect her to talk to them. Kate wanted to drink and to forget, and she most certainly did not want to get hit on by a fucking stranger in this shithole.

"Same as my friend here."

Kate whirled on her chair at the sound of Timmons's voice. "What are you doing here?"

He picked up the glass the bartender set in front of him, slapped a tenner on the slightly soggy and very sticky wooden surface, and inclined the glass towards her. "Same as you, by the look of it." He threw the shot down in one gulp and pulled back his teeth. "Getting pissed." He signalled for the bartender and held up another note. "Leave the bottle, son."

The bartender nodded and left the bottle of Napoleon on the counter.

Timmons topped them both up and tapped his glass to hers. "To another case solved."

Kate snorted derisively. "Doesn't feel like it."

"Nope." He knocked his drink back.

"It feels pointless."

"Aye." He poured another.

She sipped, staring at the bottles lined up along the back of the bar, wondering when her eyesight had started to fail and the words on the labels had begun to blur together. On second thought, maybe that wasn't her eyesight, just the brandy goggles.

"I've never felt so disappointed at resolving a case."

"This one was never going to have a good ending, Brannon."

"Maybe not, sir, but—I don't know—it doesn't feel like it's over."

"What did you expect? How did you want this to end? A big shootout, and terrorists being brought down in the streets of King's Lynn?" Timmons shook his head. "That stuff's for the films, Brannon. It was never going to end up like that." He picked up the bottle, but instead of pouring, he pointed it at her. "What he said was true, you know. The perps are dead, Ahmed's in jail, and he will be staying there for a long time. Probably the rest of his life. We all know what they do in prison to people who hurt children."

Kate nodded. It was a rough form of justice, but Ahmed would suffer before they killed him in prison. It was almost a certainty.

"The explosives are accounted for, and we know that the cell is wiped out in our area. It's finished."

"It doesn't feel finished."

"I suppose it isn't. For them, anyway. But it is for us. We've been ordered to cease and desist our investigation into Ishman Ayeshydi."

She slammed her glass back on the bar, amazed that it didn't shatter under the force. "You're joking?"

Timmons shook his head and swallowed more brandy. "Orders came in from the very top."

Kate frowned. The very top? Did he mean the Chief Constable, or higher still? MI5? The Home Office? How high up were these orders? "Sir?"

He smirked and said, "You don't have clearance." He drained his glass and reached for the bottle again. "We know as much as we're ever going to know. The bombers are dead. Ahmed confessed, and we have Nadia's diary to back it up. Ayeshydi is still on the wanted list, but that's for MI5 to take care of when he finally gets out of his undercover assignment. We just can't keep looking for him."

"If he ever gets free of his assignment." They both knew it was likely his cover would get blown at some point, and he'd end up dead. Zain Mallam was working a dangerous game, and his survival was far from assured.

Timmons nodded and tipped the bottle towards her again. "Never a truer word spoken."

The door opened. Stella, Clare, Jimmy, and Tom all sauntered in while Timmons poured them drinks and got more glasses from the bartender.

"Any news on Gareth?" Tom asked, glass in hand.

"Nothing new." Timmons poured his brandy. "Poor sod." He pointed to a table in the corner of the pub. "Shall we move this over there, people?" He didn't wait for them to answer, leading the way and sitting on the bench at the back of the room.

In dribs and drabs, they followed behind him and took their seats on rickety stools that made you feel like you were inebriated even if you weren't.

Tom sat next to Kate and caught her eye. "You okay?"

She shook her head. "Nope. Not even close."

"Stella filled us in on the way over." He clapped his hand on her shoulder. "I'd be up on charges for punching the arrogant bastard."

Kate snorted. "Wish I had."

Tom sipped his drink.

"You ever think of giving up?" she whispered into the dissonance of clinking glasses, a crackling jukebox, and angry voices.

"Every damn day." Timmons spread his arms across the back of the bench.

"Why don't you?"

"Because then I remember that there's only me who can do the things I can. And if I don't do 'em, no fucker else will."

She stared at him and tried to decipher the deeper meaning behind the words. He wasn't arrogant enough to believe he alone could save the world. But the brandy was beginning to set in, and it was making thinking harder than it should be.

"I'm not a religious man," he continued. "But I do believe that we all have something to offer. Some talent we can use to make something better. A purpose." He drank the last of his brandy and slammed the glass back on the table. "I was a shit husband and a godawful father, so I don't believe that's why I'm here. But I do believe I make a difference. I believe I've helped put some very bad people behind bars so they can't do a lot of very bad things to anyone else." He looked at each of them in turn, his gaze landing on Kate last and staying there. "Every one of you has a gift for doing the same thing. Every one of you sees different things and brings unique talents to the table, and together you solve crimes." He pointed at Kate. "If you hadn't wondered about the remote bomb thing and warned everyone, at least four more people would have died yesterday."

"But four people did die."

"Four is less than eight."

"But—"

"No buts. You did the best you could. I didn't think of that. Collier didn't, Jackson, Brown, Dalton, Palmer... They're all—were all— experienced officers, and not a single one of them thought of it. And if they did, they did nothing about it. Mallam could've done more. But he didn't. And he's got to live with that.

"I agree with you. He could've made a play there that would've warned people without risking his cover. All he had to do was what you did, just earlier. You and Stella together got the evidence we needed to get us some semblance of answers and stop us chasing our tails for God knows how long. Stopped us from wasting resources we don't have to spare, man hours we can ill afford, and fuck knows what else." He reached for his drink and frowned at the empty glass.

Tom reached over and topped it up.

Timmons nodded at him.

"Every one of you has worked damn hard on this case, fuck, on every case you've worked on, and I'm fucking proud to have you on my team." He held his drink aloft. "To resolved cases, no matter how dissatisfying."

They held up their drinks. The soft tinkle of glass filled the air, and as they began to lower them, Kate added, "To Gareth."

They all paused a moment.

"To Gareth."

CHAPTER 27

Kate popped two tablets from the blister pack she kept in the glove box in her car and chugged them down with water from the bottle, then popped a third, just for good measure. Even after a day filled with nothing but paperwork, her head was still aching from the amount of brandy she'd used to numb herself last night.

"You okay?" Gina asked.

Kate nodded. "I just don't normally drink that much."

"Rough night?"

Gina had been fast asleep by the time Kate had stumbled home. Seeing her, even in slumber, had done much to quiet the uneasy feeling in the pit of Kate's stomach. The anticlimactic conclusion to such an explosive investigation still sat awkwardly on her shoulders. She kept waiting for the rest of…something. There were still so many questions that burned. How could they be sure that Mallam was still trustworthy? How could they know he hadn't turned into the terrorist he was supposedly pretending to be? How could he look himself in the mirror, knowing he could have saved those people but he didn't? Maybe he couldn't. And she was never going to find out those answers. She was never going to know anything more than she did right now, because they'd been told to back off, to let sleeping dogs lie, and to never mention the bastard again.

It wasn't good enough. It wasn't good enough for Kate, and it was never going to be good enough for the families of those who died. Not that they would get to know anything like what she did. No one who hadn't stood inside that office last night ever truly would. And Kate wasn't sure if she could carry that.

"Sorry."

Gina took her hand. "No need." She lifted Kate's hand to her lips and kissed her knuckles. "You sure you still want to do this?"

Kate nodded. She wanted to forget about work for a while. She needed to figure out how she could let this go, or it was going to start eating her alive. There were too many emotions swirling in her guts. "I'm just happy to spend the evening with you." It was the truth. But like so many things, it wasn't the whole truth. "Have I told you how beautiful you look?"

Gina smiled. "Once or twice."

"Only once or twice! God, I'm such a bad girlfriend." She grabbed Gina's hand and kissed the back of it, letting her gaze wander over the form-fitting blue dress Gina had chosen for the evening. Long-sleeved and falling just below the knee with a modest V-shaped neckline, it was a classically beautiful dress that highlighted Gina's slim body and the deep blue of her eyes without exposing her. "You look stunning."

Gina blushed and whispered, "Thanks. So do you." She ran her fingers down the green blouse Kate had pulled out of the wardrobe to pair with her black slacks and leather jacket. "I love it when you wear that jacket." She fingered the collar, straightening it to lie flat against her collarbone before she climbed out of the car.

Kate followed her, forcing a smile to her lips as she packed her concerns into a box and shoved it onto a shelf in the back of her head, swiftly labelling it *Do Not Open—Ever* before she caught up to Gina and took hold of her hand.

Morston Hall was a large restaurant and hotel, surrounded by immaculate lawns and beautiful flowers, the scent of lavender and herbs tantalising the nose as they walked up the gravel path. It was a pity they couldn't really see them in the dark. The lighting along the path and scattered amongst the trees did little to drive back the night, but twinkled prettily against the clean, white snow that covered the expansive lawns. The flint and lime style of the hall, so typical of the area, was heavily shadowed. The restaurant itself was visible through the glass windows of the huge conservatory-style extension that had been added to the old hall. The starched white tablecloths and polished silverware indicated the level of establishment George Boyne had picked for this meeting.

"Well, this is about as far out of my price range as those glasses are from the grains of sand on the beach," Gina muttered, nerves jangling on every chord of her voice.

"Morston Hall," Kate replied. "Just screams posh, doesn't it?"

Gina slapped her belly. "Behave." She craned her neck to get a better look inside. "I'm nervous."

"About what?"

"Walking into this fancy place. Meeting him. Telling him Pat's dead. Giving him the letter. Not liking the fancy food. Worrying I'll make a fool of myself."

"Ah, so not much, really."

Gina shot her a sardonic look.

"Want me to handle the letter and tell him about Pat? I can't do too much about you embarrassing yourself, not liking the food, or the meeting him bits. Unless you want to go home."

"You'd do that for me?"

"Sure." Kate fished the car keys out of her pocket. "Home's just half an hour away."

"I meant telling him the horrible bits."

Kate winked. "I know. And yes. Unfortunately, this won't be the first time I've delivered bad news to a stranger."

Gina looked at her with such an open expression it took Kate's breath away. There was something so tender and vulnerable in her gaze, yet something a little lustful too. Kate's heart beat a little faster.

"Do you think he's already in there?" Gina asked, breaking the moment.

Probably a good thing, Kate decided. She wasn't entirely sure how the staff would react to them snogging in front of the main doors.

"Only one way to find out." Kate pushed the door open and led Gina inside with one hand on her lower back. She loved the way it felt to be able to touch Gina like this, freely, without her recoiling at such a simple, innocent touch. She'd come a long way in a short time since she'd begun working with Jodi. Kate smiled, proud of Gina's hard work, as a waiter came to meet them.

"Good evening. Do you have a reservation?" he asked with a tiny bow that tilted his body forward only a few degrees. His white shirt, starched to within an inch of its life, was tucked into black trousers, a skinny black tie hung around his neck, and an air of privilege most unbecoming to waitstaff hung around him like a bad smell. Posh restaurant, it might be... Buckingham Palace, it was not.

"We're here to meet Mr Boyne. George Boyne. Has he arrived yet?"

"I have just this moment shown him to your table." He sounded as though he was trying not to inhale too deeply. His voice coming from high in the back of his throat, making it sound pinched and a little like he was talking through a harmonica. Reedy. It was the only way she could think to describe it. Thin and reedy, like an oboe talking. "If you'll follow me, please." He waved his arm before him like a magician showing them a trick.

Well, Kate supposed, the floors were spectacularly clean. The table he took them to was in the far left-hand corner of the room. There were two empty chairs at the table and a man already seated. He had a glass of liquor in front of him and held a small square of paper in his hand.

George Boyne was a thin, wiry sort of chap with a shock of thick, steel-grey hair that had probably once been dark. He stood when he saw them approach the table and held out his hand. Eyes a startling shade of blue, like the Aegean Sea sparkling in the midday sun, watched them with amusement.

"George Boyne." His grip was firm and strong, as was his voice.

"Kate Brannon." She shook his hand and ushered Gina forward with her other hand.

"You must be Gina Temple, then."

"Yes." Gina shook his hand. "Nice to meet you."

"A pleasure. Please, sit." He indicated the chairs, and the waiter eased the chair in behind Gina as Kate quickly pulled her own in for herself.

"May I get you something to drink?" the waiter asked.

Gina ordered a glass of wine and Kate asked for water. She wanted to have her wits about her for whatever Gina might need. Besides, one of them needed to be able to drive, and she didn't need anything to add to her lingering hangover.

"So, you knew my Patricia, hey?" He was smiling, but his eyes were watching Gina. Studying her, like he was trying to get inside her head.

Kate couldn't help but smile at the possessive tinge to the sentence. Even after all those years, it seemed old George still carried a little torch for the lovely Pat.

Gina nodded. "Sort of."

He frowned. "I don't understand. I thought we were here because she asked you to give me something?"

"We are," Gina said. "But I wouldn't say I knew her well."

"Then what would you say, young lady?" George asked gruffly, leaning forward over the table, his voice a little harsh.

"That it was her dying wish."

He sat back in his chair. "She's dead?" His voice sounded deflated, hoarse, defeated.

Gina nodded.

"When? What happened to her?"

The waiter arrived and deposited their drinks, casting curious glances across them all before leaving them to peruse the menu.

"She was shopping in King's Lynn on Saturday."

His head snapped up. "This Saturday just gone?"

"Yes," Kate said, when Gina didn't respond.

"The bomb?" He whispered. "You were there?" he asked Gina gently.

Gina cleared her throat. "Yes. I was doing some Christmas shopping with a friend. I was with Pat when she—when she died."

George's face was ashen. "And she talked about me? Then?"

Kate pulled a copy of the photograph from her pocket. "Is this you?" She handed it to him.

He smiled sadly and nodded, then handed her the square of paper he'd been looking at when they arrived. It looked to have been taken on the same day. The couple was wearing the same clothes in each picture, and smiling at each other.

Kate handed it back to him. "I'm very sorry for your loss, Mr Boyne."

He shook his head. "I lost Pat a long time ago. I can't believe she had this on her when she...when she died." He looked back at Kate, then at Gina. "Why? Did she tell you?"

Gina nodded to Kate, and Kate took the copied pages of the letter from her jacket pocket.

"She wanted you to have this," Kate said gently. "I'm sorry we had to open it but it had to be checked for evidence because of the investigation."

"Of course." He took the pages.

The waiter came over for their food order, but George just waved him away, asking for another round of drinks instead.

"Would you like us to leave you alone?" Kate asked.

He didn't respond.

Kate stood, indicating for Gina to follow her.

"Have you read it?" he asked before they were even on their feet.

"Yes, sir. I'm sorry."

He shook his head. "No need." He lifted the page like a hand wave. "I knew about her bloody father." He laughed bitterly. "He was the reason I met Pat in the first place."

Gina frowned. "I don't understand."

"I was Army Intelligence. Running undercover surveillance operations on IRA suspects."

"I thought that didn't start until after Bloody Sunday," Kate said.

He nodded. "Officially. After '72, we got our own special unit. One hundred twenty men trained by the SAS. We started as the SRU, then became the FRU in the bloody '80s, but me and my men were doing the same thing back then. Trying to protect lives by rooting out those vicious bastards. And Paddy O'Shea was one of the worst you could ever come across."

"So you were using Pat?" Shock was written all over Gina's face.

Kate felt the same. She hadn't spoken to Pat, but Gina had told her every moment of their interaction. She felt like she knew her. The Pat in her head was a warm, funny woman with a strong spirit, a sense of humour, and an adventurous soul. The idea of someone using her as a young girl to get to her father irked... No, it was more than that. It made her angry. Angry that men like this had so little regard for the lives of those they used, and seemingly ruined, to further their careers and catch the occasional bad man.

She'd often wondered if they were any different to the men they were trying to stop? They both justified reprehensible actions as necessary to achieve their goals—the IRA in the name of freedom, and the army in the name of defence. The right and wrong of it all decided by the history written by the victor.

Just like Nadia. Groomed by her father, by her friend, and by someone who should have protected her. She wouldn't be remembered as a girl who was used by men with more power than her, but as a vicious murderer, the destroyer of lives, the bringer of death. And this man, the George that Pat had felt guilt over for so many years, had been doing the same. Just the same as Zain Mallam.

Same story over, and over again. Just a different set of players. *Will we never learn?*

He nodded. "That's how it started, yes. I'm not proud of it, but you don't know what we were up against. We were losing men all the bloody time because we couldn't tell who was good and who wasn't. They didn't play by the rules. So we had to start making up a few new ones."

"I can't believe her last thoughts were of you, and you were just using her." Gina's eyes were brimming with tears.

He shook his head. "No, it wasn't like that. I mean, it started out that way, of course. I was trying to get close to her father. Those were my orders. It was my mission. And it was an important one. Lives were at stake, and I took my duty, my responsibilities, seriously. I knew what Paddy had already done, and I knew there was a lot more to come from that bastard. But that all changed pretty quickly. Not Paddy, or the fact that he needed to be removed from the game, but Pat changed the way I thought, the way I acted." He smiled. "She changed everything about me, that girl did. She had a way about her." He snorted a sad laugh. "It sounds cheesy, but she really did light up a room when she walked in. I lit up when she smiled at me and said my name in that lilting accent of hers. 'Georgie', she called me. 'My Georgie'."

He tapped his chest. "Made my heart beat with something besides fear for a while. I was serious when I asked her to marry me. Serious when I said we should run away together. I would have done it for her. Given up everything for her. Abandoned my post, my responsibilities, my brothers in arms. Everything." He shook his head. "And yes, I knew what I was risking in doing so. Probably better than she did." He used his thumb to wipe away the tear in his eye. "I was a bastard, and I knew it. I had to be to fight bigger bastards than I was. Because they weren't messing around. They'd have killed me soon as look at me, if they'd known who I was. What I was. And they'd have killed her too. They'd have never trusted her, cavorting with the enemy." Sipping his drink, he shook his head again slowly. "As far as they were concerned, she'd have been worse than me in their eyes. I was a stupid English soldier who knew no better. She was one of them betraying her own, as far as they were concerned. It wouldn't have mattered that she didn't know how I was."

"It must have been very difficult, Mr Boyne." Kate swallowed the recriminations on her tongue. He had enough of his own, by the sound of it, and she didn't know what else to say. Clearly his own guilt was a much greater burden upon his soul than any words she could offer him. He was right, she hadn't been there. She hadn't lived that fear. Could she really judge him? Could she judge any of them? Mallam, Porter, Boyne, they knew more about what was happening in those situations than she did. More than Kate ever could or wanted to know. She had to accept that Boyne knew more about what happened back then and take him at his word that they were doing the best they could to end a war. Could she give Mallam and Porter the same consideration? Did she want to?

No. Not today. Today she was still grieving, still hurting. Today was a day to still hold them accountable, because history hadn't yet decided if they were right or wrong. She wouldn't be their judge.

That was for others who knew more about it. Today was a day where she would simply accept that she wasn't the one history would hold accountable. She had done all she could, and her only regrets would be in the lives others stole before she had a chance to save them. For that alone, she was glad she'd come tonight.

"It was difficult. But there was a lot worse to come." Boyne sniffed. "A lot worse. All those people. Dead. And we call it 'The Troubles'." He laughed bitterly. "Well, they certainly caused enough trouble for everyone." The paper shook in his hand as he stared at it. "And now I have a daughter." A sad smile painted his lips. "We had a daughter."

"Do you have a family, Mr Boyne?" Kate asked.

Gina was still staring at him angrily.

"Never found the right woman. I don't think I ever really looked after Pat turned me down." His smile was rueful. "Truth is, I was married to the job. After, I shipped out of Ireland for the Gulf War, then Bosnia. I ran a desk through the start of the war in Afghanistan and finally retired in 2002. What woman would want to put up with that kind of husband? I saw my peers get married, divorced, remarried. Watched them crying into their whiskey the night before a mission because their woman had done the dirty on 'em, only to find he never made it back from that mission. Nah." With a bitter smile, he swallowed the rest of his whiskey. "Not fair to me, and not fair to her. She had a lucky escape." He winked and held his hand up for the waiter. "Ladies, I do hope you'll excuse me, but I think I'll take my leave." Handing a wad of cash to the waiter he said, "Dinner is on me. Thank you for your time, and I wish you all the best."

Easing himself out of his chair, he patted his pockets, no doubt checking for keys and wallet and whatever else he carried with him.

"You don't need to go, Mr Boyne," Kate said.

He glanced at Gina and nodded. "Yes, I do. The mood I'm in right now, I'd sour the gravy anyway." He tipped his head to Kate and lifted the letter. "Thanks again for bringing me this. I can't tell you how much I appreciate it."

"Will you be all right?" Kate asked, her hand on his arm.

"Quite. Thank you. And please try to—" He glanced at Gina again. "Never mind." Then he was gone.

Kate sat down again and took hold of Gina's hand. "Well, that wasn't exactly what I thought would happen. You okay?"

Gina nodded, then shook her head. "I can't believe he was just using her, and she'd pined for him all those years."

"Didn't you listen to him?"

Gina's eyes snapped up.

"It started that way. That's how they met, but he fell in love with her. He would have given up his career for her. Risked his life for her. He loved her that much. So, no, it didn't start out all hearts and flowers, sweetheart, but it ended with them both in the same place. Both in love and stuck in an untenable position." She squeezed Gina's fingers. "Doesn't really change the story all that much, does it?"

Gina sat quietly for a few minutes. "He was carrying that picture of her. Do you think he carried it always like she did? Or just pulled it out because he was coming here?"

"I don't know. I guess we'll never know now."

"I can't believe he just left like that."

Kate laughed.

"What?"

"Well, you were just staring at him. Scowling at him, really. It felt very much like you wanted him to leave."

"I did not."

Kate stared at her. Eyebrow hitched.

"Okay, maybe I did. But it was a shock. I mean, I thought he'd tell us how they met at a dance or something. Maybe introduced by mutual friends."

"Gina, babe, he was an English soldier in what was effectively a war zone. Did you really think they met through mutual friends?"

Gina rolled her eyes. "Fine. I guess I didn't really think about the details. But it was still a shock."

"How big a shock do you think it was for him? Finding out that Pat was killed in an explosion last week and he has a daughter he never knew about."

She tutted. "Fine, he wins that one too. I handled it badly. Happy now?"

Kate pulled her closer and kissed her forehead. "Not until you smile at me." Kate understood how and why Gina had built Pat up to some sort of mythical figure in her head, some perfect angel. Quite simply, she was the first person Gina had seen die. The first person she'd sat with as the life had drained from her, and Kate knew just how overwhelming that could be. To hear that George had in any way abused the trust of that person, even if it had quickly changed for him, was simply too much for Gina to adapt to so quickly. But neither George nor Pat were of concern to Kate. All she wanted was to make Gina happy. She nudged Gina gently with her elbow. "Come on. Just a little one."

Gina snorted a quick laugh but smiled and shook her head at Kate. Kate grinned.

The twinkle in Gina's eye was back. The quirky little naughty side of Gina that Kate loved so. The look reminded her of Sammy in some ways, and it was easy to see where that child got her mischievous streak from.

"That's better. So, shall we stay to dinner, or can I interest you in some fish and chips and staring out at the lights from Hunstanton Cliffs?"

Gina's head popped up. "The cliffs? It's December!"

"Yes."

"Yes. Definitely. That sounds so romantic."

That had been Kate's thought too. Twenty minutes later, Kate pulled up on the cliff tops. The old lighthouse to the left gleamed in the orange light of the street lamps, and the moon glistened on the rushing waves as the tide advanced on its journey to the shore. The crumbling layers of rock beneath them, red, orange, and white, were safe from the erosive effects of the sea for a little while longer. At least as long as it would take them to eat their fish and chips, anyway.

The scent of salt and vinegar filled the small car, and Gina grinned as she licked grease from her lips. "This is lovely," she whispered.

Kate turned her head and gazed into Gina's eyes. "Yes, it is."

Gina laid her head against Kate's shoulder and sipped at her drink.

After a kiss pressed to the top of Gina's head, Kate rested her check against the top of Gina's and watched their fingers entwine— seemingly all by themselves. Gina's thumb brushed softly over the back of Kate's hand. It was both comforting and exciting. Especially when Gina's finger tips caressed her thigh. It felt electric, even through Kate's jeans.

Gina sat quietly. She seemed totally relaxed, at ease, even. But Kate could only focus on the touch of Gina's hand, the gentle touch of her fingers on the inside of her thigh brushing backwards and forwards, a caress that was beginning to drive her mad.

"You okay?" Gina whispered, her lips close to Kate's ear, her breath hot on the tender skin of Kate's neck.

Kate swallowed hard, fighting the arousal mounting in her body. It seemed to take less and less attention from Gina to turn her into a walking hormone, and she wasn't sure how much more she could take. The last thing she wanted to do was pressure Gina, but Christ, she was only human. If such tender, seemingly innocent touches were ratcheting her desire so much...she shuddered to think what a kiss would do to her right now.

"You okay?" Gina's voice was a little louder this time. "You're not falling asleep on me, are you?"

Kate shook her head, half in an attempt to clear it and half as her response.

"You're quiet."

"I'm just enjoying the view."

Gina squeezed her hand, unlocked their fingers, and patted the back of her hand. "Me too." She slid her hand further down Kate's thigh until she was tracing the seam in tiny increments.

Kate couldn't take any more. She gasped and gently reached down to still her hand.

"What's wrong?" Gina asked.

"Nothing." Her voice sounded a little strangled to her own ears.

Gina smirked. "You're not a very good liar, Detective Sergeant Brannon."

She chuckled. "Maybe not. But you are a very good tease."

Gina glanced down at Kate's lips, then back up to meet her eyes. "Who says I'm teasing?"

Kate groaned quietly as Gina's lips touched her cheek and her fingers continued their caress of her inner thigh.

"If you don't stop, I'm not going to be in any fit state to drive you home," Kate whispered.

Gina beamed and applied a little more pressure with her nails, scratching along the fabric. Every nerve ending in Kate's body seemed to feel that millimetre of skin that was at the end of Gina's touch.

"Well, I wouldn't want that." Gina murmured against her cheek. "I've a surprise planned for you when we get there."

Kate looked at her quizzically. "You do?"

"I do."

CHAPTER 28

Kate parked the car at the back of the house and turned off the engine.

"You're quiet," Gina said as she took Kate's hand and led her towards the car. "You sure you're okay?"

Kate nodded. "Just wondering about this surprise."

Gina grinned. "My mum's having Sammy for the night." She leant across the car and kissed Kate on the lips. Gently. Softly. But laced with promise, and Kate whimpered, not sure how much more of this teasing she could take. "I thought...well, I hoped that...we could..." Gina wrung her fingers as if nervous. Whether she was worried about Kate's response to the question she couldn't seem to ask or to the situation wasn't clear. Either way, she didn't need to worry.

Kate touched a finger to Gina's lips. "Are you telling me you want to sleep with me?"

Gina's lips twitched into a smile under her fingertip, her head dipped a little, and she watched Kate from hooded eyes. Unmistakable desire dilated her pupils, and it was suddenly very clear what Gina wanted. She kissed Kate's fingertip before pulling away and climbing out of the car.

Kate shook her head, trying to make her body do what it was supposed to. She wanted to get out of the car and follow Gina into the house, up the stairs, and slowly peel that beautiful dress off her body. But her body—her traitorous body—just wouldn't respond.

A knock on the window beside her gave her the impetus to turn her head.

Gina grinned at her through the glass and held out a hand. "Coming?"

Kate nodded dumbly and finally managed to get her body to listen to command. She stumbled from the car, and Gina wrapped her hand around Kate's, threading their fingers together. It was Gina who led them into the house and up the stairs. It was Gina who turned on the lamp beside the bed.

Kate stood in the doorway of her own bedroom and stared. It didn't look like the same room she'd left earlier. The bed had been sprinkled with flower petals and a candle burned on the windowsill. Kate's immediate concern was allayed when she realised it wasn't a naked, flickering flame dancing near the curtains, but one of those electric candles. The thoughtful touch meant more to Kate than she could have imagined.

"When did you do this?"

"While you were shouting up the stairs that we were going to be late."

"This is your surprise?"

Gina nodded. "Good surprise?"

Kate smiled. "Very." Her voice was husky and deeper than normal. "It's lovely."

Gina nodded.

"Are *you* okay?"

Gina nodded again.

"Can you speak?"

Gina grinned as she nodded a third time, and Kate laughed, tugged her towards her, and kissed her forehead.

"You don't need to do this."

Gina wrapped her arms around Kate's back. "I know. I want to." She kissed Kate's cheek. "I want it to be special."

"Any time with you will always be special," Kate said sincerely.

"Smooth talker." Gina pinched her side playfully.

"Ouch. I think I need to arrest you."

"What for?"

"Assaulting a police officer."

"Ha." Gina pushed away and stepped towards the bed. "You just love using your handcuffs, don't you?"

Kate's eyebrows shot up, and Gina turned red as she realised what she'd said.

"I meant with your work and—"

"Right," Kate drawled slowly, earning her a withering look from Gina. Laughing, she crossed the floor and pulled Gina back into her arms, but her body had stiffened. Kate wanted her to relax again. She needed to know that Gina was really here, really wanted this. Kate would rather they waited than Gina wake up with regrets. "This really is lovely, Gina. But I'm serious, you don't have to—"

"I want you." Gina slipped her hand behind Kate's neck and pulled her in for a kiss.

Her lips were warm and soft against her still-cool cheeks. But her mouth... Oh, it was hot, so hot. Her tongue slid over Kate's parted lips and teased inside. Kate moaned and held on tighter, leaning back against the cool wall behind her.

"All of you." Gina's fingers in her hair elicited shivers down Kate's spine, and she trembled in Gina's embrace. "I'm ready."

Kate had wanted this for so long now. Waited for so long, but still she didn't feel ready for the onslaught of feeling that welled up inside her. She'd had sex before, but it had never felt like this.

This was so much more. More than just the gentle caress of Gina's fingers, the brush of her tongue in her mouth. It was the trust that reached into her soul and turned her body to jelly. Gina's trust and her desire were the greatest aphrodisiac Kate had ever known, and her knees threatened to buckle. She pulled away from the kiss.

Panting, she said, "If you want to carry on with this, I can't do it standing up."

Gina smiled and nibbled on her lower lip. "You sure about that?"

Kate closed her eyes, groaned, and let her head fall back against the wall. "Positive."

Gina giggled and put some space between them. "Then I guess it's a good job we've got that big bed over there." She tugged Kate away from the wall and pushed her to sit on the edge of the bed. "Comfy?"

Kate nodded as Gina's hands went to the zip at the side of her dress. She lifted her head to meet Gina's gaze.

Gina's fingers paused on the zipper. She wanted to be confident. She wanted to be able to just let the garment fall, to let it pool at her feet, to cast it aside and throw herself into Kate's arms. To kiss and be kissed. To touch her, feel her, to surround herself in the unique smell that was only Kate. But she couldn't. She squeezed the fabric between her fingers. Fucking scars. Goddamn, stupid fucking scars.

Kate had told her so many times that they didn't matter, that they didn't detract from how attractive Kate found her or how she saw her. She didn't doubt what Kate said. She didn't doubt that Kate would look at the scars on her body and see them only as badges of her survival. Of her strength. No. She didn't doubt Kate.

What she doubted was her own ability to see past those pink, puckered lines of flesh. To see them and not remember her own fear. Her own certainty that she was going to die that night. She'd been ready to give up, to give in and tell Ally anything she could to make her stop. It wasn't the scars she saw when she looked at them. It was her own fear. Her weakness. She saw the exact opposite to Kate. It wasn't an ugly scar she worried about. She worried that Kate would one day look upon them and see the weakness she tried to hide. The cowardice she held in her heart.

Kate's eyes were filled with desire, concern, and understanding in equal measure. But there was something else that shone brighter than each of them in her eyes.

"I love you, Gina Temple." She smiled softly and reached for Gina's hand. "You don't have to do this."

"You've said that already."

"I meant it then, and I mean it now."

"I know." Gina stepped back and gathered her courage. If she wanted to be with Kate, to truly be a family with her—she needed to do this. For herself. She drew in a deep breath and lowered the zipper, one tooth at a time. Kate's pupils dilated, and Gina took courage from the desire so obvious on Kate's face. She brushed the fabric from her shoulders, down her arms, then pushed it past her hips to the ground so she couldn't use it to cover her chest.

Kate's mouth fell agape, and her tongue slipped out to wet her lips. "So beautiful," she whispered.

Gina smiled shyly. "I'm very—" her voice cracked. She cleared her throat and tried again. "I'm very glad you think so." She reached behind her back with trembling hands to unhook her bra and quickly cast it aside.

She expected the feelings of nervousness and trepidation to continue—escalate, even—as she undressed before Kate, but that didn't happen. She'd thought that Kate had made her feel special when she'd had to undress at the hospital. Clearly, Kate had been holding back. The look of awe on her face made Gina forget every worry she had. She felt worshipped as Kate leant forward and reached out a hand so slowly it was like she was approaching something precious and fragile she couldn't stand to be apart from for one second longer.

"May I?" she whispered. It was like a prayer leaving her lips.

Gina nodded. Kate's fingers were soft, her touch as sweet as Gina had always known it would be. And when Kate tugged her into her lap and wrapped her arms around her, Gina knew she was home.

"Do you remember when I told you about our first kiss?" Kate whispered as she placed tiny kisses along Gina's shoulder.

"The last first kiss?"

"Yes," Kate said and kissed her lips, taking an age to explore every inch of Gina's mouth and not breaking until they were both panting. "I want to remember every detail."

Gina nodded. "Me too." She slid her fingers into Kate's long, red hair and scratched her nails over her scalp, delighting in the shiver it generated. "Last first time."

"The last first time." There were tears of joy in Kate's eyes as she kissed her and laid them down on the bed. Every touch was a whispered promise of love, every kiss a vow pledged and agreed that this was forever.

When Kate finally slipped inside Gina's body, she claimed her heart, her soul, everything and brought them both home.

Epilogue

"Okay, this one's from me." Kate handed Sammy a huge box wrapped in paper covered with snowmen.

Sammy shook it and listened to the dull rattle. "What is it?"

"Open it and find out."

Sammy was already surrounded by a small mound of wrapping paper and packing boxes and a growing collection of clothes, toys, and sweets. But she tore into Kate's gift as though it were the first of the day.

"Oh my God! This is awesome!" Sammy opened the box and pulled out a pair of roller blades. "So cool."

Gina groaned and scowled at Kate. Roller blades and Sammy were a number of trips to the A&E waiting to happen. Kate shrugged and offered her an unrepentant grin. She sighed and shook her head. "You can take her to the hospital when she breaks something," she said quietly enough for only Kate to hear as she sat curled against Kate's side. "What do you say?" Gina prompted.

"Thanks, Kate." Sammy jumped up and ran to Kate, throwing her skinny arms around her neck.

"You're very welcome."

"Sammy, go and grab a black bag for all the rubbish. We should at least tidy up a bit as we go along."

"Okay." Sammy hurried away and was back in seconds to continue opening more gifts.

Merlin sat under the tree guarding on her own Christmas present—a large, multicoloured ball that she would roll to Sammy on occasion in the hope a game would begin.

Gina's phone rang, and Kate passed it over to her, frowning as it came up *unknown number*. Gina touched the screen to answer. "Hello?"

"Gina, it's Alison."

"Mum, new number?"

"Yes, I was just calling to tell you I'm running a little late. But I should be there in plenty of time to help with the cooking."

Kate ran her thumb across the back of Gina's neck, and Gina almost forgot she was in the middle of a phone call.

Kate smirked at her knowingly.

Gina shook her head. "No worries, Mum. We'll see you soon." She dropped the phone onto the sofa beside her and kissed Kate's cheek. "Behave."

"I don't want to." She cupped Gina's cheek with one hand and leant in for a proper kiss. The gentle press of Kate's tongue against her lips spurred Gina into action as she wrapped her hand around Kate's bicep and opened her mouth, groaning at the delicate contact and tender caress. And Gina let herself get lost in that kiss, in Kate.

Loud kissing noises from the floor and a sharp bark from Merlin tore them apart.

Sammy had her arms wrapped around her body, back to them, rubbing her hands up and down her back as she made smoochy sounds through her giggles. Bloody kid.

Kate gasped, then sprang from the sofa and lifted Sammy into the air, twirling her tucked-up form into a spin until she was hanging upside down, arms and hair trailing on the floor as she giggled louder while Kate tickled her ribs.

"Let me down, let me down!" Sammy shrieked through her laughter even as she tried to reach up and cover her tummy. Her pyjama top rode up, exposing her belly. "Let me down, Kate!"

"Nope." Kate swung her up over her shoulder and started for the back door. "I'm hanging you on the washing line so I can kiss your mum in peace."

"Abuse! Abuse!" Sammy playfully pounded her fists against Kate's back. "Gonna tell Stella, and she'll lock you up."

"Nah. She'll take pictures and save them to show your boyfriend years from now. Like, thirty years from now."

Gina chuckled as she watched them cavorting around the room, then frowned as her phone rang again.

Kate stopped, Sammy still dangling over her shoulder, as she looked at Gina.

"Unknown number," Gina said and touched the screen to answer. "Hello?"

Kate put Sammy down and sat beside her close enough to hear the voice on the other end.

"Miss Temple?"

"Who's this?"

"Sorry, it's George. George Boyne."

Gina paused a moment, and Kate moved away.

"I know you probably don't want to speak to me, after what I told you. I understand that, but I was wondering if I might have a few moments of your time?"

"Actually, Mr Boyne, I'm really glad you called. I wanted to apologise for the way I behaved last week. I had no right to do that."

"It's okay. I understand what a shock it must have been. I probably shouldn't have said anything."

"No, it's not okay. I was rude, and I had no right to be. You were right when you said I had no idea what it was like to be there. To face what you were facing. I was judgmental, and like I said, I really had no right to be. I'll work on that in future. I'm really very sorry."

George cleared his throat. "Thank you."

"No problem. So, what can I do for you today? Oh, Merry Christmas, by the way."

He chuckled. "And to you. And I was hoping I might come and see you. I've found out some things, and I'd like to talk to you about it."

"Me? What things?"

"I'll explain when I see you. It'll be easier to show you the documents and so on."

"Well, okay. I must admit, you have me curious now."

He laughed again. "Well, then you'll have to see me soon. I could meet with you today."

"It's Christmas Day."

He waited.

"I've got a dinner to cook."

"I could come to you?"

"I'm sorry?"

"I didn't mean for Christmas dinner. I just meant I could come there while you're cooking, or after, and show you what I've found."

"Just a second." She covered the microphone and looked at Kate. "George wants to come and see me."

"Okay." Kate shrugged.

"Today."

Kate's eyebrow hitched upwards in surprise. "Well, we've got six chairs and only four of us for dinner." She shrugged again. "Whatever you want, sweetheart."

"Mr Boyne. Do you have a pen handy?"

"Yes, fire away."

She quickly gave him Kate's address.

"I'll leave now. Should only be a couple of hours."

"You're keen."

He chuckled again. "Miss Temple, when you see what I've found out, you'll understand why. See you soon." Then he ended the call.

"Well, that was odd."

"When's he coming?" Kate asked.

"He said he was leaving now, so a couple of hours."

Kate's eyebrow rose. "Well, I'll start peeling some extra spuds, then."

"I didn't invite him to eat with us."

"No. But I'm not sure I could send him away to spend Christmas on his own once he's here," Kate said quietly. "He's got no family, remember."

Gina nodded. "I remember." She kissed her lips gently. "You're very sweet, Kate Brannon."

Kate clapped a hand over Gina's mouth. "You'll ruin my reputation," she said with a wide grin.

"Too late."

The next hour and a half flew by as Sammy opened the last of her presents and Gina prepared the dinner. There was a mountain of food, as per Christmas tradition. Kate wanted a traditional family Christmas, so Gina was bound and determined to do all she could to give her one.

Gina opened the oven and spooned juices over the top of the bird. The turkey was cooking well but still needed a good hour or so before it would be ready.

The doorbell rang.

"I'll get it," Sammy shouted. Then Gina heard the follow-up of "Grandma!"

"Happy Christmas, Sammy."

"Happy Christmas. Did you bring me presents?"

"Sammy!" Gina shouted through the house. "Come on in, Mum. I'm basting the turkey."

Alison staggered in with Sammy wrapped around her like an octopus, Merlin trotting along at their heels.

"Sammy, give over. Your Gran can't walk like that." The girl tutted and pulled a face but did as she was told.

Gina pushed the roasting tin with the covered bird back into the oven as her mother approached, offered her a tentative hug and kiss on the cheek, and wished Gina a happy Christmas. She was clearly uncomfortable, but Gina was still unsure if she was uncomfortable with physical affection or if it was just with Gina and would dissipate as their relationship got closer. She hoped that was the case, as she didn't seem to have too big an issue being affectionate with Sammy. But then again, that could just be Sammy.

"So, did you bring me a present?" Sammy asked again.

"God, anyone would think it was Christmas or something." Alison winked at her and plopped a bag onto the table. "I might have. Does she deserve a present, Gina?"

"Hm, not sure."

Sammy's face fell, and her shoulders slumped. "But I've been good."

Gina lifted an eyebrow.

"Mostly."

Gina folded her arms over her chest.

"Well, I tried to be." Sammy sighed heavily. "Guess it's going to the charity shop, then."

Alison sniggered. "Charity shop?"

Sammy nodded. "That's where all the naughty kids' presents get sent." She shot Gina a withering look. "Apparently."

Gina couldn't hold back her laughter anymore as Sammy dropped heavily into a chair, swinging her feet moodily. She bent and kissed the top of her head. "Go on, I'll give you a break."

"Yay!"

"But only because it's Christmas."

"Less yay."

Alison pulled a brightly wrapped box from the bag and handed it over.

"Thanks, Grandma." She tore the wrapping away to unveil a large box. "Oo. A 3-D marker. That's so cool!" She kissed Alison's cheek and ran into the front room.

"Where's Kate?"

"Shower. She won't be long." Gina pointed to a chair. "Brew?"

"Hm, coffee would be lovely, thanks." She slouched in her chair and rested her head on one hand, exhaustion evident in every line on her face and in the dark smudges under her eyes.

"You okay?"

Her mother nodded, then shrugged. "Ignore me. I just didn't sleep very well last night."

"Is that normal?"

"Only when your father tries to get in touch."

"Oh." Gina wasn't sure how she felt about that. How she felt about her father even being mentioned, let alone still being in contact with her mother. "Do you...is he...I thought you didn't keep in touch?"

"I don't. I've changed the number at the house, my mobile, everything. The only thing I haven't changed is the house, and that's because it's so bloody difficult to find somewhere else to live that I could afford to. It's so bloody expensive around here."

"If you sold the house, wouldn't you have enough?"

"When the house gets sold, he's entitled to half the value. He's not bothered now, because he's in prison and can't use it, but when he gets out, I'll have to sell or figure out how to pay him half of the value of the house. If I could figure out where to get the money to do that, I'd have sold it and moved long ago."

"I hadn't even thought about that."

"Yeah, well, half the value of my little cottage won't get me much of anything at all around here."

"Is that why he was contacting you?"

"Nope." She shook her head. "I got a letter from his solicitor yesterday. He's up for parole in February and wants me not to give a statement at the hearing or, failing that, at least do nothing to block his release."

"Bastard."

"Yup."

"So, what will you do?"

"Speak at the hearing and do whatever I can to ensure he stays behind bars."

"You're not tempted to let it go?"

"Not even a little bit. I wish he was in there for life, Gina. And I'm sorry if that sounds cold, but that's the way I feel about it."

Gina wrapped her arms around her mother's shoulders and squeezed. "I'm very proud of you. Would you like me to come with you?"

Alison frowned.

"To the hearing. I'll come with you if you want."

Alison smiled as tears slipped over her eyelids and snaked a path down her cheeks. "I think I'd like that very much. If you're sure."

"I'm sure. We'll face him together."

Footsteps at the top of the stairs alerted her to Kate's presence. Gina looked up and smiled to reassure Kate that everything was all right. Because it was. She had everything she could ever want, right here in the house. She had a wonderful partner, a precocious child, and a mother she was getting to know, and a future she was looking forward to. This was truly the happiest Christmas she could remember. Probably ever.

Gina gave Alison's shoulders one last squeeze and then stood up to finish making their drinks when the doorbell rang.

"I'll get it," Sammy shouted. Then Gina heard her ask, "Who're you?"

"I'm George. Who're you?"

"Sammy."

"Well, Sammy, I'm looking for Gina. Is she in?"

"Mum. There's an old man at the door for you."

"Show him in, Sammy."

"I'm here." Kate thundered down the stairs and welcomed George. "Sorry about that," she said. "Come in, come in. Let me take your coat." Kate held out her hand.

"Here, I brought this for Gina—I mean Miss Temple." He held out a bottle of wine. "My mother always said you should bring a little something if someone invites you to their home."

Gina put the kettle on to boil again and wiped her hands on a towel. "Well, technically this is Kate's home," she said with a smile. "But I'm sure we'll all enjoy a glass." She wrapped her arms around Kate's waist and kissed her cheek. Sammy stood in front of her, and Gina put one hand on her shoulder. "You've already met my daughter, Sammy."

"Yes." George held out his hand. "A pleasure."

"And this is my mum." Gina held her hand out towards the joining door where her mother stood. "Alison Temple, this is George Boyne."

Alison stepped forward and held out her hand. "Nice to meet you, Mr Boyne."

George stared at her, his eyes wide, his mouth agape.

Alison's welcoming smile slipped to a small frown. "I'm sorry, is there something wrong?"

He shook his head and seemed to snap out of his reverie. "No, no. Sorry. I wasn't expecting to meet Gina's beautiful mother this afternoon as well." He clasped her hand. "Forgive my bad manners."

"Nothing to forgive," Alison said, though her voice was a little subdued.

"And please call me George. Mr Boyne is so formal, and this is Christmas."

She smiled. "Of course."

"Can I get you a drink, George?" Kate asked, drawing his attention away from Alison.

"Lovely, thank you."

"Tea, coffee, something stronger?"

"Coffee would be good, if you don't mind. I'm a little chilled all of a sudden."

"Are you okay?"

He waved his hand. "Fine, fine. Just a little...well, never mind. I'm fine."

"Milk? Sugar?"

"Just a drop of milk, please."

Kate nodded and gathered cups as the kettle bubbled away.

Gina watched her go and squatted down to Sammy. "Why don't you go and play with some of your new toys upstairs?"

Sammy nodded and scampered into the front room to choose what she was taking up with her.

When she was gone, Gina pointed to the table and chairs. "Please, sit down." She waited until George and Alison were both sitting before taking her own seat. "You said you wanted to show me something."

"Yes, yes." He placed a manila folder he'd been carrying on to the table. "Before I show you all this, I should probably explain a little of where I got this information from. Or at least what I can explain."

Gina frowned. It was beginning to sound a bit like a bad spy novel. "Okay."

"I told you when we met in Cambridge that I worked for the British Army Intelligence Corps."

Gina nodded but didn't interrupt.

"Well, as I'm sure you can imagine, finding out information was very much what I did. What I do. I'm very good at it, and I know a lot of other people who are equally good at it, if not better than I am. Especially now with computers and so on."

"I'm sure you must have been to have remained in the army for so long."

"Quite. Well, after I left you last week, I had a bee in my bonnet." He smirked a little. "As I'm sure you can understand, I wanted to find out all I could about the little girl Pat gave birth to and what might have happened to her."

"Of course. That makes perfect sense, George. I hope you find her and build a relationship with her." She smiled. "You deserve it, I'm sure. But I'm a little confused, I don't understand what that has to do with me? Not that I'm not glad to have the chance to apologise for my behaviour the other day, but I truly didn't expect to ever see you again."

He nodded. "Neither did I. I thought you hated me. With reason, I might add. But I never expected to cross paths with you again either. Until last night."

"What happened last night?" Kate asked as she placed drinks for them all on the table.

"A friend of mine in Ireland found the records I was looking for and sent them to me. I got the e-mail about eleven last night. It was the last piece of corroborating evidence I needed to be sure I'd found the right woman."

Gina smiled. "You found your daughter."

His grin widened. "Yes, I did."

"Wow, that was fast."

He grinned. "I told you I was good at finding information. When I need to know something, I find out the answer."

"I'm very happy for you, George." She bit her lip. "But I still don't understand where I come into this. Why did you want to talk to me about what you found?"

He stared at the file, as though now that the moment was upon him he was questioning his own decision. He licked his lips, pulling the bottom one between his teeth, then seemed to reconcile himself to moving forward with his plan. He took a deep breath and opened the file, spreading sheets of paper across the table. "You see, I found out that my little girl was adopted by Ronald and Mary Jacobs."

"What?" Alison coughed around her drink.

"Ronald and Mary Jacobs," he said quietly, looking directly at her.

Alison paled. "It's...it's a common enough surname, and Ronald and Mary aren't unusual names either."

"Mum?" Gina said quietly.

"I was thorough in my background checks. Every detail has been checked and double-checked. I had no intention of barging into someone's life if I wasn't one hundred per cent certain it was the right person."

"You can't have been. You said you only got the information last night. You said so yourself just a moment ago," Alison argued.

"I'm sorry, I should have been clearer. I got the final confirmation at eleven last night. That was the confirmation of the checks I need to make."

"But—"

"Ronald and Mary Jacobs. Lived in Fakenham from 1970 until they passed away—Mary in 1989, Ronald in 1993. Their adopted daughter married Howard Temple in 1983, at the age of eighteen."

"Mum?" Gina quickly knelt beside her mother and took hold of her hand.

Alison couldn't seem to tear her gaze from George. "You're my father?"

George nodded.

"Bloody hell," Kate whispered. She picked up her drink and stared into the cup. "I think I need something a bit stronger now." She got up from the table and headed for the kitchen.

Gina touched her mother's cheek and drew her face to look at her. "Mum, is it true?"

Andrea Bramhall

Alison snorted. "I've no idea." She picked up one of the pieces of paper and stared at it blankly. "I was adopted. I knew that much. I told you that."

Gina nodded. "I remember."

"Is he my biological father?" She looked at George. "How the holy hell should I know?"

"I know this is a shock," George said. "But all the paperwork shows that you are the baby Pat gave birth to in 1965. My daughter."

Gina picked up the paper he held out. It was a birth certificate. Her mum's birth certificate. "You're not named as the father."

He shook his head. "Do you remember in her letter? She said she wouldn't name the father because she knew her dad would kill me for it."

Gina nodded. Oh yes, she remembered. Wow. IRA commander great-granddaddy. Army spy granddad. Murdered grandma. *I feel like I'm reading off the beginning of Gladiator. My name is Geroginas Maximus Tempilius, granddaughter to a murdered grandmother, descendant of a terrorist, mother to a problem child. And I will have my vengeance. In this life or the next.* She knew laughing at the absurdity her shocked mind was creating wasn't the correct response, but she couldn't help it. It was bizarre. The whole thing was just too bizarre.

"What's so funny?" George asked.

She shook her head and wiped the tears from her cheeks. "Warped sense of humour."

George just watched her, waiting for her to continue.

"Did that interrogation technique work for you a lot?" Gina asked, the sarcasm in her voice a little sharper than she'd expected it to be, even to her own ears.

"What happened to working on that judgemental thing?" George said, then lowered his gaze. "Sorry, that was uncalled for. Look, I know you won't believe me. In all honesty, I don't expect you to, but I truly am sorry for the way everything happened back then. I'm not sorry I met Patricia. I'm not sorry that we fell in love, and I'm especially not sorry that our love resulted in a child." He waved his hand to indicate

310

the whole room. "If we hadn't, today would be very different, don't you think?"

Kate put a hand on her shoulder and leant over to her ear. "Give him a chance. At least to explain. After all, it's not really your life this has affected. Nor your mum's really. She had a good childhood. Isn't it up to her how she wants to deal with George?"

She was right, and Gina knew it. But it didn't stop her thinking how different it all could have been. How different it should have been. Gina took a deep breath. "I'm sorry. I guess I'm still a little shocked. I just can't stop seeing it. I can't get it out of my head."

"What, Gina?" Alison asked, her voice croaky and hoarse. "What can't you stop seeing?"

"Pat." She picked up her napkin and wiped her cheeks with it.

"What about her?" Kate asked, wrapping her fingers around Gina's.

"I watched her die. I watched her die, begging me to find him, and all along she must have been thinking about the baby she gave up." The sob escaped. "You," she said, looking at Alison. "And I was right there. Her granddaughter, and neither of us knew it." Her chest heaved as Alison's tears also began to fall. "She seemed so kind. So lovely. And she died in my arms."

"And you blame me for it," George said quietly. "I understand why you're so angry at me—"

Gina shook her head and tried to swallow enough to be able to speak. "I don't blame you because she died. She was killed by a terrorist—" Gina took a deep breath and controlled herself. "I don't blame you because she died, or how she died, or anything like that. I'm not even angry at you because she made the decision to let your baby be adopted. I know my mum had a good childhood, and we all wouldn't be here today if not for that choice. I'm angry at you for using her. She seemed so sweet and kind, even after everything she must have gone through, the pain she must have felt. And she was still holding on to the happiness she had with you. I'm angry because that was a lie. Because you used her for your career. For your mission. I'm angry that you started this whole family because you were trying to arrest her father. Didn't you even think? Didn't you even consider what the consequences of your actions could be? How devastating the effects on everyone else might be?"

"You're right. I didn't think of any of those things. We were trained not to. But in all honesty, I wouldn't have let them bother me anyway. If I had, I wouldn't have been able to do what I needed to do to survive." He rested his elbows on the table and leant forward. "I wasn't thinking about the future, Gina, because I didn't know if I'd even have tomorrow, never mind next year. That's the reality for a soldier. That's the question we face every morning when we wake up. Is it today? Will this one be the last day I walk this earth? And we don't mind that. We don't question that uncertainty. Instead we answer that question with the pledge that if this is the day I am to die, let my death mean something. Let it ensure a mission, a life, a cause. Let it be for a purpose. "For their tomorrow, we gave our today." Have you heard that quote?"

Gina shook her head, but Kate nodded. "John Maxwell Edmonds."

"Exactly. For your safety, for your health, for your happiness, we would give our lives, our futures, so that you can live the life you do today. Every serviceman—every single one of us—lives that motto. Every single day." He sniffed. "So perhaps you'll forgive an old man the follies of his youth, knowing that his intentions were good, even if his actions didn't always live up to the standard you would wish of him."

He pushed his chair back from the table and stood up. Gina watched as he closed the distance to Alison and held out a card to her. "I know this is a lot to take in, and I know you will probably have questions. If you wish, we can do a DNA test to confirm what I've learnt. I'm more than happy to do that, Alison." He wrapped his fingers around hers as she took the card and gazed into his eyes.

Gina stared at them and realised what it was that had appeared so familiar about his eyes when she'd first seen him. They were a mirror image of her mother's. Of her own. Of Sammy's. *How did I not see it?*

"I would like the chance to get to know you. If you'd like." He cleared his throat. "But I understand if you don't."

"Where are you going?" Alison asked. "We made extra for you." Her voice was soft, distant. Almost like she was speaking from a long way away. She looked shell-shocked, completely at a loss as to what she should do or say.

He smiled sadly. "I think it might be best if I leave." He reached out slowly and touched her cheek. Tears ran down his face as his sad smile turned joyous. "My little girl."

Alison chuckled through her own tears. "Not so little."

He put his free hand over his heart. "I may have only just met you, and I may have missed everything a father should see in his daughter's life," he sniffed and wiped away her tears with his thumb, "but I don't want to miss any more. Not if I can help it." He leant forward and kissed her cheek.

Alison wrapped her arms around his neck and sobbed against his chest.

He held her.

Kate tapped Gina's back and drew her attention. She spoke quietly so that Alison and George wouldn't hear her. "Do you really hate him that much?"

"I don't hate him."

"Then do what you said when you spoke to him on the phone."

Gina frowned.

"Let it go." She touched the back of Gina's neck. "Ask him to stay."

"Is this another instance of you using my family to make up for the fact that you don't have to put up with all this crap?" She pulled a face as she said it to let Kate know she really didn't mean it.

Kate sniggered. "Something like that." She dropped her head and looked up at her, giving Gina the most pathetic puppy-dog expression she'd ever seen. "Please."

Gina sighed heavily. "George?" she said as he pulled away from Alison.

"I get it, Gina. I'm going."

"Please don't."

He looked at her with a frown.

"Please stay. I'm sorry I was such a bitch. I have no excuse."

"I don't want to ruin the day for you all any more than I already have."

"You'll only ruin it if you leave," Kate said. "After all, what's a family Christmas without the odd disagreement or two, anyway?"

"I don't want to argue," he said, not looking away from Gina.

She shook her head. "No more arguing. I promise. I really don't like confrontation."

George laughed loudly. "Well, you're very good at it."

She chuckled. "Thanks." She stood up and went to stand before him. "Please, stay and have Christmas with us. For years, it's just been me and Sammy on Christmas Day, and I always wanted a big family Christmas. I wanted it to be filled with the people I love, old and new." She held out her hand to Kate and felt secure and happy as Kate's fingers clasped her own and she felt the now-familiar heat of her at her shoulder.

He opened his mouth to speak but seemed unable to get the words out as the tears welled in his eyes again. Instead, he nodded and pulled her into a hug.

The first time she was held by her grandfather. She closed her eyes and tried to memorise every moment of it—the heavy weight of him against her, the strength of his arms, the scent of Old Spice and mint permeating from him as mulled wine and cinnamon lingered in the air. She breathed it in deep, the new scent of Christmas, of family. And Gina intended to remember it all.

Something attracted Merlin's attention, and she ran for the front door, her claws scrabbling across the tiles, barking as she went. Kate frowned and crossed the room, opening the door to the hallway.

"It's a card, addressed to you, Gina."

Gina frowned and pulled away from George's embrace. "It's Christmas Day. The post doesn't—"

Kate held up a handwritten envelope bearing Gina's name and nothing else. No address, no stamp, no postmark.

Kate dropped it on the kitchen counter and ran out of the house in her bare feet.

Gina stared at the envelope like it was going to bite her. She was almost convinced it would. Her heart beat wildly, echoing its frantic beat in her ears. It was so deep and so hard that her vision pulsed with each beat, like her view of the world was contracting with every pump.

When was this going to end? Why today? Couldn't she just have one day of happiness without a threat or a torment hanging over her? Over them?

"Gina, what is it?" Her mother touched her arm and picked up the envelope, frowning at it. "What's wrong?"

Kate hobbled back into the room, breathless, and limping on the side of one foot. A piece of glass stuck out of the sole. "Ow, ow, ow, ow, ow, ow." She dropped down in a chair, twisting her leg across her knee to pluck the shard from her flesh. "What does it say?"

The drops of blood falling to the floor spurred Gina back into action. "Never mind that." She grabbed a tea towel and dropped to her knees beside Kate, pushing away Kate's hands and wiping at the blood.

"Ow."

"Big baby." But she gentled her touch and studied the small cut, trying to ascertain if there was any more glass in it. It looked clean.

"Where's your first aid kit?" Alison asked.

Gina pointed to a cupboard next to the fridge. "Top shelf." Dabbing the cut, she said, "thanks" when the first aid kit was put down on the table beside her, The lid was opened, and the packet for an alcohol wipe was torn open and handed to her. She smiled up at her mum, took the wipe, and scrunched up her face. "This is going to sting."

Kate nodded and sucked a sharp breath in through her teeth at the first touch. "It might be nothing."

Gina nodded. "Yeah, it's just a little cut. I don't think you need stitches or anything."

"I meant the envelope."

"Oh. Did you see anyone out there?"

"No."

"Do you want me to open it?" Alison asked.

Kate looked at Gina as she spoke. "It might be evidence, Alison. Probably best to let me. Can you pass me a pair of those gloves from the first aid kit?"

Alison stared at the envelope she'd dropped onto the table when she went for the kit and handed over the requested gloves.

"Evidence? Why?" George frowned as he bent forward to look at the white square envelope. "Just looks like a Christmas card to me."

"Sometimes appearances can be deceptive." Kate slowly peeled open the flap at the back of the envelope and slid out a Christmas card. Santa Claus sat in a sleigh, reindeer at the front, Rudolf's bright red nose shining brightly. Just a standard, everyday Christmas card.

Then Gina saw the words at the top. "To The One I Love At Christmas." She swallowed as Kate opened it and flicked her eyes up to Gina.

To My Gina,

My was underlined several times.

Christmas is a time where loved ones are supposed to be together, but again you've ignored me. Chosen her over me. Well, I'm not going to stand for this, Gina. You are mine, and it's time you learnt that. It's time you realised that I'm the best thing for you. Not her. I see you holding her hand, letting her kiss you, letting her touch you.
I don't know how you can even do it. I don't know how you can let her touch you instead of me.
You're everything to me, Gina. Everything.
And I will be everything to you.

"It seems I have a stalker." Gina sighed. "And he's getting bolder."

About Andrea Bramhall

Andrea Bramhall wrote her first novel at the age of six and three-quarters. It was seven pages long and held together with a pink ribbon. Her Gran still has it in the attic. Since then she has progressed a little bit and now has a number of published works held together with glue, not ribbons, an Alice B. Lavender certificate, a Lambda Literary award, and a Golden Crown award cluttering up her book shelves.

She studied music and all things arty at Manchester Metropolitan University, graduating in 2002 with a BA in contemporary arts. She is certain it will prove useful someday...maybe.

When she isn't busy running a campsite in the Lake District, Bramhall can be found hunched over her laptop scribbling down the stories that won't let her sleep. She can also be found reading, walking the dogs up mountains while taking a few thousand photos, scuba diving while taking a few thousand photos, swimming, kayaking, playing the saxophone, or cycling.

CONNECT WITH ANDREA

Website: andreabramhall.wordpress.com
Facebook: www.facebook.com/AndreaBramhall

Other Books from Ylva Publishing

www.ylva-publishing.com

Collide-O-Scope

(Norfolk Coast Investigation Story – Book 1)

Andrea Bramhall

ISBN: 978-3-95533-849-7
Length: 291 pages (90,000 words)

One unidentified dead body. One tiny fishing village. Forty residents and everyone's a suspect. Where do you start? Newly promoted Detective Sergeant Kate Brannon and King's Lynn CID have to answer that question and more as they untangle the web of lies wrapped around the tiny village of Brandale Stiathe Harbour to capture the killer of Connie Wells.

Mine to Keep

Wendy Hudson

ISBN: 978-3-95533-882-4
Length: 291 pages (77,000 words)

Plagued by childhood nightmares since losing her mother, Erin embarks on a journey to rural Scotland, hoping to trace her father and put the darkness to rest. When she meets Abigail, they quickly become search partners and together pick apart fact from folklore. Erin takes sanctuary within Abigail's castle walls as her nightmares start to close in. Can she defeat them and learn to live again?

Requiem for Immortals

Lee Winter

ISBN: 978-3-95533-710-0
Length: 263 pages (86,000 words)

Requiem is a brilliant cellist with a secret. The dispassionate assassin has made an art form out of killing Australia's underworld figures without a thought. One day she's hired to kill a sweet and unassuming innocent. Requiem can't work out why anyone would want her dead—and why she should even care.

Deliberate Harm

J.R. Wolfe

ISBN: 978-3-95533-368-3
Length: 300 pages (70,000 words)

Ever since Portia Marks learned her fiancée Imma was executed in Zimbabwe, she's struggled with grief. Then a stranger tells her Imma is alive, but he's killed before she can ask questions. To learn the truth, Portia teams with two friends in the CIA. Her search takes her across continents and entangles her in a terrorist plot that will rock the globe. Portia's quest becomes a race against time.

The Last First Time

© 2017 by Andrea Bramhall

ISBN: 978-3-95533-946-3

Also available as e-book.

Published by Ylva Publishing, legal entity of Ylva Verlag, e.Kfr.

Ylva Verlag, e.Kfr.
Owner: Astrid Ohletz
Am Kirschgarten 2
65830 Kriftel
Germany

www.ylva-publishing.com

First edition: 2017

Credits
Edited by Astrid Ohletz & Michelle Aguilar
Cover Design by Streetlight Graphics

CPSIA information can be obtained
at www.ICGtesting.com
Printed in the USA
LVOW12s0724160418

573613LV00001B/34/P